THE
BIG
one

Kevin E. Ready

THE
BIG
one

Kevin E. Ready

SAINT GAUDENS PRESS
Wichita, Kansas & Santa Barbara, California

See other great books available from Saint Gaudens Press
http://www.SaintGaudensPress.com

Visit Kevin E. Ready's Web Site at http://www.KevinReady.net

Saint Gaudens Press
Post Office Box 405
Solvang, CA 93464-0405

Saint Gaudens, Saint Gaudens Press
and the Winged Liberty colophon
are trademarks of Saint Gaudens Press

Print edition ISBN: 978-0-943039-21-3

Library of Congress Catalog Number - 2014912271

Printed in the United States of America

Dedicated to Olga and the kids, who have suffered
through innumerable trips to locations in this book and gave
me the time it took to put this book together.

Powerful Earthquake!
San Andreas Fault at Redlands
M 8.5
12:44 p.m., May 6
Massive Destruction in
Redlands, San Bernardino & Riverside.
Significant damage as far away as
downtown L.A. Numerous downed
freeways, communicaitons disrupted,
total deaths +16,000.
Intense aftershock sequence.

Moderate Earthquake
M 5.5
11:51 p.m., May 5
San Gabriel Mountains
Minor damage at
Rancho Cucamonga.

Regional earthquake
activity increases
substantially
following Super Quakes

Strong Aftershock to
Century City Super Quake
M 6.7
9:10 a.m., May 7
More structural damage,
Numerous collapsed buildings.

Strong Earthquake
Off the coast of Carpinteria
M 6.3
11:50 p.m., May 6
Mease or Red Mountain Fault.
Moderate structural damage
15 to. tsunami at Santa Barbara.

Powerful Earthquake!
Northern Inglewood-Newport
M 8.1
1:13 p.m., May 6
Massive Destruction throughout the
Los Angeles region. Numerous Structural
Failures, +10,000 deaths, countless injured.
LNG plant explodes, tsunami hits Long
Beach-Santa Monica, widespread damage.

Ennosigee, fire from the center of the Earth
Shall make an Earthquake of the New City.
Two great rocks shall for a long time
war against each other.
After that Arethusa shall color red the New
River.

I:87

During many nights the Earth shall quake.
About the spring two great earthquakes
shall follow one another ...

II:46

The sun in twenty degrees of Taurus,
there will be a great earthquake;
The great theatre full up will be ruined... .

IX:83

A very great trembling in the month of May ...

X:67

Prophecies from <u>Centuries</u>

by Nostradamus, A.D. 1564

May 5th, 11:51 P.M.

Barry Warden put the book on the nightstand, switched off the light and turned over in bed. As he punched his pillow to plump it, Kathy matched his turn and edged over to him, snuggling her bottom toward him, matching the curve of his body. Spooning was Kathy's favorite way of initiating things and it had the desired effect. They both felt Barry press against Kathy's silk teddy. Barry slid his arm from under his pillow over under Kathy's pillow and then up, enveloping her, as his other arm slid around her and down her abdomen. Kathy snuggled closer into the envelopment and flexed her buttocks to acknowledge him.

Barry and Kathy had not yet settled completely into their mutual entwinement when Barry felt a movement of the bed. Barry first thought that his wife was somehow bouncing the bed, but she was snuggled right next to him and could not be the source of the movement. The question quickly passed when he heard the tinkling of Kathy's perfume bottles on the dresser. He pulled his hand away from her bully and held Kathy's shoulder. He lifted his head from the pillow and listened for the telltale murmuring roar that might indicate the ferocity of the tremor that had interrupted them. Barry felt Kathy do the same.

What had started with the bouncing of the bed soon progressed to rolling and knocking of the entire room. Kathy turned over and clutched him. She said nothing. Her excitation of sex shifted to that of fear. Barry's first thoughts of getting out of bed were suppressed by Kathy's frightened grasp and the fact that the middle of the four-poster bed was probably the safest place, with all the furniture rocking.

Barry wanted to say something, but nothing seemed appropriate. A few seconds into the quake, the rolling waves and muffled roar from beneath them were punctuated by a pair of sharp bumps. Books tumbled from the bookcase and something fell in the hallway to the bathroom. A second later there was a cacophony of smashing glass from the kitchen.

"Oh, God!" were the only words from Kathy. Barry did not speak, not from fear, but from lack of any idea what to say. No words seemed right, he merely cradled Kathy's head and shoulders in his arms. Kathy murmured a quavering "Oohh" that matched her trembling when a jarring bump knocked them from side to side on the bed.

The light from the streetlight outside their window went out. There was another few seconds of lesser rolling and shaking. The tinkling of perfume bottles stopped. Finally, all of the movement and noise ceased. Barry felt his temples pounding.

The red numerals on the alarm clock were no longer visible. Barry nevertheless reached for the table lamp next to the bed. No luck, power was out.

"You stay there, I'll get the light," Barry said to Kathy.

He took a deep breath, recognizing that his heart was racing and temples pounding.

The furniture had stayed upright in the bedroom and he had heard nothing break, so Barry felt safe to walk barefoot to the closet and feel around for the emergency flashlight he kept there. He pulled back the covers and sat up.

"How big was that?" Kathy's voice had a little girl quality to it. It was totally dark, darker than he ever remembered, since the street-light was out. Without seeing her Barry pictured in his mind the big blue eyes that would go along with Kathy saying something like that. They had only been married a year this coming month and Barry still marveled at Kathy's innocence, both perceived and real. That was part of why he loved to have her in his life. She was so far removed from the stark reality and harshness he often faced in law enforcement. Barry stroked her head one last time, then stood up and turned to the closet.

"No way of knowing. Depends on how far off the epicenter was." Barry was thinking exactly the same thing; everyone did, whenever a quake hit. ' How far away and how big?' Jargon like "epicenter," "Richter Scale," and "liquefaction" had become normal conversation terms for Southern Californians.

"Did that feel like the last big quake?" Kathy had still been in San Diego at the university when the Grapevine quake had hit. Her family's home in Granada Hills had been slightly damaged in that quake, but

Kathy had not even been awakened two hundred miles south in San Diego. Like most Californians, Kathy and her family related each to the previous ones and compared their ferocity. Barry had been on duty that morning, on patrol in his sheriff's car in Agoura Hills. That had been before he had been transferred down to his present station about the time they were married.

"Yes, I guess it was close as far as length of time. But not really as strong and it felt different in the car."

The closet was a mess. The shelves had emptied. It took several seconds to dig through and find the electric lantern. Barry flipped the lantern on in the closet and searched for his robe and tennis shoes. He usually slept either in underwear or without anything, like tonight, but Kathy usually wore a nightgown or teddy and demurely kept her robe close to the bed. This experience made him think. If they had a really bad quake he would be caught wandering around in the rubble in his Jockey shorts, or worse. If he survived, that is. But this had not been such a quake, so he dismissed the vision.

As Barry stepped out of the closet with the lantern, Kathy shielded her eyes from the glare.

"From the sound of things downstairs, you better wear shoes not slippers." Barry had her shoes, too. She already had her robe from the chair.

Barry turned the light around the walls of the bedroom. The bedroom was not too bad. The bookcase was half empty and the desk lamp had taken a tumble to the floor.

Outside the apartment, several car alarms and a single emergency siren sounded in the dark. Barry's experienced ear recognized the quaver of an L.A. City fire siren when he heard it.

Kathy sat on the edge of the bed to pull on the tennis shoes Barry offered. She started to speak, "I can't even ...," but she was cut off by the phone ringing. She went to the desk, carefully stepping over the pile of books on the floor.

"Hello." She paused.

"Yeh, Cindy, we're fine. No damage in the bedroom, just some stuff on the floor, but it sounded like all hell broke loose in the kitchen. How about you?" Kathy waited for her sister to answer.

"That's good. Let me know what happened outside." Another pause. "We're going down to the kitchen now. Call Mom and tell her we are all right, too. OK? ... Bye."

She hung up and turned to Barry. "Cindy and Jeff are all right. But Jeff is going outside to see what happened, some big crash in their neighborhood."

"Could'a been anything." Barry turned and headed out to the hall, holding the light for Kathy to see where they walked. Barry tried to picture what structures were in his sister-in-law's neighborhood.

Kathy's older sister Cindy and her husband, Jeff, lived in Marina del Rey, in their own home. Barry and Kathy were still saving for a down payment, and even then, it would not be in the Marina district. Jeff's job as an accountant, and self-employed at that, paid considerably better than Barry's as a deputy sheriff and Cindy had a good job as a legal secretary, while Kathy was still subbing and looking for full-time work as a teacher. For now, Kathy did not seem to mind the rented townhouse in West Los Angeles.

"What were you saying?" Barry asked.

"Huh?"

"When the phone rang, you were saying something."

"Uhh, I forget. It wasn't important." As Kathy spoke, she followed Barry out the bedroom door.

The cuckoo clock had fallen from the wall in the hallway. The flashlight showed it to be in pieces, the thin wood, chain weights and springs in a jumble, the little red bird a casualty of the quake.

There was total silence as they went down the stairs. They were used to the hum of the air conditioner, ceiling fan and other appliances. A shuddering thump from somewhere in the building startled both of them just as they reached the bottom of the stairs.

"Somebody opened their garage door without electric opener." Barry explained the noise to Kathy. She nodded in the light from his lantern.

The living room really was not too bad. The cable box had fallen off the TV, but the TV was still on the stand. The home theatre gear was still upright in the rack. As they walked through the living room the nearest of the car alarms shrieking outside went silent.

Barry flashed the light over the breakfast bar into the kitchen. It was as he had expected. The wine glasses that hung in the wooden racks over the counter had worked themselves loose and had crashed onto the counter and floor. Only a single glass remained in the rack.

"Great!" was Kathy's only comment.

Barry did not say anything. He had once commented on the wisdom of having the goblets hanging upside down in the flimsy wood racks here in earthquake country, but now did not seem the right time for an "I told you so." The racks and glasses had been a wedding present from somebody in Kathy's family.

The cupboards seemed to be fine. The little finger latches that the rest of the country called child safety latches, but that Californians called quake latches held tight. Barry sat the light up on the breakfast bar.

Kathy rounded the counter and entered the kitchen, reaching for the broom closet when the refrigerator roared to life. Her aquarium in the living room also bubbled again and its fluorescent light flickered. The power was on.

Barry reached over and flipped on the light switch. "That wasn't very long at all. The electric company is getting better at restoring service."

Kathy just "hmm'ed" at him, intent on the task of cleaning up the broken glass.

"I'll get the big trash can; you should put it all in there." Barry headed for the garage.

The garage was not in bad shape at all. Of course, they did not have too much in it, being newly married and the townhouse being a rental. One stack of magazines had slid off the shelving, but nothing else, almost everything had elastic bungee cords on the front of the shelves for just such an occurrence. Barry lugged the trash container over by the kitchen door and grabbed the Dust Buster from its recharging rack.

Barry entered the kitchen and squeezed between a bent over Kathy and the frig. He just eased past Kathy when the rumble of an aftershock hit. Kathy grabbed for him. They stood together in the middle of the kitchen floor. Barry noticed that Kathy's wide-eyed innocent look he had thought about during the earlier quake was really accentuated when she was scared. A young looking twenty-four, and standing without make-up in the kitchen light, clutching his robe sleeve, Kathy could have passed for sixteen. Her hair, unkempt from the interrupted sleep, hanging in blonde ringlets, added to the youthful appearance. Barry put his arm around her as they stood and waited for the temblor to stop. He could feel Kathy shake at every new tremor from the ground.

The power stayed on and they were able to watch as the short quake rattled the house. As they watched the aquarium water sloshed from side to side. Barry had not noticed before that it was low. The earlier quake had sloshed water out of the tank. The aftershock ended with a moderate bump that rattled glasses in the cupboard, but nothing broke.

Kathy let out a sighing puff of air, as if she had been holding her breath, as the last movement of the floor ended.

They stood arm in arm for a moment after the aftershock ended. Finally Kathy spoke, "How long do you think they'll keep up? The aftershocks?"

"God knows. They say we are still getting them from the last one up north. They go on for years. Who knows what they consider an aftershock, maybe this was one."

Kathy simply shook her head and went back to the broom. Barry pulled his cell phone from his robe pocket.

Seeing him with the phone, Kathy asked, "Do you have to?" She knew he was going to call the station to see if they needed the off-duty officers to come in.

Barry nodded. It was his job. With earthquakes, you could have one end of the L.A. County Sheriff's vast jurisdiction in normal shape and utter chaos in another region. In the Northridge quake, he had seen freeways ripped apart in the northwest part of the county where he had been patrolling, but some people in Pomona had not even been very alarmed. Earth tremors had become so commonplace in Southern California that many longtime residents sat through the frequent aftershocks, casually comparing one quake to another, not taking any precautions or exhibiting very much concern. It had become a way of life. On the other hand, there were also many people with the opposite reaction. Every quake brought hundreds of calls to police agencies and government offices from people with one concern or another, some real, most imagined.

Such was obviously the case tonight. The line to the sheriff's sub-station was busy. Barry clicked the phone off and went over to get the cable box picked up.

Kathy took the opportunity to take his cell phone, "I think I'll check with Cindy and see what Jeff found."

Barry nodded, and then wondered if Kathy's call back to her sister was not just an excuse to keep him off the phone and away from the chance of having to be called in for extra duty. Barry suspected Kathy did not want to be alone. She hated it when he pulled night duty anyway, even without the quake.

Barry flipped on the TV to see if any of the local stations were carrying anything. This, too, had become a habit for many Californians. He muted the set for sake of Kathy's phone call. At two in the morning it was too late for news staffs to be at work, probably the only ones at the station would be the engineers trying to recover from the power outage. However, he tried anyway.

Nothing was on about the quake, just infomercials, old movies and test patterns. He poked the remote off and turned his attention to the wet rug around the fish tank.

Barry waited for Kathy and Cindy to finish on the phone trying the radio for some news. While he waited, he spread towels on the carpet around the fish tank to sop up the water.

Timing is everything in earthquakes.

The 1933 Long Beach Earthquake caused the collapse of virtually every school building across a wide area. It is estimated that if the quake had happened during school hours that more than 20,000 students might have been caught inside the collapsing buildings. The quake was a 6.3 magnitude on the Richter Scale. Several Southern California faults, including the New-port-Inglewood fault, which caused that 1933 quake, are capable of quakes of up to 1000 times the intensity of the 1933 quake.

A quake in 1755 in Lisbon, Portugal killed 15,000 to 20,000 people. It just happened to hit when old, masonry cathedrals were filled with worshipers for All Saints' Day services. The death toll and destruction from the resulting fire in the 1923 Tokyo earthquake was magnified by the fact that it hit just when thousands of charcoal hibachi stoves were working on preparing the evening meal all across the city.

If the 1994 Northridge quake had hit at rush hour, hundreds could have been killed when parking structures and freeways collapsed. As it was, the quake, at 4:30 on the morning of a national holiday, could not have come at a better time to avoid massive casualties.

May 5th, 11:51 P.M.

"M-Mommmy ... Daddy. I'm scared."

The sound of the little girl's shrill, frightened voice cut through the low rumble in the floor and the rattle of the metal framed windows as they shook. Seconds later the baby's cry joined his sister's.

Matt Contreras had hoped the kids would sleep through this

latest temblor to hit the Palm Springs area. Obviously, this was not to be. This quake did not seem too bad, it was already dying away when the children awoke. Gloria flipped back the covers and got out of bed. Matt followed.

Matt followed his wife down the hall. The tremor ended and the slap of Gloria's flip-flop thongs on the tile floor was the only sound, except for the crying children. When Gloria turned into the baby's room, he turned the other way and went to Miranda. It was getting to be routine.

Little Miranda was standing up in her bed, still trembling with sobs. Matt gathered his daughter up with one arm and turned on the bedside lamp with the other. The girl hid her eyes from the bright light by tucking her head into his chest. She clung to Matt with a clench that made the middle of the night trip worthwhile.

"Everything is all right. Daddy's here now." The sobs died down as he spoke.

Gloria came into Miranda's room; the baby was always easier to get calmed. She sat next to him on Miranda's bed.

"Wwh .. Wwhy ... , " Miranda tried to speak through the sobs. Gloria reached over and stroked the girl's soft black hair, while Matt rocked her back and forth.

Finally, Miranda got her words out, "Why do we always have earthquakes?"

Matt answered, "Well, it is just the way the earth is here in California." He paused and a thought struck him. "Miranda, do you remember me telling you about Grandpa Cruz?"

"Yes, was he the one you said was a real Indian, not a reservation Indian?"

Gloria gave a muted harrumph at this. Both she and Matt were of mixed Indian blood. He was prone to coming up with such politically incorrect comments about Indians, Matt not really being a font of pride in his heritage.

"Yes, that's him." Matt eyed Gloria and continued. "You know, when I was a little boy he told me a story about earthquakes. A legend that the Indians told for generations about the reason the ground trembles and shakes. Would you like to hear it?"

"Uh-huh." Miranda put her head to Matt's shoulder.

"This, I gotta hear." Gloria Contreras huffed, as she settled back a little on the bed. In her eight years with Matt, he had rarely acknowledged the Indian part of his heritage, let alone tell Indian legends passed down from ancestors to his child.

Matt settled Miranda on his lap and began.

In the time before Man, the Father of All had sought to create order from the chaos that was the world. In the world, there lived many great spirits and awesome creatures. To bring order to the world the Father of All had given each spirit and creature his own realm.

The spirits were each given their own abode and they controlled the elements, Wind, Rain, Fire and the rest. The thunderbird was given the air. The great fish spirit was given the sea and the rivers. The great ram, Manuluk, was given the mountains as his home. The great buffalo, Tatuluk, was given the vast plains and wide open spaces as his domain.

No sooner than the Father of All had finished molding the world to his liking, Manuluk and Tatuluk started complaining. Manuluk said that there were not enough mountains, because, after all, he was the mightiest creature in the world and he needed more room for his home. Then Manuluk put down his great horns, rutted his great feet into the ground and pushed up a new mountain in the nearest plain.

Seeing this, Tatuluk immediately lowered his great, broad head and charged at the nearest mountain. He hit the mountain so hard that it was crushed flat and its boulders were turned to sand.

Thus, an age-old battle was started.

Sometimes, in their battle for supremacy, the ram and the buffalo would charge at each other and hit with a thunderous crash. Other times the ram's horns locked with the buffalo's and they would struggle to pull themselves free. When Manuluk and Tatuluk would crash into mountains and plains or into each other, the collision would shake the whole earth.

The Father of All attempted to reason with them saying that there was enough room for each, but they were too angry and too proud to stop. Manuluk kept pushing up mountains and Tatuluk kept crushing them. The Father of All saw that such conflict was simply a natural part of life and that the changes made by Manuluk and Tatuluk in their conflict were good, because they renewed the world and made it constantly new.

And so, even today, Manuluk and Tatuluk are constantly causing mountains to rise and fall. And people can hear the great ram and mighty buffalo and feel the earth when they shake it.

"So, each time you hear the earth tremble and the ground shake you can just say, `It is just Manuluk and Tatuluk going at it again.'" Matt finished the story and turned to tuck a very drowsy little girl back into bed. Gloria flipped off the light.

Out in the hall, Gloria turned to Matt and gave him a hug. "That was real nice. Sometimes, you really surprise me."

Matt replied, "I try."

Matt and Gloria headed back to bed to see what could be salvaged of a night's sleep.

Unable to sleep right away, Matt felt the house shake with one more set of tremors a short time later. Fortunately, Miranda stayed down. Matt heard Gloria turn and settle; she was always able to get back to sleep sooner than he could.

Matt and Gloria Contreras had purchased their modest ranch home in northeastern Palm Springs a few years earlier. They had met at Cal State University San Bernardino, married and after Matt's tour of duty as an Army helicopter pilot in Iraq they had both been lucky enough to land jobs in the area of their homes. Gloria had been raised on the Torres-Martinez Indian Reservation south of Indio. Matt had been born to a Mexican father and Morongo Indian mother, so he had grown up with a good deal of contact with the Morongo reservation, north of Palm Springs. His hometown, however, was the town of Manning, west of both Palm Springs and the Morongo Indian reservation.

Their joint salaries from his job as a pilot for the highway patrol and hers as a bank officer gave them a comfortable life, quite a bit more so than their cousins and Gloria's parents who still stayed on the reservations. Moreover, the extra money the casino on the reservation supplied to tribe members made a nice college find for the kids.

Matt finally heard Gloria's breathing slow to the rhythm of sleep. The second tremor was followed by silence and eventually Matt, too, lapsed into fitful slumber, waking at every sound and each sleep movement from Gloria, vigilant even in his sleep of the tremors from beneath the earth.

■

The Morongo Indian reservation sits in a gap in the mountains at the eastern end of the Los Angeles Basin. Two giant mountains, San Jacinto, to the south and San Gorgonio, to the North, are separated by a narrow pass. Through this pass, San Gorgonio Pass, pass both Interstate 10 and the main transcontinental railroad, as well as one of the great California aqueducts and numerous pipelines, each on their way into the great metropolis to the west.

Like Manuluk and Tatuluk, the two huge stone massifs, the peaks called San Jacinto and San Gorgonio, are locked in a centuries long battle. San Jacinto is the tip of an outcropping of mountains on the north edge of the tectonic plate or section of the earth's crust which is known as the California Plate. San Gorgonio is likewise a spur thrust out of the southwestern edge of the North American Plate. Like two interlocking pieces of a picture puzzle, the great mountains indicate a spot where the two chunks of the earth's crust have snagged each other. The northward movement of the California Plate has been stopped by the snag. The San Andreas Fault, which marks the line between the plates, takes a shallow "S" curve through the gap between the mountains. The two mountains are pushing each other with continent-building force.

This is the same force that has, in the past, uplifted the mountains of Southern California from ocean depths to thousands of feet in the air. This force is applying itself to this snag in the San Andreas Fault just north of Palm Springs. Deep within the earth, directly below the Indian reservation, the chunk of tectonic plate marked by San Jacinto is slowly pushing itself past San Gorgonio.

Small slippages along the fault line have occurred for centuries, making the area one of the most active seismic areas on earth. Every once and a while a major earthquake in the region, such as occurred in 1857 or 1992, signals some movement, but not nearly enough to relieve the stress of the moving continents.

Geologists agree that there exists the possibility, if not probability, that the blockage deep in the earth at San Gorgonio Pass holds the possibility of producing a super-quake of awe-inspiring magnitude. Even short of such a super quake, a major quake at any point along the San Andreas or the myriad of other faults in the latticework of interlocking and co-dependent faults that make up Southern California could be devastating.

■

Every child studying a globe in school has seen how the eastern tip of South America fits neatly into the western underbelly of Africa. It is quite clear that South America broke off of Africa and one or the other has been pushed away. The study of tectonics, the study of the structure of the earth's surface, has shown us what has pushed these huge landmasses apart.

Running down the middle of the Atlantic Ocean is a line of intense volcanic and seismic activity, known as a tectonic rift. A look at an undersea map shows us row upon row of undersea mountains. To the north, this undersea rift rises above sea level in the form of the volcanic island, Iceland. In this rift zone, the lava and volcanic rocks of the Mantle are constantly pushing up, spreading the rift out and pushing the continents apart. The floor of the ocean is constantly being reborn by new material being pushed out of the rift. Similar rifts exist in every ocean and are the site of volcanoes and earthquake activity.

However, not all of these rifts run exactly in the middle of the ocean. The rift in the Western Pacific runs very near Japan and Russia's Kamchatka region, causing these areas to be constantly rocked by earthquakes and peppered with volcanoes.

In the Eastern Pacific, the rift between the Pacific and American tectonic plates takes a wrong turn off the coast of Central America. It turns toward land, heading directly up the Gulf of California, splitting the Baja Peninsula from mainland Mexico. Like Africa and South America, the adjoining coasts of Baja California and Mexico once fit neatly together and are spreading apart at the rate of two inches per year.

This tectonic rift continues up the Gulf of California going inland near the mouth of the Colorado River south of Mexicali. With its power to move continents, this rift continues unabated across the corner of North America. We know it by its more common name, California's San Andreas Fault.

May 6th, 7:24 A.M.

"Wow!" Cindy Borgmann gulped as she saw the streetlight smashed and toppled in a pile at the corner near their condominium in Marina del Rey. Jeff drove around the corner and then left to the main street. A tow truck was behind a parked car that had been hit by the falling light pole.

"Actually, it was a lot more impressive last night. With all the people standing around watching and us not knowing what else was smashed out in the darkness. And then the aftershock hit while we were in the middle of the street ... ," Jeff Borgmann's voice trailed off. He pulled the car out on the Mindanao Parkway. Jeff had gone out in the middle of the night to see what the commotion was. Cindy had stayed inside, straightening up the knickknacks that had fallen and comparing notes with her sister and mother on the phone.

"So what else was damaged? I didn't get to see the TV." Cindy asked, fiddling with the gold broach on her jacket.

"Don't know of anything locally `cept our streetlight. Probably some more little stuff around though. From the TV I heard I guess some church school or something was wrecked out in Rancho Cucamonga, but not much else. I guess it was a pretty light quake. Five point something. Centered way out in the San Gabriel Mountains. Not much damage, just a lot of interrupted sleep."

"Thank God. I really hate this routine."

"Nah, not me, I really don't mind that much. These quakes are the cement of Southern California society. Everyone has them in common. You can meet a total stranger and start swapping stories about what you were doing when Whittier or Northridge hit."

"Christ, leave it to you to develop a pro-earthquake philosophy. I think you are the only one in L.A. that sees earthquakes as an asset."

Cindy checked her makeup in the vanity mirror. Her firm expected the women on the staff to be conservative, but feminine, whatever that meant. Actually, in these days of emphasis on freeing the workplace from sexual overtones, firms rarely gave voice to any such expectations. Rather, a casual hint or a discrete word from partner to senior female staffer to female employee was enough to convey the dress and grooming code to the women of Leibowitz, Smythe and Goldwasser. At any rate, Cindy Borgmann did not need to worry. Her even features, green eyes, size eight figure and business-like style fit in perfectly with the firm's image with no worry about make-up or dress. Working at the firm was the only time in her life she had not envied her kid sister's blonde hair. Her own medium brown was a better for a serious professional look. Blondes might have more fun, but brunettes are taken seriously.

Actually, as the senior partner's secretary, it would nominally fall on Cindy's shoulders to be the firm's grooming police, but it was rarely needed. Anyway, it was not the secretaries amongst the women at the firm who had the most problem fitting into the firm's expectations. The young women associates were always torn between the habits they had grown accustomed to in college and law school, the need to be stylish and feminine, or even worse, individualistic, and the need to be conservative and business-like. Cindy had seen more than one young female attorney crash and burn on the altar of fashion. Cindy snapped the vanity mirror up and straightened the silk scarf at her collar.

Jeff turned up onto the Marina Freeway. As always, he would go east to the I-405 and then north to drop Cindy off at work in Century City.

Jeff continued the conversation, "Nonsense. Lots of people benefit from the quakes or the threat of quakes. Good business for bottled water and spackling plaster dealers and for sales of earthquake preparedness kits. L.A. Business Review had an article on a person who built a ten million dollar business on shrink-wrapping dehydrated foods for earthquake kits. Most of the nine billion dollars the federal government sent out for Northridge quake relief went right into the construction industry. Contractors in Los Angeles were hurting bad after the recession until the Northridge quake boosted the construction business and brought in the federal bucks."

"Yes, and as a good little CPA you probably look at the Big One hitting us as merely good `upside potential' for mortuaries. Right?"

"Perhaps," Jeff paused speaking as he looked back over his shoulder to merge onto the I-405 northbound. "I guess mortuaries would be a growth industry. The same for selling re-cycled `Chicago brick.' Not to mention selling beachfront property in Nevada."

Cindy shook her head, "God, Jeff, how can you joke about it? You know these quakes scare me to death."

"You started it with the crack about mortuaries."

"I didn't start it, you did with the business report.... " Cindy stopped, seeing where the conversation was going.

"Enough, change subject." She said, motioning her hand in a cutting, chopping motion. It was their signal. Jeff nodded. Their marriage counselor had taught them to see an argument coming on and kill it promptly.

Jeff was staying in the slow lane. There was not much point in getting over very far between the Marina exit, the 10 freeway and Santa Monica Boulevard, especially in traffic this thick.

Cindy started out the change to a new subject. "So. What's on your agenda today?" she asked Jeff.

"I...," Jeff polished an imaginary brass button on his chest, "... am having lunch with Michael Dumont."

Cindy raised her eyebrows. "Rather lofty circles to be running in. What's up?"

"Haven't a clue. He called yesterday and said he had something he wanted to discuss. Said Don Benjamin had referred him."

"Let's see. I know the name, Dumont, of course and that he is a big wig in entertainment. But, I can't remember what exactly he is in to. Television?"

"Yes, sort of. On the side, I guess you'd say." Jeff pulled into the exit lane to Santa Monica Boulevard and slowed. "Actually, he is known for packaging total deals. If someone has a good creative project, you know, motion picture potential, Dumont is able to, up front, sell the rights to the various theatre and video markets, Europe, USA, Japan, and any merchandise tie-ins, and the television and cable rights, to the movie, sight unseen, for enough money to finance the whole project. Then, with everything financed or almost so, Dumont and his investors earn their money on the actual movie deal, as well as finder's fees from each segment of the finance package. And his latest coup has been to package whole groups of movies and movie rights together, financing the whole thing. He put together one deal that sold the rights to three published novels, Philip Shoreham's military/spy stuff, and three novels that Shoreham has not even written yet. Dumont has got the hottest author in the country writing for Dumont and Company for the next decade."

Cindy looked over at Jeff as he talked. She could see why people joked about the two of them being clones of each other. With the same hair and eyes, similar features and matching serious depositions Jeff and Cindy could have been siblings, rather than spouses. Cindy could hear the excitement in her husband's voice as he talked about his potential new client. She watched him as he drove through the heavy traffic up to Century Park East.

Cindy was glad Jeff could find interest in his work. She knew that the steady diet of tax returns and profit-loss statements for small businesses was not challenging Jeff much. Cindy had often thought that Jeff was wasting himself on small potatoes in his practice. Every day Cindy saw lesser men make bigger money. With Jeff's solid education, square-jawed good looks and bright intellect, she knew he could make it big, if given the chance. Maybe this was it.

"Any idea at all what Dumont wants?" Cindy inquired. "I hope it is something more than just some tax advice."

"Hey, I don't know, Dumont's got a lot on the table. I'll bet his taxes alone would keep most small firms busy for a stretch. But no, I think he has something more than taxes in mind."

"So where are you going? For lunch." Cindy got her purse and put it in the oversized clutch bag she always took to work with her lunch and a magazine in it. They approached her building, a smoke-silver high-rise on the west side of Century Park East.

"The Wheelhouse, on Pacific Coast Highway. Dumont's choice. You know the place, half way to Malibu." Jeff pulled into the circle drive in front of the building.

"Well, good luck. Give me a call? Tell me how lunch goes." She leaned over, offering him a cheek.

"Of course." He kissed her.

Cindy picked up her things, got out, and smiled back at him. Jeff watched her as she disappeared into the revolving doors. He found himself thinking that she had a fine figure. He did not tell her often enough.

Jeff took a deep breath. It would be a long day and horny thoughts were not the best way to start out. Keep focused. He pulled out of the drive, turned a U-turn on Century Park East and headed north to his office in Westwood.

■

In the far southeastern corner of California and farther south into Mexico, there is a landform unique in the entire world. The area is known by various names. The residents of its northern end near Palm Springs know it as the Coachella Valley, but it is more widely known as the Imperial Valley, home of the Salton Sea. It sits at the northern end of the Gulf of California. Although it is dry ground, global tectonics charts show the "mid-ocean ridge" or tectonic plate boundary that runs up the Gulf of California continuing under this land area.

A few million years ago, the Gulf of California was a third longer than now. It was subsequently divided in two parts by the dual action of the Colorado River, depositing the post-Ice Age silt cut from the Grand Canyon and the rest of the wide Colorado Basin into the Colorado River Delta, and the deposit of mud and ash spewed from an active mud volcano system under the site. The buildup of alluvial dirt filled the center of the Gulf of California with a mud flat only slightly higher than sea level. The course of the main river turned south across the delta into the southern Gulf. Eventually the northern third of the Gulf was cut off from the open Pacific by the mud flats of the delta. As the isolated water dried up this northern area became a broad flat basin, dipping to 235 feet below sea level, the Imperial Valley, or as known by the pioneers, the Colorado Desert.

The entirety of this curious region is underlain by not one, but four major earthquake faults, including the main San Andreas Fault. This tectonic rift zone is the same one that split the Baja California from mainland Mexico and is tearing California apart along the San Andreas. The entire Gulf of California area, including the Imperial Valley, is being pulled apart by the tectonic forces, widening every year by a matter of inches. It is

*also one of the most seismically active regions known,
even relative to the rest of quake-prone California.*

*This huge area of below sea level land is separated
from the waters of the Pacific Ocean only by the mud flats
of the Colorado Delta, which has an elevation of only
fifteen feet above sea level in spots. This water-saturated
sediment of the delta is the most dangerous medium for
the damaging and settling effects of liquefaction during
earthquakes. The area is also peppered with mud volcanoes, geothermal anomalies and other volcanic activity
testifying to the geologic instability. And, precisely on
top of this unstable mud plug that holds back the Pacific
Ocean, the million-person city of Mexicali has been built.*

May 6th, 10:10 A.M.

Ten men and one woman sat in the main conference room of
the Geothermal Resources Authority of the State of Baja California in
the city of Mexicali. The six Mexican managers faced five American
consultants across the polished fossil rock table. Colored graphs and
computer printouts littered the table.

"Perhaps we should start out by verifying the data," the woman,
an American geologist, said, tapping one stack of printouts.

"Miss Perkins, I know it may come as a shock to you, but Mexican engineers are perfectly capable of reading a thermometer gauge."
The engineering chief from the Nayarit geothermal plant, Miguel Ortiz,
did not hide the edge in his voice. He would not let his staff be belittled
by the Americans, especially by a woman. It was bad enough that the
Americans had been called down from San Francisco this morning for
their advice; he did not have to take any insults.

A pregnant pause was broken by Cliff Hodges, the chief consultant, "I think we can assume that the data we have is correct. There has clearly been a drop in both temperature and pressure. We need to analyze why this is occurring, what pattern it has and see what can be done about it. Obviously we have to find out if this is a freak occurrence or an onset of changed circumstances that we will have to deal with from now on."

It was now Sybil Perkins's chance to snap back, "Actually, the data I was referring to was not the temperature data. I was referring to the salinity and dissolved solids. These kind of figures are more akin to seawater than the brine they should be getting from geothermal steam.

Another Mexican, a young man in an ill-fitting sports coat, had been waiting for just this. He lifted a stainless steel canister from his briefcase to the table. He nudged it across the table toward the female engineer.

He spoke in halting English, "This is condensate from the Number Three main turbine at El Faro. See for yourself."

Ortiz cut in, "We will, of course, supply you with samples from each site. I believe spectrum analysis of such samples is part of your contract." His tone was still bordering on hostility.

Hodges answered, "Of course, if you can arrange express shipment our laboratory in Cupertino can get right on that." Hodges paused and picked up his notepad and pen. "I had a few other questions. If that's all right?"

None of the Mexicans said anything.

"OK. First. When was the first anomalous reading? Of any kind?"

The young man in the sports coat answered. "Ten days ago. *Veinte-seis de Abril.*"

"And, have there been any other indications of problems. Anything other than the readings at the plant?"

Again, none of the Mexicans spoke immediately. The young man in the sports coat twisted uneasily in his seat, unsure of whether to speak. Finally he spoke.

"Everyone has been talking about it. The mud volcanoes over by Laguna Salada have been ... have been putting on a show. They say the eruptions are the biggest in memory. That is almost ten kilometers west of Nayarit."

"Yes, but this whole area is underlain by the same geologic structure," Perkins said.

Hodges now spoke, "I think we had better mount a full scale seismic study. If the natural ground-level geothermal events are affected along with your plants' deep holes, we may be seeing something unprecedented. A change in the status quo underground."

■

"...The More Ranch, Laviglia, and Mesa faults underlie the heavily developed Santa Barbara - Goleta areas. These faults are poorly exposed, but escarpments such as the northeast-facing mesa overlooking downtown Santa Barbara is recognized as the result of an upthrust of the coastal block. Maximum vertical displacements on any of these faults is probably not more than 2500 feet. Though topographic evidence for current movement is meager, indirect evidence suggests that these faults may become active at any time.

"For example, the 1925 Santa Barbara earthquake was occasioned by the sudden slip of an offshore fault, perhaps the seaward extension of the Mesa Fault...

"The major Mission Ridge - Arroyo Parida fault zone forms the boundary of the coastal plain and the Santa Ynez block north of Montecito and is responsible, to some extent, for the sharp relief of the Santa Ynez mountain front. The Santa Barbara Riviera (Mission Ridge), a highly developed residential area built on the somewhat unstable Monterey formation, has been formed partially by movement of the Mission Ridge fault zone, which passes mostly north of the Riviera proper."

The Santa Barbara County Comprehensive Plan
-Seismic Safety Element, 1991

May 6th, 10:50 A.M.

With a perfectly manicured maroon fingernail Genevieve Dumont pushed her sunglasses back up in place and put the copy of *Vogue* that the postman had just delivered on the other chaise longue. Genevieve actually found little of interest in a magazine and fashion industry that had been central to her life so recently. She slid her hips to one side and canted her knees to the right so that the sides of her long, slender legs would get the benefit of the late-morning sun.

She would follow the sunbathing with an appropriate anointment with moisturizers and anti-oxidants. Genevieve knew that a deep tan enhanced her dark-eyed beauty. The somewhat exotic cast to her eyes and her lustrous light olive skin had always been her trademark as a model and they remained her best asset. She had become an expert at mixing the right amount of tanning with the correct cosmetics. She understood that her good fortune in having Michael Dumont as her husband was based in large part, if not exclusively, on her looks and she spent a considerable part of her time insuring that Michael remained happy with those looks.

Genevieve had been a model employed as a "hospitality girl" at a public relations suite at the Cannes Festival when she had caught Michael's eye. A fortuitous set of circumstances, namely Michael's hormones and the opportune absence of his previous squeeze, had found Genevieve on Michael's arm for the remainder of Cannes. Although a striking beauty in any sense of the term, Genevieve was slightly over the prime age for a Parisian model and she had been looking for other opportunities, visiting her parents in Aix and had wound up in Cannes. She had readily accepted his invitation to return to California with him. After a few carefully choreographed months, Genevieve managed to become the wife of the wealthy motion picture deal packager.

The newly married Dumonts had done a trendy thing amongst the Hollywood crowd and purchased a house in Montecito, in the lush hills east of Santa Barbara. With all the prestige of Beverly Hills, but none of the problems of living in the heart of L.A., Montecito was becoming the location of choice for Hollywood's elite.

Montecito was a little over an hour north of Los Angeles by stretch limo on the 101 freeway. With southern exposure on its wide beaches coupled with a cosmopolitan atmosphere that outstripped its size, Santa Barbara, with its two elite bedroom communities of Montecito and Hope Ranch, was remarkably like Genevieve Dumont's previous residence in the south of France. This fact not being lost on anyone, the high ridge covered with luxury homes above Santa Barbara was called the Riviera.

The home Michael Dumont had purchased for his beautiful brunette was on the far west end of Montecito where the low lush hills of Montecito proper rise to the heights of the Riviera. At the seaward end of a cul-de-sac running atop a high ridge, the Dumont home commanded a view of the Santa Barbara Channel and the Channel Islands beyond. Built on two levels cut into the steep slopes of the ridge, the house and garage were balanced on four steel pylons over the pool level.

The balcony on which Genevieve lounged was cantilevered forty feet above the kidney shaped pool below. Like many of the neighboring homes, their house had been built originally in the 1960's, but expanded and remodeled as the value of its location increased.

Michael Dumont had readily paid the low seven-figure price tag for the home, practically a bargain by Beverly Hills standards. The prestigious location and sumptuous decor made it a bargain in his mind. The luxurious home provided a getaway from the hectic pace of Los Angeles and a gilded cage, remote from his world of Hollywood, for this new bride for whom he had adjusted his previously carefree urban lifestyle.

Had she had her eyes open under the sunglasses, Genevieve would have seen the 270-degree view from the balcony that had so exhilarated both her and her husband on their first visit to the house with the agent. Genevieve had been entranced by the view and had never given a second thought to the unique location that afforded the view. However, like the good businessman he was, Michael Dumont had sought the advice of a pro, a structural engineer, before closing the deal.

Only the front walls of the house and garage actually were in contact with the ridge. The rear of both was perched on the four stilt-like pylons. The engineer had declared the steel I-beams of the stilts and the foundation of the house to be structurally sound. The lower end of the I-beams were securely embedded into the concrete piers sunk into the rock below on the pool level. The engineer had recommended repairs to the winding concrete stairs down to the pool, which repairs were quickly accomplished to close the sale to the Dumonts.

It was the policy of most structural engineers not to make determinations of geologic stability, which was left to be answered by a specific request to a geologist. In the aftermath of a huge landslide liability case in suburban L.A. a few years before, the insurance carriers of the engineers had excluded such evaluations from coverage under most professional liability policies. Besides, this house was no different in its essentials from a dozen neighboring houses. It was built in the same manner as the thousands of homes in coastal California that were designed to take full advantage of the marvelous scenic potential of the landscape.

There was no mention in the engineering report of the fact that the rock in which the pylons were embedded was the geologically slippery, easily stressed shale of the Monterey Formation. There was no mention in the report that the reason for the existence of the ridge itself was the location of the Montecito Fault a few hundred yards down the north slope of the ridge. With Montecito almost a hundred miles northwest of the epicenter in the San Gabriel Mountains, neither Michael nor Genevieve had felt the temblor in the middle of the previous night.

Thus somewhat oblivious to her surroundings, Genevieve turned once more to allow her nicely rounded and well-oiled buttocks to face the sun. She tugged the bikini strings up to a different spot than they had been the day before to avoid the line on her hips. She did likewise with the bra, unhooking it and allowing her smooth tan back to be open to the sun.

Had this been France she would, of course, have been topless and need not have worried about this, but Michael had, early on, informed her that her Montecito neighbors frowned on such.

Strange people, these Americans.

■

Every active earthquake fault can be viewed as a pressure release valve for the stress building up in the earth from tectonic movement. When one of these valves lets loose it creates a quake. The more stress and the longer the fault, the greater the potential magnitude of the quake.

As frightening as a single sizable earthquake might be, the real concern of many seismologists is in the massive network of interlaced faults in Southern California. Caltech scientists believe that the massive 7.5 quake at Landers, California in June 1992 started on one fault and within seconds continued by ripping up another nearby fault, causing two distinct forms of seismic wave energy from the different orientation of the faults. Three hours later a 6.6 quake hit a totally different nearby fault. Within a few hours, two strings of aftershocks had spread out from these sister quakes in the vicinity of the San Andreas, but the mighty San Andreas itself did not let loose of its own enormous stress.

The worst of all earthquake scenarios for Southern California would be if a quake on any of the potentially deadly faults caused a chain reaction of pent up energy from neighboring faults. No point in urbanized Southern California is more than a few miles from one of these faults.

May 6th, 11:40 A.M.

Deputy Barry Warden had spent the morning on relatively routine matters, back-up for a domestic dispute and a minor fender bender that needed a police report because one driver claimed whiplash. Fortunately, this area was on the opposite side of the County from the epicenter of the previous night's quake, so there had been little fallout or extra work from the quake.

The L.A. Sheriff's sub-station Barry worked out of covered several contract cities and some unincorporated areas near the Palos Verdes peninsula, south and west of Los Angeles proper and west of Long Beach. The small cities, although incorporated, contracted with the Los Angeles County Sheriff for police patrol duties. It was a good duty area. The wealthy residents of Rolling Hills and Palos Verdes were not as much of a headache as the poorer working class and minority areas that bordered them on two sides. Besides, the `rolling hills' of the Palos Verdes peninsula area were beautiful scenery. There were a lot worse assignments than patrolling these calm residential streets and their park-like greenery.

The substation had two 4x4 Explorer's among their patrol units. Technically, they were assigned to the station to patrol the small patch of the Palos Verdes peninsula that was partially undeveloped and pretty rough terrain, but in practice they were used like any other unit. Barry had pulled duty in one of these this morning.

He was parked on the side of Crenshaw finishing the paperwork from the accident. Barry snapped the clipboard down on the report and intersection sketch. He glanced at his watch. The time jived with the growl from his stomach. He decided to call in on the radio.

"Dispatch, Patrol Four-four, Over." He waited for the dispatcher to answer.

"Go ahead, Four-four." A pause, static, then, "Over."

Barry smiled, the dispatcher, Barbara Fuentes, was brand-new, still getting used to the routine. Fuentes did not quite have the radio procedure down yet. She had just transferred in from administrative office duty. Barry Warden could easily picture the duty sergeant hovering over her, cringing at every mistake, like the forgotten `Over.'

"My 10-20 is Crenshaw and Palos Verdes Drive North. I am southbound and expect to be 10-10 at Promenade Mall for lunch in five. Over." Barry reported his intention of taking lunch. He planned on doubling the lunch break with an attempt to find Kathy something for their upcoming anniversary.

"Roger, Four-four ... Wait, Over."

Barry waited.

"Four-four. Supervisor requests you keep your portable turned up for lunch. We are shorthanded and may need to interrupt your lunch. Err, ... Over."

"Roger, Four-four, Out."

The order to keep the portable radio on over lunch had come across a bit odd since it was usual procedure. Barry assumed that it was just the new radio operator and a supervisor whose patrol staff was stretched thin.

Then, thinking about it, Barry Warden realized the error might be his own. The new dispatcher might have taken his 10-10 literally, and reported to the supervisor that he was going to be off the air, rather than just somewhat unavailable, as he meant. Technically, she was right, he should have called in "10-7" and not "10-10." New bodies on the watch always took some time for everyone to break in.

Warden signaled and headed south into the noonday traffic.

∎

In most civil engineering offices in California you can find maps of Seismic Safety Zones. Recognizing the risk facing the State, the state legislature has required the state to be surveyed for purposes of determining regions of highest danger and greatest risk to buildings. The Seismic Safety System attempts to chart where the multitude of fault lines cross under the landscape in an attempt to build around the danger. Only rarely do the faults manifest themselves on the surface and to attempt to locate within a range of fifty to a few hundred feet a fault which is hundreds or thousands of feet below the surface is conjecture at best. And, if a developer wishes to challenge the location of a particular fault line, all that is necessary is to hire another geologist who is willing to go on record with a guess that the fault lies elsewhere. Seismic Safety Zones have been known to move, miraculously, a mile or more when enough money is behind a particular real estate development located near the old Zone.

Besides, the very concept that a "safety zone" a few hundred feet across is a sufficient buffer for an earthquake fault is absurd. When an earthquake fault releases its pent up energy it does so with a force that can only be likened to a volcanic eruption, or perhaps an atomic bomb, in all of human experience. The epicenters of many earthquakes, including the monstrous 1906 San Francisco and recent Mexico City quakes, are often many miles from the areas of greatest destruction. People who would never think of living on the slopes of an active volcano or in the vicinity of nuclear testing casually build homes, schools and cities so very close to the known dangers of the faults of Southern California.

May 6th, 11:40 A.M.

It was a pain that the teacher's union would not give out the job information by phone or on their website, but Kathy could not really blame them. With the fiscal austerity and layoffs that had hit California school districts, the job vacancy bulletins that the union posted on the bulletin board were popular reading for people like Kathy Warden, looking for a teaching job, but not really keen on taking one of the positions that frequently opened in the less desirable areas.

Kathy Warden's substitute teaching duties in the last year had brought her to some of the worst schools in the city and she definitely did not want to make such a locale permanent. There were many schools in Los Angeles were a young woman with blonde hair and blue eyes and Kathy's kind of looks did not feel like she fit into as a teacher. At her wedding the year before, Kathy's uncle, Harold, had described Kathy as "gorgeously cute," which was kind of a two-edged compliment in her view, but definitely not a good description for a teacher in Watts or the Barrio.

Kathy was tired of being cute. Her girlish cuteness had caused her one substitute teaching foray in the upper grades to be a fiasco. The mostly black high schoolers in Inglewood had given her no respect whatsoever. Kathy's petite, but well-rounded figure and soft-spoken manner had merely added to the problems. The unruly high school boys had been unmerciful.

Fortunately Kathy had her certificates in early childhood and special education and therefore would have a leg up for a good permanent elementary school assignment. This would be the first time she would be able to try for a full year contract. She and Barry had just finished plans to marry this time last year and she had been behind the power curve in getting applications out in L.A. for the current year and therefore had been relegated to subbing.

Luckily, Barry's job gave them enough to live on until a worthwhile teaching position appeared for her. As it was, living square in the middle of the huge Los Angeles Unified School District with only a few other employers for teachers nearby, the good vacancies were snapped up by teachers already in the system and the undesirable jobs went to the newcomers. Now, in early May, the school districts, both L.A. Unified and the many smaller outlying districts and private schools, were posting their projected openings for fall contracts. Kathy would probably have to take whatever she could to get inside the system. Maybe she would be lucky. So, Kathy went down to the Education Association offices downtown every few days to check on new openings.

Parking near downtown was, as always, miserable. But, the area near the teachers union office was not as crowded as usual. Kathy found a parking spot on the street, a real rarity.

The receptionist in the office smiled in recognition when Kathy came in. The receptionist was a somewhat portly woman who overdid her eye shadow and lipstick, emphasizing her oversized features. Kathy smiled back and went to the clipboards of job announcements on the far wall of the lobby.

"Good morning," the receptionist said, absent-mindedly checking her watch to make sure it was still morning. "Still hot on the trail of the perfect job, huh?"

"Yes, nothing yet."

"None of those you got last week panned out, huh?"

"Well. I put in the applications, but you don't hear for a while."

"I guess so, huh."

Kathy wondered if the woman could say anything without ending it in `huh.'

There was a new announcement for a special ed teacher in La Canada/Flintridge and a few other new notices, most of them out of town. Kathy also found a job announcement for a teacher at an experimental school, one of the new public charter schools, in Claremont. It would be a long drive for her from West L.A., if she got it, but it was just the kind of opportunity she was looking for. She took the interesting items to the self-service copier in the corner and started clunking coins into it.

Armed with the photocopies of the charter school notice and the few other announcements of interest Kathy walked back to her car. It was a beautiful spring day, maybe even a bit on the hot side, and she had nothing else to do, so she would head out to Claremont and put in an application.

Kathy had heard on the radio on the drive downtown that Claremont, along with Rancho Cucamonga and some other spots in the San Gabriel Valley, had been one of the areas rocked the hardest by last night's quake. But, the radio had not mentioned anything major as far as damage, so Kathy saw no reason not to go. An opportunity to teach in a progressive experimental school could not be missed.

Kathy rolled the Honda's sun roof back and checked her side mirror for traffic. Several cars passed as she watched for an opening. Finally a small opening appeared. She jerked out into the lane, earning a honk from a car behind her.

Kathy headed south through downtown to pick up the I-10 which would be best to head east on. She flicked the radio on as she started and stopped. Noontime traffic in the downtown area was dreadful. It seemed the construction projects downtown never ended and nobody paid attention to what their project did to traffic.

She cycled the radio signal search button through a rap station and two Spanish language stations before she found a news-talk station that claimed to have traffic and news reports every few minutes. The first traffic report had nothing about the 10 freeway, their traffic copter was out over San Fernando somewhere. She stayed on the station to hear the news.

"Now, with more on the earthquake that shook most of L.A. last night, we have our reporter, Herb Green, who is standing by at UCLA, where a news conference was recently concluded. Herb?"

"Yes, Bill, as you said they have just concluded a news conference here with officials from various public agencies and universities who discussed last night's quake and some interesting information that seems to have come to light regarding this quake. I have Doctor Margaret Holmes from the University of California, Geology Department and who also acts as a consultant for the State Seismic Safety Commission. Doctor Holmes, can you tell us about the information you announced here today?"

"Thank you, actually what we were trying to do today, the reason we all gathered on such short notice, was to discuss a phenomenon called `micro-quakes' which have occurred following last night's quake on the San Gabriel Fault. We really had not intended to call a press conference."

"Ah, what are these microquakes?"

"Microquakes are small seismic events that we usually associate with larger quakes, either before or after major earthquakes, but which are different from normal foreshocks and aftershocks in their duration and pattern. Most seismic experts associate microquakes with a buildup of stress in the rock structure, rather than movement in the rock structure as from normal aftershocks. Many scientists believe that microquakes could be useful in predicting earthquakes."

"So, is this a prediction of an earthquake to come?"

"No, no, no. Not at all. A few years ago we had a cluster of microquakes near Parkfield and an earthquake was anticipated and nothing happened. So, no, we are not predicting anything. We just wanted to alert everyone involved, the public agencies and scientists, that we have a rather unique situation which warrants everyone's attention."

The reporter pressed on. "What is so unique about this situation. Let's say as opposed to Parkfield or other, ah, situations."

Dr. Holmes pause a second and then spoke, "Well, what we are really interested in here, why the Seismic Safety Commission had everyone fly in to talk about it, is that these microquakes are associated with this San Gabriel earthquake, which was really a rather modest quake in relative terms, and not one likely to generate this type and level of microquake activity. We have not seen this before. And also, that the microquakes following this quake are not only in the vicinity of the previously inactive San Gabriel Fault where last night's quake was, but also on or near other faults which intersect or neighbor the San Gabriel fault, including the San Andreas."

The reporter's voice indicated he was wrapping it up. "So, if this is not a prediction, what words would you have for our listeners?"

"Right, this is not a prediction and people should not get excessively worried about this. What I always say is for people to just pay attention, follow the earthquake preparedness guidelines that everyone should know by now, every phone book has them in it. California is earthquake territory and we should be ready, now or in the future."

"Thank you, Dr, Holmes, this is Herb Green, reporting from Westwood, UCLA Campus, back to you Bill."

Kathy suffered through an overly loud commercial, exhorting her to trade in her old car, while she digested the news report. She was not sure what to make of it. On the one hand, they clearly were not predicting an earthquake, but on the other, this Dr. Holmes had clearly been waffling and doing everything she could to avoid making a prediction or really explaining what was so important to call a conference of top scientists and officials in the first place.

Traffic ground to a total stop as Kathy approached the interstate. The commercial ended and a traffic report ensued. Kathy listened in to see if they had anything that really affected her directly, such as a "Sig Alert on the 10 eastbound at the four level", or the like. There was nothing. Microquakes were forgotten in the press of the approaching freeway traffic.

■

"California is situated on the rim of the Circum-Pacific seismic belt and it is inevitable that earthquakes along the state's numerous faults will cause extensive damage and endanger the lives of people nearby. The risk to life and property is especially significant near the San Andreas fault where rapid growth and population increases have occurred in our largest urban centers over the last several decades. With each passing year, the potential for an earthquake-caused catastrophe increases as California's growth continues and the time lengthens since the last great earthquake.
California Statutes - Government Code §8871

May 6th, 11:40 A.M.

"Hi, Honey. How's your day going?" Matt Contreras heard Gloria's cheerful voice after he picked up the extension and muttered his usual monotone greeting "CHP Flight Ops, Contreras, here."

Matt was not sure when or where Gloria had picked up the habit of calling him "honey." She sounded like her mother. He was not sure he liked it, but what could you do about it? Tell your wife not to call you "Honey?" Hardly. He just let it go. There were worse things in life to worry about.

"Fine. Nothing unusual. We did a circle down over the Interstate and north to Joshua Tree for CalTrans to check for quake damage. Nothing to speak of. We thought we were gonna get to chase an escapee from the honor farm at the San Bernardino Jail, but the County chopper spotted him before we could get past Twenty-Nine Palms. How about you?"

The tone in Gloria's voice was now a bit off. "Oh, you know the usual excitement level we generate here at BankCal. Never a dull moment. We thought we had a car loan payoff this morning, but it was a false alarm, they just made a double payment." The sarcasm in her voice was clear.

"Look, Gloria, if you don't like it, you don't have to work there. We've been through this."

"Yes, we have. And you know I really do want to make this job work for me, BankCal's jumped through hoops helping me out with the fast track management program and all. It's just when you talk about flying around chasing bad guys in your chopper, it makes my world of loan applications and balancing teller's cash reports seem a trifle boring."

"Well, that's nothing a few weeks of watching tourists and truckers breaking the speed limit on I-10 wouldn't cure. Real exciting, that."

"Everybody's got their own cross." Gloria changed subjects, "Don't forget, it's Murphy's day off and I have to play manager until closing. Consuella can't stay at the house after five, so remember to get home early. OK?"

"10-4, ... er, Right." Gloria hated it when he used 10-signals, instead of English. It was a speech habit lots of cops' wives had to put up with.

She let it slide, this time. "Just, don't forget. Last time you did Consuella got real pissed. We need her happy, especially for the little money we pay her. She's a hell of a lot better than a day care center for Miranda and little Matt."

"Fine, I won't forget. Five o'clock sharp."

"OK, love ya. See you later."

"Love you, too."

Matt Contreras checked his watch. He had about an hour for lunch. He was set to go up with Captain Moody from the Riverside County Sheriff Department at 12:30. Most of the police agencies let pilots from other departments cross-qualify in each other's craft. It had been nearly two years since Matt had updated his quals in a UH-1 like the Riverside Sheriffs used for SAR. Matt usually flew the little Jet Ranger that the Highway Patrol used. He might need to use his old Army qualifications in a Huey, or its newer cousins, and he did not want to miss this opportunity keep current on the aircraft type. Even with a two hour flight, he would still be back in plenty of time to release Consuella before five.

Matt made sure his flight bag was ready with logs, area charts and his flight gear. This usually stayed in his own chopper, but he had taken it out for the flight with Moody. He called in to the CHP main office in Indio and checked out.

Matt locked the door of the California Highway Patrol's hangar office at Thermal Airport south of Indio, patted his hip to make sure the Blackberry was there and went to his car. With only an hour for lunch, McDonald's would have to do. Besides he had been meaning to try the Burger of the Month, anyway. Mushroom and Swiss.

■

Earthquakes travel through solid earth as a series of waves, not unlike ocean waves, conceptually. Every sailor can tell us that the top of a ship moves more than the bottom in an ocean wave and the taller the ship, the more the movement at the top. Simple logic tells us that the object closest to the source of a wave moves before a farther object moves. It is therefore clear that a ten story building in the path of an earthquake's ground wave will react very differently than a neighboring twenty-story building and, if close enough, the two buildings will come together with tremendous force about ten stories above the ground. While California building codes mention this problem, the state has numerous buildings close enough to "interfere" with its neighbors. Likewise, the most modern "earthquake-proof" buildings cannot withstand the collision with the tumbling rubble of a neighboring, older building which was not built to modern earthquake codes. Further, as a practical matter even the "earthquake proof" buildings are only designed to withstand collateral (i.e. indirect) damage from an earthquake in the 7.0 to 7.5 range maximum. Thus, the estimation by seismologists that several faults in California are capable of generating earthquakes in the 8.0 to 8.2 range tells us that there is a distinct possibility of experiencing an earthquake several magnitudes greater than our safest buildings can withstand.

May 6th, 12:00 Noon

"... and there were no other reports of any serious damage or injury. However, a spokesperson for the Department of Water and Power stated that they would maintain a constant watch for any changes in the current situation at the reservoir. Once again, officials indicated there is no cause for immediate concern and the efforts to lower the water level in the reservoir are merely precautionary considering the proximity of the reservoir to the magnitude 5.4 earthquake which struck shortly after midnight on a previously inactive fault in the San Gabriel Mountains."

Cindy Borgmann adjusted the volume on the radio. She wondered if anyone else recognized the incongruity of the report. Why, in normally water-starved Southern California, would they lower the water level in a reservoir that was supposedly undamaged and not in any danger, just because it was close to a quake that had already happened. Cindy was skeptical. How could they expect you to believe such reporting? What else was known, but not reported to the public? She supposed that her own dread of earthquakes was at least partly the source of the skepticism, but she still had a good point.

The radio's next report, an interview from Cal Tech, was cut off by the louder volume of the intercom. Goldwasser's gravelly voice croaked forth from the box. "Cynthia, has the FAX from Rauscher come in yet?" Goldwasser always called her Cynthia, rather than Cindy, when he had clients in his office.

"No, Mr. Goldwasser. I am watching for it. I will get it right to you when it comes in." Cindy always called him Mr. Goldwasser, even after five years. The age difference between Cindy and the senior attorney was such that using his first name would not be right. Besides, it was not just Cindy; only two of the partners, out of all the attorneys in the firm, called Goldwasser by his first name, Bernard. Only the two women who called and left their names as Mrs. Goldwasser, his wife and mother, ever dared to use the name Bernie. However, scurrilous use of the nickname "Bernie" had been known amongst associates and paralegals in the context of jokes and occasional curses, but never to Goldwasser's face. As the only "named partner" of the firm still in active practice Goldwasser and everything to do with him was the epitome of decorum, propriety and the highest-priced client billings.

This made Cindy's job a mix of both good and bad. On the one hand, she did not have to put up with the rush jobs and stress of the litigation matters the other legal secretaries did, but she did have to put up with Goldwasser's idiosyncrasies and the demands for diplomacy and client hand-holding that went with being secretary to the senior partner. And for Cindy Borgmann, just barely thirty, it was as good as she could expect. Legal secretaries did not do better than working for the senior partner in a swank Century City firm. The fact that her salary was as good or better than other women who had stayed in college for a degree, like her kid sister Kathy, added to her satisfaction. It somewhat made up for the total lack of potential of ever advancing to anything else. She would let her husband aspire to greatness. Cindy's current focus was working on developing the need for maternal leave of absence.

The radio reporter was interviewing some scientist at Cal Tech, "And, like the Northridge quake, this quake appears to be on a thrust fault at a depth and location not previously associated with seismic activity."

"Meaning...?" the reporter urged the scientist to fill in the blank.

"Well, meaning that this is probably not an aftershock of any previous seismic activity. And... very possibly is an independent event... or the precursor of other follow-on activity."

Moving in on the ever-elusive news scoop, the reporter asked, "Then this could be a pre-shock, before a major quake?"

"There is really no way of telling that. We only have preliminary information. But from past experience, the USGS has given this a twenty percent chance of being followed by similar or greater seismic activity."

"Just twenty percent?" the reporter actually sounded disappointed.

As the report ended, Cindy heard the door open and the sound of chairs being shoved back around Goldwasser's conference table. She deftly clicked the radio volume slider to zero and turned herself in her chair so that she would be facing the boss' door when everyone came out.

Goldwasser followed the group of five men out of the office. None had their briefcases with them, so Cindy knew what was up before Goldwasser spoke.

"We will be having lunch at the Century Club. When the Rauscher thing comes in, make sure we have enough copies for everyone when we get back." That was now the third time he had told her how to handle the expected fax from New York. If this were not par for the course with Goldwasser, she would be upset. But, she realized his style and simply smiled, wishing them a good lunch, knowing that hers would be spent waiting for the fax machine to spew forth municipal finance data from Wall Street.

As Goldwasser herded the clients toward elevators, Cindy headed down the hall the other way, to the employee break room to retrieve the Tupperware bowl of salad she had brought in and put in the refrigerator. Cindy looked at her watch. High noon. Rush hour for the break room.

The firm of Leibowitz, Smythe and Goldwasser had spared little expense when they had moved from downtown into the new offices in Century City a decade earlier. On the twenty-eighth floor of the thirty floors in the prestige building, the offices were top-grade in every way.

The employee break room was no exception to this. Although not done in the same oak paneled elegance of the rest of the office suite, the break room was well-appointed and equipped, not to mention well-stocked with beverages and the like. For some reason, top drawer clients expected to be offered a full gamut of beverages at meetings and depositions in the firm's offices, so law firms obliged by stocking the refrigerator. At three hundred plus minimum per billable hour for mere associates and near twice that for Goldwasser, the firm could afford to stock the wet bar. And as an unwritten employee benefit, the staff always partook of the non-alcoholic beverages and assorted snack foods as they pleased. The fifteen minutes or half hour it took for a trip to the first floor snack bar took could be billed out to clients instead if the employee did not leave the office, so no-one had cause to complain. The result of this and the time pressure most associates and other staff members were under led them to eat in the break room or at their desks more often than not.

"How goes the world of high finance?" one of the other secretaries asked Cindy as she crossed to the refrigerator. It was Dee, the tall black woman who was secretary to the firm's only African-American partner.

"Slow as usual. And I think someone ought to research the potential liability for caffeine poisoning of our clients. I think I have brought five pots of coffee in this last two hours."

"Over-dosing on caffeine is an old bond counsel tradition." Someone else, an associate, piped in. "It is the only way to survive the boredom."

Cindy smiled and retrieved her salad and a Diet Sprite. She made a place to eat between the various sections of L.A. Times strewn on the end of one table. She selected the entertainment section read with lunch.

Who knows, maybe her husband would be in the movie business soon and she might have to be up on the current movies.

■

Some of the most spectacular residential archi-
tecture in the world rests on the coastal bluffs and hilltops
of Southern California. Sadly, the same facts of nature
which lead to the dramatic vistas and splendid perches
for the homes are also the cause of their greatest danger.

The owners of these marvelous views might
wonder what caused their own bit of earth to rise above
the rest of Hollywood Hills, Encinitas, Malibu or a dozen
other geographically "desirable" areas. The answer lies
in the phenomenon which is Southern California geol-
ogy; a vast system of rifts and complex faults virtually
unrivaled on earth. Even the famous earthquake zones
of Japan and Chile are simple in comparison. In all the
world, only the Great Rift Valley of East Africa or the
mighty Himalayas compare to the network of breaches
and cracks in the earth's crust which underlies the whole
of California.

May 6th, 12:05 P.M.

The big black car purred into the deceleration lane of the 101 freeway. A bystander would have heard and felt the throaty rumble of the car's huge engine throttle down to a stop, but inside the car Michael Dumont's cellular phone conversation was not interrupted. Nor did he feel the slight tremor that shook the hill country northwest of Los Angeles, one of the swarm of small shocks that was hitting the fault system south of the San Andreas.

Nobody built a car quite like Mercedes. If price was no consideration, you could not find better transportation than this. And price was no consideration to Michael Dumont. The cost of the 550 S had been expensed as a production cost on the motion picture Dumont was handling during the car's purchase. The financial books for the movie had shown $104,000.00 for "production/staff transportation expense" and they were backed up by a daisy chain of cash vouchers and fund transfers which eventually got paid to the auto transport firm working with the film's vehicles and who also delivered the 550 S and, in turn, paid the Mercedes dealer. However, without knowing exactly what had happened it would be virtually impossible to track the destination of the money that the movie production budget had paid for. To make things even more difficult to trace, the title to the car was in an inter-vivos trust listed under the first initial and maiden name of Dumont's new wife, Genevieve.

Michael Dumont pulled the untraceable and fully paid Mercedes up to the stop light on Las Virgenes and without pausing his phone call turned south down toward Malibu Canyon. He was talking to his administrative assistant and gal Friday, Jill, giving her his instructions for the day.

"OK, then have Mindy do whatever she can to tie up the rights in New York. Tell her to let the damned publisher know he can fuck this whole thing up by being greedy." Michael Dumont trusted that either Jill or Mindy Leffertz, his New York assistant, would sanitize and deliver the message diplomatically. They knew that what the boss said and what he expected to be said by them were two different things.

Dumont jockeyed the car through the rhythmic turns that led down Malibu Canyon. A car like this made this kind of road a treat to drive. Even with a bit more speed than necessary the car hugged the winding highway. On either side of the curving road, Dumont passed the spectacular houses that populated the Malibu hill country. Houses, not unlike his own farther north, that took advantage of the dynamic landscape to perch on promontories and hillsides in order to catch the best view or command the most dramatic locale.

"Right, got that." Jill concluded. "What time can we expect you here?"

"Well, I've got this lunch thing with the new accountant. I got a late start out of Santa Barbara, so I am going right there now, to Malibu, cutting across from 101 to the coast down Malibu Canyon. Hopefully this guy will be bright enough to keep things short for now. I don't want to lay out the whole program until he is on board. Then, I promised Rupert at William Morris I would listen to some idea he has up his sleeve. He says I owe him and that it will be worth my while. He hasn't done badly by us before. That will get me to about three. I should be at the office by mid-afternoon."

"You told me to remind you to get on the Canadian Film Board grant packages, so I have them on your credenza. If you..."

"Fuck! ..." Dumont shouted, cutting Jill off. Dumont grasped the wheel with both hands and hit the brakes on pavement partly covered by sand and gravel.

The anti-lock brakes on the Mercedes did their job. The nose of the big car dipped to the pavement and it slid to a stop, barely short of the jumble of boulders and rocks which blocked the road.

A landslide cut across the road. A pall of dust still hung in the air and pebbles and rocks still rolled down the slope. The slide was fresh. Dumont was the first one to reach it.

The pile of rubble sloped from the hill to the right out across the road and into the gully below to the left where Malibu Creek ran. There was no way around it.

Dumont cussed to himself. Then, remembering the phone, he grimaced.

"Hello?" He asked. "You still there?"

"Yes. What happened?"

"I almost hit a fucking landslide in the road. Nearly bought the farm." Dumont looked in the mirror and started to pull across the road to turn around. "I'm gonna have to turn around. No way through this. Shit!"

A new streak of stones angled toward his car from the hill above. He hit reverse and backed off. Luckily, the one car that had pulled up behind him, a minivan, had anticipated the move and backed up also.

"You OK?" Jill asked.

"Yes, sure. Just some excess adrenaline. Hold on." He put the phone down while he craned the wheels to turn around. Another advantage of a Mercedes, double-cantilevered steering, let the car turn around in just over twice its footprint, a handy feature on Malibu Canyon Road this morning.

Even as Michael Dumont turned his car another cluster of small stones rolled down the slope and into the roadway. The minivan driver was hectically completing a three-point turn and following him.

Dumont got back on the phone. "Well, this will delay things a bit. I guess you should call the road department or highway patrol when we get off. They ought to have a warning up, or something."

"I will. You say Malibu Canyon Road?"

"Yes, a couple miles north of the coast. I'm not familiar with the next road down to the coast. What is it, Topanga? Whatever. I'll call back when I can. I need to turn on the Navigation."

Michael Dumont hung up and with a last look in the rear-view mirror at the landslide he headed north to pick up the freeway once again. He poked the button which to engage the Mercedes' navigation screen then hit the telephone button again, then he spoke the speed dial code for the New York office. With the extra time he had he would give young Miss Leffertz personal instructions on how to deal with the greedy publisher. And he would keep both hands on the wheel to make sure that the remaining stretch of winding roadway did not get the better of him with more surprises.

■

The San Andreas Fault takes a sharp turn to the west in the San Bernardino Mountains. This sharp turn forces the earthquake fault lines of Southern California to form a series of majestic arcs from northwest to southeast. The great faults we know of as San Jacinto, San Fernando, Whittier and Imperial all follow this arcing pattern. One such fault starts in Beverly Hills, heading south through Inglewood to Newport Beach. It caused the Long Beach quake of 1933 and, possibly, the great quakes which destroyed the Spanish missions in the early 1800's.

The Inglewood-Newport fault system does not stop at Newport Beach. It continues south in a sweeping arc precisely along the coastline all the way to San Diego. Along the way it passes directly underneath many of these precious seaside villas and, more importantly, squarely under the San Onofre nuclear power plant site, which was recently deactivated for structural and technical problems.

The northern end of the Newport-Inglewood Fault is at an intersection of six different faults, all classified by the State's engineers as being active or potentially active. With the Newport-Inglewood Fault, the Santa Monica Fault, the Malibu Coastal Fault, the Hollywood Fault, the Overland Fault and the Charnock Fault all converging within a couple of miles of each other you would think that this area would be one where the utmost caution would be used in controlling building. On the contrary, within two miles of this huge intermingling of geologic instability, you can find the main building of the U.S. Government in Los Angeles, the University of California at Los Angeles, a half dozen major hospitals, the most densely populated apartment district in California and the numerous skyscrapers of the Beverly Hills/

Upper Wilshire, Westwood and Century City high-rise complexes. In fact, the skyscrapers of Century City could not have been more perfectly positioned on the northern extension of the Newport/Inglewood Fault if their builders had intended it. Also, the Santa Monica Fault runs almost directly under the Cedars-Sinai Medical Center, as does the Charnock Fault under the huge Veterans Administration Hospital.

May 6th, 12:44 P.M.

The fax from New York had come in while Cindy Borgmann was finishing her salad in the break room. Someone had picked it up from the fax machine and put it on her desk for her. The copy clerk would not be back in the copy machine room until one o'clock, so if she were going to have the copies waiting for Goldwasser when he returned she would have to run the copies herself.

Cindy shook the last of the moisture from her freshly washed Tupperware salad bowl and tucked it into her canvas clutch-bag. She picked up the fax and shuffled through the stack. Nothing interesting, as usual, just certificates by auditors and verifications by underwriters and their attorneys.

She put the cover sheet in her in-box and with the sheaf of fax papers in her hand headed for the copy room, down the hall across from the break room. She could hear that most of the employees were still in the break room, talking and watching television as they had been moments before when she left.

Like most things in a modern office, making copies had gotten more complicated in recent years. Not more difficult, just more complicated, since the new copiers could save many steps and time, but they took more complicated instructions to do the work quicker. When they installed it the Xerox sales staff had given the Leibowitz, Smythe and Goldwasser staff a three hour course in how to run the new copy system, which could copy, color, staple, collate, bind, scan, store on disk, email or whatever, but needed computer panel input instructions to simply photocopy. Cindy took a deep breath and stuffed the fax into the input tray. As she touched the touchscreen to indicate the number of copies she felt the big machine shudder. When she reached over to poke the staple icon on the screen the floor under her feet quivered. Once and then again.

Cindy's first thought was enunciated by a shout from someone across the hall in the break room, "Quake!"

Cindy had felt minor quakes in the building before, but usually even aftershocks which other in the LA area felt quite strongly were minimal here. Someone had once commented that the building's quake dampening foundation was the reason for this. Apparently the building was built on huge rubber bumpers which protected it. Cindy's thoughts were on this as she felt the deep rumbling shakes in the floor.

Then, beginning subtly, then not so subtly, she felt the pit of her stomach tighten, a feeling mixing dizziness and the gutty sensation of an elevator starting grew. Cindy had grabbed the front edge of the big copier when the first vibration shook her. Now, as the feeling of light-headed movement grew, Cindy felt the movement through her hands and the copier. As though she were on a huge ship at sea and the copier were the railing of the ship, she felt the rolling motion. It increased.

"Oh, my God!" was someone's quavering moan from somewhere outside the door.

Cindy thought of moving somewhere safer, but she did not know where that might be, She stood frozen, gripping the copier. Now the rolling grew to a point were standing was an effort.

There was a crash from the hall, something crashed loudly, jarring the floor even through the quake. Someone screamed across in the break room, a woman. Then a man shouted, "Here. Come over here." Cindy had no idea what has going on there, but as the swaying increased and crashes multiplied in the office, she felt the need to be with others.

She turned part way around and realized that to leave the room she would have to leave her grip on the copier and walk across the rolling floor. The ten feet to the door seemed a long way. As she looked for the door behind her, the lights flickered. Again someone screamed from the break room. This was all she needed to encourage her.

Cindy let go of the copier and lunged for the door. Only as she staggered forward, almost drunkenly did, could she see that the swaying of the building was also swaying the copy room door, which now swung closed in a arch. The combined effects of her headlong lunge, the flicker of the lights, her staggering gait over the rocking floor and the swing of the door led her to wobble toward the swinging door's edge. She tried to put her arm out to block the swing, but missed. She hit the arching door on the right side of her body. Cheekbone, jaw, breast and thigh all hit the door with a thud. Cindy fell to the floor, her hand came up to her face, to touch the pain in her cheek, but as she moved her vision narrowed and the rumbling and noise from the crashes in the office moved into the distance. Cindy did not pass out, but felt the peculiar disembodiedness and loss of senses that was the precursor of unconsciousness.

Beneath her the floor still rolled. In only a few seconds, full consciousness flooded back on her. The full pain of the impact with the door also flooded back in. She cried in pain. And fear.

Cindy now lay sprawled in the copy room door. She had only a moment to look up and all she could see was the ceiling of the little room and the hall outside. Then, in another flicker, the lights went out. She now lay in total darkness.

The floor now lolled back and forth with a dizzyingly slow rhythm. The door swung once again, this time banging her leg. Her body actually rolled from side to side on the floor. All around the furniture and contents of the office flew and bounced and crashed. Cindy heard the sound of glass breaking as unknown objects crashed into windows.

Somewhere to here left, down the hall toward reception, she heard a scream. It was the same as many she and others had uttered, but different. This scream was a young woman's scream. Was it Brenda, the receptionist? The scream started nearby in the office and then whined off into somewhere else, dying away as it went. The sound was unmistakable, and chilling. Someone in the office had fallen out of a window.

In the horror, the pain and the fear, Cindy Borgmann was overwhelmed. She covered her aching, bruised face in her arms and curled into a ball in the doorway. Cindy sobbed a whimpering cry she never remembered doing before. Even as she did, she felt the copy room reverberate as the metal paper supply cabinet fell to the floor, bouncing off of the copier as it fell. If she had not come to the door, she would have been under it.

As she lay curled in her fetal ball, waiting for the skyscraper to stop its rolling, Cindy's thoughts flicked from person to person in her family, husband, sister, parents, friends. Where were they? How were they? Would she see them again? Was the building falling over? When would it stop swaying and reverberating?

It seemed like forever.

■

Barry left the gift wrap counter at the jewelry store and went out into the courtyard of the mall. He took the escalator down to the street level where he had the Explorer parked in the yellow zone. Nobody would ticket or complain about a sheriff's vehicle left overtime in the loading zone.

Barry tucked the silver-wrapped box into his pocket. He had found an anniversary gift for Kathy at the jewelry store in Promenade Peninsula Center. He had the gift, gold heart shaped earrings, gift-wrapped. He would keep it in his locker at work until the anniversary at the end of the month. He made a mental mote to make reservations somewhere for the anniversary dinner.

Lunch had been uneventful. Despite the warning from the new dispatcher, he was not interrupted by the radio. He had used the earphone in the restaurant to keep the other calls from bothering the patrons.

The escalator was about halfway between floors when the shaking began. The escalator jerked and protested the extra torque of the load. With his hands on both rails, Barry could feel the escalator quiver. It stopped. All around him in the mall he could hear shouts, yelps and screams as customers discovered the floor move beneath them.

At first, neither he nor the other people were much concerned, they all had felt quakes before. Then, as the rolling intensified and the duration extended, everyone started to talk, to shout and walk, then run toward the nearest cover.

Barry, standing as he was on the escalator, had to wait for the people below him to move. He looked above him, his chief concern being the skylights in the mall high above them. He was not alone. The woman in front of him, while looking up, tripped over a hastily dropped bag on the escalator and fell. People behind him crowded in. It was only his uniform that kept the people behind from elbowing through and over Barry and the fallen woman.

"Get her out of there," a man shouted.

"Move!"

Barry did not answer, he just grabbed the woman by her arms and picked her up bodily.

They finally got down the escalator. Leaving the escalator, it became harder to run, as the shaking of the floor became more pronounced. High above him, there was a crash of broken glass. He looked quickly toward the skylights. They were in place. Somewhere above on the upper decks of the mall, a plate glass window had shattered. Barry hoped the cause was the quake and not a running body. The sound of the glass redoubled the screaming.

There was a cluster of pushing, screaming people at the double doors to the street. Barry was ready to intercede and bring order to the throng, but as he hurried up the rolling stopped. It had lasted about maybe forty seconds.

Barry realized the lights were out. The only light now came from the doors and the skylights.

Barry backed away from the door. With the end of the rumbling, the crowd had settled, although still intent on leaving the mall. He backed up to the wall outside the Abercrombie & Fitch and cupped his hand over his ear to hear the radio earphone.

As he listened to other units call in, Barry Warden looked around the inside of the darkened mall. There did not appear to be any damage, except to business, the mall was almost empty already.

It was evident from the calls on the radio that the long rolling quake had scared the hell out of everyone. But it had apparently not caused much damage, at least in this part of Los Angeles.

His opportunity to report came on the radio. "This is Patrol Four-Four, Over."

"Go Ahead, Four Four." It was the new dispatcher, Barb Fuentes, again.

"I am on foot in Promenade Peninsula Mall. Checking on possible damage. Over."

"Roger, Dispatch, Out."

His circuit through the mall had turned up nothing untoward. The window had been broken by a mannequin that had fallen, the only casualty. Barry Warden reported and was told to continue his patrol.

He was sitting at a light on Hawthorne Boulevard listening to the AM radio in the Explorer, starting to get an idea of the destruction the quake had wrought in the San Bernardino-Riverside area when the police radio crackled his call sign. "Patrol Four-Four. Dispatch, over." It was the duty sergeant's voice. Barb must be at lunch. Barry clicked off the AM radio.

"This is Four-four, over."

"See woman, Mrs. Westover, at 12517 Savoy Ridge Drive regarding possible vandalism. Over."

"This is Four-four. Let me guess. Broken glass and housewares, no sign of forced entry. Right? Over."

"You got it, Four-four."

"You don't have any more urgent for me. Especially after that quake? Over."

"No. Looks like our area got by pretty well. Nothing major reported. But it sounds like they had some bad stuff downtown and out east. Inland Empire got the shit kicked out of them. Eight point on the scale. But, for now, we get to treat a vandalism break-in as a serious incident report and you get to check it out, OK? Over."

"Roger, Four-four, out."

Barry shook his head. Both patrol officers and the dispatchers were getting tired of the scheme. A magazine article on earthquake insurance published after the recent quake was to blame for calls like this.

The typical homeowner's insurance did not cover damage from earthquakes and if there was an earthquake endorsement on a policy it usually had a deductible amounting to something like ten percent of the total value insured. Therefore, the slight damage from minor quakes would not be covered. So, the writer of the article had suggested that the good citizens turn in police reports on vandalism for the damage and get it covered that way.

It was obviously insurance fraud and the insurance companies were aware of it, but that did not stop a whole new crop of otherwise upstanding homeowners from committing the fraud every time the ground shook. The advice the sheriff and other police agencies had gotten was to simply note in the report that there was no indication of forced entry and add the term "possibly earthquake related" to the report. It was amazing how irate the homeowners who tried the scheme got at that term in a police report or how quickly they shut up when the officer mentioned he knew about the magazine article and that the insurance companies did, too.

Savoy Ridge Drive was a cul-de-sac in Rolling Hills, a private road up in the hills. Barry Warden turned the Explorer south to pick up the cross street.

The talk about the damage downtown had made Barry think of Kathy. He knew it was her day to check out the teaching job lists, but she was usually done by mid-morning. She was probably back home by now. He would call her at home when he finished with this call.

■

The massively destructive Mexico City quake occurred a considerable distance from the area of greatest death and destruction in the city itself. The Fukushima, Kobe, Northridge and Loma Prieto quakes all had areas of profound damage clustered in certain regions far removed from the center of the quake. The reason for this is liquefaction.

Liquefaction occurs when seismic waves strike an area where the earth is saturated, or nearly so, with groundwater. The effect is most often compared to the quivering of a bowl of gelatin, which continues long after the movement of the bowl itself ends. Mexico City is situated on an ancient lake-bed and the force of the distant earthquake was magnified by the liquefaction effect on the soil there.

From downtown Santa Barbara to downtown San Diego, hundreds of critical areas and buildings in Southern California rest on soils which are perfect mediums for liquefaction. Many inland areas such as the central San Fernando Valley and parts of the central Los Angeles basin are ideal liquefaction zones. Freeways and airports built in tidal areas and former swamps, as the city of Oakland well knows, are prime candidates for liquefaction's destructive force. After both the Loma Prieto and Northridge earthquakes destroyed complete sections of several freeways, one California Department of Transportation structural engineer pointed out that from the 101/33 Freeway intersection in Ventura to the Interstate 5 and 8 interchange in San Diego that four fifths of the freeway interchanges in Southern California are located in prime liquefaction zones.

May 6th, 12:44 P.M.

The intersection under Interstate 10 was crowded. The traffic lights to the two on-ramps and off-ramps were not working. Two motorcycle cops were trying to sort out the mess. Their efforts were not showing much success.

Kathy briefly considered alternatives to the freeway. Having grown up and learned to drive in Granada Hills she had learned to always consider the surface streets when L.A.'s vaunted freeways choked to a stop. However, if any other traffic lights were out the regular streets would be even worse than the jammed freeway. Besides, she was not sure if she had any idea of what streets to take through downtown and East L.A. Not all of L.A. was as easy to navigate as the monotonous square block pattern she knew from the Valley. It took the better part of ten minutes to get through the intersection and up onto the ramp to the eastbound freeway.

The freeway was moving in the rhythmic stop and go that was so common for L.A. commuters. Kathy tugged on the seat belt to give her some more room and settled in for what would probably be a long trip out to Claremont.

She thought of calling the school employment office by cellphone, but she had no hands free unit, she had not thought of calling before she left the teacher's union office and found the traffic so clogged up. The radio report had said that the San Gabriel Valley was hit harder by the quake in the middle of the night. She had no idea whether the office she needed to reach for the job applications was open, but she would take the risk, hoping that determination and perseverance in getting to the office might count for something.

She pulled into the second lane out which immediately ground to a halt following that corollary to Murphy's Law that says whichever lane you enter will stop and the lane you left will start moving. Kathy glanced at her cellphone clock on the seat beside her. Plenty of time. The start and stop routine continued all the way across and past the downtown area.

As she approached the interchange with the Golden State Freeway, Interstate 5, the pace picked up a bit. Apparently the north-south freeway was taking some of the pressure off the 10. The Honda was moving at about thirty miles an hour when Kathy felt it start to bounce. She immediately saw a thousand taillights of the cars ahead of her flash red, as did her own. Screeching to a stop just behind the car ahead of her, Kathy heard countless tire squeals and several impacts.

Now, setting still in her car, she again saw and felt the bouncing that had stopped the traffic. Her car and those around her were slowly swaying up and down. Ahead, she could see the four lanes of cars heading up the slight incline toward the huge interchange between the I-5 and I-10 freeways. The thousands of taillights of the stopped vehicles undulated in what was clearly a wavelike motion.

Kathy watched in awe, comprehending, but not fully believing what she was seeing. She could see the massive transition ramps curving into and away from the intersection of these two huge elevated highways swaying like sapling trees in a wind.

After several swaying pitches to and fro, the highest of the arching spans, in curious slow motion, tilted, tottered a moment and then fell, out of her line of vision, toward the freeway below. Several cars and what appeared to be a delivery van were on the span as it fell. The concrete pillar that had supported it was sheared off near the top, like a broken pencil. Even in the rolling of the quake, Kathy felt the earth shake as the huge section of roadway hit the elevated freeway ahead of her. Kathy found herself screaming as she watched. She put her hands to her face for a brief moment and then, in panic, she looked out the sunroof above her as she thought of whether something might fall on her. There was nothing. She was still many hundred feet from the over-head interchange structures and ramps.

Through the sunroof she heard the deep rumbling sound. In the floor of the car under her feet she could feel the sound that went with the rolling motion. A deep rumbling, not unlike the feeling of riding on a train or a subway. Kathy felt trapped in the car, nowhere to hide, nothing to protect her.

She looked quickly to either side to see what her fellow motor-ists were doing. An older women to her right was gripping the steering wheel and starring in wild-eyed horror ahead of her. A man in a truck to her left was looking around and when their eyes met he raised his eyebrows to convey the awestruck bewilderment they both felt.

After a short pause, or rather a brief lessening, in the motion, Kathy felt what seemed like sharp shocks, which literally bounced her car on its springs. Then, without warning, she felt the car lurch side-ways and slide into the car to her left. There was a muffled retort from somewhere and her vision was suddenly clouded by a flash of silvery white. Her shoulder, arm and head slammed into the car door on her left. All around her were crashing sounds and she instinctively covered her head with her arms, but her arms became tangled in something. Something covered her head and blocked her vision.

After a few seconds in abject fear, Kathy was relieved when, in a puff of white powder her car's air bag deflated as quickly as it had inflated to protect her from what it had perceived as a vehicle impact. And, an impact was exactly what she saw as she wiped the dusting of powder from the air bag from her eyes. Around her she saw that the interval between her car and its neighbors was gone and the vehicles to her left and right were now pushed directly up against her car doors. The truck bed of the truck to her right had crashed through her passenger side window.

Kathy felt as though she were sitting sideways in her seat and this feeling was confirmed by the sight, ahead of her, of the vehicles about tens rows ahead which were lifted up tilted to the right. At the far left edge of the freeway she could see bare, broken concrete and jagged reinforcing bar. It looked as though the section of roadway she was on had tilted off the left. To her left front she could now see the city street and warehouse buildings below this elevated portion of Interstate 10.

With the windows now shattered from the impact Kathy could hear the woman in the next car screaming. Turning, Kathy saw the woman, eyes closed tightly, screaming like she was on a roller coaster ride.

A rumbling shudder announced another rolling undulation. Kathy's view of the ground wavered wildly. The roadway lurched violently once more and Kathy felt the sickening motion of falling. As she saw the section of freeway ahead of them move upward out of her vision, Kathy joined the woman in her screams. They were falling.

Kathy's world went black mid-scream.

■

When an earthquake occurs under or near the ocean and the seismic wave energy is transmitted to the water, a phenomenon known as a tsunami or seismic sea wave occurs. Such tsunamis can travel thousands of miles in open ocean and when they reach land they can impart tremendous energy and destruction.

In 1964 the tsunami from the Alaska quake hit northern California causing eleven deaths, injuries and damage to property. Many occurrences of destructive tsunamis have been reported in the border areas of the Pacific. Often the primary damage from Japanese area earthquakes is from tsunami damage.

On June 15, 1896, a tsunami from an undersea earthquake hit Sanriku, Japan with a wave 110 feet high. 27,000 people died. The March 11, 2011, Tohoku Earthquake in Japan produced a 133 Foot Tsunami and killed 16,000 people.

On December, 21, 1812 a major earthquake, presumably from the Newport/Inglewood Fault, hit colonial Spanish settlements in Southern California. A ship offshore near Santa Barbara reported a tsunami wave of over fifty feet hitting the coast. Estimates of the earthquake's magnitude at 6.5 to 7.5 are consistent with a tsunami of fifty feet given the distance. The patchwork of faults on shore in Southern California is matched by a similar system underwater. Major faults such as the Newport-Inglewood fault, which continue underwater for part of their course, could produce massive tsunami effects in coastal areas. Also, each of the islands off the California coast has at least one seismic fault in its vicinity. In fact, the islands are the products of earthquake faults.

May 6th, 12:44 P.M.

The Wheelhouse Restaurant, viewed from the outside, was a nondescript cluster of cubes and angled roofs on the beach side of the Pacific Coast Highway between Santa Monica and Malibu. It was painted varying shades of battleship gray and its total lack of architectural style give a hint at its heritage as an often remodeled and enlarged beach shack. In the late '70's the owners had tried to get permits to tear it down and rebuild with a modicum of design and style. However, a partnership of surfers and environmentalists intent on preserving the status quo, irrespective of style, had stymied the rebuild and actually got the place declared an historic landmark based upon an obscure piece of surfing trivia regarding the building, thus preserving the architectural blight on the coast.

The current owners of the restaurant tried to make up for the outside by making the inside decor presentable. Nautical memorabilia and lots of lacquered wood and polished brass, generously intermixed with plush carpets and good upholstery, gave the place a measure of warmth and ambiance. The pay-attention-to-details cuisine and generous drinks rounded out the restaurants assets. The Wheelhouse was the preferred place to meet for business on this stretch of coast. It was also particularly noted for its Singles' events on Saturday nights in the dual bars on each of its levels. It was in one of these bars, near the entrance, that Michael Dumont found Jeff Borgmann waiting for him.

Michael found Jeff easy to spot. Only a CPA, or an attorney, would be wearing a dark gray suit, white shirt and a colorless bland tie to a beach-front restaurant on a warm spring day.

Michael wore his usual California attire for a business day. Pleated slacks and a overly large polo shirt that showed off his tan and the gold chain he always sported around his neck. Only in the evening or at formal occasions did Michael Dumont ever wear anything roughly approaching a suit.

Michael walked up to Jeff and offered his hand, "You would be Mr. Borgmann."

"Yes, Mr. Dumont."

"It's Michael." He never used Mike.

"Jeff."

Michael Dumont raised his arm toward the balcony that overlooked the beach. "Let's sit outside, it's a beautiful day."

"Sure."

As the two men approached him, the head waiter for the balcony area, a small Mexican with a huge smile, nodded recognition and mumbled "Mr. Dumont," as he turned and led them to a table by the railing, but under the overhang of the roof, shaded from the noon sun.

Jeff took off his coat and folded it over the empty chair. Both men sat down.

"Anything to drink?" the waiter asked as he opened menus. Michael ordered an Arnold Palmer and Jeff copied him.

"Your waitress will be right with you, with your drinks."

Michael patted a napkin into his lap. "Sorry about the delay. I was coming down from Santa Barbara and the road coming across from the freeway to Malibu got hit by a landslide, almost hit it."

"No problem. I had not been here long. My last appointment ran late," Jeff lied. "You live in Santa Barbara?"

"Yes, just bought, up in Montecito."

"Beautiful area."

"So is Marina del Rey," Michael added, letting Jeff know he had been researched.

Jeff looked at Dumont. "You do your homework."

"I earn a rather good living, doing my homework."

The iced tea and lemonade concoctions came and both men ordered sandwiches.

When the waitress left, Michael turned to Jeff and spoke, "Since we are running a bit late, let's cut to the chase and tell you why I wanted to talk to you."

"Fine with me." Jeff sat back to listen to the wunderkind of deal packagers explain how deals are packaged.

"So, ever since the Buchwald case, everybody and their uncle thinks they are the expert on what should be paid above the line, below the line, as a net profit, gross revenue, and so on. All the Big Six firms and their ilk don't want to risk an embarrassment by getting tied up in another fiasco where the accountants are looked at as co-conspirators with the production companies, and the smaller accounting firms, the ones who know what is going on with the motion picture business, all have allegiances with the big studios and production partnerships. All the while, the deep pockets who are sitting there with the money I need to finish financing for a project are scared that movie finances are always crooked and they, the investor, will be taken to the cleaners." Michael left the loose end for Jeff to grab.

"So, you want someone like me, who isn't beholden to the big studios, to set up an accounting structure, that you can show to potential investors and give them warm fuzzies that a cutthroat industry is not going to screw them. Right?" Jeff conjectured.

"Almost, ..." Dumont was cut off by the unmistakable jumping of the table between them and the deck on which they sat.

Several tables near them were occupied and there were at least four expletive declarations of "Quake!" from the patrons at the other tables.

"Here we go again." Jeff said as he cleaned his mouth with the napkin and gripped his chair's arms. The quake had now risen to a rolling and buffeting of the entire building.

Glasses and silver rattled on tables. Several glasses fell off tables to the wooden deck and broke.

Jeff, Michael and the other patrons rose to their feet as the balcony shook with bone rattling ferocity. Jeff looked above him, doubting the strength of the overhanging roof.

Several customers started to run from the balcony. The only exit was through the restaurant.

"Think we should get out of here?" Dumont shouted above the rumble.

Jeff was on his feet, his hands on the railing. "Nah. If this old place goes I don't want to be inside. If it starts to go over. I am going for the beach." He indicated the sandy beach fifteen feet below the balcony.

Michael Dumont looked down and raised his eyebrows. "Maybe," he had to shout to overcome the rumble and rattle of the shaking building. He did not seem sure about the option of jumping to the beach.

"Look!" a woman a few tables away screamed, as she jumped up and pointed seaward.

Both Michael and Jeff looked out and saw the cause of the woman's fear.

The waves on the beach, which had been lapping gently forty feet out from the balcony when they sat down moments before, were now twice that distance or more, and the water was clearly flowing out away from the shore. Clumps of kelp and rocks, usually below water were visible in the wake of the retreating ocean waters. They could see one rather large fish was landlocked and it flopped about in protest.

"Damn, it's getting set for tidal wave, like in Japan. We have to get out of here." Jeff shouted as he grabbed his coat. He cocked his head and motioned Michael to follow him.

"What?" Michael yelled to Jeff, following after him through the swinging doors, off the balcony.

Inside people some people stood around the restaurant, huddled in doorways and others knelt under tables. The hanging lights in the main dining room were swinging in unison. With the number of people inside, Jeff waited until he and Michael had crossed the main lobby before he shouted over his shoulder, "Get out, Tidal wave coming." Then he remembered the other name for it and shouted, "Tsunami."

More people were clustered outside the front of the restaurant. Michael and Jeff passed them on the run. Jeff shouted his warning again as they passed. Many of the people understood and followed Jeff in his run for the parking lot. The run was awkward, as the ground still shook and rolled. The parking lot asphalt was pleated and cracked.

"We have to get away from the coast," Jeff warned, shouting back to Michael who followed his run down the entrance ramp to the parking lot.

"The valet has my car keys," Michael shouted back.

"Come with me," Jeff yelled as he headed for the second row.

Jeff stopped at his Buick, popped the automatic door locks and told Michael, unnecessarily, "Get in."

As Jeff put the keys in the ignition, Michael asked, "How long do you think we have?"

"No idea. You saw how fast the water was going out. Who knows when it will come back in or how fast. I saw those videos of the tsunamis in Thailand and Japan, and they move real fast and ..." He did not finish. The car started and Jeff smoked rubber heading toward the entrance. He could still feel the quake but now as wobbling bumps felt through the tires.

He did not stop at the street, no cars were moving on Pacific Coast Highway, but many cars were stopped, waiting out the quake and avoiding the tumbling pockets of stone that rolled onto the highway from the cliffs and hillsides above.

Jeff finished his last sentence, "Tsunamis can be huge, can cover buildings, ships, whatever. We have to get to high ground."

"Yes," Michael said. "I saw those videos, too."

They could both see the limestone cliffs above the beach area. Only an occasional driveway cut into the cliff face interrupted the highway and these might not get them far from the ocean. The nearest cross street was a half mile south.

The bumping of the earthquake stopped as Jeff sped toward the intersection, the quake was over. They could see cars and trucks stopped in and around the intersection, but could not see it clearly.

Jeff saw one car, then another go by on the other side of Pacific Coast Highway, racing as he was toward some hoped-for exit, but to the north. His heart fell at this sight and what it meant for the chances of getting away from the coast at the intersection.

He raced toward the intersection and had to brake heavily. As he had feared, the intersection was blocked. Somewhere, above them in the hills to the right that the cross street led to, something blocked the whole line of traffic down to the beach.

The two lanes ahead of him were also blocked with cars waiting to turn. No one was trying to go straight down the highway. Their way was blocked.

"Look! Down the coast," Michael Dumont shouted.

To the south, Jeff Borgmann could see the cliffs of Santa Monica and the ribbon of highway that led to them. Now looming to the left, he could see a frothing swell of gray water as high as the cliffs themselves.

The wave rolled toward them, not so much as the curl of ocean wave that surfers sought, but more as a simple mass of water from a giant overturned bucket.

"Can we outrun it?" Michael yelled, too loud for the inside of the car. His eyes were wide with fear.

"I'll try!"

Jeff started to turn around, cramping his wheel, but in his rear-view mirror he could see the taillights of cars which were now stopped on the other side of the highway, going northbound. He could see the steep bluffs that lined the highway all along Malibu had careened onto the road in a landslide.

"No way," He mumbled, more to himself than Dumont.

They were trapped.

Michael Dumont leaned forward and looked up to the cliffs above them.

"Can we make it up on foot?"

Jeff Borgmann did not answer, he just shook his head slowly, watching the wall of water roll up the coast toward them.

Michael opened the door. "I'm gonna try."

In his rush, Michael had left the passenger door open. Jeff

reached over and closed it. He then fastened his seat belt and put the car in park.

The wall of water approached at unimaginable speed, faster than a car could travel up the coast from Santa Monica. Jeff saw buildings and cars and billboards rolling in the hundred foot high froth of seawater.

In the last instant, out of the corner of his eye Jeff saw Dumont. Michael Dumont was about ten feet up the sandy slope, clawing at the dirt and rocks, making little headway.

Jeff Borgmann gripped the steering wheel tightly and pushed his body back into the seat, his head braced against the headrest. He closed his eyes and forced himself to think of Cindy and not the mountain of water that raged up the Pacific Coast Highway.

■

The point at which the initial rupture occurs and the first earthquake waves radiate is referred to as the focus or hypocenter. The position on the earth's surface directly above the focus is called the epicenter. Seismic waves are produced near the edge of the rupture as it spreads out from the focus, releasing the accumulated strain energy. Consequently, if the magnitude of energy released is significant, as is generally the case for large earthquakes, there will be relative movement between the two sides of the fault at other locations besides the immediate vicinity of the epicenter.

Santa Barbara County Comprehensive Plan

May 6th, 12:47 P.M.

Genevieve Dumont had become rather good at the American art of channel surfing. She now used the skill to flick from channel to channel, gleaning whatever she could of the earthquake she had just felt.

It had been the first quake of any size she had been through, the little aftershocks she had felt while staying down in LA had been nothing, compared to this. Earthquakes were rare, but not unknown in France. She had certainly never experienced anything like what had just occurred.

She was just finishing her shower, which had removed the last of the gelatin facial she had applied after the morning sunbathing. Genevieve had just reached to turn the water lever off in the shower when she felt the shower enclosure move and then she felt the queasy motion.

At first, Genevieve thought that the shower stall was moving and then in a moment of abject fear, she assumed her whole house was sliding off its stilts into the ravine below. She raced from the bath, heading for the front door, only remembering her nakedness at the door. At the door she stopped, turned to look across the house to the tiers of glass patio doors, which gave her a view of the world outside, the neighboring hills which remained in place. She saw that the house was not sliding. She could now feel the movement beneath her, the rolling waves of motion that rocked the house.

The distance from Santa Barbara to the epicenter of the quake in San Bernardino attenuated the massive quake to the point where she felt the cyclic S-waves of the quake, but not the punctuations and bumps of the P-waves.

Genevieve had stood, dripping wet, on the tiles of the entrance-way, her feet planted, experiencing the quake like a child on a new carnival ride. Her initial fear had left her, but she kept an eye on the terrain beyond the glass doors, for the first time fully appreciating the unique architecture of the house.

When the quake subsided, Genevieve Dumont went back to get her robe from the bath. She then went to the wall-size television Michael had installed. She had no way of knowing that at about the time she flicked the remote control the first time, that she had just become a widow.

Now, with the remote in one hand and her diet soda in the other, Genevieve searched for information on what had just happened. It was only a few minutes before a report from some laboratory in Pasadena had fixed the earthquake on the San Andreas fault east of San Bernardino. Two of the usual Los Angeles stations were nothing but static and one of the others reported they were on emergency power, because of a blackout, but it only had an announcer speaking. Genevieve tried the CNN channel she usually preferred, but it only had a photo of a correspondent and a voice reporting from the CNN building in Los Angeles.

Finally, she went back to the station in LA which now had video from a helicopter. It was flying east from Los Angeles and they showed the destruction of freeways and some buildings.

It was only with the views of destruction that Genevieve's thoughts turned to Michael. He was in LA.

She muted the TV, put the remote down and picked up the cordless phone on the end table. She hit the speed dial key for Michael's office.

A sterile female voice responded, "Your call cannot be completed at this time due to a circuit outage. Please hang up and call again when circuits are available. Please ..."

Genevieve hung up and pushed speed dial number for Michael's cell phone.

"Your call cannot be completed ..." A different female voice, but still emotionless, spoke for the cellular company.

Genevieve exchanged the uncooperative phone for the remote again and turned on the sound. There was some picture of fires and wrecked buildings in cities she did not recognize.

The sound had just come on the television when a thump from below jarred Genevieve and her surroundings. The cordless phone, sitting on its base, fell over off the table.

The floor quivered and Genevieve prepared herself for the waves of another quake. But, after the first few seconds, this quake did not resemble the first. In a few more seconds the house was rumbling and shaking chaotically. A lacquered china cabinet crashed to the floor, smashing china on the ceramic tile floor of the dining room.

Genevieve Dumont rose to her feet. This time she needed to steady herself. It was near impossible to stand.

The television quit abruptly. As it died, the full rumble of the quake became apparent to Genevieve.

A sharp bump hit the house, then another. She lost her footing and went to her knees. Her earlier fear about the house resurfaced and just as she looked out the glass doors and resounding shudder hit the house. Her view out through the doors shifted. The house was moving. The right side was going down.

Genevieve Dumont turned on her knees and scrambled for the front door, her bare feet struggling to gain foothold on the carpet and then the slick tile floor of the entrance. She was on her feet by the time she reached the two small steps up to the entranceway. As she stood, she felt the house rock once more. The floor jumped below her feet.

The front door was locked. She fumbled with the knob, thankful for the curved brass handle to hang on to. For now the house shuddered and shook continuously, pounding on her feet from below. She felt dizzy and unbalanced, feeling the floor shift under her.

The door took two hard pulls to open. She flung it back and ran out. Her second step out of the door tripped her. There was a new foot wide crack between the porch and the sidewalk. She turned her ankle in the crack and went down to the ground on the sidewalk, skinning her knees and hands.

On hands and knees on the sidewalk, she felt the earth move. Behind her she heard and wrenching tear as metal and wood ripped apart.

With her rear foot in the crack between the sidewalk and porch, Genevieve could feel the porch move backwards, away from her. She pulled her foot away and instinctively rolled away from the porch.

She was now on her back on the sidewalk, near the circle drive. She looked back toward the house and saw the roof line and front door receding from her.

The sidewalk still rumbled beneath her. She again scrambled for footing and struggled to move away into the driveway.

Genevieve got to her feet and ran a short way up the circle drive to the left. The ground still swayed, making the run clumsy. She turned toward the house.

She turned just in time to see the front of the house slide out of sight. One of the pylons pierced the roof as the house slid down over it, then it too yielded and followed the house down the slope.

In those few seconds, the whole house and garage disappeared. Below, out of her line of sight, she could hear a rending of wood and concrete as the house hit the lower pool level.

In the same few seconds, the last quivers of movement died out in the ground beneath Genevieve.

A bizarre silence followed. No rumbling, no crashing, no sound. Not even a bird in the trees across the drive.

Genevieve stood numbly in the driveway, encompassed by the silence and the utter horror she had felt. She stood in her open black satin robe, knees and elbows bloodied from the scrapes and scrambling, at the edge of a cliff that had, moments before, been her multi-million dollar house.

Genevieve Dumont stood there. Just stood. In her shock and disbelief, there was nothing else to do.

■

A fault, in its simplest terms, is simply a scar on the earth from a previous release of seismic energy, an old earthquake. Some faults show themselves clearly, like the thousand mile long wound the San Andreas Fault leaves across the length of California. Other faults are known only by secondary evidence, uplifted bluffs or landscape anomalies. Some, like the extension of the Whittier Fault which cuts close under downtown Los Angeles and the specific fault generating the 1994 Northridge quake, are unknown until they manifest themselves in a sudden, unexpected quake.

May 6th, 12:48 P.M.

Kathy Warden's first flicker of consciousness was a thought of the pain in her arm and ribs. She tried to open her eyes, but felt something on her face. Trying to lift her right hand to brush whatever it was away, she felt her arm blocked by something. Finally, she shook her head and curled her lip to blow her breath up on her face to get rid of whatever was on her eyes. It worked. The dust and dirt flew off of her face. She held her breath and squinted as dust settled.

Finally, she could see around her. The steering wheel was in front of her, but everything was misshapen and skewed. And she was laying on her side, as was the car.

Outside, beyond the now missing windshield, she could see things, but it took a few moments to recognize them in the dust and dark shadows around her. Actually, the windshield was not missing, it was in a pile of glass fragments laying just in front of her face. The large flat yellow mass that filled her view out the front of the car and to the side out of the sunroof was the top of the truck that had been next to her on the freeway.

The thought of the freeway brought a flood of memories back to her. Varying from the thought that she was still alive to the stark recollection of falling sideways, unable to get out of the tumbling the car, off of the elevated freeway, she was overwhelmed and verged on passing out again. Kathy closed her eyes, set her jaw, and then opened her eyes and continued to look about her, taking stock of the situation.

She was on her side, the arm rest on the door was pushing into her left arm and ribs. Everything was misshapen and skewed because the little Honda had been crushed sideways. Sunlight was coming from somewhere above and to her right, but she could not see any opening. Her purse, which had been on the passenger' seat was sitting in front of her, its black leather powdered with the dust from the air-bag deployment and the dirt of the crash. Her cell phone was nowhere to be seen.

The vinyl dashboard was crushed together in front of her, pushed over against the steering wheel. That was why she had not been able to lift her hand to her face. The passenger door and seat were likewise pushed halfway across the car, nearly pinning her shoulder. Above her, through the passenger side window, she could see what looked like the bottom of a car, perhaps its transmission.

Kathy was able to turn her right arm, pulling it between her body and the steering wheel. Then, brushing crushed glass out of the way she pushed on the door below her, she lifted herself up and pulled her left elbow out from under her. She winced in pain as, after her left arm was free, her ribs settled back on the armrest. At least her arms were free.

Somewhere in the jumble outside her car, Kathy heard some-one moaning in pain and the sounds of voices.

"Hello. Is anyone out there?" She shouted above her. "Hello!"

She heard movement behind her, out of her vision.

"Yeh. I hear you," someone called, a man's voice. "Where are you? Say something else."

"I'm here, in my car." Kathy shouted as she twisted to try to see out the back window. There seemed to be more light coming from there.

"Which car? I can't tell." The voice seemed closer.

"Silver Honda ... Civic." Kathy shouted. She thought a mo-ment, then added. "I'm near the top of the yellow truck."

"OK. Hold on. I think I can make it." She heard more move-ment behind her, definitely closer and then a screeching of metal against metal.

With entire width of the driver's side of the car now just the width of the steering wheel, Kathy had little room to turn in, but she was able to pull her hips up and pull her body upright by pulling on the top of the steering wheel with her left hand. Now, turning her head she could see out the back of the car. The rear window was shattered and hanging in shards from the edges.

With another screech and the sound of metal bending, she felt movement in the car's frame. In a moment, she saw a man's head and shoulders appear sideways in the rear window.

"Wow. You're really jammed in there. Can you get back here?" the man asked.

"I hope so. I just don't have much room to turn."

The man was pushing the broken glass out of the rear window.

Dust clouded up as the glass fell. Kathy could now see that it was the truck driver she had seen on the freeway above.

"You ain't hurt any, are you?"

"No, at least not seriously."

"Your lucky, the way your car is pinned. That other lady up above is hurting. We can't get her legs out and she's bleeding all over..." His voiced trailed off as he pushed closer in the window.

He reached in toward her. "Come on. I'll help."

Kathy turned and tried to grasp something above her, finally getting a handhold on the window frame of the passenger door. She twisted her hips and wiggled up as much as she could.

Kathy yelped in pain as her leg rubbed through the pile of glass fragments below her. She now felt his hand behind her shoulder, supporting her through the headrest.

"Careful. Careful. Take it slow," her rescuer cautioned.

Kathy took a deep breath, wiped her hair out of her eyes and pulled on the door again. Slowly her hips and legs slipped up through the space between her seat and the wheel. If the sunroof had not been open she would never have been able to squirm out of the front seat. Now half-crouching on the door she crawled through the space between the seat and the open sunroof to the back. As a last thought, Kathy reached back between the seat and pulled her purse out of the broken glass below the seat. Still no sign of her cell phone.

They were standing on asphalt pavement, but around them and above there was nothing but jumbled cars. Her own car was somehow on the bottom and others stacked two or three high all around. The man turned carefully and eased through a crack between the yellow truck and another car to sunlight, pushing the screeching metal fragment she had heard out of their way.

"I got her," he yelled to someone ahead. "She's OK."

Something wet dripped onto Kathy's face. She wiped it off and, then, remembering what the man had said about someone bleeding up above she looked at her hand. It was not blood. But she could clearly smell the gasoline fumes on her hand.

Kathy wished she were wearing something other than her suit and dress shoes as she maneuvered the jagged metal and glass debris all around. Sunlight proved to be only a short distance around the truck's rear end and up over the crushed rear trunk and fender of another car. She stopped when she saw, through the back window of this car, that the owner was still in the car in the driver's seat. There was blood on the back of the headrest. The roof of the car was crushed in by the back corner of the yellow truck. The driver was obviously dead, as Kathy might have been. She crossed herself and mouthed a long unused prayer.

Kathy followed the truck driver up over the last chunk of wreckage. Arms reached for her out of the sunlit hole above her and she was pulled out into the light.

■

Under the Uniform Building Code a new building with a proper seismic design is engineered to withstand a lateral movement of about seven percent of its height, either through absorbing the energy or isolating itself from the force by moving with it. That is, a two hundred foot building should be able to withstand a lateral movement of fourteen feet in either direction without collapsing.

That the building can withstand such forces is somewhat re-assuring until you consider that when the seismic waves of the earthquake hit, a secretary working on the top floor of that 200 foot building, along with her desk and typewriter, are being flung back and forth in a twenty-eight foot arc as the building sways, for as long as the earthquake lasts.

Best estimates for the duration of maximum energy release for a 7.5 to 8.0 quake on a southern California fault are 35 to 65 seconds.

May 6th 12.48 P.M.

The building's swinging slowly ended. Cindy was not sure how long it took. She lay on the floor, eyes shut, fearing the worst, sobbing, barely conscious, possibly not.

Eventually, the sobs, like the movement, ended. Cindy Borgmann unwrapped her arms from her head and tried to catch her breath. She heard movement in the blacked-out building and a flicker of light from the hall.

The copy room door swung past her and someone flashed a light in her eyes.

"Cindy?" a young man's voice asked. "You all right?"

"Huh? I don't know." She started to sit up.

The voice was Terry, a college student who worked as the firm's courier. He now held a flashlight to the floor, so she could see to get to her feet. She was unsteady.

Seeing her dizziness, Terry suggested, "Come on in here and sit." He took her shoulder and maneuvered her across the hall to the break room.

In the light of the flashlight, Cindy could see several people in the break room. Dee was kneeling next to someone laying on the floor.

"What happened?" Cindy asked.

Dee answered. "Refrigerator toppled. It caught Heather and she's still out. You OK?"

Heather was one of the newer employees, a pretty young woman, engaged to marry one of the patent law associates from a boutique firm a few floors down.

Cindy answered Dee, "Sort of. I managed to slam into the copy room door going full tilt."

Then Cindy thought about the moaning scream she had heard during the quake. "What about Brenda? Anybody see Brenda? I thought I heard ... "

No one spoke.

Finally, Terry cleared his throat. "That's where I just went." He paused. "The whole reception area is gone. Looks like the big reception desk slid sideways, ripping the carpet up. It slid right through the windows. I think that's what we heard. There is just bare cement floor between the front hall and the elevators and all the windows are gone."

Another silence ensued.

Cindy put her hand to her face, and then to her shoulder,

checking out her own injuries. Her eye was swollen badly, cheekbone tender and her jaw rebelled at opening. She would also have a bruise on shoulder and hip, but nothing more serious.

Dee spoke with a nervous quiver in her voice, "Terry can you bring the light over here? Something is wrong."

"Sure." He walked over, avoiding the overturned tables and chairs. He pointed the light toward where Dee crouched near Heather.

"Oh. My God!" Dee cried, averting her eyes.

"What?" Cindy asked, rising to see, as did others in the room.

Terry now bent over Heather, reaching out to touch her neck.

"She coughed up blood," Dee observed.

Terry moved his hand from Heather's neck to open one of her eyes. He shook his head.

"She's dead." Terry said in a hushed tone.

"No!" Dee cried.

Cindy walked over and stood behind Terry. From here she could see the blood pooling in the girl's mouth and rolling down on her face. Cindy averted her eyes.

Roberta, an older woman, a paralegal, stepped over to take the crying Dee in her arms. Roberta asked, "Should we do CPR, or something?"

"This isn't something CPR will help." Terry surmised.

There was a long silence, interrupted only by Dee's hushed sniffling. Cindy ended it by walking over to the linen drawer by the sink and picking out a clean dishtowel. She unfolded it and gently lay it over Heather's head and shoulders.

Cindy spoke. "Terry, I think we need to get out of here. Before your light is all used up."

"Huh. Uh, Yeh. Right... You're right."

"Did you check the rest of the office? Besides the reception area?" Cindy swallowed hard, thinking of Brenda.

"Yes. On this side. Lots of the partners' offices have broken windows and everything messed up. Mort and Billings are OK, they are over across the lobby by their offices. They said they would check out the far corridor."

"What should we do?" Roberta asked. "Get out of the building?"

"It is twenty-eight floors down and the elevators are out, no electricity." Terry commented.

Cindy thought, then spoke. "He's right, that'd be tough. I think we should all get in another room," she could not help looking down at the dead girl, "Somewhere safe and hopefully closer to daylight. Maybe we can check the radio and get some idea of where things stand."

"What if there is another quake, an aftershock?" Dee asked, back with them again.

"Well, maybe somewhere close to the sunlight, but not right near the windows," Cindy suggested.

"Your office." Dee suggested, indicating Cindy.

Cindy thought. "Yes, I guess." She had light from Goldwasser's office, but no open window areas. And she had a radio. "That's as good as anyplace. And we can get in the main hall if there is another quake, I think it would be safe there, no windows, no furniture."

Roberta spoke again, "I still think we should get out of the building. Get outside."

Terry answered, "Maybe later, right now we need to figure things out. Besides, outside is just as dangerous if we have another quake, with glass and stuff falling out of the buildings." He stopped short at this, everyone thought of the same thing when he said " stuff falling out of the buildings."

Cindy spoke, "I agree, let's go down the hall. Maybe we can see who else is still in the offices. Then we can decide what to do. I want to know what the radio is saying."

"Me, too," Dee added.

"Well, let's go." Terry pointed his light to the door.

Nearly everyone gave Heather a last look as they went out.

■

"Using sophisticated satellite-oriented Global Positioning System receivers it has been determined that Oat Mountain in the Santa Susanna Range both grew taller and moved during the 1994 Northridge Earthquake. It is now 14.8 inches taller, 6.2 inches farther north and 5.5 inches west."

Andrea Donnellan,
Geophysicist, Jet Propulsion Laboratory

May 6th, 1:00 P.M.

Matt Contreras glanced at the man in the co-pilots seat. Contreras saw the same look on Captain Nathan Moody's face as he felt himself. Something combining awe and fear.

Neither man said anything. They just watched the terrain below them.

They had lifted off from the Thermal airport for Contreras' qualification flight and everything had gone like a charm for ten or fifteen minutes. Then, the Riverside Sheriff's frequency they kept active in the right earphone went crazy. Frenzied reports of a huge quake, shattered buildings, fires, deaths. They had been heading due East and Moody ordered him around to the West, and as they swung around, Contreras and Moody saw the telltale puffs of dust from the ground. Quakes often puffed dust geysers out of the open earth, both Moody and Contreras had seen them during the little temblors that peppered the desert region of California. These were not the usual size.

They tried to raise someone on aircraft frequencies, but the towers in Thermal and Palm Springs were not been up on the radio. When they came over Palm Springs Airport they could see why there was no traffic to worry about and nobody up on the radio. Nothing could even lift off from Palm Springs, some of the runways and taxiways were a jumble of errant concrete chunks, like a overturned box of dominoes. It was also clear why the tower was off the air, the concrete pillar that served the air traffic controllers was tilted crazily to the east, its glass missing and jagged cracks crisscrossed its height. Whatever had hit the ground had been mighty.

The Sheriff's frequency they had first gotten word of the quake on was in disarray, a bunch of patrol units reporting to each other without any control. No dispatch was on the circuit. Moody flipped the radio to the other local agency frequencies, Everywhere it was the same. Chaos.

"Isn't there an Emergency Ops Freq. I seem to recall..." The crew chief, Deputy Pat Barnwell, sitting in back, spoke up on the cabin intercom. Contreras had forgot he was on board.

"Yes. But it is probably no better." Moody grabbed a red vinyl binder from under the co-pilots seat he sat in. He thumbed quickly through the book, then mumbled "Appendix E." At last, he found what he was looking for.

"Yes, there it is. Emergency multi-channel transponder on San Jacinto Peak. Incoming freq ..." He flipped the frequency wheels on the UHF radio. "... and outgoing freq. There, should be tied into Riverside County E.O.C., if they're up yet."

The radio snapped to life with a sign-on call by the Hesperia Police Department. This was followed by another.

"This is Riverside City Fire Department alternate headquarters. Reporting minimal damage at this location, but we are unable to reach three stations including Main Headquarters. Over."

Two other emergency offices, one in Hemet, one in Cathedral

City signed on and reported.

"I guess the transponder is working if Hemet can talk on the same UHF circuit as Cathedral City. Huh?" Barnwell said from the back seat. The two cities were on opposite sides of the tall San Jacinto Mountain range and would normally be out of range for the largely line-of-sight UHF radio.

"Yes, I guess so," Moody replied. "Let's see if it works for us."

Moody thumbed the mike switch and signed on, "This is Riverside Sheriff Air Two. We are not assigned to this net, but we are airborne over Palm Springs and cannot reach our ground control. Can you tell us the situation on the ground? Over."

"This is Riverside E.O.C. Don't mind the intrusion. Glad to have you. We can use some eyes out in the world. We had a huge quake on the San Andreas fault. Riverside and San Bernardino, really everybody in the county, are hit bad. Don't know how bad yet. Maybe you can help us on that. What is your craft and crew status? Can you do some recon for us? Over."

"Roger, E.O.C. Riverside Air Two is a Uniform Hotel One November equipped for SAR with CHP Officer Contreras at the stick and Captain Moody, Riverside Sheriff Department, in second seat and in command. Deputy Barnwell in the jump seat is SAR and EMT qualified. We are at ninety percent fuel, fully operational and we are at your service. Over."

Following the direction of the Emergency Operations Center for Riverside County, Contreras first circled to the south and checked on the status of a huge fire between Rancho Mirage and Cathedral City. They only noticed two or three fire strike teams at the fire. They continued on toward Indio.

As they flew they heard other reports from the length of the county. Everywhere, each locale seemed to have its own unique problems. During one lull in the radio traffic, Contreras asked Indio E.O.C. to relay to the CHP office, if they could, that Contreras was alive and well on-board the Sheriff's copter. They agreed. The CHP offices had not come up on the county's emergency operations net yet, as would be expected by now. Contreras was concerned for his buddies. He was not able to see the CHP building through the pale of smoke from the fires in Indio.

"E.O.C., this is Riverside Air Two. Over." Moody did the radio work.

"Roger, Air Two. E.O.C."

"Air Two has completed the circuit down to Indio. We have at least two dozen fires in the built up areas, stretching from central Palm Springs to Indio. The one in La Quinta looks worst. Possibly as many as thirty homes and a big building, maybe the clubhouse at the golf course. Lots of quake damage, but we cannot see anything major except for the Esplanade Royale Hotel which looks to be about half collapsed. They appear to need lots of help. Urban Search and Rescue, if you have it."

"Roger that, Air Two. We are ... Wait one, Air Two."

While they waited for E.O.C. to come back to them, Contreras turned the chopper to the north toward the interstate north of Indio. They went down low over the worst of the fires in Indio, a fire that engulfed parts of several blocks. They could see a geyser of fire coming up out of the center of the largest street in the area. A gas main had blown, taking the surrounding homes and businesses, including a gas station, with it. They could see fire trucks, but no hose lines.

"No water?" Moody said, more of a statement than a question.

"Air Two, Ops/E.O.C, Over."

"Air Two."

"Air Two, we would like a recon of the area between Whitewater and Banning. We don't have any phone contact with the area and no ground units have reported. We're ... hold on, Air Two, we're having another aftershock."

Contreras and Moody looked at each other, both of them considering the curious thought that there had been no report from the ground between Whitewater and Banning. The main quake was now the better part of an half hour past and the fifteen miles between the two towns was a straight stretch of interstate highway. How could they not have ground reports?

As they waited for Ops to come back, they, once again, saw the tell-tale tufts of dust cloud arising from numerous places on the earth below them. In the thirty seconds it took them to reverse their course with a 180 turn to the north, the open ground north of Indio was almost obscured by the pale of dust rising up. It must have been a pretty big aftershock.

While they waited for E.O.C. to come back to them they heard another call on the radio net. "All stations this net, this is Palm Springs E.O.C., we are signing off. Our building is in danger of collapsing. We will report back when able. Out."

Finally Ops came back on the radio, "Air Two, this is Ops/E.O.C., are you still with us?"

"Roger that."

"We had another hefty bump here. Thought we might have gone off line again."

"No, read you loud and clear. We are turning toward Whitewater. Current 10-20, I-10 at Washington. ETA Whitewater ten to fifteen minutes."

"Roger. Air Two, request you proceed best speed. Out."

As they increased altitude and headed west they could see the same telltale clouds of dust rising from the Indio Hills to their right. Somewhere within those hills the scar of the San Andreas fault passed, but the could not see it. They could barely make out the Interstate below them.

"Looks like a rough one," Contreras said for want of anything more informative.

A guttural "Hmphf," was Moody's only reply. He was peering through the binoculars ahead of them.

They were following the interstate up from Indio. The traffic was light and just cars, not the usual mix of big rigs. They heard a report on the Sheriff's operational net that still sporadically chirped in their right ear that the Interstate was closed somewhere east of Indio with a fallen overpass.

The helicopter was a few miles past Thousand Palms, with the smoke plumes from Palm Springs rising from the west when Moody blurted, "Jesus H... ." He trailed off and did not finish the epithet.

"What?" Contreras asked, he could not use the binoculars while flying the copter.

Moody took the glasses down and turned to Contreras in an unnecessary move since they spoke over the headsets. "There is a cliff across Highway 62 north of the 10."

"A cliff?"

"Yes, a fucking cliff." Moody had the glasses up again. "A cliff right across the highway. And its worse than that to the north and west."

At this, Contreras looked north. He could now see the smoke from Desert Hot Springs. It looked worse than La Quinta and Indio. Between there and the chopper he could see North Palm Springs, where Gloria, Miranda and the baby were. It seemed to be without fire.

Contreras had the helicopter going full throttle and it was only minutes before he, too, could see what Moody had seen earlier. A dark, jagged scar crossed tan earth and cut through the four lane highway that headed north from the Interstate north to Morongo Valley. Matt Contreras saw the track of broken ground heading east and north of the "cliff." Some roads and the nearer buildings of the North Palm Springs area were broken and many were places were burning. All he could see of Desert Hot Springs was the pall of smoke, or perhaps dust.

"Can you take the stick for a minute?" Contreras asked Moody.

"Sure." Moody grabbed the control between his legs felt the movement for a minute and then said, "OK, got it."

Matt Contreras took the other pair of binoculars from between the seats and looked to the left. It took him a minute to get his bearings and then he saw the cream colored rectangle of the BankCal building where Gloria would have been when the quake hit. It looked fine, from here. Matt followed the line of the streets over and up to where he figured the house must be. He could not really tell much, but there was no fire in the area, just smoke from the north, and no cracks in the earth like across highway 62, that he could see. He worried a minute about what Consuella might react like in an emergency. He had no idea what the old lady might do.

"Home?" Moody asked.

"Yeh," was Matt's answer. "Seems all right."

"My family, my wife and daughter, are in San Bernardino today, shopping for graduation and prom," Moody said without emotion. The question of what it was like through the pass in San Bernardino was left hanging, They had both heard the reports from the fire and police stations destroyed in the city of Riverside, which was twice as far from the San Andreas as the city of San Bernardino. They had heard nothing from San Bernardino, which was in another county, on another radio net.

Matt took the controls back from Moody.

As he watched the scene roll under him, Matt heard Captain Moody report in. Moody, with the binoculars, could see much more than Matt and obviously knew the area on the ground.

"E.O.C., this is Air Two."

"Ops/E.O.C., over."

"E.O.C., Air Two is approaching Highway 62. We can see the highway is cut about a half mile north of the interstate. There is broken ground running to the east along Dillon Road. We can see numerous fires in the area to the north. Do you copy? Over."

"Copy."

"There is a big back-up west-bound on the interstate and numerous vehicles wrecked on and off the road both on the 10 and 62. A black and white, can't tell if it's CHP or sheriff, is sitting off the road with its lights flashing near the break in the highway."

Just as Contreras saw the next problem, Moody was reporting it. "There is a flow of water running down the Whitewater River wash. It is coming from the side of Painted Hill. Looks like the Colorado Aqueduct broke. And there is a major fire just below Tipton Road. It appears to be gas. I think there is a pipeline there. Over."

"Roger, proceed up I-10 and report."

Both Contreras and Moody could now see the cause of the back-up. Just beyond the Whitewater interchange and the park the interstate was totally blocked by a jumble of vehicles and broken roadway.

Contreras turned the helicopter to the west, straight up San Gorgonio Pass following the Interstate. Or rather, he followed what had been the interstate, for below him the highway he had driven and flown over a thousand times had ceased to exist.

The valley floor was a litter of tumbled chunks of concrete near the track of the highway and toppled towers from the huge forest of wind generators clustered in San Gorgonio Pass' eastern gateway. The tall towers of the transcontinental electrical transmission line that went through the Pass from the power plants in Arizona and Utah to Los Angeles joined the thousands of white windmills in piles on the ground. Cars and trucks were scattered along the track of the highway.

As they flew over Whitewater they could see a group of people on a stretch of highway waving at the chopper. They seemed to be stranded above the water flowing down the wash and the fire and smoke from the burst pipeline to the south. Moody called in a report of the stranded people as Contreras continued west.

The winds from the north-east pushed the smoke from the pipeline fire and the city fires in Desert Hot Springs and clouds of dust churned by the quakes into the Pass. The deep cut of San Gorgonio Pass was hazy and visibility was severely restricted. They could only see a mile or so ahead. The stiff tail winds through the pass sped the helicopter's progress, but made for a rough ride.

Beneath them, an eerie scene unfolded. In places, the ground was the jumble of broken highway, buildings, vehicles and power lines they had seen at Whitewater. However, as they approached the narrowest part of the Pass, the ground changed. It took on the appearance of a newly plowed field. They could clearly see the track of the San Andreas Fault and for fifty to two hundred feet on either side of the deepest crease there was fresh, roughened earth. The rear end of an eighteen-wheeler poked up out of the earth as though some absurdist farmer had planted it. There was no sign of the cab for the truck nor the road it had traveled on.

At Rushmore Road the track of the fault turned and cut across the interstate. The roadway southwest of the area of greatest devastation was fifty to sixty feet beyond the roadway to the northeast which should have led directly to it. The entire southern half of the Pass had slid past the north, crunching everything in its path.

The tiny village of Cabazon seemed to have been directly on the fault. The Morongo tribal center and the nearby casino were flat, totally flat, as though neatly folded by a giant hand. The two factory outlets malls just beyond the casino were a jumble of stucco, broken wood beams and piles of debris. Both the town and the interstate for two miles beyond it were unrecognizable from both the turmoil and debris and the dust and smoke that now blanketed the valley floor.

Again Moody reported in the grizzly news. "This is Air Two. We are over Cabazon. The town is totally destroyed. Survivors visible. Some structures appear to be on fire or threatened, a brush fire is covering three sides of the town. Surface travel appears to be impossible. Over."

A new voice came on the net, "Air Two, Moody, this is Sheriff Hodges at the E.O.C. Would you please clarify your report from Cabazon. What shape is the interstate in, and how about the railroad and the power lines? This is very important, we need to know."

Moody cleared his throat in preparation for the report to his boss, then he keyed the mike, "This is Air Two. Sheriff, the interstate is gone. I mean, it isn't here anymore. In places you can barely see where it even was. The railroad is gone, too. So are the power lines and we think the gas pipeline went up in flames below Whitewater. We haven't seen a building left standing or a passable road between North Palm Springs and here... we are coming up on Banning. The entire San Gorgonio Pass is impassable as far as we can see. Over."

"God! OK, thanks, continue to report. Out."

Contreras now said nothing to Moody, he just flew on toward Banning, his childhood home. After having seen Cabazon and the other cities, Contreras had a horrible tautness in his gut about Banning. His parents and sister still lived there. From somewhere in his memory of childhood hiking trips he knew the main San Andreas fault turned north-west toward San Bernardino after Cabazon and he kept this in his mind, hoping that the worst of the destruction he had seen would have missed Banning.

He should have had the beacon from the Banning airport in sight, but in the smoke from Cabazon and points east he could see nothing and nobody was up on the assigned radio frequency for Banning airport. It was only three miles between Cabazon and the airport, but he was almost over the airport before he saw it.

The single runway was rippled and fractured just like the interstate. Fires spewed from the airport hangar. Any thoughts of landing at Banning for fuel on the return were hopeless.

Beyond the airport Contreras could see his hometown. It was recognizable, but eerily different. In a moment he could see why. The smoke cleared to the west and he could see both Banning and some of Beaumont, farther west.

Both towns, Banning and Beaumont, sat in the valley floor at the west end of the Pass. With hills on both the north and south that rose into mountains higher up, the two small towns were nestled in a flat-bottomed valley and adjacent plateau. Except that, it was no longer flat-bottomed. Across the width of the valley, Contreras could see a rows of undulating hillocks. Houses, buildings and sections of pavements lay akimbo, tossed about like miniature village scenery a child would use with his electric train. Railroad freight cars along the siding in Banning lay in a zigzag pattern on either side of a rippled rail bed. Banning had not faired much better than Cabazon.

Contreras turned a bit to the north and flew over the section of older houses just north of the main street of Banning, the neighborhood where he had grown up. He could see the businesses he recognized on the street, but except for the relative direction from these, he would not have been able to recognize the location of his parents' house. Two blocks of houses were on fire, although not his parents side of the street. The old house appeared to be standing, people stood out in the street. He hoped they were his parents. It looked like it could be. He could not go lower to see in the smoke of the fires.

Two blocks farther on, he passed directly over the schoolyard he had played on as a boy. He could clearly see a rupture in the earth to the north, bigger than the one that had cut Highway 62 on the other side of the pass. The brick school itself was flat, a pile of rubble. The ground to the north of the crack was broken and chunks of green sod topped clusters of tiny hills. To the south of the crack, he could see, on the open ground, groups of children sitting in circles in the schoolyard. Nearer the school, he could see people walking among a row of tiny bodies arranged on the grass. Contreras prayed they were resting, but he feared that was not the case. He thought of Miranda.

He could see no emergency vehicles near the school. Then, he could not see a passable road around it either.

As Contreras turned south to pick up the course of the Interstate again, Captain Moody called up Ops/E.O.C. to report on what they had seen at Banning. The Operations Center did not answer. As Moody repeated the radio calls to E.O.C., in vain, Contreras watched as fresh plumes of dust rose from a hundred points in the rubble of Banning and the fields to the west. This aftershock seemed bigger than the earlier ones.

In 1935, C.F. Richter devised a scale to define the magnitude of an earthquake. It is one of the most widely known and recognized measurements of physical properties, following only weight, temperature, voltage and the like. Virtually everyone in California has some concept of what "a 7.4 on the Richter Scale" means, although it is usually misunderstood.

There is no upper limit to the Richter Scale or the newer systems like it, although since there is an actual limit to the amount of strain that rock can endure, it is reasonable to assume that there is an upper limit for the magnitude of an earthquake. In California, this limit is usually assumed to be 8.5.

A difference of decimal one point on the Richter scale is a difference of 30 times the energy. An increase of a one whole digit on the Richter scale is indicative of a tenfold increase in the amplitude of seismic waves produced. Accordingly, the difference between the magnitude "4" earthquake that virtually every Californian has experienced and a quake the size of the Great San Francisco or Alaskan quakes is more than a million times the magnitude.

May 6th, 1:00 P.M.

Genevieve Dumont née Fortier, fashion model, new bride, *beauté extraordinaire*, and member by marriage of the Hollywood in-crowd, surveyed her domain. That domain now consisted of the wrinkled and cracked asphalt of the crescent drive and a sidewalk leading to a cliff. Her sole remaining personal possession was a black satin robe, which she now tightened around her.

Genevieve stood barefoot and clad in only the robe. She had stood in shock as the last trembling remnants of the quake died. There had been other sounds, not unlike the crashing of her own house. After the turmoil of the quake, the tearing apart, the mind numbing fear, she simply stood for several minutes, occasionally blinking, uncertain of what to do. Shock, both clinical and figurative, enclosed her consciousness.

A thought crossed her mind, `What if I had not put the robe on before I turned on the television to watch the news? I would be standing here without any clothes.' She wanted to laugh at the thought, but she could not. Then she thought, `What if I had still been in the shower when this earthquake hit? I would be down below, crushed in my house.' She wanted to cry, but she could not.

The thought of her house led her to amble forward toward the edge of the cliff. The cliff edge was nearly straight across, the front of the house had fallen cleanly away. Part of the flower bed the gardeners tended for the Dumonts had fallen over, also; the remaining flowers trimmed the cliff edge. The sidewalk jutted out in mid-air beyond the dirt. She dare not go too close, but she had to see below.

Genevieve walked slowly, feeling the vertigo that a cliff edge or building ledge often gave her. She had never felt the vertigo on the balcony of the house, but now, after this, she would always have a different feeling for heights, and things suspended.

When she got as far as she dared go, she looked down. The wreckage of the house covered the pool area and the hillside around and below where the pool had been. Only one of the four pillars that had held the house on the slope was still standing, the one on the left. The other three girders had ripped out and fallen down with the house.

As the girders pulled free of the earth they had pulled the dirt and stone with them. The dirt rolled down and now partially covered the twisted scraps that had been the house.

To the right she could see the rear bumper of her beautiful green Jaguar poking out of the pile of roofing tiles and splinters of garage siding. The car appeared to be nose down where the deep end of the pool had been. Between the lip of the cliff and the wreckage below there was nothing but loose, moist dirt, the stairway that had run down to the pool was nowhere in sight.

A few feet below the jutting sidewalk Genevieve could see two metal pipes, bent and splayed. The larger pipe spouted a steady stream of clear water down toward the remains of the house like a bizarre decorative fountain. From the smaller pipe she could only see a flow of distortion in the air, masking in a quavering haze the view of points beyond. The pipe was venting gas. Now, as she listened, attuned to it, she could hear the hiss of the gas and smell it. She retreated back from the edge, up the driveway.

As she walked up the drive, Genevieve felt pain in her knees. She bent over to look. Both of her knees were bloodied, from the scrapping on the sidewalk as she escaped the house.

Bending over, looking at her knees, Genevieve Dumont gave thought to the predicament in which she found herself. Although her usual vanity kicked in and brought thoughts of lack of clothing, make-up and stringy just-washed hair, she quickly turned her thoughts to greater problems. Without her house, her car, her purse or even any identification, she was alone in a place in which she knew hardly anyone. She had not been able to get in touch with Michael. In addition, she dreaded the thought; she had no idea if he was all right himself.

Genevieve's thoughts now raced. How could she get help salvaging the house, her possessions? How could she get something to wear? Where was Michael? How could she get money, identification, food? What if she could not find Michael? The satin robe now flapped in the stiff ocean breeze, chilling her private parts. This seemed a priority. Clothes.

There was only one thing to do. She would visit the neighbors she had disdained to get to know the last three months, and ask for help. She looked around her, up and down the tree lined drive. She had never considered the distance to the other stately homes in the neighborhood, but it now appeared great as she trudged off, barefoot, up the drive. Gravel pebbles poked her soft feet. Genevieve decided to try to the left, the big houses on top of the hill. The ones on the right, set on the edge of the ridge as her own had been, were not anywhere to be seen.

■

A magnitude 5 earthquake will cause damage to certain structures and widespread minor damage. A magnitude 6 earthquake will damage most structures within a reasonable distance of the quake and in certain danger areas, such as liquefaction zones. A magnitude 7 quake will damage or destroy all but the most lucky or stringently built buildings. High priority buildings, such as hospitals, if built new today would require design consideration that would keep the building from collapsing in a magnitude 7 quake, although building design guidelines do not deal directly with earthquake magnitude in their considerations. Most engineers assume that virtually any man-made structure, particularly complex ones, will be damaged or destroyed in a magnitude 8 or greater quake.

Both the leading seismologists and the Las Vegas bookmakers give the average Californian about even odds for experiencing a 7 or 8 magnitude quake at close range in a lifetime.

May 6th, 1:13 P.M.

The sensation first came to him as the odd feeling of unbalance, that he could not put his feet down in the places he wanted to. Deputy Barry Warden had finished the bogus vandalism report and he was heading to the Explorer, walking quickly over the solid asphalt of the road, but his shoes seemed to be touching different levels and angles of the ground with every step. He had little time to think about the odd sensation. When he was a few feet behind his vehicle it started to bounce and he had to brace his feet wide apart and lean against the rear of the 4x4 to keep his balance. Now he could hear the pervasive rumble that he had heard before, only louder. Here in the open he could clearly hear it coming from the East, toward Long Beach.

Barry Warden watched in awe as the asphalt of the road rolled in waves up the hill toward him and off behind him toward the ocean. Chunks of roadway curled up and crumbled as the waves passed by. Thirty feet in front of the Explorer a geyser of water spouted up from such a crack in the road. Windows broke in nearby houses and a chimney gave way up the street, adding to the din of rumbles. A child screamed. Somewhere to his right, with a splintering crash, part of a house gave way to the movement. Then another identical sound came from the other side of the street. With a quick glance over to the left, he could see a roof-line slump toward the ground.

Several people ran into the street, including the woman in the house behind him from whom Barry Warden had just been taking the questionable complaint.

After a while, ten seconds, perhaps, of rhythmic rolling the character of the quake seemed to change; now a chaotic shaking of everything took place. The Explorer was now bouncing so awkwardly that he gave up his balance point and stood alone in the street. Barry remained on his feet, but only by staggering back and forth and moving his weight around on his feet, like a boy in a carnival fun house ride or a slightly punch-drunk boxer. A cloud of dust rose from the ground and the fissures in the pavement. The waterspout rising from the crack in the street pulsed in response to the shaking.

Now, while the earth still shook, in the sky in the East, out toward North Long Beach, there was a flash of light, so bright he could feel its heat of his face. It was followed straightaway by a new sensation of pressure that he felt in his eyes and eyelashes and with his ears popping.

Not more than a few seconds later a deafening blast shook the ground and reverberated the air around him, shaking his body like a toy doll. Caught off guard by the blast, Barry lost his footing and fell backward, landing on his butt.

A woman screamed. Others joined her.

The source of the blast was just out of sight over the hill behind the houses to his right. Barry assumed from the force and heat of the blast that a house on the street in the next canyon over had been destroyed in a gas explosion. He had vivid memories of seeing videos of the many such fires and explosions up in Northridge in '94. But, why had there been a delay between the flash and concussion, if it was so close?

With a last quiver of the ground, the tremors died out. His ears were ringing from the concussion of the blast and his tail-bone ached from the hard landing. The sound from the ground died, as did the movement. Barry waited for it to start up again.

It did not. Now, in the far distance he could hear another sound. A roar, rather than a rumbling. Fire? And it, again, seemed to far away to be a house on the next street, but it did seem to be the sound of a fire, somewhere.

Unseen, in the backyards of the houses near him, a deep bellowing howl of a dog let loose.

Barry had no idea how long this had all taken. It seemed like several minutes, but he knew better. The quakes always seemed longer than they were.

Deputy Barry Warden pulled himself to his feet. His butt was sore, but he was not injured. He brushed the small gravel pieces and sand from his hands and the seat of his green uniform pants. He stood a moment and looked around him. The broken water main, the distant vague roar and the dog howling were the only sounds, but these seemed quiet in this stillness after the quake and that god-awful blast ended.

Up and down the street people ran to each other. Some hugged one another. Others sobbed and cried openly. Deputy Warden saw several heading toward his vehicle.

The geyser of water from the street died. The water now simply gurgled up out of the broken pavement and flowed down the hill through the plume of mud and sand that had been left by the torrent. Apparently the water pressure feeding it had died. Barry could imagine that this was not the only break in the water system and pressure could not be maintained in a sieve of broken pipes.

Barry weighed his next step. Check the neighborhood and see if he could help anyone? Certainly, he should check the houses that he had heard go down? He was sure to have to deal with the people who now would look to him as a savior, an authority figure in the chaos.

First things first. He would follow procedure and report in. Then he would quickly see what he could do in the neighborhood.

Barry went to the car to call in. Other sheriff deputies already were calling in as he opened the door of the Explorer.

"Dispatch, this is Patrol Three-Seven. Over."

No answer. Three-Seven repeated the call. Still no answer.

Then, "Any station, this is Patrol Three-Seven, Radio Check. Over."

There was a cackle of static and bursts of voice fighting the radio's squelch as several chimed in to answer the radio check. Finally one voice won out in the chaos and continued.

"...stations this net. All stations this net. This is Sergeant Rivera, Three-niner. I am assuming net control. Repeat. I am assuming net control. I am three blocks from the substation, just off Pacific Coast Highway and all I can see at the station is dust and smoke. I don't think Dispatch is with us."

Rivera's voice paused, then continued. "Everybody calm down and lets do this by the numbers. All stations will report. Give your 10-20 and status. First, if anyone knows what the hell happened near the Harbor Freeway, let me know. All I could see was a flash and the blast and now a mushroom cloud a mile high is there."

Barry looked straight ahead through the windshield to the East. As Rivera had said, he could see a boiling, churning ball of black-gray and red rising into the sky.

Before the status reports could start coming in, someone crackled onto the net and announced, "10-33, Patrol Four-Six." Barry Warden recognized it as Janet Mortimer, a patrol officer.

Rivera answered the emergency call, "Roger, Four-Six."

"I'm on Avalon, north of Sepulveda. Officer down, badly burned. McNeely was outside the car taking an accident report when the quake hit. I stayed in the car. Then during the quake something flashed and exploded. Fire just swept through here. Everything is on fire. I put the fire out on McNeely, but McNeely's really bad. The people in the cars, too. My ear's are bleeding and I can't hear too well ... Everything is on fire, as far as I can see. Houses, brush, and the gas main cracked on Sepulveda ..." Her voice trailed off and the radio clicked off to static and then silence.

Rivera cut in, "Roger, Four-Six. Is anyone able to assist Four-Six? Over." There was a long silence.

"This is L.A.P.D. Seven Edward Five out of San Pedro. Couldn't raise anyone on our tactical so we were listening in. We are just south of

Sepulveda on the Harbor. We can ETA at Four Six's 20 in three minutes."

"Roger that, thanks for the assist."

The reports started to come in when Barry was interrupted by a woman running up and pounding on the Explorer's window.

"Help me, help me. My God, the whole roof. It fell... my daughter is in there. Please help me."

Barry held one finger up, nodding urgently to her, indicating he would just be a moment. Then, at the first break on the radio, he broke in and announced, "This is Patrol Four-Four. My 10-20 is the 12 - 500 block of Savoy Ridge Drive, Rolling Hills, report of victim in collapsed building, Request fire-rescue assistance, if available. I am 10-6. Out."

He did not wait for a response. Barry got out and ran to the building on the right that the woman pointed at, to check out the situation. A brisk wind had sprung up in just the last few minutes, blowing into the East. The wind and the dust tossed up by the quake made it hard to see.

"Around in back," the woman shouted from close behind him. She was almost keeping up with him even in her housecoat and slippers.

Barry's heart sank as he rounded the corner of the house and saw that a one-story addition at the back of the house had pulled away from the house and now lay folded flat on the ground, nothing more than a pile of scrap wood topped with a roof lying tilted across some unseen lump below.

`If the woman's daughter was under there ... God! ...,' he wasted little time on the thought as he rushed to peer under the eaves and roof gables that lay in the grass, trying to catch sight of the girl.

■

If properly mixed with air, the contents of an industrial Liquefied Natural Gas (LNG) or Liquefied Propane Gas (LPG) storage tank is capable of generating equivalent destructive energy to a small atomic weapon. In one five mile radius area in southern Los Angeles County there are several dozen such tanks, as well as the LNG container ships docked at the piers in Long Beach and the Port of Los Angeles and the off-loading facilities for them. The refineries, harbor facilities and tank farms are bracketed directly between the Palos Verdes Hills and Cherry Hill Fault Zones and within five miles of seven epicenters of recent 4.0+ quakes. They are in prime zones for liquefaction. Also, in every direction from this industrial zone, there are tracts of wood-frame residential dwellings. The working class residential communities in Wilmington, Carson and North Long Beach are immediately adjacent to the tank farms.

May 6th, 1:13 P.M.

The tank was as unobtrusive as could be expected for an object as large as it was, on a hillside overlooking the eight-lane I-405 freeway. Unlike some tanks in the area which were proudly emblazoned with logos of oil companies or utilities, this tank was simply off-white. From a distance, you could not see the streaks of rust that flowed down from welds in the frame or the nameplates of its interstate pipeline owner on the fence surrounding it.

It was just one of a half dozen or more similar globe-like tanks the pipeline company used for storage and transshipment of the natural gas it collected from the nearby Los Angeles refineries and the port facilities in Long Beach and San Pedro just to the south. Depending on the vagaries of the spot price for natural gas on the market and the time of year, the tank and its neighbors might be full or empty. It happened that in the beginning of May after a particularly warm winter the tank and its neighbors sat nearly full, waiting for markets and weather to make the contents more valuable to the pipeline company.

With the combined effects of the years of built up stress deep within the Earth, the energy released by the huge quake on the San Andreas to the East and the aftershocks, the Newport-Inglewood Fault had taken all it could. Now it let go with its own temblor, slightly less than the horrendous release of seismic energy from the San Andreas to the east, but still in the range of what could be considered a great quake. And, this great quake was situated squarely under the Los Angeles basin.

The tank took the initial shock of the Newport-Inglewood quake well, all things considered, but, like the Fault itself, with the combined effects of the continuing waves of movement and the sudden slippage of part of the hillside a few feet downward, the double-walled tank split itself open along a lateral seam about halfway up its side.

Pressurized natural gas in its liquid form spewed forth. When it met the warm air it instantly vaporized, thus expanding its volume a thousand-fold in a matter of seconds, sending an ever-expanding front of shimmering gaseous turbulence in every direction.

Nearby workers who stood in the open waiting out the quake's fury were quickly enveloped in the nearly invisible cloud. Oxygen was displaced by the heavier cloud of gas and the workers quickly fell to the ground, chests heaving, soon unconscious and oblivious to what was to come.

In the first moments of the rupture when the gas was not fully mixed with oxygen from the air, it was incapable of ignition. In fact, cars and trucks on the freeway and the boulevard which passed through the tank farm, deprived of oxygen, stalled as the cloud surrounded them, while their drivers choked for breath. Gas spread out thousands of yards in every direction, pooling in the low areas, slowly mixing with the surrounding air. As the force of the expansion dissipated and the air mixed in, the invisible gaseous mass achieved proportions that were combustible. Then something ... sparks from a loose muffler on the freeway, a lit cigarette, a pilot light or refinery flare ... it did not matter, something set the leading edge of the gas cloud off.

The portion of the gas cloud which was properly mixed with air ignited in a single explosion almost instantaneously across the outer surface of the entire distended pancake of space that the gas now covered. The intermixed gas and air had become an efficient high explosive charge a half-mile or more in diameter. The enormous concussion and flash could only be compared to an atomic bomb, or perhaps the quake, which had engendered it, in its magnitude.

The shock wave, traveling faster than the speed of sound, obliterated everything in its path. Much of the face of the earth itself for a great distance in every direction was instantly wiped away. Vehicles, aircraft taking off from the airport down the freeway, buildings, soil... everything was blown outward in the globular wave of shock. The gas which had not been able to ignite due to lack of oxygen was also blasted outward, only to ignite again when the broiling fire storm mixed it with air once more. Everything flammable was soon consumed; trees, grass, buildings, vehicles and the corpses of the victims; not to mention the nearby oil refineries and the other gas released by gas mains broken by the quake.

Within the gas cloud, the intense heat and force of the pressure wave imploded back upon the off-white tank that had first given way to the quake. The tank, with its remaining contents and the contents of dozens of neighboring tanks, both with natural gas and petroleum distillates, on the hillside and surrounding area were crushed and vaporized in the twinkling of an eye. The inferno was thus fueled anew. But without air within it to ignite, the mass broiled into a firestorm as air was sucked into the center by the power of the flames and the force of the atmosphere that rushed back in to fill the void pushed outward by the initial shock wave.

A mushroom cloud of pure fire rose into the air. To feed the fire, winds of hurricane force were sucked back into the firestorm and rising mushroom cloud. The winds fanned the secondary fires that consumed the debris and spread the conflagration further.

In a metropolis still shaking from the latest earthquake, the rumbling from within the earth had been joined by the ferocious detonation and the following roar that marked the consumption of huge areas of the cities of Carson, Long Beach and the adjacent region. Windows cracked for many miles around. For those in the immediate area who were lucky enough to escape the inferno, eardrums ached and bled from the overpressure of the shock wave. Everyone in the Los Angeles Basin heard the sound, millions jumped in fright and thousands cowered in fear of whatever new cataclysm was upon them.

■

To attempt to design buildings and public works for an earthquake zone is to gamble. The only truly safe course of action would be to not build or build somewhere else.

A California design engineer and architect must make a number of dangerous assumptions. What magnitude of earthquake is the building likely to be subjected to? How long will the future earthquake last? What are the chances that the earthquake will occur within the life expectancy of the building? Obviously, the answers to each of these questions flaunts Mother Nature's ability and propensity to do the unexpected.

May 6th, 1:13 P.M.

Cindy Borgmann followed Terry down the dark hall of the law office. Each step was a sharp pain in her upper thigh. It was nearly impossible to limp in high heels. Dee, Roberta and the other two secretaries followed them toward Cindy's office.

No one said anything. They simply followed in the dim light cast back by Terry's flashlight. All of the doors in the office that had been open slammed shut during the earthquake, so everything was pitch dark. Cindy realized this about halfway down the hall.

"You know, we don't need to walk in the dark. All this row of offices have windows," Cindy said as she reached for the nearest office door. The door handled turned grudgingly, but the door would not open, even with a push from her shoulder. Something blocked it from within. Terry was already at the next door down the hall, which he tried.

The light from the office pierced the hallway, overtaxing eyes accustomed to the dark. It was the first sunlight the women had seen since the quake. Cindy walked up to where Terry stood at the door.

As Terry pushed the door open, Cindy noticed that it was Madeline Jankowicz's office. The female partner's white burlap Danish furniture was tossed asunder, the glass topped pedestal desk was shattered. Law books were strewn everywhere. Cindy turned back up the hall, following Terry. The others each peeked into the office as they passed.

Now Cindy could see light ahead near her office. It looked like Goldwasser's door was shut like the other offices, but the hallway entrance from the reception area had no door.

"Hold a sec. I want to get my purse," Roberta called from her spot at the rear of the group, she had reached her secretarial station. Terry stopped and flashed the light back toward Roberta. Cindy walked on the dozen or so feet to her desk. The light from around the corner in the reception area was now enough to see by.

The entire contents of Cindy's desktop was on the floor; potted plant, picture of Jeff, pencil can, phone, papers, files, everything. The furniture had not moved, however, and the L-shaped desk was still in place, as were the files cabinets, both the ones behind her desk and those across the hall. Her radio was hanging off of the credenza, suspended by its cord.

With the toe of her shoe Cindy pushed the pot, plant and potting soil under the desk so that nobody would trip as they followed her. She bent to pick up the telephone set. She cringed in pain at the motion. Her hip and leg protested the bend. She decided to fore go picking up the papers and the wedge of wood tone plastic and brass that announced "Cynthia Borgmann".

Terry came up behind her, the women behind him. Cindy walked over to open Goldwasser's door.

She was ready for the light from the opened office this time, but not the view. Cindy stepped back in shock.

Instead of the massive oak furniture, burgundy carpet and the two tiers of full length windows of the corner office, she saw only the carpet. The huge executive desk, conference table and the several chairs were all gone, victims of their own expensive design which included casters for ease of movement. In all of the once familiar office only the built-in bookcases and credenza section remained.

The floor-to-ceiling windows and their metal frames were also gone for the most part. She could see the places where the conference table and desk had rolled and crashed through the windows. The post at the corner of the room and two sections of window on either side of it were all that remained of the exterior walls of the office. The heavy burgundy draperies, suspended from the ceiling rails, now framed openings into mid-air, twenty-eight stories up.

Cindy's head reeled at the thought and sight of the office. If anyone had been in this office during the earthquake, they would have been ... like Brenda.

Goldwasser's office was on the northeast corner of the building. From her position at the door in the corner of the office, Cindy could see out the openings to the east and north. The neighboring high-rises across the street on the eastern side of Century Park East and those to the north toward Santa Monica Boulevard appeared to have faired about the same as the building she was in. Some whole floors had glass totally broken out, some places were randomly broken and other places untouched.

Cindy wanted to venture out into Goldwasser's office to see the ground below, but she could not summon the courage. The now-empty office was a place to be feared. What if another quake hit when she was out there looking down?

Sirens whined in the distance. The sound came not only from the open windows in Goldwasser's office, but also from behind her in the lobby, where Brenda had been.

The view east from Century City covered all of Beverly Hills and Los Angeles beyond. A few tongues of smoke rose above the city skyline in the east, but other than the glass knocked from the neighboring buildings, Cindy could not see any evidence of the quake.

"Damn!" Roberta said from just behind her. Cindy jumped in surprise at Roberta, clutching the door frame to Goldwasser's office.

Roberta touched Cindy's shoulder and reassured her, "Sorry, didn't mean to scare you."

"I'm OK. It is just spooky. Seeing this."

"Tell me about it." Roberta moved back over where Terry and Dee were holding Cindy's radio.

"You'll have to pull the cord to get the batteries to work," Cindy recommended.

Terry pulled the cord from the back of the radio and static filled the room. He turned the dial.

"I still don't know that we shouldn't just take the stairs and get out of here," Roberta said. "Look out there. Everything, all the other buildings are like ours. We don't have a phone. And no one can do anything for us up here."

As she spoke, Roberta's voice became a whine, verging on panic. "I think we need to get out of here."

"Let's just hear what the radio has. Maybe we can find out how bad things are. Then we can go down the stairs or whatever. OK?" Cindy walked over next to Roberta as she spoke to her.

Roberta nodded. One of the other secretaries muttered her agreement. Dee walked over and put one arm around Roberta, speaking as she did. "Bobbie, I agree. Let's hear whatever we can and then get down. Its going to be quite a trip. Twenty-eight floors. We might as well, who knows ..." She stopped talking as Terry found a station.

The radio blared and Terry adjusted the volume, "... and we have not been able to get any official confirmation of that report. Our reporter, Marcia Tillotson, in Pasedena, did hear that the Cal Tech Seismology Center was confirming the location of the epicenter east of San Bernardino, but not the report on that tremendous Richter scale reading out of Golden, Colorado."

"So what was it, damn it!" Terry cut in with what the others were thinking. Roberta shushed him.

The radio continued, "With the massive power outage we still have not fully regained our links ... Whoa! . . there goes an aftershock ... a big one, just now hitting our West Hollywoo broadcast center."

Even as the words came from the radio, the floor started to oscillate. The effect of the shock on the upper floors of a skyscraper through the building's quake-dampening system was obviously slower than on the ground at the radio station.

The floor gave two quivering lurches which sent everyone staggering.

Terry shouted, "Everyone in the hall. Away from the windows and doors."

Terry pushed Roberta and Dee ahead of him. The other two

were already stumbling back into the hall. That left only Cindy, who tried to follow.

The floor shook with a thunderous knock. It felt to Cindy as though she had jumped several feet down onto a concrete floor, but her feet her still in place on the carpet. The knock sent her reeling toward the file cabinets across the passage from her desk. Terry and the radio hit the cabinets just beside her. Dee and Roberta were already on the floor. All around them a deep rumble, combined with a constant shattering of glass and tearing sounds from every direction, created a wall of noise. From the open windows of the reception area came the rumbling, roaring crash of a building falling somewhere outside. The roar joined the din, as did several screams from within the hallway and building.

Another powerful knock, stronger than the last, hit from through the floor, before Cindy could regain her balance. She flew backward against the file cabinets. The top of the cabinet hit right below her shoulder blades. The air was knocked from her lungs and she slumped toward the floor. As she hit the floor, another hammering blow from the building slammed her against the far wall across from Goldwasser's door.

Stunned, breathless and battered as she was, the sight of Goldwasser's open door brought a scream to Cindy Borgmann's throat. She clawed the carpet for a grip to keep herself from being flung out into the open office.

Cindy scrambled away from the open door, but in the opposite direction was only the entrance to the lobby, which was open, too. Cindy's feeble crawl away from the open door stopped short. She rolled onto her back on the carpet, paralyzed by fear, pain and disorientation.

Cindy turned her head toward the hall. She could see Terry and the others there, eyes wide and faces ashen. Even as she thought of making it to the safety of the hallway, she felt a series of throbbing bumps jar the floor under her back. The bumps were in rhythm. Bone-jarring rhythm.

After five or six bumps the light in the room shifted dizzyingly. A waft of air blew in through the open door and up her skirt. A sickening feeling of momentum joined the bumps and the flow of air. The rhythm of bumping continued, ever stronger.

Cindy Borgmann lifted her head and shoulders to look down toward her feet and the door to Goldwasser's office. The movement of lifting her head seemed to push her body up off of the floor. The rushing feeling of movement and wind now climaxed. In her last moment of life, Cynthia Borgmann saw the rubble-strewn pavement of Century Park East rushing at her through Goldwasser's office door.

In coming days, television viewers world-wide would marvel at the cellphone video shot by a golfer on the seventh tee at the Los Angeles Country Club, just across Santa Monica Boulevard from Century City. Excusing the staggering gait of the cameraman as he struggled to remain on his feet, unsuccessfully, during the full fury loosed by the Newport-Inglewood Fault directly beneath him, the video clearly showed the buildings of Century City in their death agony.

The video caught the dusty collapse of part of the Century City Shopping Mall and the four skyscrapers on Avenue of the Stars that brought each other down by collapsing upon one another. But, none of the video was quite as enrapturing of the viewer as the graceful demise of the smoky silver bank building on Century Park East as it rhythmically folded its lower floors like a stack of cards, then slowly slid sideways until its upper floors slammed into the boulevard with a thunderous crash that was heard clearly via the golfer's camera, a half mile north.

■

Like California's seismic engineers, the insurance industry is engaged in a monumental gamble. They are betting that the "Big One" that everyone fears either will not happen, will not happen soon or will not be as bad as it could be.

Each year, the California Insurance Commissioner, knowing the momentous risks facing the industry, issues a report outlining the level of property insurance, earthquake insurance, the insurance reserves and reinsurance support available to the insurers and estimates the ability of the insurance industry to cover potential earthquake damage. As in the architects' estimation of a building's ability to withstand an earthquake, the Insurance Commissioner's estimates do not assume a worst case, or even close to it.

Many scenarios are spoken of in these estimates, but the unspoken bottom line of the official insurance estimates is that if a catastrophic high-magnitude quake would hit a central urban area, such as downtown Los Angeles, most major insurance carriers along with their re-insurers and financial backers, world-wide, would have unfunded insurance liabilities far greater than the financial assets available. This would not only affect property insurance, but life and health insurance as well, since the companies and re-insurers are the same and since a catastrophic urban quake would probably lead to heavy death-tolls and severe injuries. The collapse of many insurance companies after the recent hurricanes would be minuscule compared to the effect on all companies after an urban earthquake in a major well-insured city.

Since the insurance industry is a major funding source for financing of business and commerce, the direct result of a catastrophic urban earthquake in California might be world financial collapse. The only way to prevent such an occurrence would be for the government to declare a moratorium on insurance coverage for the disaster. Thus, if the worst thing happens and the Big One strikes, a likely outcome might be for the insurance coverage meant for just such a disaster to fail utterly.

May 6th, 1:13 P.M.

Kathy Warden emerged from the shadow beneath the wreckage of the vehicles from the freeway and stepped into the bright sun of mid-day. She was not prepared for the sight that greeted her. The two men who grabbed her hands and pulled her up over the last hurdle of wrecked automobile stood on crates that had spilled from the broken cargo box of the big yellow truck. Other people helped her catch her balance and climb down from the crates.

A cluster of people stood around her. Kathy blinked and looked around at them, not knowing what to say. Someone else saved her the trouble.

"You OK?" one of the men on the crates, a burly older man with a thick Mexican accent, asked.

'Yes, I'm fine, Thanks." She nodded to him and then to the truck driver who had come in to get her. Again she said, "Thanks."

Both men mumbled words she did not comprehend back to her.

Another bystander, a black man who was bleeding from a head wound, asked the truck driver, "You see anybody else?"

"Nah, just her ... and the first guy in the Caddy." He paused respectfully. "How's the old lady up above?"

"No change. The young guy went back up, but it ain't no use.

We need one of them Jaws o' Life things to get her out. Hope the rescue guys get here soon."

The conversation went on around her, but Kathy's eyes were focused beyond the group. To her left and right the elevated portion of the Santa Monica Freeway lay in ruin. Some sections, like the one she had been on, had collapsed sideways, some balanced on shattered supports and some still towered, untouched, on their rows of concrete pillars. Just to her left was one such section. People crowded near the edge watching the wreckage below that they had avoided, even though stranded on a freeway to nowhere, suspended in space.

To her right, toward the Golden State Freeway, there were several sections that had matched hers in falling sideways, cement support columns splintered and crushed. Each section had dumped its vehicles in a jumbled line of wreckage. Some sections had only partly failed, leaving some cars and occupants balanced in the air. One section had simply pancaked itself flat into the ground. Everywhere the survivors turned rescuers and scoured for people trapped in the wreckage. However, Kathy saw no emergency vehicles, save one L.A.P.D. squad car which topped the pile of wrecked cars two sections to the east.

As she finished looking around, Kathy once again tuned in the conversation of the people around her.

"What do we do now?" Someone was asking.

"I guess wait until the fire department or somebody shows up. Not much else we can do."

"What makes you think anybody is coming. If it is this bad here, It could be worse elsewhere. And who says there is much left of the fire department? And, if there is why would they come here? I think we're on our own." The truck driver gave voice to everyone's fears.

Before anyone could reply, they heard a cry go up from another of the clusters of people who stood in the city street near the wrecked freeway sections. Kathy and the others on the street turned to see what was happening.

Two sections up ahead, near the wrecked police car, the people were running away from the pile of wrecked cars. A fire could be seen lapping at the stacked hulks of vehicles.

"That's all we need," the truck driver shouted to no one in particular.

In only a few seconds, the fire spread to several neighboring cars. Then in a muffled "whumpf" the tank of one car exploded in a fireball. As they watched the fire leaped to the next section.

"Everybody back. The whole mess is ready to go. Gas everywhere," again it was the truck driver who shouted.

The older Mexican man now shouted up to someone above them. "Hey, kid, get out of there!"

Kathy and everyone else now ran back from the fallen roadway and piles of cars. The non-freeway side of the street they were on was lined with older warehouse and factory buildings. Kathy followed the main group of people toward a side street between two warehouses. As she ran, she heard the muffled "whumpf" of a gas tank exploding behind her. The group slowed as they approached the side street. They turned to see behind them.

Kathy was shocked at how fast the fire had spread. In the short time it had taken them to run to the end of the block, the fire had passed down the line of wrecks most of the way to the yellow truck, feeding on gasoline fumes from a hundred ruptured fuel tanks.

Kathy now saw that the Mexican and the truck driver had waited to help a young man who just jumped down off of the yellow truck's cab. He must have been the one they had spoken of helping the injured woman trapped in the wreck above her car. That older woman they had spoken of would still be in the wreckage, with the fire approaching.

The young man seemed to hurt himself in the jump and the other two men grabbed his shoulders and helped him away from the spreading flames. A retort from an explosion behind the yellow truck knocked the running trio to their knees, but they quickly scrambled to their feet and raced toward the side street where Kathy watched.

The whole line of fallen freeway and smashed vehicles now belched thick black smoke as tires, gasoline, cargo and interiors of vehicles joined the conflagration. Flames leaped hundreds of feet in the air. Kathy could tell that her car, behind the yellow track would certainly be in the fire now.

Kathy could see people on one section of freeway that still stood upright run from the flames now right below them. At first, it appeared they might be all right, but then the vehicle nearest the inferno caught fire and the blaze spread up to the standing section. The section of freeway must have been already awash with spilled gasoline for it only took seconds for the whole stilted section to catch fire. That section of roadway was directly over a storage yard full of machinery. The people caught on the elevated section had no choice but to jump the fifty feet to the jumble of machinery and wreckage below. Kathy watched in horror as many hesitated at the edge of the freeway a moment too long and the next exploding gas tank on the section spewed burning fuel on them. Many burning bodies fell or jumped the last fifty feet to the ground. Kathy turned away from the scene and ran a few more steps up the side street. It was only then that she realized that from the side street in the East L.A. warehouse district that she had a full view of the downtown Los Angeles skyline to the northwest.

Kathy had only a few seconds to acknowledge the unexpected view when a voice nearby, perhaps the truck driver's, shouted a new warning from behind, screaming over the roar of the fire and explosions. "There's a tanker truck over there. If it goes up we might be too close."

The crowd of people she had run with to the side street now again moved as one up the street between the warehouses. Kathy Warden ran with the crowd.

Half way up the block, the crowd slowed and many turned to look back, as did Kathy. They now could only see a small portion of the fallen freeway, part of the yellow truck and the edge of the still-standing section. But, above the warehouses roofs on both sides of the street she could see the billowing smoke and flames coming from every direction. The whole freeway was on fire.

The acrid smoke made breathing a struggle. Kathy blinked through tears at the sight of the smoke and flames of the thousands of cars and trucks burning. The roar of the inferno a block away and the explosions of each succeeding gas tank now joined each other in one long rumble.

It took Kathy and those around her a few seconds to realize that the rumble of the inferno on the Santa Monica Freeway was not the sole cause of the vibration in the ground. A couple of stomach wrenching bumps were joined by the first shouts of "Quake!" "Here it goes again," and "Oh, my God!"

Kathy's scream joined those of others. The ground seemed to rise up at her. While many around her fell to the ground, Kathy managed to remain on her feet. She staggered drunkenly toward a chain link fence that rimmed the back lot of the warehouse to her left. The act of staggering to the fence saved her life.

The first pounding blow of the earthquake had shattered the integrity of the brick warehouse on the right side of the street. Those in the crowd who had the misfortune to stagger right were instantly smothered in a crashing shower of bricks and concrete from the shattered facade of the warehouse.

Kathy first clutched the wire of the chain link fence to keep her balance. Then she held on tightly, out of fear. Abject fear.

She managed to turn her head just in time to see the whole wall of the warehouse across the street crash to the pavement. A dozen people from the crowd were under the falling wall.

A billow of choking dust blocked Kathy's view of anything further. The cloud of dust enveloped her and everything in the street. Her next breath brought a spasm of coughing, and the coughing forced her to take another lung full of the foul, dusty, smoky air.

As she struggled to control the coughing and get her breath, another shock from below knocked her free from her grip on the fence. Kathy fell backwards onto the sidewalk.

The sidewalk and the ground buffeted below her. She heard the rumble from the ground merge with the continuing roar from the fire behind her, and the ever more frequent crashes. Another crash joined the din, as some nearby building joined its neighbor in a pile in the street. The old brick buildings of the L.A. warehouse district were not holding up well in the quake.

Kathy felt the pieces of concrete in the sidewalk below her crack and twist in the continuing waves of the quake's fury. The ground itself rumbled an almost mechanical roar.

The utter pandemonium of the noise, the crashing, the shocks and shaking of the ground, the screams of the injured and fear-stricken people was overwhelming.

Someone staggered over Kathy's prone body, kicking her in the leg, and stumbled away into the dust cloud.

The kick of the stumbling feet jarred Kathy into action. She pulled herself to her feet by pulling up on the fence wire.

Kathy hung on to the fence with one hand and covered her mouth and nose with her blouse collar with the other. Breathing through the cloth she was finally able to catch her breathe. She still could not see anything well in the dust and smoke. Her eyes burned at the effort.

Kathy Warden hung onto the fence, which swayed in the waves from the earth. Behind her, a shrill voice of a woman crying out in pain pierced the rumbling of the earth, the crashing of debris and the roar of the fire in the freeway wreckage.

Then, the woman's shrill cries stopped abruptly. The rumbling from earth and fire and the shouting of everyone else did not.

■

The best available data indicates that the San Andreas Fault in the vicinity of Palm Springs has, historically, had a major quake every 220 years or so. The last major quake on this stretch was in 1680, or 315 years ago. This section is primed and ready for a major quake.
Kerry Sieh, Geologist
California Institute of Technology (Caltech)

May 6th, 1:13 P.M.

Genevieve Dumont would have been far more self-conscious of her current predicament had she not spent several years on Parisian fashion runways in clothing more revealing than the flimsy robe she wore as she hiked up the hillside drive.

Gravel on the roadway cut into her feet and the patches of un-gravelled asphalt burned hot in the mid-day sun, forcing her to walk in the narrow sandy path along the edge of the road. She chose the right side of the road, the left side dropped sharply into the steep ravine that had just swallowed her house.

The road, Camino Espinazo, was a horseshoe drive ending and beginning on Alston Road, an east-west street linking Santa Barbara to Montecito. Camino Espinazo arched seaward around the ridge line circling the large estate that occupied the top of the ridge and servicing the ring of expensive homes bordering the ridge, of which her own house had until moments before been a part.

At the first curve around the hillside, Genevieve looked back for a last look at her house. All that she could see was the mailbox and driveway. From this view, nothing remained of her home or the two other houses farther down the road toward the Pacific. Instead of the houses she had always seen driving in around this curve, she now had a clear view of the islands across the Santa Barbara Channel.

The drive now turned uphill more steeply and Genevieve had to walk on the road and its gravel and hot asphalt, hedges crowded her off of the roadside path. Behind the hedges on the right was the wrought iron fence of the big estate on the hill. Finally, she saw a driveway.

The driveway curved dropped away from the road out of her vision. She climbed the last stretch of road to the driveway and looked down to the house.

The house was about the same size as her own, but not as well kept as hers had been. The driveway was blocked by a chain locked between two posts, upon which a real estate sign hung. A picture of a middle-aged women with over-teased hair smiled vapidly from the sign which urged Genevieve to "make on offer." A pile of a half dozen sun-yellowed copies of the Santa Barbara News-Press littered the drive-way. Genevieve sighed and turned back up the hill.

As she rounded the top of the next hill, Genevieve could see the next house. Her step quickened as she saw a Land Rover in the driveway with people around it.

It was a big, white house and the yard was lushly landscaped. Occupying a wide terrace on the hillside, the house had a large manicured lawn on either side of the circle drive leading down from the road. A woman was unloading the vehicle. Another figure had just disappeared into the house as Genevieve turned down the driveway.

Genevieve took advantage of the thick grass and cut across the lawn rather than the hot driveway pavement. Now, finally approaching someone else, on their property, she became aware of just how much of her long legs were not covered by the short black robe and she clasped her hand over the open edges of the front of the robe below the tie.

The women was unloading a grocery bag from the rear hatch of the Land Rover. The front door of the house stood open behind her. She looked up as Genevieve Dumont sauntered toward her across the grass. Genevieve smiled. The woman, an attractive, but matronly blonde in a khaki jumpsuit, smiled back, but somewhat quizzically.

Genevieve spoke with a hesitation, her French accent growing with her nervousness, "Hello, I am Genevieve Dumont, I live down the street."

"Hi, I'm Natalie Weld." She reached forward to offer Genevieve her hand.

Genevieve risked letting the robe go and shook hands. She saw Natalie's eye flash downwards and back to her face.

Genevieve continued, "I, ah, my house, ... I was wondering if you might be able to assist me. The earthquake," her French tongue struggled with the word, "the earthquake ruined my home."

"Oh, My!" Natalie interjected as Genevieve continued.

"I, unfortunately, have nothing else left to wear."

Natalie took a moment to recognize what Genevieve had said, then she gave a look of wonderment and sympathy, "Oh, you poor dear, of course we can help. Our house is a mess too, but not ruined. You mean it is totally ruined?"

Genevieve nodded, "Yes, totally ruined. It fell down in the *valle*." She pointed to the ravine below the woman's home.

"Oh. All the way down. Everything? My goodness!"

Before either women could speak again the earth moved beneath their feet.

Slowly at first, and then with a growing ferocity, the ground oscillated. Up and down, then quivered and repeated the undulation. Genevieve balanced like a passenger on a trolley bumping over a rough street. Natalie backed away from the vehicle as its springs started to squeak from the bouncing.

There was a clattering crash from within the house. It was followed immediately by a girl's shriek.

Natalie turned and ran toward where the front door stood open, shouting as she ran, "Kiki!"

Genevieve took a few steps to follow the other woman, not really thinking about it, just acting. Then, as a cloud of white dust spewed from the front door, both women stopped short, Natalie bringing an arm up to protect herself should the dust and debris hit her.

A second later a teen-age girl ran headlong from the door, colliding with Natalie, who caught her arms and swung her around to maintain balance.

Natalie pulled the girl out away from the house, near where Genevieve watched. The last vibrations of the earth were ending as Natalie stood next to the coughing girl, stroking dust from her face and hair. Genevieve stood blinking and breathing deeply, her heart pounding in the quake's aftermath.

"Kiki, what happened?" Natalie asked.

"The chandelier ... the ceiling. I was feeling the earthquake, watching the chandelier swing from the doorway when the whole ceiling fell in. I thought the house was falling."

"God, you scared me when you screamed. I thought I lost you." Natalie Weld continued stroking the girl's sandy blonde hair and then she jerked the girl out to arm's length, "Where's Ted?"

"He, he was in the back yard. Feeding Frisco."

Natalie now stood, shouting in a loud, commanding voice, "Ted. Ted. Do you hear me? Ted!"

On perfect cue, a tow-headed boy, a few years younger than the girl, rounded the corner of the house, his pubescent voice cracking as he screamed, "Mom, quick, you've gotta come. The ocean ... Hurry!" And with that, he spun and headed back around the corner of the house.

The girl followed first. Natalie looked to Genevieve with raised eyebrows. Genevieve shrugged, not fully comprehending. Then the two women trotted off behind the girl to see what had so excited the boy.

The grass of the front lawn sloped down at the side of the house, past a huge fig tree, and out onto a lower terrace of grass. This was where they found the boy, pointing out across the ravine toward the coastline and the city of Santa Barbara below.

The scene was the same as from Genevieve's property. The ravine and the green folds of the Montecito Country Club immediately below them, stretching out toward the beach. Santa Barbara's famous curve of sand, palms and hotels ended on the point below the far-off Mesa with the harbor and Stearn's Wharf on the coast to the left and the downtown area of Santa Barbara on the right.

The first look at the view seemed the same as always. But as Genevieve tried to focus on the familiar landmarks she had difficulty. Stearn's Wharf no longer jutted straight to sea, now it was crooked and truncated. And, it did not start on the beach. It seemed to be out in the harbor. The coastline, the beach itself could not easily be seen. At least not where it should have been.

The entire center of Genevieve's view was glistening with the light of the sun reflected on water that should not have been there. She could see water on both sides of what she knew to be the 101 freeway, which should have been five or six blocks inland from the beach. The freeway itself was a watery river through islands of buildings.

Genevieve tried to grasp what had become of her adopted hometown. It appeared that the entire beach-front area was wreckage. She could see the glint of sunlight on water halfway across the city. She looked for the twin landmarks of the upper side of the city, the towers of the Courthouse and the Arlington Theatre. They were not standing were she knew they should be. The quakes had done to the city what they had to her home.

"I saw it come in," the boy recounted for them. "A really big wave, just went whoosh," He supplied the motion with his hand, "And it went over everything."

The boy stopped speaking as another very light aftershock quivered for a few seconds and stopped. No one spoke, until Ted asked his mother, "Ma, who's she?" indicating Genevieve.

Natalie Weld startled out of her contemplation of the scene of Santa Barbara, broken and flooded. "Oh, yes, aah, Miss Dumont, wasn't it? Yes, Ms. Dumont, this is Kiki and Ted, my daughter and son. Children, this is Genevieve Dumont, our neighbor from down the street." Genevieve noticed that the American woman gave proper French pronunciation to Genevieve's name. "Ms. Dumont ..."

Kiki did not wait for her mother to finish the introduction, she stepped up to Genevieve and extended her hand, "Yes, wow, glad to meet you. I heard you lived down there. I saw a magazine article on your wedding, in People. Smashing dress. I loved the picture, you were beautiful. And your husband is a real hunk."

Genevieve smiled an embarrassed smile, "Thank you. Unfor-

tunately, that wedding dress is with everything else, down in the ruin."
She pointed into the ravine.

Natalie spoke, "Mrs. Dumont's house was wrecked in the quake.
We are going to help her a bit. Ted, could you run through the house
and unlock the patio doors in my bedroom. With the chandelier down
we don't all need to traipse through the foyer."

Ted gave a quizzical look, muttered "Chandelier?" and then took
off at a run around to the front of the house.

"Kiki, let's see if we can find Mrs. Dumont something to wear."
Natalie spoke as she ushered her daughter and Genevieve toward the
nearest French doors. Genevieve noted how Natalie had switched from
Ms. to Mrs. in addressing her when she heard she was married. Genevieve chalked this up to culture, she was beginning to like her neighbor.

■

In earthquake preparedness brochures and in the front of telephone books California residents are reminded of the need for a source of clean water for up to 72 hours after a quake. They are asked to store water and make use of the water stored in water heaters.

Water department planners estimate that a truly catastrophic quake could be much worse. A magnitude 6 or greater quake is capable of rupturing underground water mains. A major earthquake could cause enough destruction to require weeks or months for restoration of service. The 1994 Northridge quake resulted in disruption of water service for thousands of people, some for several weeks. The absolute failure of water and sewer services in Kobe, Japan after their 1995 quake was one of the biggest dangers to public health.

Even if local water service could be restored, another problem remains. Southern California is a desert. The bulk of its major water sources come through pipes, canals and waterworks systems from other areas many hundreds of miles away. And, every single water transportation system into Southern California passes through at least one and often several fault zones capable of a magnitude 7 quake. Destruction of underground piping and the complex pumping system of the California and Colorado River Aqueducts and the other major water diversion projects could require months to repair.

May 6th, 1:15 P.M.

The quake continued with alternating powerful thumps and lesser quivering of the ground. When it finally died out, Kathy continued to stand still, clutching the chain-link fence for fear that the quake would start up again. It did not.

With the final waves from the earth, a new sensation came to Kathy Warden. The smothering smoke and dust gave way to a cool mist falling on her skin. The wafts of watery mist alternated with gusts of hot, smoke-fouled air. The nature of the sounds filling the street around her also changed. As the deep rumble of the quake ebbed, it was replaced by the muffled gurgle and rushing sound of a broken water main. The tumult of the fires and explosions up the block at the freeway continued. The victims shouts and screams struggled to be heard of above the other noise.

Kathy had been covering her mouth and nose in her blouse in order to breath in the cloud of dust the collapsing buildings had billowed out. She had been forced to close her eyes for the same reason. When the mist touched her she uncovered and looked about her, wiping her eyes with the back of her hand.

There was break in the water main half way up the block toward the freeway. The spray and mist from the geyser of water was already knocking down the dust cloud, at least on this block.

The freeway was a churning mass of fire, belching a billowing cloud of acrid smoke skyward. At times the fire would spurt outward as another gas tank exploded.

The fire of the freeway gave forth a constant rumble, but a rumble far different from the rumble of the quake. Now, above even this rumble she heard, from the south beyond the freeway, a greater sound, an explosion. It was far away, echoing, but its power was clear, like a long thunder clap. That it was so clear above the noise of the freeway fire and explosions made it all the more terrifying. What could explode with such force? Kathy had no idea.

As she was looking south toward the sound and the freeway fire, Kathy became aware that the large building to the right which had blocked her view of the freeway when she had first turned around to look was no longer there. Neither was the other building across the street which had first fallen. Kathy turned toward it and finally became aware of the other people on the street.

There had been a crowd of several dozen people fleeing up the side street from the freeway when the quake started. Now there were roughly half as many standing, sitting and laying around the street. Some pulled themselves from the periphery of the brick pile across the street. Others stood, like Kathy, trying to comprehend the chaos around them. A couple ran around, searching for someone they had lost in the chaos of the quake.

Kathy was just starting to take stock of the piles of rubble, the injured people and the chaos surrounding her when a young man in a brown package delivery uniform halfway up the block toward the freeway started screaming and running toward her.

"Gas! Gas! Run for it. The gas main broke, too." The man's words could barely be understood as he shouted and ran past her. It took Kathy a moment to comprehend. Several other people near where this man had started now ran along behind him.

Kathy considered whether she should run also, or go to help the others, injured in the street and under the rubble. The decision was made for her when a particularly large explosion from the freeway shook the ground and flashed fire in all directions. This convinced her to run from the gas main break, which she could now smell for herself.

Kathy ran as best she could in the smooth-soled ladies' heels.

The scattering of bricks and debris and the occasional break in the pavement itself made running even more difficult. Kathy slowed to step up over a raised chunk of sidewalk when the gas exploded behind her.

The sound, the flash and the force of the explosion hit together. Like a stick figure in the wind, Kathy was thrown forward by the force of the blast. She landed face down on a stretch of sidewalk that was thankfully unbroken and relatively clean. The chunk of raised sidewalk shielded her from the rolling fireball that followed the blast's shock wave, as did the coating of mud on her clothes and skin from the dust and the spray from the water main.

Someone had not been so lucky. A yowling cry, a man's cry of pain, immediately followed the concussion of the blast. It came from somewhere behind Kathy, on the street between her and the freeway.

Kathy was in pain herself and she was struggling to catch her breath. The force of the blast and the impact of landing chest-first on the pavement had knocked the breath from her. Although she had been able to cushion her fall with her arms, her chin had hit the pavement and she had bitten her tongue. Kathy Warden lay face-down on the street, breathlessness and pain immobilizing her.

The initial blast of the gas main instantly retreated into the steady noisome furor of a pillar of fire erupting from the street. The yowl of the injured man also stopped in only a few seconds. By the time Kathy was able to roll over and sit up, there was no sound from the unseen man. Her view of the street was dominated by the sight of a geyser of water arising from the same car-sized crater in the street, as did a pillar of fire.

Kathy Warden sat frozen in place, sitting on the broken pavement. Her thoughts were a useless jumble, unable to concentrate and comprehend the calamity. Thoughts and half-thoughts flashed through her mind. Ideas of running, fleeing, sobbing, helping other people, praying, doing anything ... something ... cycled back and forth in her consciousness. But, still she sat, half mesmerized by the spectacle of the twins columns of fire and water that arose from the ground she had crossed only moments before.

Kathy's first move other than sitting and blinking was to bring the sleeve of her dress jacket up and wipe the grit from her mouth. A smear of mud brown and deep crimson smudged the sleeve when she looked down. The realization that the red was not lipstick, but her own blood, brought her out of the shocked stupor.

Kathy fingered her lip, then rolled her tongue in her mouth, finally determining the bitten tongue as the source of blood. She leaned over and spit the blood, grit and saliva to the side. A peculiar thought crossed her mind. This was the first time she had spit in public since a junior high softball game had required it to get rid of a mouth of second base sand. Not that this scene could really be considered public. Certainly nobody was paying any attention to her in this cacophony of fire, death, and horror. She dismissed the strange thoughts about the un-ladylike act and spit repeatedly until the last salty taste of blood was gone. Then, she rolled to her bruised knees and stood up.

Kathy's body recoiled at the effort of standing up. The combined effects of the freeway wreck and now two successive meetings with the pavement of the warehouse street made the first movement painful and stiff. Both of her knees were scrapped and an ankle was slightly sprained.

In front of Kathy, back up the street where she had come from, the twin columns of fire and water had a backdrop of the wall of fire and black smoke coming from the freeway. The freeway, a far as she could see both left and right, was engulfed in fire that spouted viscous black smoke. Now that both the warehouse on the left and right were laying in rubble, she could most of the I-10 Freeway and some of the Golden State Freeway. It was all ablaze. The wall of smoke from the freeway lifted as high into the air as she could see.

In the center of her view, Kathy could see one charred corner of the yellow truck at the edge of the fire. Her own little Honda would be right behind it, in the heart of the fire. Kathy turned her back on the freeway to see the view behind her.

Kathy Warden's jaw dropped at the spectacle she now saw.

She had noticed the view of the downtown skyline as she ran up the side street after the freeway collapse. However, she had not paid any attention with the ensuing earthquake and explosion to that view. Now she saw it.

Framed by columns of smoke from many fires, both nearby and throughout the downtown area, the skyline could be clearly seen against the bright afternoon sky to the west. The unforgettable scene which would soon be flashed worldwide, this view, the symbol of the great L.A. earthquake, the "Big One," now held Kathy Warden entranced.

The most astonishing thing was the sight of the once-majestic silver-blue BankCal building laying over against two of its neighbors, like a huge Thanksgiving Parade balloon somehow deflated. Several more buildings, which, to the mind of a native Angeleno should have been visible, were not to be seen. One lesser building also tilted over in imitation of the BankCal building. None of the once shimmering mirrored facades were without missing glass, most were entirely devoid of windows.

Worse yet, was the view of the entire east-side mercantile district which lay between Kathy and the high rises of downtown. These older brick buildings resembled a scene from post-War Germany. Girder skeletons, missing their brick skins, were everywhere. Many had smoke rising from them.

To the left, however, Kathy could see the beige spindle of City Hall, still standing, apparently undamaged. Kathy could not see the courts buildings, which should have flanked City Hall.

Another explosion behind her snapped Kathy from her view of the city. Something in the warehouse rubble to her left had ignited and blown up. She turned in time to see the arching flight of a canister of some kind, on fire, and flying through the air like a Fourth of July rocket.

This latest flare-up pushed Kathy into action, moving away from the gas main fire and the conflagration of the freeway beyond. The continued glare of the intense heat was already threatening to scorch her skin and clothes, or so it felt. She trotted off, up the side street, as best as she could considering the body aches, unsuitable shoes, and the debris in the street. As she ran away, finally getting her wits about her, she felt foolish at having stood in shock as she had only a few dozen yards from the blazing pyre.

The exertion of jogging up the block finally wiped the last cobwebs of shock from Kathy's mind. She passed several people. One woman sat on the curb, staring at Kathy with a wide-eyed glare Kathy understood only too well. Kathy passed the woman and did not stop running until she was around the corner at the end of the warehouse block.

Kathy ran on until she was beyond the street corner. In the shadow of a corrugated steel warehouse that had withstood the quake undamaged she paused, leaning with one arm on a "loading zone" sign. Her chest heaved from the run and the bad air.

This side street and its buildings had less damage than those around the corner on the street up to the freeway. Twenty to thirty people stood in the street, some talking and crying with each other, others, like Kathy, just stood, trying to comprehend the calamity.

Across the street a swarthy man, perhaps Iranian or Arab, ran from the frame of one building that did show damage. Its brick facade had fallen away and revealed the twisted steel frame. The man motioned frantically to a group of similar looking men who stood in the street in the spaces between parked cars. Kathy could not understand the language, but from the reaction, she could tell he had found someone in the wreckage. The man and two others ran into the building taking with them a length of metal railing from the fallen facade.

Kathy could see that the other men had been standing in a group surrounding two prone figures. What appeared to be a man and a woman lay in the street. Another woman knelt beside them, tending their injuries.

The sights and sounds of the city around Kathy were unnatural. The afternoon sun shown in a cloudless sky, but the sunlight was muted and the sky was not blue. Columns of smoke from the freeway a block behind her and a dozen other fires across the city in front of her rendered the sky a smoky gray-red. The smoke from the huge freeway fire to the south blocked much of the mid-afternoon sun. One of the big ten story warehouses between Kathy and the high rises of downtown now billowed smoke and flame to rival the freeway fire.

Something else to the north near Union Station belched black smoke and flame. Maybe the 101 freeway had wound up similar to Interstate 10 where she had been.

The sounds were simply wrong. The sound of traffic was an

ever-present aspect of life in Los Angeles. She could hear no traffic. Instead, the rumble of fires and lesser explosions joined together in an uncanny murmur. The murmur was joined by the chirping and wailing of several alarms, both in cars and buildings. The effect of the unfamiliar sounds and the sights of destruction was surreal.

Finally, Kathy recognized a familiar, although eerie sound. A single siren sounded in the west. It was the first siren she had heard, which seemed odd in such a calamity. The sound of the siren made her think of her deputy sheriff husband. What was he doing? Was he OK?

The thought of Barry led to wondering about others. Her parents, sister Cindy, Jeff... Kathy realized that she had not thought of Barry nor anyone else since the first tremor had hit her in the car on the freeway.

When she was still in high school her family had set up a plan to call Grandma in Phoenix in case an emergency like this happened and separated the family. No one had spoken of it in years. Now, Grandma was in a nursing home and probably would not be much help as a news gatherer and message taker. Kathy wondered if the phones were working. Would she be able to reach Barry? Cindy? Her folks up in the Valley?

"You OK, Miss?" A man's voice broke into Kathy's thoughts.

Kathy startled at the voice, removed her hand from the signpost and turned to the voice. A small, but handsome, middle-aged man with his arms full of boxes stood looking at Kathy. His tie was pulled loose from his neck and his face was covered in dirt. Dust coated his white dress shirt and rendered the sweat stains under his arms as muddy rings.

He spoke again before Kathy could respond, "I thought maybe you were hurt, the way you were standing."

"Uh, well, no ... No, I'm OK. I guess." Kathy involuntarily brushed at her clothes as she spoke. Just now realizing how grubby she must look after the freeway wreckage and the sprawling on the street during the quake and explosion. The suit she wore for the possible job interview was unrecognizable, coated in mud. Her stockings were tattered. She felt strings of wet hair sticking to her cheeks.

The man nodded at her and motioned with his head toward an open door in the building next door down. "The bathroom is the first door on the right. You can clean up if you want. The water is just barely trickling out. Feel free." He did not wait for a response, moving off to the small pickup truck at the curb with his boxes.

Kathy hesitated a moment before taking up his offer and going into the building. It was a narrow one story building, indistinguishable from the others in the neighborhood. A sign painted above the transom stated "Villanova Importers - Wholesale Only."

Kathy walked into the doorway. The lights were out, the only light came from outside. She could see rows of warehouse shelving, most of which had discharged their contents, hundreds of boxes, in the aisles. The office space on the left was a mass of ledger books and catalogs which had flown from the shelves along each wall. On the right hand wall rows of racks displayed various types of clothing, but now about half of the hangers were on the floor below. As promised, there was a single doorway between the racks on the wall.

The bathroom was dark and smelled heavily of pine disinfectant. Once Kathy had closed the creaky door the only light came from a small cobweb-covered window in the front of the building.

The small oval mirror on the wall disclosed why the man had thought Kathy was injured. Her hair and face were covered in mud and dust. The effect was magnified by the sparse light, but she looked horrible nevertheless. Her ash blonde hair could barely be seen under the muddy brown coating on it. One eye seemed swollen and her chin was bruised. Blood mixed with dirt on her chin.

Two grayish towels hung from a wire coat hanger next to the mirror. Kathy reached for one, then tried the other. Both were damp from previous use. She took one from the hanger and started to work on the dirt.

The water was, indeed, a bare trickle. And it seemed to lessen a bit more while she waited for it to soak a corner of the towel.

She had managed to keep a tight grip on her purse throughout the entire ordeal. It was oddly comforting to have the personal items in the purse with her in a world the had become so unhinged. Her little rat-tail comb was right where it belonged. Kathy unsnapped her gold hairpin which had held her long page boy away from her face and used the towel to try and get most of the grit out of her hair. With the comb and hairpin she twirled her hair into a roll behind her head. It was too dirty, wet and stringy to hang free.

Kathy could see in the mirror that her efforts had been worthwhile; except for the bruises on brow and chin she looked fairly presentable, relatively speaking. That is, except for her clothes. The cream-colored suit was beyond hope. Her consideration had just reached her torn hose and shoes when the bathroom rattled and knocked in its frame. Her quake-spawned jitters pumped adrenaline for a moment until the knocking was followed by a voice.

It was the man's voice. "Uh? Miss? I have ..." He paused. "I have a suggestion."

He wanted her to open the door. Her nervousness from the whole series of events now led to worry over the intentions of the stranger. Here she was in his office, his bathroom, amidst this chaos. Finally, she decided that she had nothing to lose in opening the door to see what he wanted. Why, she was not even sure the door was locked.

The man was standing outside with his hands full. As she opened the door wider he handed a box and two hangers of clothes to her.

He spoke, "I assume you are on foot and from the looks of your clothes. I thought this would help."

She now saw the what he had handed her was a pair of jeans and a matching denim shirt, along with a pair of blue and white Nike's, the box labeled size 7 1/2, her size.

"No, really. I couldn't," Kathy objected.

"Hey. I won't hear it. I insist." The man held up his hands as if to block any attempt to return the items. "I figure that if I help you out, then someone will be helping my wife and kids out. Wherever they are in this god forsaken mess of a city. I guess you would call it a Jewish version of Karma."

By now Kathy had checked the tags on both pants and shirt. Both would fit her. "How did you know my sizes."

"Well, I inherited this business from my father, we moved out form the East. I have been judging the sizes of people's clothes since I was a kid. By the time other little boys were wondering why girls wore bras, I could tell you their cup size at one glance." The man smiled, his New York accent showed itself as he told the story of his youth.

"You just get yourself out of those wet, dirty things. I have a couple of warehouses of clothes, or at least I did have, before this all happened." He motioned outside toward the ruined city. "No, you don't worry about it. Just get into these clothes. It will make it easier to get through that mess out there. Oh, and here." He reached over to a display of sock samples and grabbed a pair of white gym socks which he tossed onto the pile of clothes in her arms.

"If you will excuse me, I have work to do. Trying to collect some of the expensive stuff in case the fires spread down here. It looks like all of wholesale district around the Mart is on fire. And, I think they've got paint in that one back behind us. Could go up and take this block with it." He moved off into the back of the building, ending the discussion of whether Kathy would use the clothing he had given her.

Kathy went back into the bathroom and started the process of getting out of the muddy suit and shredded pantyhose.

■

In 1992, the Los Angeles riots tested the abilities of authorities to handle a massive civil disturbance in an urban area. At that time the police and National Guard had a fully functioning governmental system and infrastructure to support it. If an element of society will loot and burn when the lights are on and the police and fire departments are only minutes away, what can be expected when darkness and disaster have the authorities' full attention? The Northridge earthquake had some looting, but it was minimal. However, the worst high-crime areas were, by and large, spared the major damage.

At any given moment in Los Angeles County the number of known criminals in jail, on probation, work release and pre-trial release far outnumbers the police personnel. As with all other public safety organizations, in time of natural disaster the police forces of Southern California put their emphasis on protection and saving of human life and put less effort into crime control unless absolutely necessary. Without telephones, utilities and transport, a post-catastrophic earthquake Los Angeles will be a chaos unlike anything anyone has ever seen and only part of that chaos will be caused by natural forces.

May 6th, 1:20 P.M.

"OK, Everyone! On three ... One, Two, Three!"

Barry Warden grunted with the strain as he and the others lifted on the eaves of the collapsed roof. To his surprise the roof lifted with less difficulty than he had feared. He had the help of the five neighbors that the woman had recruited to help find her daughter. She had rounded them up while Barry had tried to hear any sound from the trapped girl.

There had been no sound; no indication that she was still alive in the collapsed room addition.

As the roof moved, Barry could see that they were really only lifting the near half of the roof, the other half settled back on the far side. It was balanced on something waist-high inside the rubble, perhaps the remains of the fireplace whose chimney has now strewn back across the lawn. Stressed timbers groaned and cracked as the six people pushed up on the eave.

Two women, the girl's mother and, Mrs. Westover, the woman Barry had taken the vandalism report from stood behind the others holding two redwood picnic table benches. As the roof lifted, the women struggled to push the ends of the benches in place under the edge of the roof. The near edge of the roof was now about shoulder high, enough to get under it to find the girl, but still precariously balanced.

"OK, now keep it balanced. Let the props take the load, but keep it balanced." Barry spoke as he moved his hold from the eave to one of the benches. The bottom of the bench pushed into the sod, but it held.

The mother wasted no time in scrambling in under the roof. Barry made no attempt to stop her, especially since her efforts were immediately rewarded by movement under the pile of broken gypsum wallboard.

The woman pulled at the wallboard and from underneath it a figure arose. A teenage girl, in a sweat suit and curlers, covered with dust struggled to pull free of the rubble. She appeared to be crawling from under a pool table. Perhaps the "Duck and Cover" drills California school children trained in twice yearly had paid off for her.

"Hurry, get her out quick, This won't hold long." Barry urged, stepping in to pull on the debris also.

The mother pulled her daughter the rest of the way out from under the pool table, quickly brushing the chalk white gypsum from her face, so she could see. Then they both scampered out of the rubble. The girl did not seem hurt at all.

When they were clear, Barry did not wait, he shouted to the others holding and balancing the roof, "Everyone back off, I've got it." He waited a moment, looked around him, and added, "Way Back!"

When everyone was fully clear of the area of the precariously leaning roof, Barry tested the balance of the bench and then quickly turned and ran back himself.

The room addition's roof stayed for a moment in place and then slowly swung to the left. It and the benches they had balanced it on crashed heavily to the ground, half on the remains of the foundation and half on the grass. A billowing cloud of dust spewed forth. Barry and the other onlookers turned their faces away, choking on the dust and spitting the dust grit out.

The dust cleared quickly, the strange, stiff breeze still raced to the east. The mother and daughter were still hugging. The mother mouthed words of thanks as Barry started to move off. One of the other neighbors, an elderly man, clapped a hand on Barry's shoulder in thanks and congratulations. This clapping resulted in another puff of dust. The neighbors stood in clusters, talking and gesturing, some hurried off toward their own houses. Barry walked back towards the Sheriff's Explorer.

He had not paid attention to the radio during the time he had struggled to free the girl, but now he heard his call-sign squawk from the portable radio on his hip. The voice was Sergeant Rivera's, the new dispatcher had still not come back on line.

Barry thumbed the mike key and answered. "This is Patrol Four Four, over."

"Roger, Four Four, what is your status, we need you to free yourself up at your current location."

"I am free here, victim was rescued."

"Roger, we need you to roll to the Harbor UCLA Med Center, they have some major problem with security and setting up triage for the victims, not really sure what's the status. I have E.O.C up on the command radio, they gave this the highest priority."

"There has got to be someone closer. I'm several miles from Harbor Hospital."

"Roger that, but you have the only operational 4x4 vehicle. You are about the only one who can travel with road conditions what they are."

"What happened to Espinoza and Ruppert?" Barry asked, knowing the two deputies who had taken the other Explorer that morning.

"No report since the quake. We think they may have been caught in the quake or in the fireball."

`Fireball?' He had heard the first reports about the fire and Barry wanted to ask more about this, he had obviously missed a lot while he had worked on the toppled roof.

"Roger, Four Four is on the way to Harbor."

Sergeant Rivera's voice came over once more, "Barry, don't stop for anything. Get to the hospital. We have got to help the most people we can, you can't help everyone. Just get to Harbor where you can help the most people. OK?"

Barry had no idea yet why the sergeant had said this, but he responded, "10-4," and climbed into the Explorer.

Barry had not traveled more than a few hundred feet before he fully understood the importance of driving the 4x4. The rolling waves in the street he had felt on Savoy Ridge Drive left little damage on the soft asphalt there, compared to what he found on the main boulevard down the hill. Chunks of cement and asphalt were tilted and uplifted in a pattern of even rows across the width of the street. Few cars were moving. Even the Explorer scraped bottom on the larger chunks of pavement. As Barry struggled with the driving, he caught glimpses of the damage as he past through the lower stretches of the Palos Verdes hills heading north.

Damage was everywhere. Buildings, trees, signposts, houses, utilities ... It seemed everything was broken. Pools or flows of water from the cracked street showed the state of the pipes in the ground. The scent of gas in the air confirmed the underground situation. This area of Palos Verdes had underground electrical and phone wiring, so there were no toppled utility poles, but this did not mean that these utilities were undamaged or that a broken underground power main could not spark one of the gas breaks. It would also make repairs to restore service more difficult.

The radio was a constant stream of reports. Damage, death, and injury. Finally, Rivera ordered everyone to keep the channel clear for command traffic. There was obviously too much damage and injury for the L.A. Sheriff to report each case by radio.

Clusters of people were everywhere on the boulevard. Some struggled with unseen tasks in the rubble. Others shouted and waved at the police vehicle, trying to get him to stop.

The first major intersection north of Savoy Ridge was a real mess. A small tractor-trailer rig emblazoned with a McDonald's logo had apparently been turning into a strip mall on the right side when the quake hit. It was three-quarters of the way across the intersection. Barry could not tell what had stopped the rig, the fallen traffic signal poles or the torn pavement, but it was obviously immobile. This problem was compounded by the people from the strip mall and the neighboring McDonald's who were now trying to get out of the parking lot, either around the disabled truck or over the curb. A VW van had high-centered on the upthrust lip of the curb and was stuck. People were shouting and gesturing at the hapless driver of the VW.

Barry thought of stopping and trying to lend order to the scene, but Rivera's orders were clear. Barry quickly looked for an alternate route.

To the right, the strip mall parking lot was hopeless. Several storefronts and sections of roof were collapsed. The cinder-block building had not taken the quake well. Even as he watched Barry saw a crowd of men pushing people back away from the dry cleaners on the end. Barry could not see the reason for their haste, but now even some drivers in the line to get out of the parking lot left their cars and run back up the boulevard.

One option remained for Barry. He turned into the used car lot on the left and drove up through the rows of fluorescent flagged cars.

He had almost reached the end of the car lot when a figure stepped into his path. Barry slammed on the brakes. The figure was a tall, mustachioed man in a plaid suit. Barry rolled down the window, already angry at the arrogance of the man.

The man spoke first, shouting and gesturing wildly with his arms, "Hey, whatcha doing? Aren't you gonna do something?" With this he pointed at the truck in the intersection.

Everything in Barry's ego wanted to lash out at the car salesman, to scream back at him. But, his training taking the fore, Barry did not.

"Yes, I am going to follow my orders. I am just one man and I have ... I have a job to do elsewhere." Barry paused for just a moment, thinking. "If you want someone to do something. I would suggest you get into that tow truck," Barry pointed to the wrecker on the far side of the car dealer's lot, "and get to work, there is going to be lots of stuck, stalled and damaged cars that need to be moved. I suggest you get going. Now, get out of the way."

The man blinked at Barry, but backed out of the lane in front of the Explorer. Barry continued, but had to turn up the sidewalk, since the cars waiting on this side of the intersection still blocked his way. In his last glimpse of the car dealer's lot in the rear-view mirror, Barry saw the man taking off the cheap suit jacket and walking toward the tow truck.

Barry smiled to himself as he turned off of the sidewalk and back out across the boulevard. He flipped on the Explorer's emergency lights to get two waiting cars to try and back up enough for him to clear. He had to waive them back as they did not understand that he wanted to go across the street. The boulevard was separated by a grassy median strip here, but the Explorer bumped up over it easily.

The mess at the intersection to the south had kept this stretch of road free of traffic, at least on this side. The stretch of the boulevard seemed to have fared better than higher up, less damage, just a mild washboard effect on the pavement. The boulevard curved down into a tree-lined canyon to the north, no further buildings on the east side. Barry was just getting ready to shift into second for the first time since the quake when there was a bright flash in the rear-view mirror and a blast shook the Explorer.

Barry hit the brakes. He could feel the glare of heat on the back of his neck. He turned in his seat, trying to get a view behind him. Unable to get a good view, Barry set the parking brake and climbed out to see.

The dry-cleaning store had blown up. The whole downhill end of the strip mall was in flames. A half dozen cars and the back of the McDonald's were also aflame. The dry-cleaners burned with an instance white-yellow flame. Several secondary explosions, probably cleaner fluid, spread the flame and smoke higher. Here, a block away, the heat was searing on Barry's face.

Barry was torn between the automatic reactions of heading up to the strip mall to help and calling in the explosion on the radio. But, he was under orders by the duty sergeant to do neither. We watched for a moment as the tractor-trailer driver turned a paltry $CO2$ extinguisher on the burning VW on the curb. Barry realized that whatever he could do himself would be just as minuscule, in relation to the scope of the disaster. He hoped that whatever pressing duty waited at Harbor Hospital was worth ignoring all of this.

Deputy Barry Warden followed orders rather than instinct. He turned his back on the burning strip mall, started the vehicle and maneuvered it down the rippled surface of the boulevard out of the Palos Verde Hills toward the flatlands of South L.A.

■

Aside from the myriad of hospital, airports and other critical facilities which sit astride the earthquake faults, there is a peculiar habit of placing nuclear facilities in harm's way in Southern California. Both Diablo and San Onofre nuclear power plants are on top of faults, or nearly so. But, military facilities are of particular interest from the standpoint of earthquake safety.

The nuclear submarine base at Ballast Point in San Diego is located on a finger of land sticking out into the Pacific and forming San Diego Bay. The finger of land is itself the scar tissue of a massive ancient earthquake fault. Recently discovered evidence indicates that the Ballast Point area is an elongation of the Rose Hill Fault, which is considered an active fault by some seismologists.

The most disregard, or ignorance, of earthquake safety by the military is the case of Naval Weapons Station (NWS) Seal Beach. Not only is this the primary repository of conventional ammunition for the U.S. Naval Forces in the eastern Pacific, it is also the main nuclear weapons storage site. It is located on tidelands which are the worst possible areas for liquefaction. It is also located squarely on top of the Newport-Inglewood Fault. The nuclear weapons storage igloos at NWS Seal Beach could not have been built more directly on the state's Almquist-Priolo Seismic Hazard Zone for the area. But then, the federal government has no requirement to pay any attention to the state government's seismic safety laws.

May 6th, 1:40 P.M.

The President was in Ohio, stumping for his party's candidate in a special election to fill a vacant House seat. The high school gym was bursting with political well-wishers and the curious. The President was toward the end of a typical speech for such occasions, when one of the several somber men in overly conservative suits clustered around the podium broke ranks and ascended to where the guests of honor were seated.

The casual observer would have assumed him to be Secret Service, having the ever-present earphone and tiny colored lapel badge, but this man was different. He was slightly older, had shorter hair and he had a heavy black briefcase chained to his arm. Everyone listening to the speech was surprised when this man walked briskly up to the President, took his arm and pulled him away from the microphone, whispering in his ear. However, insiders from the President's staff were not simply surprised, they were in shock. They knew what this man's function was.

This was the Army officer who kept the President in constant contact with the Pentagon. He was jokingly referred to as the keeper of the red button. He or one of his fellow officers were never more than a few paces from the President, but no one had ever seen them interfere in the President's activities. The unspoken fear they associated with this keeper of the nuclear weapons codes and satellite communications system was not soothed when the President made a quick and enigmatic apology to the crowd, shook hands with the congressional candidate and raced his stunned entourage to the waiting limousines.

Much of the short ride to Air Force One at Wright-Patterson Air Force Base was chaos. The officer's limited communications capabilities raised more questions than were answered. It seemed that the West Coast had been attacked, with at least two nuclear hits reported. The sight of Air Police with flak jackets and automatic weapons blocking the main gate to the air base did not help the nerves of the presidential party. The huge installation was on war alert. Aboard Air Force One the President was finally able to get a fuller picture of the disaster that was unfolding and to try to take control of the situation which had placed the nation's armed forces at DefCon 5, imminent war alert.

The Communications Duty Officer at the Naval Weapons Station Seal Beach had just gotten his communications equipment back on line from the most recent quake using emergency generators when he heard the blast from the explosion in north Long Beach. Finally going outside the small reinforced concrete building that housed the NWS Comm Center, he had just rounded the northeast corner of the building when the first shock wave of the massive explosion of the Carson tank farm hit. Between the airborne concussion he felt and the rising mushroom cloud he now saw to the northwest there was only one thing to do. The young lieutenant went inside, looked up the appropriate form message blank, sat at the Satellite Communications terminal and reported a nuclear explosion in Long Beach with the following message:

ZZZ

OPREP THREE PINNACLE TRAFFIC

FM NWS SEAL BEACH CA [OPS/COMM]

TO NMCC WASH DC

PINNACLE AIG

OPREP-3 PINNACLE

SUBJ: NUCLEAR EXPLOSION LONG BEACH CA

PROBABLE NUCLEAR EXPLOSION SIGHTED LONG BEACH, CA. UNKNOWN SOURCE. UNKNOWN CASUALTIES, SHOCK WAVE AND MUSHROOM CLOUD SIGHTED FROM SEAL BEACH NWS. SIGNIFICANT STRUCTURAL DAMAGE THIS STATION.

SITREP TO FOLLOW.

THIS IS NOT RPT NOT EXERCISE TRAFFIC.

ZZZ

Such was the report the Air Force brigadier on duty as the Duty Officer in the National Military Command Center (NMCC) received. Following the standing orders to confirm anything of this type, the general immediately went to work confirming the report. Neither Navy SOPA Long Beach nor the Army Reserve at Ft. McArthur in San Pedro answered his first calls, which was itself an oddity. With added urgency, the general called the Marines at Pendleton. Again, no answer; just a female voice repeating over and over that the Federal Interagency Telephone Network Exchange for Southern California was temporarily inoperative, please call back later. Civilian telephone lines were no better.

He was getting ready to call March reserve air base on SatComm when the following hard-copy message was pushed in front of him:

ZZZ

OPREP THREE PINNACLE TRAFFIC

FM COMNAVSURFPAC SAN DIEGO CA

TO NMCC WASH DC

PINNACLE AIG

MY SITREP ONE TO NWS SEAL BEACH OPREP-3

SUBJ: CASUALTIES SAN DIEGO

CARRIERS CONSTELLATION AND KITTY HAWK CASREP UNABLE TO GET UNDERWAY. CRUDESGRU THREE REPORTS TWO CRUISERS AND THREE DESTROYER/FRIGATES UNDERWAY PRIOR TO ATTEMPTED SORTIE, ALL OTHERS CASREP. TWO SUBPAC UNITS ARE BROKEN ARROW RPT BROKEN ARROW. USS JOHN PAUL JONES REPORTS POSSIBLE TSUNAMI ETA HAWAII 0400 TO 0700 ZULU. UNKNOWN PERSONNEL CASUALTIES, MINOR CASUALTIES TO BUILDINGS AND EXPECTED CIVILIAN CASUALTIES.

SITREP TO FOLLOW.

ZZZ

Both Seal Beach and San Diego had failed to put the earthquake in perspective, only its aftermath. A flag officer, the admiral in San Diego, had now confirmed the lieutenant's report from Seal Beach without commenting on the nuclear aspect. Why, the admiral had two nuclear subs on the rocks at Ballast Point himself, perhaps one of the ships at Long Beach had gone "Broken Arrow," meaning nuclear weapons had been critically damaged.

To the navy officers in California the quake was obvious. To the general in the Pentagon it was not, critical damage to nuclear weapons units and a reported nuclear attack were all he needed. Mention of tsunami did not deter the man at the Pentagon. All the general knew was that a mushroom cloud was rising above Long Beach and except for five ships the bulk of the Pacific Fleet was presumably destroyed in San Diego Bay.

The final event that spurred the Air Force general into action was an automatic computer alert from the super-secret satellite intelligence nerve center outside Reston, Virginia. A satellite had picked up the infra-red signature of the massive explosion of the LNG tank and interpreted it as a "nuclear explosion, probability high." To the general it was clear the bases on the West Coast were under attack. He ordered a DefCon 5 alert and started the course of events which would ruin the President's day.

The fact that several military bases and the Naval Air Stations at San Diego, Point Mugu and El Centro are all in prime earthquake hazard zones and reported their casualty status in the next ten minutes using preprinted casualty report forms that failed to mention earthquakes did not help.

It would take some time for the military to straighten out exactly what had happened in Southern California. Actually, the pieces were finally put together with the help of cable news reports that started flowing into NMCC shortly after the OPREP-3 message.

■

*On October 4, 1990, a liquefied propane gas
storage tank facility in Ekaterinburg, Russia exploded.
The resulting fireball and mushroom cloud made many of
the million residents of the city think a nuclear attack had
occurred. The city's subway stations soon filled up since
they were the designated atomic bomb shelters for the
populace. Hundreds of people were killed and injured in
the explosion and the secondary damage brought about
by the immense shock wave such an explosion creates.*
Krasnaya Zvyezda newspaper

May 6th 2:00 P.M.

In a world that had become dangerous and alien over the past
hour, the street sign seemed like a familiar beacon.

Pico Boulevard.

A similar sign stood not more than six blocks from Barry and
Kathy's apartment in West L.A. That was, of course, many miles away
across the city, but this sign gave Kathy some idea of where she was.
Until now she had walked with only a vague idea of where she was going,
avoiding the fires that seemed to be spreading to the north and east.

In the half hour since Kathy had changed into the denim outfit
in the clothing warehouse near the freeway she had only travelled a
dozen or so blocks. Every other block was closed by either a fire or some
collapsed building obstructing the way.

The area she was in now was the garment district. Kathy had
been here before with her mother and Cindy on shopping trips. The
immigrants, primarily Iranians, Eastern Europeans and Orientals, who
owned the myriad of shops were well-known for their willingness to
sell samples and wholesale merchandise tax-free for cash to virtually

anyone. It was L.A.'s worst kept shopping secret. Now, though, it was very different from the bustling place she remembered.

It was still busy, but the activity was centered on people trying to break through the gridlock at the intersections and the rubble piles. Many of the old brick buildings had crumbled. People crawled over the rubble. Some were obviously looking for victims in the ruins. Others, filling their arms with merchandise. It was not always clear whether the people filling their arms were rightful owners or just scavengers.

The question was answered, at least partially, when, at the corner of Pico and Los Angeles streets, a group of teenage girls threw a brick through the window of a store displaying beaded and sequined gowns. The girls seemed oblivious to the onlookers, some of whom went over to check out the new window opening after the teenagers had taken their fill. Kathy Warden, deputy sheriff's wife, momentarily considered the idea of joining the group mentality of the looters, before shaking off the thought and running through an opening in the gridlocked intersection.

Kathy was midway across Los Angeles Street when the next aftershock hit. Shouts from people nearby alerted her to the tremor. She had planned to stop on the opposite corner, but a scattering of bricks falling from the already damaged face of the corner building caused her to dart into the street instead. A screech of brakes from a delivery van, itself darting across Los Angeles Street, greeted her abrupt move.

Another whine of brakes followed on the street behind the van. A silver Volvo sedan was not able to stop in time to avoid the van. Kathy turned in her tracks just in time to see the slight impact.

The driver of the van looked back in his rear-view mirror considering the situation. Then, shaking his head at Kathy, flipped her the bird and roared off up Pico to the west. Kathy could see a broken headlight on the Volvo. The dark haired, mustachioed man in the Volvo threw up his hands in disgust and, likewise, gunned his car down Los Angeles to the south. The opening in the gridlock was more important than a fender bender. Neither driver wanted the trouble of stopping in the chaos that was gripping downtown L.A.

The little aftershock which had led to the incident had stopped. Kathy blinked at the departing vehicles and shrugged off the rude gesture and the new experience. The bystanders who had viewed the accident were already turning their attention back to various salvage, rescue or looting tasks.

Kathy Warden turned back to the west, up Pico. The afternoon sun hung as a red orb above the street, the smoke of a thousand fires filtering the sunlight through as a blood color. The immediate stretch of Pico Boulevard in front of her seemed relatively clear. The van was already out of sight. But, several blocks ahead Kathy could see the flashing of several emergency vehicles. These were the first she had seen since the big quake. Something big must be happening for so many emergency vehicles to be in one place, when the whole city was so devastated.

Kathy took a deep breath and headed toward to lights. Somewhere, off in the south county, Kathy's husband would probably be flashing the same lights, dealing with the same problems. Kathy worried about him. In bad times like this, men like her husband were called on to do more than she wanted to think about. Kathy tried to put thoughts of Barry out of her mind.

Another public telephone stood on the sidewalk ahead. Kathy picked up the receiver. Like all the others, it was dead. She went on, toward the flashing lights.

■

Scientists at the University of California, Berkeley believe that waves of seismic energy from earthquakes may be focused or channeled by subsurface anomalies like sedimentary strata or subterranean outcroppings of exceptionally hard rock, as well as layers of the earth's deep mantle. They believe this explains why the Loma Prieto earthquake focused so much destructive force in San Francisco and Oakland when both cities were far from the quake's origin.

This focusing effect, along with the liquefaction phenomenon, may also explain why there is a history of many pockets of utter devastation interspersed with untouched areas at significant distances from earthquakes such as Mexico City, Kobe and Northridge.

May 6th 2:15 P.M.

Barry Warden had left the burning strip mall far behind him in the Palos Verdes hills, but as he negotiated the rippled and cracked asphalt of the Palos Verdes Drive the stench of smoke grew rather than lessened. In the breaks in the rolling hills he could see the eastern sky was filled with smoke. And, although he passed an occasional car carefully heading down out of the Peninsula area toward the L.A. basin, he saw not a single car heading up into the hills. Either the roads were blocked ahead, or something else prevented traffic from heading into the heavily populated area.

This time of day, especially after an event such as the quake, the roads should be full. With tense curiosity Barry peered through what had now become an ever-present pale of smoke to try and see what the smoke and scattered reports on the radio foretold of the cataclysm that had hit to the east.

The radio squawked again. "All units, this is Sergeant Rivera. I have confirmed that substation has collapsed and we have multiple casualties. Patrol Three-Four and Patrol ... Uh? Well, Patterson, forgot your call sign. You're the closest units. We can use your help here, when you can break free. All other units, switch to Interagency Tactical Channel One. Torrance PD is taking over net control and dispatch duties for all Sheriff units until further notice. Repeat, switch to Interagency Tactical Channel One and report your 10-20, status and current duties to Torrance Dispatch. Out."

Deputy Barry Warden checked the laminated plastic chart that hung from the radio to see what frequency Interagency Tac One was on. The only other time he had ever used an interagency channel was to coordinate all the officers coming in city-wide for a slain L.A.P.D. officer's funeral at Green Hills Memorial Park. He thumbed the freq switch until the diodes glowed the right number. The thought of that funeral with the sergeant's talk of casualties at the sheriff's substation made Barry wonder who the casualties were.

Not a single car could be seen at the two larger intersections he crossed, the ones that connected through to Lomita and the other cities below. Barry did encounter some traffic at Western Avenue and he considered taking this cross street north toward the hospital. But, the quickest route to Harbor UCLA Medical Center and the route the L.A. County Sheriff's usually took was up Vermont. In the crazy-quilt of jurisdiction in Los Angeles, the Sheriff's deputies usually kept as much as possible within the patchwork of small cities and unincorporated area in which they had direct jurisdiction. There was no use in patrolling L.A.P.D.'s beat. So, Barry headed across to Vermont, rather than take

Western, which would have been entirely in L.A. city turf all the way to the hospital, which was once again in county jurisdiction.

An awesome panorama unfolded as he headed down the last sweeping curve of Palos Verdes Drive. The first thing he saw was the columns of smoke rising out of the former Navy base housing complex to the right. Then, as the road turned a bit more, he saw just east of the Navy housing, a petroleum tank farm, or what had been a tank farm. Collapsed by the force of the quake and the main tank farm explosion just to the northeast in Carson, this tank farm had joined the several other petrochemical plants in the Long Beach-Wilmington area in the inferno that now filled Barry Warden's view.

From this vantage point on the hillside Barry should be able to see a panorama stretching from the Harbor area out across Wilmington and Carson all the way to the Dominguez Hills. But, all that could be seen was a wall of smoke and fire rising higher than Barry could see in the sky. In all directions, south toward Long Beach and San Pedro, as well as to the left in Carson and off toward Compton, all that could be seen was fire, smoke and destruction.

It was an urban landscape like nothing other than a Cold War era nightmare. Seeing this, Barry could understand the radio call he had heard from Officer Janet Mortimer just after whatever explosion had caused this. The plaintive call from the injured deputy had come in from an area Barry estimated would be right in the middle of the inferno he now watched.

Barry slowed to a stop halfway down the hillside. The nearby Navy Housing, he could now see, was not only burning, but most rows of the frame townhouses were flattened into the slope of the hill. Even the trees lining the street were broken and leaning into the west. The blast had twisted and broken the pines and oaks like pencils.

The residents of the housing project were standing in the streets, watching the buildings burn. Abandoned garden houses lay useless nearby.

The check-in calls were proceeding on the new Tactical Net. It seemed to Barry that only about half of the Sheriff's units that should be checking in with Torrance PD were doing so. Where was everybody?

Barry could also see, at the bottom of the hill, the major intersection where Palos Verdes Drive ended. It was clear why no traffic had met him coming up into the hills. The entire intersection was awash with flames and spurts of ferocious fireballs. A gas main, apparently a major one, under Normandie Avenue, had blown. A dozen blackened husks of cars and trucks littered the intersection. To the east and west he could see traffic backed up. People were out of their cars, some running, some milling around, some tending the injured. Nothing was moving.

There was a pause in the radio traffic, so Barry took the opportunity to check in. "Torrance Dispatch, this is Sheriff Four-Four, Over."

The squelch on the radio hissed at him, he heard the new dispatcher repeat his call sign. "Four-four, Dispatch, Over." Barry noticed something odd about the voice. The deep, baritone and firm inflection of the voice was not the usual dispatch voice you would expect.

Barry answered, "Four-four, here. My status is, one officer, uninjured, and fully operational four wheel drive patrol vehicle. I am under orders to proceed, best possible, to Harbor UCLA Medical Center. My 10-20 is just south of the Anaheim/Normandie intersection on Palos Verdes. It appears impassable. Gas main blew out. Big jam-up."

"Roger, Four-four. County Emergency Services has apprised us of the situation at Harbor Center. Wait one, Four-four." The solemn man's voice on the radio did not sound like a regular dispatcher, more like the Torrance Chief of Police, from the tone of authority he evoked. "Things are getting pretty bad at the Medical Center. Near riot and they have nobody for crowd control and security. All jurisdictions have been asked to assist. Top priority. Neither Carson or Compton PD's can help. Uh, Standby, Four-four."

Barry waited for Torrance to get back to him. His wait was interrupted by a blast from the east that shook his vehicle. Somewhere in the wall of smoke that marked the tank farms to the east toward Long Beach another tank gave way. Barry did not have time to look, as the radio sputtered again.

"Four-four. L.A.P.D. Unit Seven Edward Seven is inoperative in the vicinity of Western and Anaheim. Two L.A.P.D. officers from that unit are available assist you at Harbor Center, but you have to go get them. That is about eight blocks north-west of you. Take cross street," he paused, "Senator Avenue or President Avenue to avoid the block below you at Normandie and Anaheim. You are authorized Code Three. Do whatever you have to get up to Harbor."

"Roger. Consider me Code Three, Out."

The mature voice from Torrance continued. "LA Seven Edward Seven. Did you copy? You are assigned to Sheriff Four-Four. Secure your vehicle and equipment and proceed with Four-four to Harbor Medical Center. Over."

Barry's suspicions about the identity of the Torrance dispatcher continued to ring true. Whoever was on the dispatch horn at Torrance on Tac One was a senior officer able to switch into a mode of giving orders to a half dozen different police agencies without missing a beat. While at the same time, this new net command, had the presence of mind to order another agency's cops to remember to secure their broken vehicle before transferring to another car.

"This is Seven Edward Seven. Roger, out."

Just before Barry was able to put the Explorer into gear to turn around and find Senator Avenue, he felt the truck shake again. At first, he was not sure if it was an aftershock or another explosion. It continued longer than an explosion would have. The Explorer quivered with this latest aftershock. Of far less intensity than the earlier shocks, but quite long, this quake had no effect discernible to Barry, other than to set the bystanders in the Navy housing and down near the intersection in motion, running away from the remains of the buildings and burning vehicles.

Deputy Warden took a deep breath and started the U-turn to go get his new passengers. As he turned, he flipped on his lights and siren, the `voice' from Torrance had told him to go Code Three.

■

The vast below sea-level basin, the Imperial Valley, which remained from the prehistoric drying up of the northern end of the Gulf of California remained dry for most of the next few millions of years. Then, in 1905, the early American settlers made an error in judgment while building an irrigation system from the Colorado River. Their error caused the floodwaters of the great river to be diverted for some time from its course into the Gulf via Mexico and up into the Valley, cutting the New River canyon (hence its name) and forming a huge inland lake. The mistake was corrected, returning the flow of the Colorado to the Delta and the ocean, but subsequent irrigation of the farms in the valley replenished the waters of the Salton Sea. The accumulated salts from the farm runoff rendered the new lake, the Salton Sea, highly saline. The irrigation system started in 1906 eventually developed into the most complex land reclamation projects ever conceived. The combination of the irrigation, hot desert weather and the fertile soils of the former seabed made the Imperial Valley one of the most productive agricultural regions on earth.

May 6th 2:15 P.M.

Gil Echeverria's lunch bounced on the seat of the pick-up, partially eaten and now cold. The single lane road that rimmed the top of the dike along the All-American Canal was rough. The Imperial Irrigation District (I.I.D.) employees like Gil were the only ones supposed to use the restricted roads on the dikes, but everyone knew the locals did also. This afternoon the road was empty. Echeverria sped along the road, his well-practiced eyes flicking from the road to the canal walls,

checking for breaks or fissures in the canal and dike. He had been riding these canal roads over twenty-five years, first as a laborer and now
as an experienced old hand responsible for watching out for the canal.

Gil's attempt to eat the hamburger on the seat had first been
interrupted by the initial quake. He had just gotten his order from the
Wendy's drive-through in Calexico and turned north onto the main
highway when the rolling started.

At first, the quake had been rhythmic, bouncing the truck on its
springs. Stopping the truck, Gil had watched the broad highway to the
north of Calexico roll in successive waves from the north. Buildings,
utility poles and the signs that lined the commercial strip oscillated
with every succeeding wave from the ground. Some of the structures
protested the rolling by collapsing, others simply rose and fell with the
earth beneath them.

Then, after a long minute of the even rolling the motion seemed
to get confused and chaotic, like the waves from a pebble dropped on
a pond's surface, concentric at first and then jumbled as they reflect
from the shore. The rolling turned to a violent shaking. The white I.I.D.
pickup shook and the tools in the truck bed rattled. Gil Echeverria held
tightly to the wheel.

When the motion finally ceased, Gil had to ignore the damage
all around him in Calexico and the temptation to drive over and check
his own house. He turned off the highway and headed north through
the residential district toward the canal. His job as a Field Inspector for
the District required him to check for damage to the canal after a quake,
whether the small quakes that were commonplace in the Imperial Valley
or the monster quake he had just experienced.

Gil's normal area of responsibility was from Calexico east. The

All-American Canal took a jog north from its normal course right along the Mexican border to by-pass the city of Calexico. The broad canal that supplied the life-giving irrigation water to the whole valley followed the sea-level elevation around the rim of the valley from its source on the Colorado River in Arizona far to the east.

In the first half-hour after the big quake, Gil had followed the canal from Calexico east for several miles. He had seen fires and smoke from the damage the quake had wrought in the city of Mexicali, a few hundred feet south of him, across the border into Mexico. Looking over the high fence that separated the two countries just beyond the canal, Gil had not been able to see anything where he should have seen the upper floors of the new medical office building in the eastern section of downtown Mexicali. He did see plumes from a half dozen fires south of the border.

After he reported no damage in his section by cell phone to the District headquarters, Gil had been ordered to continue his inspection to the west of Calexico. The Water Master at headquarters had reported a drop in water level west of Calexico, the worst of all possible places. The man assigned to that stretch of canal had not reported in after the quake, so District headquarters had called on Gil.

He was now heading southwest from where the canal crossed under the highway north of Calexico and headed back towards the border. He saw nothing out of the ordinary from the highway all the way down to the gate station west of Calexico.

Headquarters had obviously thrown the switch, closing off the canal's control gates; east of the gates the water stood still. West of the gates the great canal was an empty, muddy trough.

The reason for the loss of water was clear once Gil's truck approached the rim of the New River canyon. The canyon had been cut down through the flat plain of the Imperial Valley by flood waters from a huge irrigation project mistake in 1905-6. The waters of the All-American canal had to be piped across the expanse of the broad gorge in the earth so that the canal could continue its sea-level route around the valley on the other side. The huge suspended pipes now dipped steeply into the New River gorge ahead of him.

Gil Echeverria pulled the truck to a stop at the end of the road by the pipe outlet header. He punched the Water Master's number into the phone's handset and waited.

"Operations, Water Master."

"This is Echeverria. I'm at the east side of the New River Gorge. The canal is empty past Station Sixteen and I can see the pipes at New River are damaged. I am getting out to inspect now."

"OK. Keep us posted." The phone clicked dead. Gil wondered at the abrupt reply, he would have figured Operations would have wanted to know more or have some instructions. He got out and walked forward to the metal rail at the side of the pipe inlet at the edge of the canyon.

The sight was not what he had expected. Normally less than a hundred feet deep and three hundred wide, bottom of the New River canyon was usually an expanse of sand and sage brush with the narrow flow of polluted water that came across the border from the untreated sewage of urban Mexicali. Now, the whole of the chasm was a boiling froth of red-brown water and floating debris.

The steel latticework support columns for the canal's pipes were straining to withstand the raging flood waters coming across the Mexican border. The third column out had obviously succumbed and been carried away with the water, dropping the pipes down and thus breaking the canal's flow.

Gil's thoughts raced. 'Where could such a mass of water be coming from?' He knew that the canal system on the Mexican side was small compared to the All-American and this flow was ten times the size of the water in the All-American at peak capacity. It could not be a canal break in Mexico. Had a dam on the Colorado River broken? If so, why was it flowing this way and not to the delta and the ocean.

"What in the hell? ..." Gil gave voice to his question.

As he watched, he paid closer attention to the debris floating by. He saw wood, boxes, furniture, a cow's dead carcass and ... then he saw it. He saw an uprooted tree floating by with a person hanging on, bobbing and spinning in the churning froth. The person's clothing had a bright floral pattern, maybe a girl or woman.

Echeverria had only a minute to think, to digest the sight, when a groaning creaking sound came from the huge concrete housing of the pipe header next to him. He saw an almost imperceptible tilt forward. Then a greater tilt.

The concrete slab under the guard rail where he stood cracked. Gil ran back, stumbling over his own feet, to his truck. As he turned again toward the canyon, the whole structure of the pipe outlet tipped forward, folding the huge steel pipes like toilet paper tubes, and fell off into the torrent. The raging waters had undercut the soil of the canyon wall under the end of the canal.

Gil jumped into the pickup and hurriedly backed it up the access road, out of harm's way. Then he picked up his cell-phone.

He hesitated a moment before dialing the I.I.D. number. His own son's family, his grandchildren, lived in Brawley, downstream on the New River.

Gil Echeverria called the District office. he would make the call quick and then call to warn the kids.

■

> *Current law requires all police and fire stations, hospitals, emergency service centers and the like to be built with the highest level of seismic-safe construction. Roughly half of the public buildings of this type in California were built before the laws were strengthened in the '70's. A good percentage of the buildings on the top danger list of unreinforced masonry structures are public buildings. Like private business, public agencies have a hard time coming up with funds to pay for seismic upgrading.*

May 6th 2:15 P.M.

The jarring whine of a chainsaw filled the air. Kathy Warden, startled, jumped and turned left to see the source of the painful sound that filled the intersection of Hill Street and Pico Boulevard.

The chainsaw was being wielded by a fireman. He was one of a dozen or so uniformed firemen who stood in the driveway of the firehouse on the south side of Pico. Some of them held two long timbers in place against the upper corners of the overhead doors of the fire station. The one with the chain saw seemed intent on cutting into the door.

Kathy finished her trot across Hill Street and walked further. She came directly across Pico from the fire station. From here she could see the reason for the firemen's activity.

The frame of the fire station door was skewed sideways, matching the crazy angle of tilt of the whole building. The overhead door, with its panels splintered, had been crushed sideways and instead of being a square opening was now somewhat trapezoid shaped.

The timbers were obviously insurance that once the jammed

door was cut out, that the door blockage was not the only thing holding the building or the front wall up. A man was standing on a ladder against the door wearing only his blue uniform pants. Kathy now saw that several of the firemen were only partially clothed. The one on the ladder was drawing in fluorescent orange chalk on the door, marking out an area just big enough for the fire truck Kathy could see through the broken windows in the door. The firemen were having to rescue their own fire truck from its quake damaged station before they could get out and help the victims of the quake.

Kathy joined several other people on the north side of the street watching the firemen work. She covered her ears to hold out the sound. Finally, she moved off down Pico, not wanting to witness what would happen if the timber shoring was insufficient.

Ahead of her, the flashing emergency lights were now closer. They seemed to be parked in the middle of Pico Boulevard with some kind of bright green backdrop across the street, the view clouded by dust in the air.

The next block of Pico, between Olive and Grand, was closed to traffic by a pile of debris from a collapsed building, or rather the collapse of a whole row of buildings on Olive. Another traffic jam had developed as the people trying to go north up the one way street and those trying to turn off Pico met. There did not seem to be any movement north toward the high rises of downtown. This, and the blockage of Pico had stopped all movement of cars. Several people were out of their cars peering over the traffic ahead and cursing. The shouting matches and honking symptomatic of a downtown traffic jam added to the din raised by the chainsaw down the block and the many sirens that could now be heard to the south and west.

Kathy clutched her purse and the plastic bag that now held her dirty clothes and heels. She took advantage of the jam to squeeze across between cars and then scamper over the lower end of the brick pile across Pico. As she maneuvered over the bricks and debris Kathy Warden gave another silent thank-you for the tennis shoes and blue jeans she now wore.

Just beyond the rubble pile, two women, they seemed to be well-dressed business women, sat on the curb beside a FedEx drop-off box. The women were hugging each other and softly sobbing. They did not look up as Kathy and the other people heading on foot up and down Pico walked by.

Seeing the two women sharing whatever their grief was had a peculiar effect on Kathy Warden. It made her feel utterly alone, not just `feel', as she really was all alone. And at that moment seeing the women, being alone meant not being with her big sister. `Where was Cindy? Was she OK?' Kathy shook off this round of thoughts about Cindy, and then Barry, and her folks.

The intersection at Grand was empty by comparison to the last. No cars seemed to be coming down Grand and Pico was clear all the way to the cluster of emergency lights several blocks ahead. Only a few cars, which seemed to be leaving the area, and the pedestrians could be seen.

The reason for the lack of traffic was obvious when Kathy got a clear view from the sidewalk on the northeast corner of the intersection. To the north, up Grand and toward downtown, building after building, mostly older buildings, lay crumpled. Some fell across the wide street, others had simply collapsed upon themselves. A few people walked through the rubble, but no one seemed to be working on rescuing the people who must be trapped.

Behind the nearby buildings, Kathy got another view of the destruction of the skyscrapers she had seen earlier from the freeway area. Closer now, and without the smoke that had blocked her view before, Kathy could see the limp hulk of the BankCal building as it sagged against two neighboring buildings. The big, gold BankCal logo hung tenuously to the top, propped against the neighboring building.

From this angle Kathy could not see the other leaning building she had seen before, but now that they were only a few blocks away, the sight of the thousands of panels with missing glass on virtually every high rise in the city gave Kathy the horrifying thought of what it what it must have been like to be on the streets of downtown when the quake hit. Anyone running out of the collapsing buildings into the street would have been showered with tons of splintered glass, falling from hundreds of feet above them.

South on Grand, Kathy could see a huge crowd of people. Some of those who had walked up Pico with her now turned south also.

"'Scuse me. Miss? Can you tell me where the hospital is?" Someone behind Kathy spoke in a thick accent.

Kathy turned to see a young Hispanic woman with a young girl in her arms and a little boy hanging onto her leg as she walked. Kathy opened her mouth to answer, but before she could speak a man who had been walking nearby spoke.

"I think that is it. Right there." He pointed down Grand Avenue beyond the crowd, to a building with a huge sign on its top floor labeling it "Cali__rnia Medi__l Ce__er."

"You need help with the kid?" the man asked.

"No, I can make it."

"Hey, it looks like you can use some help. I'll take her." The man put out his arms and the woman hesitatingly shifted the child's weight over to the man. As she did so the girl cried out in pain. The man cringed at the girl's cry and the mother spoke soothing words to the girl in a foreign tongue, not Spanish, maybe Oaxacan Indian or the like. They moved off across the nearly deserted Pico and Grand intersection. The little boy, who had momentarily let go of his mother's leg, blinked at Kathy and ran off to follow the others. As he ran away, Kathy realized the little boy was wearing only a T-shirt.

Crossing Grand Avenue herself, Kathy had to go into the middle of Pico to avoid a building that seemed in eminent threat of collapsing. Across the open parking lots north of Pico she could now see the whole scene ahead with the emergency vehicles. But, it took a while to figure out what was going on. A large RV-type emergency vehicle, surrounded by police cars and ambulances, stood in the middle of Pico. Hundreds of people could be seen moving around. Some police seemed to be shepherding the crowd southward. Ambulances were loading injured and pulling away.

A bit behind the crowd, a single yellow crane worked off to the right, lifting something from a slopping mass of girders and panels that had once been the Los Angeles Convention Center. The Convention Center's elevated walkway over Pico Boulevard had fallen part way to the ground, and was slung lazily over street, still attached to the south side at the second story. That was the green mass Kathy had seen earlier.

Beyond the hulk of the Convention Center, the over-crossing of the Harbor Freeway over Pico was likewise caved in. A city transit bus hung precariously off the edge of the roadway.

Nearer to her, at the end of the block ahead, Kathy could see the source of many of the crowd of people. They seemed to be coming up out of a grating in the sidewalk at the corner of Pico and Flower Street. A sign directing people to the Metro Blue Line station hung on a light pole directly above their exit hole. Even with what she had been through in the last hour, Kathy had to cringe at the thought of being underground in the subway during the big quake. But, these people had been lucky, they were climbing out on their own.

As if to punctuate the thought, another quivering aftershock sent Kathy and everyone else she could see hurrying away from nearby buildings. Everyone was getting used to the routine.

■

Most financial institutions will find it impossible to operate for some time following a major urban quake. Aside from the obvious problems of operating ATM machines, funds transfers and credit transactions in cities without phone service or electricity, financial institutions will find it nearly impossible to maintain liquid funds to operate. These institutions rely on incoming payments on debts due to them and deposits to replenish cash to operate. Closed businesses and unemployed, homeless, injured or dead consumers do not make loan payments or regular deposits. It is likely that hard cash will be required for people to live and function in a post-quake period and people who rely on using ATM's, credit cards and open banks will be strapped to find actual cash. Even if they are physically able to remain open, banks will have a difficult time maintaining cash liquidity and supplying cash to depositors, let alone credit seekers. Only massive infusions of cash from the Federal Reserve system will allow banks to function. Finally, the entire financial system relies on electronic funds transfers and Internet functionality. In a post-quake period the existing telephonic and computerized systems could be inoperable. The Federal Emergency Management Agency and the Federal Reserve system have contingency plans for such an eventuality, but estimates of time to get an emergency system operating are measured in weeks.

May 6th, 2:30 P.M.

Gloria Contreras was torn between conflicting responsibilities. Her duties as the manager of the BankCal branch were interfering with her natural reaction of heading home to check and see if her two children were safe.

Consuella was perfectly capable of handling the normal routine as a sitter, but Gloria had no idea if the house was even OK. She had been able to see only smoke when she had tried to see in the direction of their housing development from the back door of the bank. With the phones and cell phones out and rumors and stories flying about the awesome quake, doubts and worries about the safety of her home and children flooded Gloria.

The piercing racket of the workmen's power saw and hammers echoed through the darkened bank building. The arrival of the contractor's truck shortly after the quake was one of the few aspects of the BankCal Disaster Response Plan that had worked so far. In the wake of the Rodney King riots and the Northridge Quake and Loma Prieto quakes in the '90's, the big banking chain had undertaken to train its staff and prepare for the worst in future quakes and other disasters, both natural and man-made. The BankCal Disaster Response Manual lay open on Gloria's desk in the dim light from the single unshattered plate glass window and the one empty window frame that still awaited its plywood cover from the workmen.

Gloria had reread the manual and its sections on security, personnel problems, communications and restoring operations. It had not been much help. Her assistant manager, Ron Murphy, and her chief teller had been on lunch break when the quake hit and she had heard from neither of them since. Both of her loan officers and two tellers, all parents themselves, had insisted on going to get their children from schools and daycare centers. She did not need the manual to tell her she might as well let the "non-essential personnel" go home when the bank was without lights and computer connections. The branch's management intern, Brian Kowicky, had followed Gloria's instructions in clearing the cash out of the ATM machine outside which had been damaged along with the windows and the entire brick wall on the front of the bank. The two remaining tellers, after closing their drawers, were now helping the intern straighten the interior of the bank. Desks, potted plants, literature racks and computer terminals had all crashed about the lobby when the quake had hit.

Gloria herself had been sitting in a stall in the ladies' restroom when the quake hit. The sensation had been as if she were sitting inside a big cardboard box that someone had dropped and then kicked. After a momentary feeling of light-headedness, she had been slapped hard against the wall of the stall, winding up on the floor in a puddle of toilet water that had sloshed out in the initial thump.

The electricity went off almost immediately and the emergency light up in the corner of the restroom clicked on. The train-like rumble of the quake had continued. Gloria braced herself against the stall walls. After one particularly hard thump both of the sink basins and numerous ceramic tiles tore from walls of the bathroom. Falling ceiling tiles gave the impression that the whole building was caving in.

Gloria had found herself muttering, "God, how long?" as the quake continued to roll under her. As repulsive as it was to sit on the wet floor of the toilet stall, she was unable to get to her feet, so bad was the shaking and rolling.

After an interminable time the quake had stopped as abruptly as it began. One moment she was being jostled around and the next all was silent and still. Only the peculiar hum of the emergency light broke the total silence. The dust sifting down from the ceiling tiles sparkled in the glare of the emergency floodlights. The spray from the broken sink pipes added to the puddle on the floor as Gloria struggled to her feet on the toilet floor.

The shower of water as she turned off the sink water at the little wall spigots cleansed the toilet water from her clothes, at least Gloria hoped so. Her wet silk blouse clung to her like transparent lycra. Her long black hair molded flat in its wetness to her head and neck. The electric hand blower was useless and the paper towels lay in a soggy pile in the water puddle. A few minutes after the quake, the totally wet bank manager attempted to salvage her dignity by running from the restroom to get her jacket from the desk. There had been no dignity in her trot through the overturned furniture and chaos of the bank lobby. Everyone had seen her.

Gloria had relived the fear of the initial quake with each of the three strong aftershocks that hit in the ensuing half hour. With each aftershock, she stopped breathing, temples pounding and heart racing, waiting for the horror to end. The first aftershock had actually done much of the worst apparent damage to the bank building. Most of the bricks that now lay in piles at the front of the bank had fallen as the workmen boarding the windows broken in the initial quake scrambled out of the way.

The communications section of the disaster manual was, as yet, the most useless. The phones and dedicated computer modem lines were totally lifeless. Not that this really mattered since all of the bank's phones and computers, except one laptop computer, needed electrical power to operate. Gloria's cell phone simply announced, "All cellular circuits are busy, please try your call again later" no matter what number was dialed. Without any phones or computers, all of the planning that went into the disaster communications plan was worthless and without communications the planning for restoration of banking operations was worthless. A modern bank without the ability to talk to its central computers and other banks was a rather useless entity.

All of the records for Gloria's branch were handled in the regional office of BankCal in San Bernardino. Without a computer connection with them, Gloria's staff had no idea what account balances were. The signature cards would tell who had an account at the branch, but the bank had centralized, "freeing" the local bank of keeping voluminous paper records. Without the interconnection with the nationwide banking network the ATM machines, credit card cash advances and all other electronic banking functions were inoperative. Gloria knew that once the big safe was closed today that for security purposes it could not be opened until power was restored to the building. Following the Manual, she put the requisite cash reserves in the alternate manually-operated safe in the back room.

The sound of shattering glass startled Gloria. Looking quickly around the bank lobby Gloria was relieved to see that it was Brian dumping a dustpan of broken glass into the trash can under the deposit slip table. Seeing Gloria look up, the husky youth walked over to her desk.

"I got just about everything cleaned up that I can without a vacuum working. Terry and Jenny were wondering what else needs to be done." Brian wiped heavy sweat from his brow as he spoke. The noted heat of Palm Springs had started early this year. The air conditioning was, of course, inoperative and the heaviest of the work of righting furniture had fallen on Brian. He looked tired.

"Let's check the list, again. I'd kind of like to get out of here myself." Gloria thumbed the tab on the manual marked Emergency Closing Procedures.

∎

The siren gave a final chirp as Barry flipped the switch off, but he kept the emergency lights on as he pulled over to the curb to pick up the two L.A.P.D. officers who waited for him. They had a pile of gear collected on the sidewalk, apparently having decided to take the gear with them instead of securing it. As Barry hopped out to help them load the stuff into the Explorer, he saw why they had chosen to take the things with them.

The L.A.P.D. cruiser, Seven Edward Seven, sat half-crushed under the bricks of a collapsed building. A donut shop sign had crushed the cruiser's light bar and roof.

Barry nodded a welcome to the two officers, a black man and woman, both about Barry's age. They had their arms full of portable radios, body armor, first aid kits and scatter guns. Barry opened the back window of the Explorer and they put the equipment on top of that which Barry already had there.

"I guess the proper thing to say is `Welcome Aboard,' or something like that," Barry ended the awkward comment by offering his hand to the man, "Barry Warden."

The lean black policeman, who stood half a head taller than Barry, smiled and took the offered handshake," Jamil Allen."

Allen turned and gestured to the woman, "And this is my partner, Alisha Walker."

Officer Walker shook Barry's hand and smiled.

"I hope you weren't in there when that happened." Barry indicated the stricken police cruiser with a nod.

Alisha Walker answered, "Unfortunately, I was. In the passenger seat. Jamil had got out to make a personal phone call. I thought the world was coming to an end." As she spoke Barry took note of the woman's light coffee complexion and pale green eyes. Her coloration was closer to Barry's than her black partner, Jamil. Barry had often wondered why everyone, himself included, always considered anyone with any smidgen of African blood to be black, rather than white or whatever. Like Obama, the "first black President," when he was as much white as black. That always seemed sort of racist to Barry. He helped them load the last of their gear into the Explorer.

The L.A.P.D. officers did not bother locking the car, as the windows were gone from the smashed roof. They climbed into the Explorer. Alisha rode in the back seat. Barry flipped the siren back on and they headed north.

Now that he was in a more built-up area, Barry could see an increase in the effects of the quake and the explosion. Houses and buildings, frequently whole rows and blocks, had been hit hard. Seeing the traffic, unmoving, to the north on Pacific Coast Highway, known as PCH, Barry turned east on a side street.

As they headed east, the effects of the blast became more pronounced. Whole rows of the old, post-war tract houses showed damage, some lay over on their side.

There did not seem to be a lot of people around. Mostly children and a few adults. This was a working class neighborhood and the mid-afternoon catastrophe had not found many people home. Unfortunately, many of them worked in the expanse of industrial areas to the east, where the explosion had hit.

Their lights and siren had cleared a path across the jammed PCH. Just as Barry found the opening across PCH, Jamil called out.

"Look, looters!" Jamil pointed to the right.

A group of youths were running from a small corner appliance store, apparently thinking that the approaching siren and light of the sheriff's vehicle was meant for them.

"Looks like we put the fear into 'em," Alisha said.

"Yeh, for two minutes. They'll be right back. Their kind is probably just practicing for the big game, come tonight," Jamil Allen added.

Until now, Barry had not fully considered the scope of the problem facing the city as far as looting and lawlessness went. Of course, every police officer, or for that matter, every citizen, always considered the possibility of some looting in a disaster. But, from what Barry had already seen, this was different.

"You think its gonna get bad tonight."

"Yes, real bad. Why shouldn't it? Nothin' to stop it," Jamil answered. A call on the radio interrupted him, he continued when it finished. "From what I heard on the radio while we were waiting for you, one of the kids from the donut shop had a Walkman ... Anyway, the whole city has been flattened. They said we lost whole skyscrapers downtown."

"And that the real heart of the quake didn't even hit us. It was somewhere out east. Riverside or San Bernardino or somewhere," Alisha added.

Barry realized that he had not reported in after picking up the two passengers and heading back north towards the hospital. As he reached for the microphone, he passed a group of people trying to carry someone injured. They waved at him trying to get his attention. He knew he should not stop, the whole city had problems. He had to ignore these people and stick to his assigned task. He did just that and keyed the microphone.

"Dispatch, this is Sheriff Four-four, Over." He waited for an answer, turning north on Normandie, now, off of the cross street.

"Roger, Four-four." The same authoritative baritone voice answered.

"Sheriff Four-four has the crew of LA Seven Edward Seven embarked, heading north vicinity Normandie, approaching Lomita Boulevard. Proceeding to Harbor Medical Center."

"Roger, Four-four, report your status upon arrival. Out."

Barry had an idea, he called back to the "voice" in Torrance. "Torrance, this is Sheriff Four-four. We are kind of in the dark out here, in the field, about what the big picture is. You know, the scope of what happened. How bad things really are. Can you fill us in a bit? It would sure help. Over."

There was pause and then, "Roger, Four-four, Wait. Out."

"Good idea," Jamil said, "I was kinda feeling like a mushroom myself."

"Yes, I've been feeling kind of like an ignorant orphan ever since Division went off the air. I ..." Alisha was cut off by the radio."

"All units this net, this is Chief Corcoran, Torrance PD," Barry smiled at this confirming information. "As Sheriff Four-four requested, we are going to try and fill you in on the, ah, big picture. We should have done this sooner, but ... Anyway, here goes.

"Word we have from L.A. County Emergency Services and, uh, commercial news sources, is that we have been hit with what they are calling a `swarm' of great quakes. The first, just before One O'clock, was on the San Andreas Fault a few miles east of San Bernardino. That one was huge, Eight point Something. Then, about a half hour later, maybe less, we had two, or maybe three, they can't tell, additional quakes that measured between 7.8 and thereabouts on the Richter Scale. It looks like these quakes were on the Newport/Inglewood Fault under Culver City and on the Elysian Park Fault right square under Downtown L.A. With another big quake right about that time reported somewhere off the coast toward Santa Barbara.

"All of L.A. County is without power and telephones. Gas and water mains are busted all over. Most of you on this net are aware of and probably dealing with the big gas or petrochemical explosion in East Carson. Besides that one, we have reports of a half dozen other refinery, factory and tank farm fires and huge sections of the urban area are on fire. Fire units reports no line pressure for water in most areas.

"You folks probably know the situation in the streets better than we do. You're spread thin. And you may be it, without backup, for the time being. The Governor, and the President, have declared an emergency and the Guard and Reserves are going to be called up. But you know that takes time. Lots of roads are out, or jammed up. Both the Harbor and 405 freeways are cut in several places. Big fire reported on the 91.

"Well, that's about it for the overview. You're all pros, do your job. Make the citizens help out, if you can. We'll do whatever we can to get you and the people out there help as soon as possible." A pause, then, "Corcoran, Out."

■

"There are five major areas along the Santa Barbara Coast which are subject to inundation if an earthquake were to occur off shore [including the Santa Barbara City-Harbor area]. In planning of all coastal installations and developments, it is recommended that a 10-foot high sea wave be considered and that a conservative contour elevation of 40 feet be used as a basis for establishing the tsunami risk limit."

Santa Barbara County Seismic Safety Planning Element

[The majority of downtown Santa Barbara is within this inundation risk area. There are historical references to a fifty foot tsunami wave in Santa Barbara in the early 1800's.]

May 6th, 2:30 P.M.

Genevieve Dumont felt much better. Proper clothes made a big difference.

Natalie Weld had found a mint green jogging suit that, although not really Genevieve's usual kind of attire, was infinitely preferable to the scanty black robe. The teen-age girl, Kiki, had supplied a pair of sandals that fit Genevieve.

Genevieve now sat in the Weld's kitchen with Natalie, Kiki and Ted. The boy was trying to get some news on the battery-powered radio. There seemed to be few stations on the air. What they did get on the boy's boom box was difficult for Genevieve to understand,

"... declaring a state of emergency ... preliminary indications ... contradictions as to the exact epicenter. ..." Genevieve wished she understood English better, the excited announcers on the static filled radio were impossible to understand.

Genevieve had just taken a sip of the iced tea Kiki had made when the refrigerator roared to life and the ceiling fan began to spin.

"Good. Now we can get some TV," Ted shouted as he clicked off the radio and ran out of the kitchen. Natalie and Kiki got up to follow. Genevieve left her tea and went with them.

The Weld's family room was as big as the house Genevieve had grown up in back in France. At the far end, beyond the pool table, sunken fireplace and piano, Ted Weld was already flicking through channels when Genevieve came into the room. The wide screen television was nestled between shelves of books, mementos and trophies. By the time Genevieve had walked the length of the huge room, Ted had found a station with quake pictures. Everyone gathered wordlessly in front of the set.

"Cable is still out, but the DirecTV antenna works." Ted explained.

A scene from a helicopter hovering above a city was shown. The announcer explained, "These are live shots from San Bernardino which is now believed to be the closest to the original quake epicenter."

Genevieve watched in astonishment as the pictures of crushed buildings, flattened freeway overpasses and fires flashed on the screen. Although she had watched her own home slide into oblivion, seeing this massive destruction was amazing to her.

"Oh, my God!" Natalie Weld put her hand to her mouth as the televison switched to a ground view of a collapsed building. A woman's legs could clearly be seen sticking up out of the rubble.

"Where is that?" Kiki asked.

"They didn't say. Shhh!" her little brother hissed as he poked the volume higher. Then as a shot of the news anchor came back on, Ted poked up another news channel.

The new channel brought a different airborne view, flying above what looked to be fallen skyscrapers. Genevieve had just started to recognize what she was seeing when the newscaster confirmed it. "... and the Century City area was the site of this scene of destruction. With unknown numbers of casualties, the scene is almost without ..."

"*Mon Dieu!*" this time it was Genevieve who cried out.

The Weld family all looked at their house guest as she stared wide-eyed at the screen.

Genevieve Dumont pointed to the television which was now directly over Avenue of the Stars and its four flattened highrises. Choking back tears, she said, "That was it. I know the building. That was my husband's office."

Genevieve Dumont had no way of knowing that Michael had never even made it to his office that morning.

■

"Look, Mr. Sloan. I know it is impossible, I'm just trying to tell you what I see," Gil Echeverria had given the same description three times in the last fifteen minutes. "The entire pipe crossing for the All-American Canal has been washed away. I've had to move my truck back twice while I've been standing here, I'd say the walls of the new River Gorge have been washed away a good hundred fifty feet on each side. You've got a hell of a lot of water coming in from somewhere down south."

Gil did not really know who it was he was talking to, it was not one of his supervisors at I.I.D. This Sloan fellow was someone the guys at I.I.D. had connected him to after the second round of describing what was happening.

Sloan's voice came from the handset of the truck's phone, "What can you see to the south?"

"Well, you know the New River canyon comes northwest out of Mexicali just west of Calexico. It's the same thing clear to the border. I'd say the undercutting is getting pretty close to the border crossing in downtown Calexico, but I can't see around the turn east into Mexicali. However, from what I remember of downtown Mexicali, the New River really isn't much besides a low spot through downtown, not a gorge like it is on this side of the border. This much water going through the city has to be real bad. I can see some people in the water, along with trailers, junk, lots of debris."

"You say `people?'" Sloan asked.

"Yes, I'd say at least ten in fifteen minutes, but could be more, you can't see that much in the muddy water."

"And you say the water doesn't show any signs of letting up?"

"No, sir," Gil figured Sloan must be someone worthy of calling `sir.' "If anything it's increasing. You know, the way the banks are getting eaten away by the water, well, the canyon is just as full now as it was when the canyon was half this size, and maybe deeper, too."

"Thanks. I want you to stay there. Keep yourself safe, move back if you have to, but you are our eyes on this. We've got a lot of problems across the county with the quake already, but it looks like the quake may be old news. We've got to figure out what is happening down there where you are. We'll be in touch."

The phone went dead. Sloan had mentioned `the county,' but that did not give Echeverria any idea about who it was giving him orders to stay on the banks of the torrent-filled chasm. Maybe some politician. Gil had seen some political yard sign about "Sloan" somewhere?

It did not matter. Gil backed the truck up another thirty feet and started using the phone to call his kids in Brawley and his wife, at work in El Centro.

Gil Echeverria had spent his life roving the canals and irrigation ditches of the Imperial Valley. He had a sense of what was happening with the New River. Gil needed to make sure his family was warned and told to head for his house in Calexico. Gil knew very well that although Calexico was the farthest south of all the towns in the Valley and the closest to this flood before him, that Calexico was also the only town in the whole valley that was above sea-level.

■

The moderate (6.4) San Fernando quake in 1971 totally destroyed the San Fernando Veterans Administration Hospital and so severely damaged the nearby Olive View Veterans Hospital that it had to be demolished. Forty-four people were killed in the San Fernando VA Hospital collapse. Construction standards for California hospitals were raised after the 1971 hospital failures. However, the authorities in charge of these hospitals should have known of the danger even before 1971, for many decades the closest earthquake fault had been named and shown on seismic charts and planning maps as the "Hospital Fault."

May 6th, 3:14 P.M.

The horrible traffic snarl they had crossed at Sepulveda was nothing compared to that which Barry saw ahead as he approached the hospital.

He had put the Explorer into Low-4 gear and used the railroad right-of-way as his route around the crush of traffic at Sepulveda. But the railroad turned west at 228th and from there he saw nothing but stalled traffic to the north, past 223rd and on to the hospital grounds.

Looking at the hopelessly gridlocked intersection at 228th and Normandie, Jamil quipped, "I'd offer to get out and direct traffic, but I figure this intersection to be about a hundred fifty yards out of my jurisdiction.

"Maybe so, but I think the jurisdiction boundaries blurred somewhat when my substation and your division went off the air. We both seem to be taking orders from Chief Carmichael, now." Barry replied.

"Corcoran. It's Chief Corcoran," Alisha corrected from the back seat. Both men in front harrumpfed acknowledgment.

With Barry's lights and siren going full, the cars in the intersection begrudgingly managed to edge forth and back until Barry could squeeze the Explorer through.

Turning east, they could see a thick wall of smoke between them and the freeway.

"Looks like the whole development over beyond Vermont is on fire," Jamil said. Barry, too, could see flames from that area licking into the sky. "That's a fairly new development. Figured they would do better."

Alisha replied, "Maybe for the quake, but fire doesn't care if the house is new. And all them new house tracts all jam the houses so close together."

"With the fire that close and the traffic on Vermont, I think we had better go north here." Barry's words gave little warning of his turn. Jamil had to put his hands on the dash to brace himself as Barry turned north on Meyer.

"Sorry, about that," was Barry's apology for the turn.

With all of the adjacent streets, Vermont, Normandie, and probably Carson to the north, clogged it had been a good thing they had come in on the side streets to the south. .

It was Officer Alisha Walker who saw Harbor UCLA Medical Center first, "Oh, My God!"

The Harbor UCLA Medical Center stood alone, a block from the Harbor Freeway. A major teaching hospital and the primary public welfare hospital in the huge area encompassing much of the southern half of Los Angeles County, Harbor UCLA was the keystone for providing public health services to a million people or more. Although the dozen or more private and lesser hospitals served the neighboring areas also, it was to Harbor UCLA that the bulk of the emergency services planning was focused. It was for this reason that the structural failure of the hospital would be so devastating.

Approaching from the south, Barry Warden saw the problem immediately. The west side was shorter by one floor than the rest of the huge hospital.

It looked to Barry like the ground floor level's supports had given in at the far west end and the upper floors had settled down. Fortunately, the upper floors had not pancaked down in a pile, they had merely tilted down, still attached to the rest of the building and still at the proper interval. Barry wondered if the people on the ground floor had gotten out.

Barry had been in that wing several times. It was where the temporary medical hold lock-up and the duty deputies' offices were, on the first floor. That explained the urgent call for police help.

Barry pulled the Explorer onto the grass at the south end of the hospital's Vermont Street parking lot. A large crowd of people ringed the parking lot. Some of them staring through the chain-link fence that surrounded the hospital complex, others, several hundred of them, were already inside the fence ringing the triage area. In the lot itself, which had been cleared of cars, figures in white walked and ran between rows of prone bodies. Some of the bodies were being carried onto and away from the parking lot. Many in the crowd that waited could be seen holding bodies in their arms or carrying makeshift stretchers. Barry assumed that the same was true at the main north entrance.

Figures in white could be seen holding their arms aloft, begging the crowd to move back and for those arriving to take their turn. A few dozen doctors and nurses were trying to do triage for hundreds, if not thousands, of people in an open area and the on-looking crowd of many times more was pushing the bounds of orderliness. The crowd that was inside the fencing stretched all the way back to the main hospital building and as far as Barry could see toward the Vermont/Carson intersection beyond.

"One of you want to work on getting the crowd out away a bit. And, someone needs to check the front entrance. Off to the north along Carson. I'll call in and be right there." Barry said.

"You got it." Jamil said as he started out.

Alisha was half-way out of the Explorer when it started rocking more than it should have with her exit. As the aftershock was felt by the crowd, a roar of screaming went up. And, the crowd mentality took charge and everyone started running. The boundaries of the triage area disappeared as those people next to the building ran out away from the structure. In an instant, a thousand people were running, screaming and tromping, across the parking lot already littered with the injured.

The two L.A.P.D. officers were already running off toward the chaos. Barry had to wait for a Torrance PD unit to finish their report to Dispatch. The shaking below him had stopped, but a riot was now in full progress in the parking lot triage area in front of him.

Barry finally got his chance to talk on the radio net, "This is Sheriff Four Four, uh, and L.A. Seven Edward Seven. Harbor UCLA Medical Center. Officers need assistance, Civil disturbance, Code Red. One thousand plus in crowd, repeat, one thousand plus. Request all available assistance. We need crowd control and additional medical triage, immediately. Over."

Torrance took a moment to respond, then, "Roger, Four Four,

County Emergency Services will be apprised. We have no other units available. Over."

"Roger, this is Four Four, out."

Deputy Barry Warden understood. He and the other two officers were it. They would have to "hold the fort" until some county bureaucrat on the radio in downtown L.A. decided this little corner of chaos deserved help. He wondered where this problem stood on top of the priority list facing L.A. County Emergency Services tonight. And, he wondered how help could get to him, even if someone sent it, on the hopelessly jammed and damaged streets of this metropolis.

Barry Warden checked to make sure the hand held radio was on his shoulder strap. Then, he reached for the dashboard and unclasped the long, black nightstick. He put an extra Mace can in his pants pocket. The loud-hailer from the back of the Explorer would probably be needed.

■

On July 28, 1976 at 3:42 a.m., a 7.8 magnitude quake struck directly beneath the city of Tangshan, China. The Chinese authorities reported one quarter million deaths, but independent sources estimate three quarters of a million people died, two million people were left homeless and there was untold billions of dollars in damage. Many of the deaths resulted from a 7.1 aftershock which hit when people were going into previously damaged buildings to rescue others, salvage belongings and collect the dead.

May 6th, 4:30 P.M.

Olympic Boulevard was not much better than Pico had been. Traffic, both cars and pedestrians, clogged it, snaking around rubble piles. Honking, shouting and the ringing of building alarms filled the air, along with the smoke.

Kathy Warden had experienced the smoke from the fires at the freeway and the gas main explosion, but that smoke had risen into the sky. Now, the very air around her was heavy with choking smoke. At times, the air smelled of burning wood, like a barbecue. At other times, Kathy could smell the heavy putridity of burnt rubber. The light wind out of the east did not help at all. It just brought more smoke, and a burning of the eyes.

Kathy had crossed over from Pico to Olympic, just before she got to the Convention Center. It had looked to her as if everyone was being herded south by the police there and Kathy wanted to go west, toward home.

Olympic Boulevard had presented her two problems, the traffic and the rubble. Like the cross street over from Pico, virtually every building on Olympic had some kind of damage. Many buildings, they seemed to Kathy to be mostly the older ones, were in ruins, blocking the sidewalks and one or two lanes of the wide boulevard. Other buildings, including the taller glass high rises, were in various stages of destruction.

The glass of the first tall building Kathy encountered close at hand had been entirely stripped from the upper floors and now lay in neat, shining crystalline piles around the buildings perimeter. Other debris -- office equipment, furniture, papers, boxes and parts of the buildings -- was mixed with the glass. Some piles were many feet high and they covered parked cars, trucks, shrubbery and ...

Kathy blinked in horror at the first corpses she saw. They lay were they had fallen in the quake. Kathy could not believe the scene.

Some of the corpses were nothing more than pinkish-red lumps in the crystalline piles of glass. Other bodies lay by themselves, where they had managed to run after being hit by the first shards and before they succumbed.

On the corner nearest Kathy, a bright blue BMW convertible was stopped partially on the sidewalk against a litter bin it had crushed as it crashed to a stop. The driver of the BMW, a young women, was still in the car. Her body slumped forward into the steering wheel. Behind the driver's seat, braced between the headrest and the convertible cover, was what appeared to be a computer monitor or TV, smashed in its fall from high above. The young woman's head tilted to the side in a sickening angle, without movement. A thick piece of plate glass stood erect in the trunk of the BMW where it had sliced through the sheet metal as it landed.

Kathy glanced skyward at the building. The building was at

least ten stories high. Not a single window remained. Draperies wafted out of the open window frames. In at least two places, Kathy could see furniture, a sofa and a long desk, hanging precariously on the edge of the upper floors of the building.

She could also see smoke coming from two of the upper floors of the building. Other than the smoke, there was no movement in the whole building. Whatever survivors had been in the building had gotten out and left the building and its corpses for someone or someday else.

A cacophony of honking broke Kathy Warden's concentration on the glassless building and its victims. The traffic on the intervening street had ground to a total halt. All traffic seemed to be westbound now, everybody leaving the downtown area. Kathy continued her walk west also, carefully checking behind her to see that no maniacal driver tried to use the same path on the left hand periphery of rubble that Kathy and the hundreds of other pedestrians were using.

The number of pedestrians had been increasing for the last two hours that Kathy had walked through downtown L.A. Around her, Kathy could see that some of the people were injured. Many people carried children or possessions and quite a few assisted or carried victims.

Kathy trudged on, avoiding bricks and debris. Sweat and the choking air stung her eyes. The sun itself was no longer hot. It was now only a orange-red glow in the western sky, having been lost behind the smoke of Los Angeles burning. However, the heat was oppressive. The heat, and the thoughts, the worries, the fears.

No one among the people walking with Kathy was talking. Even people who apparently knew one another just marched on in silence.

The underpass on Olympic under the 110 Harbor Freeway was still standing. Nothing was moving on the freeway above, though. Kathy had seen the sagging break in the freeway just south at Pico. Nevertheless, it did seem to be flowing pretty well to the north. A steady stream of vehicles was turning off Olympic to the northbound 110.

Kathy and the others, both in cars and pedestrians, who crossed under the freeway were greeted by a barrage of flashing amber lights and barricades. The southern half of the boulevard was blocked off a block ahead, forcing the oncoming cars to turn south on a side street. This explained the lack of traffic coming up Olympic.

A large sign, which looked like it had been made, sometime before, for this exact purpose, had been erected in the middle of Olympic Boulevard. It said, "Good Samaritan Hospital --->."

A police officer stood in the middle of the street, stopping the cars heading west to let groups of people on foot cut across the traffic and head north to the hospital. Many of the cars also turned north.

As Kathy exited from under the freeway, she considered the options ahead. Olympic Boulevard would have two-way traffic ahead. With so many the cars turning north here, it seemed that the north side of the street would be safest to negotiate around any rubble. She decided to wait with the group of people behind the Good Samaritan sign. She would cross over to the north side of the street and then head west again.

While she waited to cross, Kathy watched two men from a Department of Water and Power truck stopped on the south half of the street. They stood with their hands on their hips, looking at something which Kathy had not noticed until now.

There was a gaping hole in Olympic Boulevard directly between her and where the oncoming traffic turned south. Looking closer now she could see the steady stream of water flowing from the hole in the street to the storm drain on the far side of the street.

A minivan and a Volkswagen were the last cars to be signaled through by the cop before he signaled the slowly moving traffic to stop. The shrill tweet of the police whistle signaled the pedestrians to cross, but they did not immediately move. Most of them, Kathy included, were trying to keep their balance and glancing hurriedly around to make sure they were safe here in the middle of Olympic Boulevard. The Water and Power workers scurried quickly back from the edge of the broken water main hole, out of respect for this stronger than usual aftershock. Kathy had to brace her feet apart to remain standing. But she was getting good at this. However, her heart still raced with each tremor from the ground.

Kathy saw the first bricks tumble onto the north side of Olympic Boulevard just as the traffic cop's whistle started a frantic series of loud tweets warning of the danger. For a brief moment, Kathy stood transfixed, watching the front and side of the building on the northwest corner of the intersection crack and crumble to the ground. Then, with the other pedestrians and the traffic cop, she ran back toward the empty southbound on-ramp to the freeway. Those nearby in cars were not so lucky.

Kathy stopped short of the freeway overpass, as did the others, and turned to see behind her. Her first sight was of the minivan and Volkswagen disappearing into the expanding debris from the building and its accompanying cloud of dust.

The wrenching screech of metal and crashing roar of tumbling bricks somehow blotted out the quake itself. The cloud of dust, spotlighted by the headlights from the traffic coming under the freeway churned out and filled the width of the boulevard.

The ferocity of the collapse ended as suddenly as it had begun.

Soon, the only sound was that of traffic on the other side of the freeway, oblivious to the new obstacle that blocked their way on Olympic.

The dust cloud slowly settled and drifted out until the headlights pierced its gloom and Kathy could see the awkward pyramid of bricks, steel and wood that now stretched well past where she had just been standing in the middle of the street waiting to cross ... waiting to cross to the sidewalk on the north side that no longer existed. She tried to think if there had been anyone waiting on that sidewalk before the aftershock. She could not remember.

As the last loose bricks tumbled to the pavement from the slopes of the debris pile, the traffic cop and the two public works employees ventured forward, sleeves to their mouths to block what dust they could. Slowly, the others with Kathy also edged forward.

The three story office building no longer existed. In its place stood a pile of bricks and concrete, pierced by steel reinforcing rod and wood. The pile was less than half the former building's height.

The Volkswagen had been partially pushed out across the street by the falling, rolling architecture, but the push had not been enough. The rear engine compartment was all that now showed. The oval rear window of the old VW was filled with bricks. The body of the car was under the slope of debris. The minivan could not be seen.

The cop ran to the edge of the debris at the VW's rear bumper. There he hesitated, looking up, surmising the stability of the ragged pile of brick and steel. Satisfied, he reached for the first chunk of mortar and brick in the VW's rear window. One workman ran over to help and the other ran off up the street, shouting something as he ran.

Two men standing near Kathy also ran up to help uncover the VW. The rest milled forward, uncertain of what to do.

Kathy, herself, debated whether to come forward and help. It was the same quandary she had felt earlier in the day. Should she ... could she, Kathy Warden, do more to help the others in this disaster. She had been the recipient of help, by the truck driver and again by the kind clothier, but she felt inadequate to pitch in to rescue, or nurse, the victims. She had her own needs, her own injuries, her own fears. She had no skills to help. She was just one young woman. Not strong. Not brave. Just scared. Lonely. Hungry. Hurt. And, all she wanted to do was get home.

`What could she do?' The others could handle it.

Some of the people near Kathy watched the rescue attempt. The other workman came back up the street with a big scoop shovel. Others who had been waiting to walk across Olympic took advantage of the blocked traffic to cut between the new debris pile and the hole in the street to head west.

Kathy realized that she had probably just seen someone die. The bloody bodies by the glass building had been one thing, but seeing those cars with people in them crushed was another. She shivered.

Kathy took a deep breath, wiped sweat and accumulated dust from her brow and trotted diagonally across Olympic around the collapse. The minivan could not be seen on the other side of the debris pile. That whole side of the pile was covered with a billboard that had earlier advertised Asahi beer from the top of the building.

■

Like most California governmental bodies, the southernmost county of Imperial requires important public buildings to be constructed under stringent anti-earthquake engineering standards. The brand-new County Administration Building was, thus, considered to be "earthquake-proof" when it was hit by a moderate earthquake in 1979. The bulk of the building's structure remained intact, but two ground supports on one end sheered off, causing the whole building to tilt sideways. Nobody was seriously injured, but the new building was rendered useless, a total loss. Interestingly, the seismic strengthening, which had failed to resist the relatively moderate earthquake, proved remarkably adept at resisting the dismantlers' jackhammers. It took many months and high-explosive charges to finally level the ruined building. An identical county building in Santa Barbara County was hastily reinforced after the collapse of its sister building. Both county seats have known earthquake faults directly under them.

May 6th, 4:30 P.M.

Deputy Barry Warden felt like he needed to be in a dozen places at once. He, the two L.A.P.D. cops and the two hospital guards still at work at Harbor UCLA medical Center had been struggling for over an hour to control a situation that a hundred police or even riot troops would have trouble handling. There was no sign of the deputy sheriffs who should have been in the collapsed west wing.

The chaos he had encountered when he drove up had only multiplied as time passed. The cars parked and abandoned by those coming to get help at the hospital had now totally blocked both Vermont and

Carson, and with that, the off-ramp to the east from the Harbor Freeway was blocked. However, the traffic blockade that prevented the incoming injured from getting to the hospital was probably the only thing that kept the hospital staff's triage attempts from grinding to a complete halt.

Barry had stationed himself at the south side of the hospital, where the most of the triage was taking place. The worst of the injuries were coming from the fiery cataclysm to the south and east in Carson and Long Beach. It was not uncommon for people with their clothes burned off to stumble forward out of the crowd assembled around the hospital.

It did not take long to see that traditional triage, which they had been trying to carry out in the parking lot, a multi-level prioritizing of casualties waiting for medical care, was ridiculous in their circumstances. The doctor in charge had made it clear that there would only be two choices. Anybody in a life and death situation who could be helped would be the only ones who would be handled by the medical staff. The walking wounded, the lesser injuries, and even those with broken bones would be turned away or would have to wait. Those deemed beyond hope, unannounced to them or their families, were sent to the upper level of the back parking garage. The many DOA's and the "criticals" who died at the hospital were sent to the lower parking level. The west end of the hospital had been abandoned and only the east half was working on generator power.

The throng gathered around the building was, amazingly, obeying the bright yellow "Crime Scene-Do No Cross" tape he had strung between the landscaping bushes on the south side. The crowd was filled with those waiting for loved ones inside, including those waiting for those persons relegated to the parking structure. Those injured who did not justify immediate treatment waited on the grass and amongst the crowd. Others gave up and left to find help elsewhere.

The decision was made that only the staff and the injured could remain inside the cordon. Everyone else must wait outside. Barry wondered what would happen if the real story of the triage got out.

They had stopped doing the triage in the open parking lot. That was just an invitation for further riot, especially after the new triage rules were invoked. A single checkpoint was set up in the middle of his "police line" through which everyone gaining admittance must pass. The other cops and hospital staff had similar setups in place at the north side of the hospital. It was Barry's job to see that this fragile system kept working.

"Where do I go?" a woman's voice asked. Barry turned around to face a young nurse. Her tear-streaked face looked something like Kathy's. Barry blotted out that thought, he had no time for that now.

At first, Barry thought the young nurse was cradling a child in her arms. As he looked he saw that her right arm was in a sling and she was cradling it in her left. She answered his look with, "Broke it in the quake."

"Where do you go for what?" Barry asked her back.

"They said I should help with triage since I can't work on patients with my arm. Where do I go?"

"Well, we have two spots. Up there," he pointed to the checkpoint on the west walkway, "we do the admitting to the hospital grounds, sort out the walking wounded and less critical. Over around the corner and in the hall," he pointed toward the building and then, continuing softly, "we separate out the critical from the, ah, the hopeless. Take your pick."

The nurse nodded and walked toward the checkpoint on the walkway. He watched her go, but his attention was drawn to a scuffle that had sprung up at the far northwest corner, nearest the front gate, where the crowd was thickest. He ran over, nightstick drawn.

"Stop pushing!" someone shouted.

"Hey, watch it."

Barry heard the shouts from just outside the yellow tape as he ran up. He arrived in time to see a man emerge from the crowd, pushing and jostling, and receiving the same from the crowd.

Barry had his nightstick cocked, ready to enforce his perimeter line when he saw what the man carried in his arms. A little boy, maybe five years old, hung limp in his father's arms. The boy's T-shirt was soaked in blood. His head lolled backward, but the little body gasped for breath, air rasping in his throat. The crowd nearby quieted when they saw what Barry saw.

Without saying anything, Barry lifted the yellow tape and pointed the man toward the checkpoint. Turning his back on the crowd Barry walked back to his chosen vantage point near the checkpoint.

After a few minutes the man walked out of the hospital with a group of other people leaving the triage area to wait in the crowd.

Barry wondered if the little boy would go to the east wing or to the parking garage. However, he really did not want to know.

■

The Good Friday Earthquake which hit Alaska on March 27, 1964 had the destructive energy of 10 million times the energy of the Hiroshima atomic bomb. An area of coastal Alaska the size of all of Southern California was uplifted, in places by as much as 50 feet.

May 6th, 5:10 P.M.

Gloria drove slowly around the curve toward her house. It was still beyond the curve, out of sight. After the destruction and fires she had seen on the way from the bank, a lump of dread anticipation clung in her throat. Her slowness was not only a response to the anticipation, but also the many road hazards she had encountered in the half-mile trip over from the BankCal building on Palm Drive. The sight of several of the houses in the big housing development, the majority of which were identical, except for color and trim, in various stages of fire or quake damage made matters worse.

By the time she rounded the last turn and saw the familiar blue and gray trim, Gloria Contreras was fully prepared for the worst and muttering prayers for her children under her breath.

The house seemed fine. In fact, all of the houses within a block of hers were fine. The only sign that anything was amiss in her immediate neighborhood was the fact that the occupants of many houses were sitting on their front steps. But, nobody was sitting on Gloria's porch. Her heart fell.

Gloria pulled the little Pontiac into the driveway and gathered her purse, the cell phone and the emergency manual she had brought home to study. It had taken a long time to get the bank secured, guard in place and employees instructed on tomorrow's plans. She did not know if Consuella would stay or not. It was now after five, and even in the best of times Consuella wanted to leave at five.

Gloria was half way up the walk when her questions were all answered in one quick flurry. Consuella stormed out of the house with her purse and the sewing bag she always brought with her in her arms, ready to leave. Consuella was letting loose a barrage of machinegun-like Spanish at Gloria. The rudimentary Spanish Gloria knew, from growing up half-Mexican and from business Spanish classes, was no match for the rapid pace of words the old Mexicali-born woman now threw at her. Before she could slow Consuella down, Miranda ran from the front door shouting, "Mommy, Mommy."

Miranda had not yet finished her hug of Gloria when she started speaking as fast as Consuella had, "Mommy, did you feeeeelll it? I saw fires from the backyard. Did you? ..."

Consuela pushed past Gloria on the sidewalk and headed for her old rust colored Chevy.

Gloria's attempts to shush her daughter so that she could talk to Consuella before the old woman got all the way to her car required Gloria to touch Miranda's lips and raise her voice. "Miranda, I need to talk to Consuella. We'll talk in a minute, OK?"

"Consuella, Wait! Slow down! I need to know ... Consuella!"

When she reached her car, the old woman turned and, in broken English, said, "You are late again. I have family, too. Everything OK. No electric', no agua." She turned and opened the car door. Before getting in, she turned to Gloria once more and added, "And the baby needs diapers. Papel! No coton. No agua por la lavadora." She lapsed into Spanish as she finished, sat down and shut the car door.

Gloria's attempts to say more were drowned out by the sound of the Chevy coughing to life and pulling away. Gloria stood blinking at the departure. At least the old woman had stayed until she got home.

Miranda was going a mile a minute, telling her of the day's experiences as they walked hand in hand back up the walk to the house. As they walked, both Gloria and Miranda waved at Jessica Seligman, the neighbor girl about a year and a half older than Miranda. Jessica was sitting by herself on the porch next door. The girl waved back, somewhat forlornly.

Gloria went inside to check out her house. When she opened the front door, she heard the baby crying. It was reassuring to hear him, even crying. Now all Gloria needed was Matt.

There had been remarkably little damage inside their house. With all the quakes, big and little, they had in the Palm Springs area, Gloria and Matt had gotten pretty good at securing furniture and avoiding knickknacks on shelves, the worst culprits in a quake.

Miranda was in the breakfast nook, off the kitchen, eating a sandwich Gloria had made from rapidly warming food from the inoperative refrigerator. The sun had just set behind Mount San Gorgonio and Gloria had utilized the last of the sunlight to go around and collect candles, matches, flashlights and batteries from their hiding places in the garage and kitchen cabinets.

Pausing from her collecting, Gloria tried the telephone and cell phone again. She was thinking of making contact with someone from BankCal, but also hoping to dial Matt's cell. No luck.

Gloria looked out the front window, fleetingly thinking she might see Matt drive up. He had promised to be home at five. Under the circumstances, she probably could not hold that against him. But, what were his circumstances? Where would a Highway Patrol pilot be in a disaster like this? When would she see him?

As Gloria gazed out the window, she saw little Jessica still sitting all alone on the front steps of her house, arms wrapped tightly over short sleeves in the rapidly cooling dusk air. Something was wrong. She had been there, alone, for a long time.

Gloria went outside, crossed the driveway and waved to Jessica. She knew the little girl well. Jessica's mother and Gloria regularly exchanged baby-sitting services.

As she approached the little girl, Gloria spoke to her, "Hey, Jess. What's up?"

Jessica started to speak, "My ... My Mmm ..." Sniffles started and Jessica could not get the words out.

Gloria put her arms out to the little girl, who ran toward her. After a moment's hug Jessica finished, " My Mommy and Daddy didn't come home."

Gloria knelt down and held Jessica out to where she could see her face. "And you have been sitting here all afternoon. Why didn't you go inside?"

"They made us leave school and my key is in my backpack and they wouldn't let us go back into the building."

Gloria knew Jessica's parents owned a dry cleaning store in Desert Hot Springs. Working staggered hours with her husband, Jessica's mother usually came home right after Jessica got out of the elementary school a few blocks away.

"Jessica, I think you should come over to our house and wait for your parents. I'll fix you some supper. OK?"

"Okay." Jessica moved to follow Gloria, "D'you think Mommy

and Daddy are OK? I heard everybody at school talking about how bad the quake was ...”

“Don’t worry. They are probably just making sure things are fine at their store. I had a lot of problems at my work, too.” Gloria lied. It had now been several hours since the quake and Seligman Dry Cleaning was only a couple of miles north, her parents could have walked home to make sure their little daughter was all right by now.

■

Sybil Perkins had never felt so alone in her life. Alone and totally isolated from everything.

Technically, she was only about a mile from the American border, but she might as well have been on Mars. And, technically she was not alone, but the young man with her did not stop the empty feeling she had as she stared out at a cataclysm of biblical proportions. Perhaps lonely was not the right word, but heartsick, dreadful and foreboding did not work either.

After the meeting in Mexicali, she had decided to see the mud volcanoes the young Mexican engineer had spoken of. While the rest of the American consultants had paired off with their Mexican counterparts to review engineering data she had taken the opportunity to pursue her specialty, geologic structures. The young Mexican, Esteban Lopez, who had first spoke of the mud volcanoes accompanied her.

Although only a few miles, as the crow flies, from Mexicali the mud volcanoes were physically remote. On the opposite side of the landmark volcanic mount south of Mexicali, the mud volcanoes were a thirty mile trip across the salt deserts of Laguna Salada.

Sybil was at the volcanoes, eating a burrito with Esteban, at the shack that served as a visitors center at the volcano site when the quake hit that afternoon. It had been spectacular.

They had run from the shack at the first sign of the temblor. Her excitement as a geologist had been tempered by the stark fear of the situation. The quake had rolled on and on. The mud volcanoes had spurted into the air hundreds of feet. Even the locals who made a living at the volcanic attraction ran in fear.

They ran for her rental car, afraid that some of the boiling mud might fly on them. She had found it difficult getting the key in the rental car's lock, so hard was the car bouncing.

At length the quake had died down. The quake was obviously a major one. Sybil had no idea of how big. She knew that the sediment of the Mexicali region was prime liquefaction medium, so the constant rolling she felt could either be the direct result of the quake or the reflection locally. Her first thoughts were of the opportunities the quake would present in her chosen field of interest.

Her first disappointment was that the Mexican rental car had a inoperative radio. She would have to wait until she got to Mexicali to find out more about the quake. The mud volcanoes were still spewing huge geysers as they drove north.

The narrow two-lane macadam road passed through Laguna Salada from west of Mexicali to the resort of San Felipe on the Gulf of California to the south. The road was broken and barely passable after the quake. The trip north to the major highway, Route 2, between Mexicali and Tijuana was slow. Route 2 turned out to be not much better; its concrete slabs had twisted and settled in the quake.

Then, just west of the Mexicali among the poor farm laborer's tenements of Nueva Colonia, Route 2 had disappeared into a half-mile wide torrent of water. She could go no further.

Sybil Perkins tried to remember what this river crossing had been like on the trip down, she could not even remember crossing a river on the way down to Laguna Salada. In fact she was sure she had not. Now, they were trapped on the far shore of rapidly growing flood that ran north across the American border separating them from Mexicali.

"What in the hell is going on?" Sybil asked, not really expecting Esteban to answer.

"The only thing in Baja with this much water is the ocean," Esteban said looking across the widening chasm of water.

"The ocean. We've got to be forty miles from the ocean."

"*Si*. But, the swamps of the delta come almost to the southern edge of Mexicali. The elevation of our geothermal plant at Nayarit is only two meters. If the earthquake caused a subsidence, the delta might be draining this way, and the ocean with it."

"If this is the ocean, then this would ...this could ..." Sybil could not finish the thought.

"*Si*. It could be a flood to make Padre Noah proud."

■

Another curious phenomenon of earthquakes is a "seich." Rocked by the force or the waves of motion from a quake, a body of water, whether a swimming pool or a lake, will rock back and forth gaining momentum as it rocks. Swimming pools have been known to pour up out of their sides and lakes overflow their dams and shore-line. The seich effect has been known to cross hundreds or thousands of miles from the epicenter of the quake.

May 6th, 6:00 P.M.

"I've got the beacon." The sun was low behind the mountains in the west when Matt Contreras finally sighted the Palm Springs Airport.

"Yes, me, too." Captain Moody sounded as tired as Matt felt. They had switched seats at Moreno Valley when they refueled, so it was Moody who turned the Huey directly toward the occulting blue and white light that cut through the smoky haze of the Coachella Valley.

By this time of night there should be plenty of city lights along the whole arc of cities ringing the valley from Palm Springs to Indio. The airport beacons were among the few lights they could see in the twilight. The only other lights were vehicles or the glowing square patterns that represented houses, buildings or blocks on fire. The electricity was obviously out, the airport and the beacon had to be operating on emergency power.

Now that they were passing the Palm Springs airport, it was about time the check in with Thermal's tower. Matt had not thought about it, but they had no idea how the little airport south of Indio had held up to the quake. They had been turned north toward Banning when they reached Indio earlier in the afternoon. No one from the Thermal area had been up on the emergency services radio net.

Matt set the frequency and did the call-in, "Thermal Tower, this is C.H.P..." Matt caught his error and re-keyed the microphone. "Correction, this is Riverside Sheriff Air Two. Over."

Only static answered his call. They waited.

Matt called again. "Thermal Tower, this is Sheriff Air Two. Do you copy, over?"

"Sheriff Air Two, this is Thermal."

"Sheriff Air Two requests clearance to land. West Hangar Area. And, please notify the Services truck for refueling at the County Hangar. Over."

"Be aware that Thermal does not have any control or ground operations working. We have only this radio and no lights. You are cleared to land West Hangar area, but with extreme caution. Repeat. We have no approach control, no lights. The tarmac is broken and may be hazardous to land on. We have no telephones. You will have to contact Hotchkiss Flight Services yourself after landing. They have the only pumper truck that can pump its own fuel out of the tanks without electricity. And, watch out for the mud on landing, and standing water in the low spots. You are cleared to land without further contact. Thermal, Out."

Matt and Moody looked at each other, amazed at the curt communication they had gotten from the ground and the reference to "mud." Where had Thermal gotten mud and standing water? After what Contreras had seen this day, he had no doubt that everyone on the ground had more than enough problems to deal with and just about anything could be expected.

They had spent the day over the cities on the far side of San Jacinto Peak and the mountain range that split Riverside County. Between their own observations and the reports that came in over the radio, it was clear that the worst damage, as expected, was nearest the San Andreas Fault. Matt Contreras had seen entire subdivisions of houses folded flat in the cities of Riverside and Moreno Valley. But, nothing had compared to the sheer geologic havoc that they had seen in the San Gorgonio Pass on the way out and back into the Coachella Valley.

Matt's own house, below him now in the darkness, was not much farther from the San Andreas than some of the badly hit areas they had seen, but the gist of the reports they had heard on the emergency operations circuit was that they epicenter of the quake had been somewhere near Redlands. This explained the great damage in Banning and Beaumont in the Pass. And, it gave him hope that his home and family had been spared.

As they dipped lower toward the airport, the smell of smoke increased. The hot winds that had fanned the fires in Moreno Valley and Riverside had kept the smoke low, below flying altitude. Now, coming in low, the smoke was, at times, choking.

"Tough to judge distance against the horizon, with no lights." Moody said.

Matt answered, "Yeh, the lights make it tough. No reference points with the city lights out."

Captain Moody murmured agreement. He reached down and turned on the landing lights. Then, after a pause, he flipped another switch. Matt could feel and see in the reflection of particles in the air as the huge arc lights came on below him. This search and rescue unit had an advantage other aircraft did not. Its search lights could light the whole airport without any need for ground lights.

Moody explained, needlessly, to Matt, "No ground lights, might need 'em."

They came in from the northwest. The sheriff's hangar was next to the CHP building along with the other general aviation hangars on the west side of the airport. Matt Contreras craned his neck to see the ground as Moody flew in an arc around the little airport. The glare of the chopper's lights lit the ground, casting eerie shadows as the helicopter moved.

In spots, the concrete squares of the runway apron were tilted and twisted like poorly laid floor tiles. The heavier concrete of the runway itself seemed better, but several of the taxiways so rough it appeared they might have been prepped for removal by heavy equipment.

Matt saw the crew of the Life Flight choppers surrounding one of the red and white Allouette helicopters. They had a portable generator and work light going, apparently trying to do emergency work on the air ambulance. The air ambulance service would probably be as important a function as could exist this evening in Southern California. Perhaps only outweighed by the few urban search and rescue teams that existed. Bloodhounds, paramedics and mobile cranes were probably hot properties.

The only building Matt could see that had been destroyed was the cinder block structure that housed the parachute packing and electronic repair services at the end of the hangar row. It looked like it had been swatted flat by a huge hand. The metal frame "Butler" buildings and hangars had taken the quake's impact pretty well.

Matt's hangar and office looked fine, as was Moody's. But Matt could see what they meant about mud and water. The whole area was glistening with wetness.

Moody settled the Huey into a relatively smooth section near the sheriff hangar. Moody started the shutdown routine and the rotors and turbines started to wind down.

Matt looked around. In the lights from the chopper he could see the walls of the hangar.

"Jesus, look at that!" he said to Moody. He pointed to the hangar, where a high water line could be seen. Piles of soaked trash cluttered the ground. There had been a flood of some kind.

"How in the hell do you have a flood in Thermal?" Moody asked. "There isn't any river, nothing, 'cept the irrigation ditches, for miles. Where do you get enough water for a flood? Looks like about two feet of water on the wall?"

"No idea."

A jumpsuited figure from the Sheriff's hangar ran out to affix the tie down straps as the engines and rotors spun to a stop. Matt Contreras climbed out. He walked over to the ground crewman with Moody. A wet ocean-like smell filled the air.

"Where'd all the water come from?"

The crewman shook his head and shrugged, "They say the quake sloshed it out of the Salton Sea. I guess Mecca got hit a lot harder. Strangest thing, huh?"

Contreras and Moody could not believe it. They looked at each other and then the crewman. Moody scraped his foot on the muddy ground as if to confirm the mud for himself.

Mecca was a small town halfway between Thermal and the big saltwater lake to the south. That lake, the Salton Sea, was five miles away, across the flat farmland of the Coachella Valley.

It must have been some slosh, Matt thought as he walked to his own hangar to check on his aircraft.

■

On July 9, 1958, an earthquake in Alaska generated a wave that surged over 1,700 feet up a coastal mountainside at Lituya Bay.

May 6th, 6:15 P.M.

"I'll try to make this as quick as possible. But, we've got some major decisions to make, some big problems ahead, and everyone needs to know what's up." The hospital administrator, Dick Perry, looked at each person in the group as he spoke. "First, we've got some new faces. Everybody ought to know who they're working with."

Perry pointed at Barry Warden and Alisha Walker, "Deputy Warden and Officer Walker, have taken over the task of security. Hopefully, some help will be coming on that front soon." Jamil Allen had chosen to stay out front of the hospital rather than come to the meeting.

Perry now pointed to one of two men in coveralls next to Barry, "This is Pete Valdez, County Public Works, he's working with John Holmdahl, our facilities manager," Perry pointed again, "to keep things running and make sure the building stays put." Perry's attempted smile was pitiful.

"Most of you know, Dr. Frames, E.R. Chief; Dr. Milborn, Pathology; and Chief Nurse Gates." Perry finished the introductions and took a deep breath. "First, I think we need to hear from John, that's really why we had to call the meeting right now."

The facilities manager looked around nervously. "Well, as you all know the west wing of the hospital is a total loss, Pete doesn't think we can even risk walking in there. That's why we moved the temporary morgue to the west parking garage. The real problem is that the reserve fuel oil tanks for the emergency generators and hot water system are in the basement, the boiler room, in the west side of the building. The generators themselves are the noisy things you hear in the auxiliary building in the south parking lot, they are fine. The lines to the reserve tanks are cut and we can't even get to the boiler room. The emergency generators had a total operating time without refueling of about six hours. That's already up. Pete's men have managed to siphon diesel fuel from the few diesel cars in the parking lot, but that is only going to get us a couple of hours. I figure that if nothing happens to change things, the hospital will go dark in two hours, maybe earlier. And, very unfortunately, the emergency power only runs to the main hospital building, with all of this huge influx it would be nice to be able to use the paramedic training center, the med and nursing student housing and the medical office building to treat patients, but as of yet, the only electrical power is the main building which is half ruined. If we can solve the fuel problem, the next thing we will do is run temporary power lines to the other buildings. For now, even the main building is at risk."

"Isn't there something they can ..., somebody, who can get some fuel in here?" one of the doctors, Dr. Morrissey, interjected.

Perry cut in to answer, "We have been talking to the County Emergency Services people on the microwave link. They know the problem, but it doesn't sound like they are in any shape to send help. They say there are high-rises that fell over downtown. Tens of thousands injured. We're on our own for a while." Eyebrows raised in the assembled group, no one in this group had been monitoring the news of the disaster. News of the extent of the tragedy came as a shock.

"Diesel fuel? That's what you need?" Alisha asked.

"Yup. Plain, old ordinary diesel fuel. Why? Got some ideas?"

Holmdahl asked.

"I'll work on it." the policewoman answered.

Perry took back the floor of the meeting, "Well, we'll see what happens there. But, we need to be ready for the worst. Dr. Frames, how's triage going? What should we do if we're gonna lose power?"

"Christ, if we lose power it is going to be hell. Even with the strict life and death triage we're still beyond full up. It is getting so you can't walk in the halls. You've all seen it. We're beyond the ability to treat most of the new patients coming in. I say the most humane thing is to turn new patients away, tell them to go elsewhere." The Emergency Room chief threw up his hands.

"We've got people on the lawn, who've been waiting hours with broken bones. Now, we seem to be getting a huge rush of horrible burns, just now getting in here from the big blast out in Long Beach. If we close down new admittees, the people outside will go nuts. We nearly had a full-fledged riot a couple hours back. You close down and all bets are off. There is no `elsewhere' for these people. Everywhere is just as bad." Barry said.

"The decision to close down may be out of our hands if the power goes off. I can't do anything for a critical burn patient or internal injuries in the dark." Dr. Frames paused. "We lose electrical power and Dr. Milborn's morgue will start filling up fast."

Barry noticed Alisha slip away from the group as the hospital's managers turned to subjects of medical staffing and supplies.

■

The January 1995 quake in Kobe, Japan resulted in over 300,000 refugees, $90 Billion in damages and over 7000 dead. Prior to this quake Japan was considered a model in earthquake preparedness. The failure of some earthquake resistant construction technology, the huge traffic jams after the quake, the poor response of the Japanese authorities to the immediate needs of quake victims and the utter destruction of a modern urban area left many to doubt the ability of any nation or people to prepare for a major earthquake in a congested urban area.

May 6th, 6:15 P.M.

The darkness was premature. And eerie.

An unnatural twilight was descending on Los Angeles. Cars turned on their lights as they drove in just two opposing lanes down the once broad Olympic Boulevard. The two lanes wound their way between piles of bricks, abandoned vehicles and those places where the boulevard was impassable from the quake damage. Smoke hung everywhere. Fires still burned in virtually every block of the old buildings. The dark yellow-gray of the sky above was unlike anything Kathy had ever seen. It seemed the overcast was from the smoke and dust, and not from any clouds.

Kathy trudged on, block after block. The foreign lettering on shop signs got more numerous, until, past Alverado, the curious oriental lettering on signs became the rule. Kathy was on foot, in what she assumed to be Koreatown, and it was rapidly getting dark. The steps of the library at Westmoreland Avenue seemed like a good place to stop, rest and take stock of her situation.

Kathy sat on the concrete rail and put her purse and the plastic bag on her lap. She looked around. The number of people walking had diminished somewhat from the large crowd that had crossed under the freeway from downtown. And the crowd had changed, too. Or maybe it had not actually changed, but Kathy was now aware that her fellow travelers were decidedly ethnic. In the minute, she watched, thinking about this, she saw only three people whom she could consider white. They spoke hurriedly in a guttural Middle-Eastern tongue.

Kathy Warden felt hopelessly tired, bewildered and definitely out of place. And, with the light of day having slipped away she was still half a city away from home.

Seeing a pay phone by the library, Kathy tried it, more out of habit now than out of hope. It was dead.

"Little lady need some help?"

Kathy jumped at the sound of the man's voice in her ear. In the moment of fear, she missed her footing on the broken sidewalk and fell to the ground next to the phone booth.

A dark figure stood over her, reaching down toward her.

"Hey, sorry to freak you. Here, let me help." An unshaven face ringed by stringy black hair peered down toward her and a hand grabbed her arm, pulling her to her feet.

The stench of body odor blotted out the smell of smoke in the air. The hand on her arm did not release her. Now, she found herself nose to nose with the man. The alcohol on his breath merged with the body odor. Kathy's throat tightened to wretch, but her stomach was empty, so she just gagged.

"You O.K? Not feeling well? Need some help?" he said. With the aspiration of the word "help" the smell of rum flooded into Kathy's face.

Turning her face aside and gulping, she tried to pull her arm away from the man's grasp, "No. Thank you, I'm fine. you just scared me. . I'll be fine."

The man stood uncomfortably close to her, still holding her arm. He wore an oily camouflage field jacket several sizes too large for his skinny frame. The field jacket covered a tattered sweater and nondescript dark clothes. The neck of a rum bottle poked out from the field jacket pocket.

For a brief moment, Kathy looked into the man's face, waiting for him to release her arm. He was white, probably in his thirties, and spoke without an accent. His sunken eyes were glazed by alcohol and looked out from under a brow coated in sweat and the dust of the quake. His sallow features showed no hostility, but neither were they the face Kathy would turn to for help, in any circumstance, let alone now.

Kathy had to grab his wrist and remove it from her arm. The wrist she grabbed was moist and clammy. She involuntarily wiped her hand on her jeans as she turned to move away.

He followed her.

"You live around here?" He asked, she did not answer. He continued talking as Kathy turned onto the sidewalk, "A good lookin' gal like you ought to be careful. Gettin' dark fast. Not a real good neighborhood. You want me to escort you?" He ended the question with a wheezing cough.

"NO! I'll be fine. I don't need your help. Uh, thank you."

The man now shuffled beside her as she crossed the next street, close enough to brush her arm when she slowed to step over debris at the curb.

Kathy continued on. They were in an area of older buildings, some of which still stood, some were flattened. People stood in groups near some of the buildings. Some people dug in the ruins. The traffic still struggled both ways down Olympic Boulevard, now not much more than a two-lane path through the rubble of one of Los Angeles' older sections.

The man continued to follow close beside Kathy. She tried to ignore him by looking around her. Many clusters of people, what looked like family groups, stood in front of the buildings. They were apparently afraid to go inside with the continuing aftershocks. Kathy saw that many of the men in the groups near the shops and stores of Koreatown carried guns and clubs cradled in their arms. The shopkeepers watched the passing crowd closely.

Kathy wondered how she could rid herself of the man who had attached himself to her. She had not seen any police, but, anyway, the man had not done anything, yet. He was just annoying her. Kathy continued on, approaching a spot were the building's fallen facade lay stretched out well into the street. The cars heading west were driving over the outer edge of the brick pile, so it was necessary for those on foot to crawl over the pile itself. As Kathy started over she felt the drunk still shadowing her, just behind.

She heard the man stumble, the crunching of bricks joined by his curse upon them, "Fuck. Fuckin' rocks!"

Kathy did not stop, hoping the man's drunken clumsiness might lead to him giving up on following her. She rounded the top of the brick pile and headed back down to the sidewalk beyond.

She heard the man get back to his feet and hurry to catch up. Bricks rolled down the pile behind her as the drunk hurried down toward her. Kathy started to hurry herself, to get away, when she heard him curse again. The drunk's falling body rolled into her ankles, knocking her back over him onto the brick pile.

The impact on the brick pile dazed Kathy. Brick chunks and wood poked her back and the cloud of dust from the fall filled the air. Kathy was coughing and trying to free her legs from the tumult the drunk was making below her, when someone grabbed her arms and pulled her away from him.

Two men helped Kathy gain here feet on the sidewalk. One of them yanked the drunk to his feet.

"You alright?" the man at Kathy's arm asked her. He was an older oriental who spoke with a trace of Korean accent.

"Yeh. Ok. He just tripped me up."

The drunk was now speaking also, "Fuckin' rocks. Jus' couldn't . . " Then fingering his field jacket and the broken rum bottle cursed again, "Fuck!"

The other man who had helped Kathy up, a younger Korean, came back to where Kathy stood. He spoke with an American accent, "He with you?" He seemed incredulous.

"What? No. He's been following me. I told him I didn't want any help. Not from ..." Kathy stopped.

The drunk now staggered toward Kathy, "Gee, Miss, sorry about that. I missed a step. Hope I didn't hurt you."

The younger Korean stepped between them. Kathy now saw he carried a baseball bat. "Just leave her alone. You've done plenty already. Why don't you beat it." He punctuated the last with a push from the bat on the drunk's arm.

The drunken man protested, "I was just helping her along. No reason to ..."

He was cut off by the young Korean, "She doesn't want your help. Get the hell out of here, go sleep it off." He ended his words with a bolder threat from the baseball bat.

The drunk stumbled back from the bat wielder and careened off between the slowly moving cars on Olympic, earning honks from the cars as he stumbled through them.

Kathy collected her purse and bag from the brick pile and brushed dust from them and her clothes as best as she could.

"Thanks a lot. I didn't know how I was going to get rid of him."

The older man spoke, "We know his type, hanging around. He is not alone. Lots of his kind. It is not safe for a young lady. No police. No streetlights."

The younger man joined in. "Yup. I don't know how far you're expecting to go, but it is not safe. Especially for a woman alone. You should stay here, my wife could ..."

"Really, I think I will be all right." Kathy put the bag under her arm to go. "Thank you for your help."

The young man shrugged and smiled a wry smile, "OK. It is your life. Good luck,"

Kathy smiled back and turned down the street. Fear, the darkening night and the newly strange city enveloped her as she walked through the rubble. She really did not know why she had refused the offer to help. Partly, she just wanted to head home, and, partly, the Koreans were strangers, too.

One block ahead, she reached Vermont, but the major cross-street was a mess. One of the corner buildings on Vermont had collapsed on a city bus. She could see this in the headlights of the vehicles gridlocked in the intersection and the glow of flames from a major fire in the block beyond Vermont. The whole block looked to be on fire. From a block away the flickering heat of the fire could be felt of her face.

The traffic could not go north on Vermont because of the transit bus carcass in the street. It looked like Kathy could walk north a block, around the fires on Olympic.

Without traffic and shaded from the light of the fire by the buildings, the block north on Vermont was dark. Very dark. An orange glow from the city's fires reflected from the low-hanging smoke, but this was not enough to light Kathy's way.

With her eyes not yet accustomed to the change in light from the fire's glare to darkened street, Kathy went slowly. There were a few people walking ahead of her, but they were at a distance. She heard someone working on a car ahead of her on this side of the street, wrench banging on metal. After a moment's thought, she was not sure they were working on a car or stripping it. She decided not to find out, she would cross over to the west side of Vermont.

The instant Kathy Warden stepped from the curb, she heard, smelled and felt the danger, but, too late. The scuffle of gravel behind her was instantly joined with an arm encircling her neck, tightly. As the arm crushed the air from her throat, her struggle for breath brought a familiar putridity to her nose. The rum-laden breath on her face hissed at her, "Quiet!"

Something cold and sharp pushed into Kathy's cheek. "You scream or fight and I cut. Got it?"

Kathy was pulled backward out of the street. She struggled to keep on her feet as she was pulled into the dark alley.

The choke-hold on her throat brought ringing to her ears and flashes of light, pulsing stars, to her eyes. Her consciousness was slipping.

"I can't breath," she struggled to whisper, her voice a rasp.

"Quiet!" he ordered again, but the grasp loosened a bit.

Her assailant stumbled on something in the alley or in his drunkenness. His now familiar "Fuck!" followed. Twenty feet into the alley he pushed Kathy toward the wall, shifting his grip to his hand on her throat, but keeping the cold point on her face.

"Remember, you scream, you bleed. Understand?"

Kathy tried to nod, but the point on her cheek prevented it. Instead, she hissed a "Yes" through clenched teeth.

"Get down!" the man ordered her as his hand on her throat pushed her down toward the ground.

Kathy bent her knees and knelt. Reaching down for balance she dropped her purse and bag. She felt that they were on a pile of cardboard boxes. The hand on her throat pushed her back out of a kneeling position onto her back. The man's weight came down on her. His face snuggled into her neck, smelling her, tasting her skin. The fetid stench of her assailant enveloped Kathy.

His mouth came up to her ear, "Fuckin bitch don't need no help, huh? Now I'm gonna give you some help. Some real fucking help."

The man shifted his weight on her, moving around. Thoughts flashed by her. What would he do if she fought him. Could she? He was drunk. How fast could she kick him, hard, in the balls, and run away? The struggled to remember the self-defense class she had taken. What should she do? But Kathy could do nothing, the drunk kept the cold point (the broken rum bottle?) on her face and then her neck.

The hand on her throat now moved down. First, it cupped her breast, squeezing hard, and then went down, probing between her legs and then fumbling to release the man's own belt and zipper. All the time the sharp, cold edge pressed against Kathy's neck.

The man's tongue tried to find Kathy's mouth, its wetness running up her chin as she turned her head. "Kiss me or you get cut," he hissed as he made the point on her neck poke deeper. Kathy stopped her attempts to avoid his tongue on her mouth, but she set her jaw, unable to cooperate further.

Now, his other hand was on her crotch, trying to open the button-fly jeans, drunken fingers fumbling on the buttons. The rotten breath surrounded her, his tongue and saliva all over her face. He rubbed himself against her thigh as he pulled at the buttons.

The buttons were finally open and the man was working into a frenzy, pulling down on Kathy's pants, pushing against her. Kathy felt his body jerk and shudder against her. `An orgasm?' she thought, thankful that he was premature. Then the man's whole weight fell on her, motionless.

A second later the weight of his body was pulled from her. His body fell beside her. Kathy saw a baseball bat arc downward for another shuddering blow. Kathy cringed for the blow, she curled to the side covering her head, but the blow fell only on the body of the man at her side.

A flashlight clicked on in the alley. Kathy could now see that the bat wielder was the young Korean man. Another young oriental was with him. He reached out to help Kathy to her feet. Kathy uncoiled from her fetal position. She could barely stand. She was shaking and sobbing. For the second time in ten minutes, the young man pulled her to her feet.

Kathy stood up on her own and then realized her pants were open. The men in the alley turned to give her privacy and she buttoned up, her hands shaking as she did. Her sobs kept her from catching her breath fully.

The young man bent to pick up Kathy's purse, which he gave her. He spoke, "When you left, we saw him follow on the other side of the street. So, we followed and ..."

Kathy found that she could not answer; she was quivering, her teeth chattering with fear, shock and sobs.

The man put his arm around her. "You'll spend the night with our family. It isn't safe out here." It was an order, not an offer.

Kathy did not argue, this time.

The other young Korean with the flashlight went over and kicked the drunk in the ribs. He did not move. They left him in the alley.

Kathy thought she felt an aftershock as she walked with the men back down Vermont toward the lights and fire on Olympic. Nevertheless, no one else seemed to notice, so she assumed it was her legs shaking. Kathy clutched her purse and then she noticed that she did not have her clothes bag anymore. It was back in the alley. She did not mention it to her rescuers. Her business suit and heels did not seem very important anymore.

■

In disaster planning documents distributed to California public agencies by the state, the local governments are warned that they may not receive significant outside assistance in case of a major quake for up to seventy-two hours. After the 1994 Northridge quake, some areas were without power for several days. If generation and transmission facilities are also damaged, electrical power restoration could take weeks. Most power generation and major electrical transformer stations in southern California are located in areas deemed to be significant danger areas for liquefaction damage from quakes.

May 6th 7:15 P.M.

LAPD Officer Alisha Walker rode on the running board of the Kenworth truck. Barry first saw it as the truck turned from southbound Vermont and waited for the crowd at the south entrance of the hospital to part and let the truck through. Alisha had waved to Barry as the truck drove in, heading for the utility building in the back parking lot.

By the time Barry walked back to where the generators were, John Holmdahl had a garden hose in the Kenworth's saddle tank siphoning the fuel out into a red plastic container. The truck driver was talking when Barry came up behind Alisha.

"... 'bout thirty gallons each side, but they ain't but half full. I been sitting in that god-damned traffic for six hours." The burly black man had a heavy, southern accent, but the sign on the Kenworth's door said "Hank Mitchum Trucking, Arcadia, California." The truck had a short bed stake trailer with rolls of fencing wire on it.

"If we can get thirty gallons from them, it will give us another hour." Holmdahl said.

"Well, if you leave me something to run on, I'd be glad to go out and rustle up some more fuel. There's got to be somebody with diesel around here. The truck plaza over in north Torrance on the 405 for sure does."

"But maybe they don't have power to pump it out," Alisha said.

"Then you gotta make do. That's all. Gotta make do," the truck driver said, scratching his chin.

A sound of an explosion came from the east. Everyone standing at the utility building turned to see a fireball rising in the air beyond Vermont, from somewhere over on the far side of the Harbor Freeway.

"Bet that's the gas station on Figueroa," the truck driver guessed. Nobody disagreed.

■

"Any suggestions?" Sybil Perkins asked.

"No, if Highway 2 is closed to Tijuana, we are pretty much cut off," Esteban Lopez said.

"Well, it certainly doesn't look good from here."

Sybil and Esteban sat, parked at the side of the Mexican highway, watching traffic ahead of them turning around to head back east. In the dark, they could see nothing of the road ahead.

"What is up ahead? What could be causing the problem?" Sybil asked.

"Oh, that's easy. What is causing the problem? A bad road, full of sharp turns, that climbs into the mountains. At best of times, with no quake, it is, ah, how to say, a real experience. Often people cross the border, those that can cross the border, into the U.S. just to use the

American Interstate 8 to drive over to San Diego and then down into Mexico again, to get to Tijuana. Now, after a quake like that ..."

"Yes, I get the picture." Sybil Perkins let her frustration show in her voice. "What else can we do?"

"Well, we certainly cannot go east, the water does not look like it is going to stop. And if my guess is correct, the water is cutting right across the delta, so you can't go south around it. If they can't open this up," he gestured ahead, at the mountain road out in the darkness, "then we are cut off, from everything."

"Great. And I suppose there's no way to get across into the U.S."

"Not legally, and not by car."

"Any place we can find a motel?"

Esteban Lopez thought for a long moment, and then he spoke. "The only place we are not cut off from is San Felipe, on the coast. It is probably ninety kilometers south and you know what that road was like just down to the mud volcanoes. I am not sure if this car would make that journey."

"Great. Just great. Biggest geologic event in my lifetime, and I'm marooned in the desert. No radio. No place to sleep."

"It could be worse."

"How?"

"If, as I said, my guess is correct, about the delta settling and the ocean coming in, it would seem quite possible that my home in south Mexicali is being washed away in that flood. A little delay in getting news of the earthquake does not seem that important to me."

Sybil Perkins had nothing to say.

■

In May 1970, a 7.8 earthquake hit the Peruvian cities of Chimbote and Yungay. The initial earthquake killed only a few hundred people, but a landslide which swept through the mountain valley a few minutes after the quake wiped out, quite literally, entire cities. Between sixty and seventy thousand dead were estimated.

May 6th 8:45 P.M.

The lights of the hospital dimmed to yellow then blinked out. It was, of course, not unexpected, just unfortunate.

Barry Warden had appointed a `posse' of six men from the waiting crowd to take over maintaining the crowd perimeter on the south side of the hospital. With the potential shutdown of the hospital looming, Barry had been trying to concentrate on what should be done to keep the crippled hospital functioning and what, God forbid, should be done if they were forced to close down.

The fuel siphoned from the one Kenworth truck had kept the generators running almost an hour.

A city that had been hit with multiple petroleum tank fires was not a good place to find extra diesel fuel. Besides, with the traffic jams that clogged every street, there was no way to get the fuel to the hospital if they had found some. Unfortunately, all of the jammed up vehicles were autos, more diesel trucks like the one Alisha had found were not to be seen. Professional truckers knew enough to keep off the streets at such times.

Anticipating the loss of power, Barry had gone out to the Explorer and traded his nightstick for the big metal police flashlight. It was just as effective a weapon and the light was going to be needed. He had pulled the Explorer in closer to the hospital, near the rear entrance loading dock, and parked it.

He had just checked on his `posse' at the checkpoint and was heading back through the main hallway of the hospital when the lights went out. The group of six men in the posse was down to four, the two others had found out that their injured relatives had died so they had left. The crowd outside was still getting bigger, milling restlessly in the smoke filled night.

Dr. Frames had already announced, using Barry's battery powered bullhorn, that they were, indeed, not going to be taking any new patients. It would be hard with all the additional injured who arrived constantly, but they were packed, without staff or supplies to handle any more. Now they would be turning away people and those they had would be treated in the dark until morning.

It would be tough, and certain to be the cause of many a heated argument at the entrances. Americans were used to top medical care and immediately available care. In the aftermath of the quakes today, they were not getting either.

Picking his way through the hospital hallway now, Barry could see that the decision had been the only one possible. Bodies lined the hall, every spare inch was being used. Somber figures in white crouched over the injured patients. Teams with stretchers moved through a hospital lit only with the emergency lanterns by the exits and a few flashlights. Most of the light came from the windows, the reflected light from the traffic and the fires that now seemed close on the other side of the Harbor Freeway. Moans and cries echoed in the hall.

The thought that everyone who had been admitted was one of

the critical life and death cases made things more stark. Everyone who lay in the hall had been determined to be a savable life, under normal hospital situations. But, they did not have a normal situation. They had lost the lights needed for surgery, sterilization and x-rays. The great teaching hospital had become a warehouse of the injured and dying.

"Could you shine that light over here?" A voice from an alcove off of the main hall asked. Barry stepped over several people to get close enough to light up the alcove.

A doctor was kneeling on the floor next to someone. Barry saw that it was Dr. Morrissey, the doctor who had spoken out about getting help at the staff meeting. The doctor pointed at the person's head. "Up here."

Barry flashed his light on the patient's face. It was a young black boy, maybe twelve. Looking closer at the face the doctor wearily shook his head and passed his hand down over the boy's face, closing the dead eyes.

"Thanks," the Morrissey said softly, motioning Barry to go on.

■

In October 1995, scientists disclosed that they had discovered what was probably a new fault, running from the San Andreas near Wrightwood under the San Gabriel Mountains to the Los Angeles suburb of Azusa and perhaps beyond. The survey which found the new fault used sonic air explosions to try and map unknown faults, such as the previously unknown fault that caused $20 Billion in damages and 61 deaths in January 1994.

May 6th, 8:50 P.M.

Kathy Warden had barely been able to see the face of the old oriental woman who had presented Kathy with the paper cup of soup, a matching cup of coffee and a large chunk of bread. The flickering light cast by the four candles in the large room did not shed enough light to identify the chunks she had found in the soup. She recognized the cubes as tofu and the slender noodles, but she could only hope that the amorphous blobs of slippery material were pouched egg. However, the soup stock was obviously based on chicken broth, it was hot, tasty, and Kathy had not eaten in over twelve hours. She emptied the cup quickly.

The young Korean man, he had introduced himself as James Kim, had taken her from the alley back to the vicinity of the brick pile were the drunk had tripped her. There, after a conversation in Korean with the other men gathered there, James Kim had escorted her back across a vacant lot to the single story wood frame building she now found herself in. The building seemed to be a factory or workshop. Of fairly new construction, it had obviously been selected by the neighboring Korean families as the safest place to wait out the aftershocks. The brick pile the drunk had tripped her on was the remains of a brick building of the type that predominated in this neighborhood.

James Kim had shown Kathy to a corner by a work table. A young boy had run over and presented Kathy with a blanket and run off. Kim had left her there and gone back outside.

There were probably twenty to thirty people in the building which consisted of the one big room and another smaller room in the corner. They sat in several groups. Some children already tried to sleep on the floor. The adults talked softly together. Kathy could not make out anything that was said. Kathy noticed that several prone figures were laying in the far corner. Women knelt next to these prone figures, tending to them. Kathy saw people coming and going from the building. The population of the building grew slowly as the evening wore on.

A radio was playing in the room in the other corner. Occasionally people from the various groups would get up and go to where the radio was. Kathy thought vaguely of going over to hear the radio, too, but the trauma of the alley and earlier in the day had left her with little curiosity and no gumption to join the circle of strangers around the radio. Kathy Warden wrapped herself in the blanket and curled up in the corner next to the workbench.

One of the blanket-cloaked figures returning from the radio walked over in front of Kathy and stopped. A young woman's voice spoke, "Mind if I join you?"

Kathy looked up, unable to see the speaker's face, "No, feel free."

Kathy straightened up, moving closer to the bench to make room for the young woman in the space along the wall. The young woman put a hand out on the next bench down and swung herself to the floor next to Kathy rather clumsily.

The woman's blanket pulled down as she sat, revealing that she was breast-feeding a baby. The young woman pulled the blanket back in place, settled back against the wall and put her hand out to Kathy. "Hi, I'm Sally, Sally Kim."

Kathy reached forward to shake the offered hand. A twinge of pain in her shoulder showed on her face as she spoke. "Kathy Warden."

"You're hurt."

"No, not bad. Just a collection of bumps and bruises. It's been quite a day."

"Yeh, for sure." Sally spoke with a slight "Valley girl" accent like Kathy herself had affected in high school. Now, in the candle light Kathy could see that the young mother could be no more than twenty, probably less.

"Jim told me what happened in the alley. You gonna be OK? Need to talk it out?" The girl said, shifting the baby to the other nipple.

"No. Fortunately he, ah, James, got there in time. Nothing, ah, bad really happened."

"Yeh. Well you were lucky."

"Sally? Is James your ... are you related? You know, same name."

The girl laughed. "Yes. But the name wouldn't help you know that. Most of the people in this building are Kims, or related to them. `Kim' is like `Smith' to Koreans. Especially with Korean-Americans in LA. James, ahh, Jim, is my cousin by marriage, his aunt is my mother-in-law. Or, you know, his father is my husband's uncle. Whatever."

"Oh." Kathy paused a moment, not really sure if she wanted to continue the conversation. She decided she did. "What's the news on the radio?"

"Not a whole lot new. None of the main L.A., ya know, the regular stations are broadcasting still. They've got a Korean station from

Orange County on now. That's why I left. I don't speak Korean very well. Mostly just enough to understand what Mom said when she got mad at us kids. But, they had a news station from San Diego up a little while ago that was pretty good."

"Tell me. I haven't heard anything about what happened. Just what I've seen on the streets downtown."

"Oh. Well, they say the big one, the first quake was out in San Bernardino. An eight point three. Then I guess two big quakes hit LA, besides the little aftershocks. Seven something. Both here, downtown, and out in Culver City or maybe Century City, I forget. You saw the buildings downtown, huh? Ah, the freeways are dead meat. Lots of fires. They say the National Guard is coming in, and federal troops, too. The San Diego station had a story about the Marines from Pendleton having to fly up because the nuclear plant at Capistrano was leaking or something and the 5 Freeway wasn't safe.

"Wow. I thought they closed the nuclear plant down there."

Sally shrugged as she pulled the baby from her breast and cuddled it in her arms, rocking side to side. She continued. "Ah, let's see ... Oh yeh, real big explosion in Long Beach. Chemical plant or something. Lots of people dead and ..."

The girl's news story stopped as a quiver of movement rose up through the floor. The aftershock lasted only a few seconds, but enough for Kathy's adrenaline to jump. She had not been inside before this aftershock. Visions of all the wrecked buildings crossed her mind as the aftershock shook sawdust from the workbench before it ended.

"How old is your baby?" Kathy asked, hoping to fill the silence left by the quake.

"Three months."

"Boy or girl?"

"Boy. Yeh, just three months and already he has saved his Mommy's life." Sally cooed, snuggling the baby closer.

"What do you mean?"

"Today. I had just come back from the store, after the first quake I thought I would stock up. Had him in his car seat and thought I would leave him there while I carried the groceries into the house. He saw me close the car door and let out a squeal, really loud, wouldn't let me leave him. I went back to the car to get him. Just then the bad quake hit, flattened the apartment building. If I hadn't gone back to the car, I woulda been dead."

"Gee. And you lost your house, ah, apartment?"

"Yup. Everything."

"But, your family's alright, though."

"Yeh, I guess. Me and the baby. My husband works in Commerce." Sally's voice cracked as she finished. "We haven't heard from him." She put her head back against the wall and sniffed, wiping away a tear.

"I haven't heard anything from my husband either. He is down in South Bay. At least I think he is. He's a cop. Deputy Sheriff."

"He's probably OK."

"Yes, I hope."

Thoughts of missing husbands quieted both of the young women.

They waited in the dark, listening to a far-off siren that finally stopped. The radio in the corner room had been shut off, the occupants of the workshop were getting ready to try to sleep.

The silence of the workshop building was broken by a blast

outside. Then another identical blast followed.

"Gunshot?" Kathy said.

"Shotgun, I think." Sally said. "My guess is that Jim's vigilantes found themselves a looter."

■

In the area-wide electrical outage that followed the Northridge quake, Santa Barbara residents found that only two service stations in the whole city had portable generators with which to power the gas pumps.

May 6th, 10:10 P.M.

"Officer?"

Barry turned to the voice. He was standing by the Explorer behind the main hospital with Jamil Allen, who also turned.

A hospital worker in a white smock ran up behind them. They could just barely make out his face in the light cast by the fires in the overcast sky.

"Yes. What's up?"

"Dr. Milborn said to tell you. We think someone is in the temporary morgue in the garage, they're a ... rummaging, picking the pockets of the, ah, the dead people, the corpses. We thought it might be best to tell you. It is all dark back there. You know, we , ah ... "

"Right. Got it. Be right there."

As the hospital worker left, Barry turned to Jamil. "Well, you been out to the morgue, yet?"

"No. I thought I would avoid that pleasure if at all possible, but it looks like that won't work. Huh?"

"Nope. You think we need to wake Alisha?" Barry said as they walked across the main drive toward the parking garage.

"Nah. Let her sleep, she'll get her turn later. You take the south entrance, I'll go in the front." Jamil Allen said, pointing to the nearest entrance to the two-story parking building. "Lets keep our lights off until we see something. No use letting 'em know were coming"

Barry joined Jamil Allen in clicking off the flashlights.

The temporary morgue was in the lower level of the parking garage. The darkened structure had only minimal light coming from the outside. Twenty feet down the ramp, Barry regretted agreeing to keeping the flashlights off.

He waited at the bottom of the ramp, trying to adjust to the total darkness. Barry's heart pounded, entering a dark building, knowing it to be full of dead bodies, knowing that somewhere the `perps' might be waiting. Yes, his heart was pounding.

He could now make out the outlines of the few cars on the level. The parking structure was designed on two levels with each level sloping up and down on the left and right so as to allow access to either level from the ground level drives. Jamil would be coming in on the lower level, Barry was at the top of a section leading down toward where Jamil was.

As his eyes adjusted to the light, Barry could see the occupants of the building. Row upon row of bodies, carefully lined up along the east wall. Hundreds of bodies. Barry had been watching the stretcher bearers come and go for hours now, but he had not envisioned this scene.

He had little time to think about the dead. He heard the scuffling on feet echo in the lower level.

"Stop. Police!" He heard Jamil's voice boom from below to the right.

The sound of running feet escalated with the shout. Barry estimated three or four persons were running up the ramp toward him. Following his training, he held the flashlight out at arms-length to his left, so that anyone shooting at the flashlight when he turned it on would not be shooting directly at him. His 9mm pistol nestled in his right hand, Barry waited until the sounds of running feet were forty feet ahead of him. He turned on the flashlight and shouted, "Halt! Police!"

Three youths skidded to a stop on the ramp ahead of him. One of them, closest to the row of cars of the left, dove between to cars and Barry could hear him jump over a car's hood. Barry resisted the temptation of moving the flashlight over to the left to follow the escapee. He kept the light on the other two, shouting again, "Don't move! Hands up!"

Jamil ran up the ramp behind their quarry, gun drawn. Barry walked in closer. Jamil had his flashlight trained on the two youths, also. Barry could see that they were two black kids, maybe sixteen years old. The boys were clad in identical black plaid hooded sweatshirts. Gang colors.

"Over to the pillar. Slowly." Jamil said. A cement pillar stood ten feet to the right. The boys shuffled over.

"We didn't ..."

"Shut up!. You talk when we say. Spread 'em and reach high on the pillar. Other side, you."

The boys followed Jamil's order and stretched their arms high on the concrete pillar. Jamil sat his light on the ground, but aimed at the pillar and the perps. He moved in to frisk them with his empty hand.

The sound of running feet echoed in the parking structure. The third kid was making his getaway.

Moving quickly up and down legs and torso, Jamil found no weapons, but from each boy he took three or four wallets from the sweatshirt pockets.

"A little robbing from the dead, huh?"

"Hey, man. We ..."

Jamil cut the boy's comment short with a pistol in the ribs. "I said shut up. You ain't in no place to yap."

The boy dropped his head.

Jamil continued, "Jesus Christ, how fucking low can scum go. Robbing the corpses in a morgue. That's sick."

Jamil kicked the wallets into a pile on the cement floor and walked a circle around the pillar. One boy followed him with his gaze.

"What you looking at?" Jamil shouted. "You keep your fucking grave-robbing eyes on the ground." He continued to pace around the pillar, stopping to ask Barry, "Well, deputy, what do you think we should do with these little bastards."

Barry understood the tone of Jamil Allen's voice and he answered, "Not really sure. It's a bad night to take them all the way to Metro."

"Yeh. I got an idea. Over here by the wall." Jamil motioned toward the east wall, near the end of the line of corpses. The boys pulled their hands off the column and walked slowly to the wall, looking around warily.

When they reached the wall Jamil shouted again. "OK, drop! On the ground!"

One of the boys turned to Jamil and started to speak, "Hey, what's the ..." He stopped when faced with the police officer's gun planted in his cheek.

"I said `On the floor.`" Jamil's voice growled.

The boys started to kneel, Jamil pushed the nearest in the butt with his heel, knocking him to the floor. "OK, now roll over on your backs. Next to the others." The boys were now almost in line with the corpses along the wall.

"You can't ... What's the ..."

"I said `shut up.'" Jamil again made his point by gesturing with the gun. The boy was quiet, rolling over next to his comrade.

"I've been on the force a long time and seen some real scum, but I never saw anything like you bastards who break into a morgue and rob the dead. How'd you feel? Shit, I ain't never been so fucking mad." Jamil now fumed in sanctimonious anger. "There's only one thing to do with your kind. Deputy, you sure you want to watch this."

"Sure, why not. But first, make 'em put there hands across their chests, like the other stiffs."

"Hey, you can't ..."

"Why the fuck, can't I?" Jamil shouted, raging mad. "We got a thousand dead people in here. You think someone's going to do an autopsy to see how you two scum died. You trust your buddy to tell where he was tonight? You think anyone cares how two grave-robbing punks wound up in here?"

One boy was now in tears, blubbering. The other stared, his eyes round in the light from the flashlight. Barry could see the boy's jaw quivering.

It was Barry's turn. "Hey, you know, I'm not really sure we should do it like this. In here. It's too close to the hospital. All the injured people. The noise."

Jamil followed the lead. "You're right. On your feet. We'll take them out to the back fence. That'd be better."

"Please, man. I'm sorry. You can't ..." the blubbering one cried.

It was Barry's turn again, "Maybe we ought to give 'em another chance. Maybe ..."

Both boys saw the opportunity and started pleading at once, "Yeh, let us go."

"Jesus, please."

"Well, maybe ..." Jamil paused, apparently considering his course of action.

Barry stepped forward, motioning toward the ramp, "You two, or your friends, set foot at this hospital again, you're history. You got it?"

"Yess, officer. We're gone."

"Thanks."

Both boys were running so fast they tripped each other up and they slid on the cement floor near the up ramp. They were up the ramp and out of sight in a few seconds.

Barry looked at Jamil. A broad smile creased Jamil's face. Both men burst into laughter, stopping quickly as they realized where they were, in an improptu morgue.

Jamil took the stolen wallets from the floor and stacked them on the chest of the nearest corpse. He joined Barry walking toward the ramp.

"You know, you did a pretty good job acting. I almost believed you myself," Barry said.

Jamil Allen put his hand on Barry's shoulder. "Well, Deputy. there's a funny thing about that. I tried out for a part in Othello in high school. Over at Centennial High."

"Yes, and ..."

"The drama teacher offered me a spot on the stage crew, painting sets. I never have been able to act."

They were at the top of the parking ramp, ready to cross over to the hospital when they heard the honk of the Kenworth's air horn. It was turning in the entrance, heading toward them. The two peace officers waited in the driveway for the truck to pass and followed it at a trot.

The Kenworth pulled to a stop by the utility building. Barry and Jamil ran over and were waiting when the driver cut the engine and dismounted. Barry shined the flashlight between the stacks of the truck to see a half dozen fifty-five gallon barrels had replaced the rolls of wire he had seen earlier. He saw the label "#2 Diesel" on each barrel.

Hank Mitchum was grinning from ear to ear. Holmdahl and two of his custodians had come out of the utility building, too.

"Fuel? Where'd you get it?" Barry asked.

Hank Mitchum raised his eyebrows and looked at Barry. "Well, Officer... Deputy, isn't it? My guess is that you'd be happier not knowing the answer to that question?"

Barry nodded knowingly, "Forget I even asked."

Twelve minutes later Holmdahl threw the switch and Harbor UCLA Medical Center lit up.

∎

On Saturday morning, May 21, 1960, an earthquake measuring 7.7 on the Richter scale hit southern Chile. A half hour later another 7.7 quake hit the same area. These two temblors, while on the scale of great quakes in their own right are generally considered to be only foreshocks for the events of the next day. On Sunday afternoon, May 22nd, within the period of seventeen minutes three massive quakes, measuring 7.8, 7.8 and 9.0+ on the Richter Scale hit on faults close to the fault which had released the previous day's quakes. This "swarm" of great quakes, culminating the strongest quake ever recorded, are considered clear evidence that great quakes on adjoining faults can trigger one another, given the right circumstances.

May 7th, 12:14 A.M.

The clunk of the front door bolt closing woke her. Gloria Contreras had fallen asleep on top of the bed covers, still wearing her robe and slippers. Something had kept her from getting fully into bed until she knew about Matt.

She got up. As she walked down the dark hallway, Gloria heard Matt bump into something, rather hard. A softly muttered curse followed.

They met in the kitchen where Matt was taking off his muddy boots. Without saying anything they embraced. After a long moment Matt spoke.

"So, how was your day?" The flippant tone of voice Matt used to try and make the question humorous did not cover the fact that his voice sounded dog-tired.

Gloria tried to match his attempted humor with mock sarcasm, "You're late!"

Matt let out a breathy "Ha. Ha." They gave one last squeeze to their hug.

Gloria pulled away and snapped on the little battery powered fluorescent trouble light she had set on the counter. Matt commented, "Looks like you've got things pretty well organized."

"Yeh. I stripped all of Miranda's toys for batteries. You want something to eat? Where'd you get muddy feet?"

"It's a long story."

"Oh. Well. You wanna eat? Or do you just want to sit and talk?"

"Both. But first, I need to go to the bathroom. Bad." He turned to go down the hall.

"Whoa. Wait. Take the bucket." Gloria put out an arm to stop him from leaving and reached for a pail on the counter next to the light.

"Bucket?"

"Yes," she handed him the plastic mop pail, half full of water. "No running water. You need this to flush. It is from Miranda's wading pool. There is a two liter bottle of water from the water heater on the sink, if you need to wash or brush your teeth."

"Wow. Little Miss Preparedness, aren't you."

"I try." Gloria said, using one of Matt's favorite lines.

Gloria made Matt a sandwich. The meat and mayonnaise from the fridge were now fully warm. She would have to sort things out in the morning. Some foodstuffs would save for a while, some would not and would have to be eaten right away, or thrown out.

Matt came back in. He was now only in his undershirt and boxers, the CHP uniform had been shed.

Matt said, "I checked in on the kids. And, I couldn't help noticing that our population of little girls seems to have doubled."

"The Seligman's never came home. Jessica was all alone. So ..."

Matt already had his mouth full of sandwich, so he just nodded his understanding.

Gloria picked up the trouble light and motioned to Matt, "You need this to eat? We should save the batteries."

Matt shook his head `No.'

Gloria switched it off and sat down next to her husband in the dark. They had a lot to talk about. She started.

"Guess what I was doing when the Big One hit?"

For Californians, the phrase would soon replace the old question, "Where were you when 9/11 happened?" as a lead-in for nostalgic conversation.

■

The restoration of electricity to the Harbor UCLA Medical Center was, like many blessings, a mixed one. While the hospital was still remained a blackened, damaged hulk, the gathering crowd of injured and those who had pulled the injured from the earthquake's rubble and carried them to the hospital had begrudgingly accepted the excuse that the hospital was full and no one could be admitted when the hospital had no power to treat patients.

Now, with power restored from the emergency generators, the hospital stood out. With the only electric lights for miles around the ten-story hospital stood as a beacon, a beacon of hope to a million residents in the blacked-out city. In the broad flat basin of southern

Los Angeles the only lights in the night sky came from this building or from the fires that still raged in the area of the great gas explosion toward Long Beach and elsewhere.

Word spread from those who did not really know the facts, that at Harbor UCLA you could get help for the broken bones, burns, concussions and the panoply of injuries the huge quake had caused. Even emergency crews, after laboring hours to free trapped victims, would load those victims on ambulances and paramedic vehicles for transport to a hospital that was already bursting at the seams. What else could be done?

Barry covered his ears as the bullhorn squealed. Officer Jamil Allen took the bullhorn down and adjusted the volume wheel before trying again. "Please stay on the far side of the paved street. We have to keep the street open. We will get to everyone in turn. Please stay back."

Taking the bullhorn down, Jamil muttered over his shoulder to Barry, "This is fucking hopeless. Nobody's going to listen."

"What choice? They've got to."

Jamil shook his head and spoke again into the bullhorn. "The hospital can only treat critical cases at the present time. Additional help should be coming soon. If you have what you feel is a critical injury, go to the checkpoint at the rear or front entrance of the main building. If you have been asked to wait, please wait on the far side of the street."

Barry saw that those in the throng on the street that Jamil had been talking to were unable to move back. The crowd behind was pushing too far forward.

Jamil turned to him again. "This isn't going to work. There is just too many. It's only going to take one hothead, one rowdy group to set the rest of these poor bastards off. This is gonna blow."

"Yeh. It's surprising it hasn't already." Barry looked out into the crowd. He had no idea how far back it went. They had managed to clear the waiting crowd out of the eastern end of the sprawling hospital ground, but there were thousands waiting in the west, across the main drive. The huge hospital complex stretched for a quarter mile beyond the main building, filled with old Army barracks converted to student housing and classrooms, and several auxiliary buildings. From what Barry could see, much of the complex was filled with the waiting crowd. "Hank Mitchum said they were triple parked way back five blocks on Carson and that was two hours ago. It's just getting worse."

"And no reason for it to get better anytime soon."

Barry pulled the radio from his belt. "Let's see if they've got any magic ideas yet, " he said to Jamil.

"Yes, and like maybe some back-up. They can't all be in this bad a spot. Can they?"

"God knows." Barry adjusted the squelch on the little radio and keyed it on. "Dispatch this is Sheriff Four-four. Over."

"Roger, Four-four. Over" Barry was somewhat surprised to hear Corcoran still on the radio, Barry had not been paying much attention to the radio's message traffic for some time. The Torrance chief was obviously staying on shift as long as his field officers were.

"This is Four-four. Chief, I know we have said this earlier tonight. It is the opinion of the officers here at Harbor that the situation is ready to get totally out of hand. We have a crowd of thousands waiting. The hospital is full, they can't even treat the critical cases they already have. They started taking a few new cases, the bad ones they think they can help, but we've got thousands of people in the streets who can't get help. It's a powder keg. Over."

"Roger. We understand. We will try to convey the seriousness of your situation on up the chain. We will dispatch two cars, I think they're gonna be city staff vehicles, not black and whites. We've got six or eight reserve officers and POST cadets, who we can send for crowd control. That's the best we can promise from here. But, we definitely will convey your problem to County Emergency HQ. We've already heard the Hospital Administrator there at Harbor on the County Emergency Ops circuit begging for help. They know downtown that you need help, but ..."

The Torrance chief did not finish his sentence.

Barry finished, "Roger, Four-four, Out."

Jamil had been listening. "Cripes, reserve cops and cadets? That's our back-up?"

"Well, it's better than nothing."

"Oh, really. I'm not sure I want a trainee or a trigger-happy do-gooder reservist who only puts the uniform on for July 4th standing between my back and that crowd there." Jamil flung his arm out toward the masses waiting to the west to emphasize his point.

Jamil Allen had just finished his gesture when a flood of light came from a building two blocks west in the hospital complex.

"Looks like the Public Works guys got the power line rigged to the Professional Building," Barry said. "Holmdahl said they were trying."

"So what's the plan for that building?"

"More of the same. The E.R. doc said they have X-rays and stuff over there. You know, medical offices, waiting rooms."

"Oh, great, waiting rooms. They don't have enough doctors or nurses to treat what they have now. But now we got waiting rooms. What's next? They want us to go through that crowd with one of them little number machines, giving out numbers and telling them to sit in the waiting rooms?"

Barry did not answer Jamil's remark, they were both turning toward the sound of an altercation near the rear checkpoint. Someone was shouting. Barry and Jamil both headed for the checkpoint, but Jamil stopped when he saw the crowd react to the altercation by milling forward.

"You check it out, I'll try to hold the crowd back," Jamil Said to Barry as he turned to face the crowd with his bullhorn. They were already milling forward, gawking at the developing problem.

Barry ran toward the checkpoint. He could see several people in white coats facing someone carrying a body. The figure with the body in its arms turned to face Barry on his approach from the side. Barry could see that Dr. Morrissey was one of those facing the figure.

The figure was a husky man of thirty-five or so. He had longish blond hair and was wearing shorts, thongs and a sleeveless tank top. He was well-tanned and muscled. In his arms was the body of a young girl, without clothes and covered in a chalk-white covering of dust. In the man's right hand was a chrome-plated revolver.

"Whoa, far enough." The man turned the gun on Barry, who had his own weapon in his hand.

Before Barry could say anything he heard the sound of the bullhorn squeal behind him and Jamil exhorting the crowd back across the road.

Barry spoke, "Put the gun down. That's not going to solve any-thing."

"You bet it is. Don't play no piss ant games with me. This is all that's left of my life here. My daughter. I just pulled her mother and her out of our house. My wife is dead. I'm not gonna let no fucking bureaucrat tell me to wait while my daughter dies, too. Somebody's gonna help her right now, or else. You got it." The man looked quickly between Barry and Dr. Morrissey who stood closest. "If my daughter dies, too, I don't have any reason to live. I'll use this if I have to."

Morrissey started to speak, but Barry motioned him back, "Look, mister, the gun is not going to work for you here. You use it and I'll use mine. That isn't going to help your little girl."

"Neither is waiting for this asshole," he pointed the gun hand toward a paramedic at the checkpoint, "to let her die across the street."

Barry nodded and gestured with his gun, "OK, look, we've got ourselves a standoff here. It isn't helping anyone. Why don't you give me the gun and we'll promise to do everything we can for the girl, your daughter."

"Nah. I keep the gun until she gets the help."

"Huh-uh! Not a chance."

Dr. Morrissey cut in, "I and my people don't treat patients with guns at our backs. You might as well shoot me now and see how that helps her."

"Why should I trust you?"

Morrissey said, "Why? ... Because that's all you can do. Because it's my duty. Because it's the only hope your daughter has."

The man looked at Barry and then back to Morrissey. He said nothing, but dipped his head to show his acquiescence, his bravado was running out.

"Bring a gurney, " Morrissey shouted over his shoulder.

The man shifted his grip on the pistol grip, holding it so Barry could grab it.

The gurney arrived and the man laid his daughter on it. He gently stroked the girl's head as she was rolled off toward the building. The man turned to Barry.

"What now? Am I under arrest?"

"Put your hands behind your head and walk," Barry motioned the man back towards the back of the building. When they had rounded the back corner, walking out of sight of most of the waiting crowd, Barry said, "Stop. This is good enough."

"So?"

"So, you just assaulted a police officer with a deadly weapon. You know that's worth a prison sentence right?"

"I guess so. Right."

"Well, I wanted to get you over here so the rest of the crowd doesn't get any ideas about mimicking what you did. That could have gotten really ugly out there. You know that?"

"Yeh."

"Well, my part of the bargain you made with the doctor is that I won't arrest you, if you promise to sit right here, out of sight and wait to hear about your daughter." Barry indicated a cement wall by the hospital loading dock, "I don't want that crowd to know that they can get by with doing something like that and getting away with it."

The man blinked at Barry, not believing what he heard, "Why aren't you arresting me? I mean, not that I want it."

"Why? Because I've got only one set of hand-cuffs, no way to get you to a jail, no back-up, no time for the paperwork, and ... Frankly, because I probably would have done something the same as you did, if I had to. And, I've got bigger problems than one poor S.O.B. trying to save his kid's life. I have to worry about the ten thousand others out there."

"Do I get my gun back?"

"Don't push it."

Barry turned his back on the man, who sat quietly on the loading dock. Barry decided to let Jamil know how things had concluded and then make a circuit along the north side of the hospital, maybe check out how the big intersection at the northwest corner of the hospital complex, Carson and Vermont, was doing. He could still hear the honks from the crowded intersection and possibly from the other one just beyond that went to the Harbor Freeway, but maybe things were easing up in the middle of the night.

Barry walked back to where Jamil stood near the street. He holstered his own service pistol and pulled the cylinder catch on the chrome revolver he had taken from the man. It was an expensive collector's model Colt .44 with engraved scrollwork. The six cartridges fell out in Barry's hand. The bullet casings were also chrome plated, magnum loads. The bullet tips were slit-jacketed hollow points. Not illegal, but so deadly that cops were forbidden to use such a load in service weapons. The weapon that the guy sitting back on the loading dock had drawn down on Barry with was not a Saturday night special. It was a rich man's weapon. A weapon designed to kill, rather than wound. It made Barry wonder if he had made the right decision in letting the guy go. For a brief moment, Barry was as incredulous at his own decision as the man had been. He pocketed the bullets, realizing as he did the he still had the earrings he had purchased for Kathy in his trouser pocket. He had not noticed the lump all night. He wondered when he would get to give the gift to her and where she was. At home? He hoped.

■

Two hundred twenty blocks north on Vermont, Barry's wife was spending a fitful, uncomfortable night. The single blanket on a hard floor, the closeness of strangers sleeping in an unfamiliar place and the repeated murmurs of small aftershocks left Kathy Warden to toss and turn, alone with thoughts, worries and fears. She tried to plan what she would do in the morning, but, other than keep walking toward home, she had no idea of what she should do.

Memories of the alley kept intruding in Kathy's mind. Vivid memories of the attack, the revulsion, the fear, and the reeking smell of the man's breath as he tried to violate her. Kathy kept trying to sweep the memories from her mind, but the only thoughts she had to replace it with were those of the destruction she had seen that day.

Even when Kathy was able to drift into a short bit of sleep, she was soon roused by a dream or memory of explosion, or quake, or the movement of those sleeping nearby. People who, like her, struggled with blankets and nightmares.

The unanswered questions that careened through Kathy's mind were even harder to deal with than the fearful memories. She knew nothing of Barry; or her family, Cindy, her parents. What about her home, she had seen enough destruction across the many blocks of downtown Los Angeles to feel that her own home out west might be lost, too. She realized that the town home itself really meant nothing. What little she and Barry owned could be replaced, easily. She started to think that maybe her quest to walk west to her home was not the highest priority.

Barry. She wanted to see Barry.

Where would Barry be? How would he try to reach her? If she was not at home, he could not reach her. Maybe she could reach him. How do you contact a deputy sheriff, during an emergency? Who would know where Barry was?

At length, it was this thought that Kathy Warden found to occupy her mind, until real sleep finally came to her. Kathy decided to concentrate on getting in touch with Barry. Whatever it took, she would get to Barry. The thought that he might not have survived the quake was rejected. Kathy knew Barry was alive she just needed to find him. She could not let herself think anything else.

◼

Genevieve Dumont had no problem sleeping. The guest room at the Weld home, Natalie called it the "garden room," was spacious and comfortable. Natalie Weld had come up with a loan of sleeping apparel to rival Genevieve's own. Genevieve's objections to staying the night had been rejected by Natalie Weld, "Of course, you will stay. I'll not hear of anything else." Genevieve did not argue too stridently on this, for it was clear that she had little alternative to being Natalie's house guest.

Nor did thoughts of the terrors of the day interrupt Genevieve Dumont's sleep. Natalie had taken care of this with the little white and pink capsule she had given Genevieve with the glass of Perrier on the nightstand, "This will help you relax."

Not only did Mrs. Weld's sedative relax Genevieve, it made her absolutely oblivious to anything for nearly twelve hours, including the moderate aftershock that woke the rest of the household at midnight.

◼

At 2:00 P.M. on the afternoon of February 4, 1975, municipal authorities in Haicheng, China ordered all buildings in the metropolis evacuated due to a prediction by local scientists that an earthquake was imminent. At 7:25 P.M. a 7.3 magnitude quake destroyed ninety percent of the buildings in the city. There was little loss of life thanks to the evacuation.

May 7th, 2:30 A.M.

The coffee from the partially functional hospital kitchen was losing its effectiveness for Barry Warden. With the arrival at one o'clock of the seven new officers, the reservists and trainees the Compton chief had sent to the hospital, Jamil had taken the opportunity to join Officer Walker who was catnapping in the staff break room in the utility building. Barry had promised to get some sleep himself, but so far had not.

The new officers were not the problem Jamil had worried about. The reservists were from the Carson city police department. Apparently, the Carson city government had been so devastated by the explosion in their city that the Carson police, like the sheriff's deputies and the LA city police in South Bay, had also been put under the emergency joint dispatch\command from Torrance.

The POST (Peace Officer Standards and Training Program) cadets actually turned out to be from Barry's own department, prospective Los Angeles Sheriff's deputies from the peace officers' academy at Compton. The reservists were armed, so Barry and Jamil had assigned them to the checkpoints, the two at the front and back of the hospital and the new one at the entrance to the professional building two blocks west. The cadets were unarmed, so Barry assigned them the task of directing traffic and trying to clear out the cluster of illegally parked cars that surrounded the hospital and getting traffic flowing again at the intersections on each corner. These were two functions that, although critical to keeping the hospital complex operating, had been ignored until now in the crush of dealing with the crowd.

Barry was sitting in the Explorer, watching two cadets do an adequate job directing traffic at Carson and Normandie at the hospital complex's far northwest corner. He had just started contemplating the loss of oomph from the last cup of coffee when he heard gunfire erupt to the east, toward the hospital. The gunfire came in two distinct groupings. The first was the quick, staccato burst that could only come from an automatic, maybe a machine pistol like a MAC-10. This was followed after a pause by multiple shots from a heavier weapon, maybe a large caliber handgun, and then another burst of automatic fire.

Barry quickly considered his course of action. He did not know what was going on at the scene he did not want to race into the field of fire. However, he knew he was the only experienced officer who was awake at the hospital.

Barry flipped on the emergency lights on the Explorer, that would be sufficient for the two blocks he needed to go to get to the hospital entrance, if that were the source of the shots fired. The radio was busy with a call from some Torrance officers to their dispatcher. Barry decided to break in.

"Break, This is Sheriff Four-Four. Multiple shots fired, vicinity of Harbor UCLA hospital, Carson and Vermont. Repeat. Shots fired. Carson and Vermont. Situation unknown. Automatic weapons fire." Barry was already approaching the entrance when he said this so he ended, "Sheriff Four-four, requesting back-up. Out."

"Roger, Four-four. Acknowledged. Out." It was no longer the Torrance Chief of Police, he had finally gone off the air.

The traffic in the two blocks between the intersection and the hospital entrance had cleared to the side as best they could for the Sheriff's vehicle, but the crowd that had been standing between Carson and the hospital entrance was now moving out into the street as Barry approached.

Just as Barry slowed to keep from hitting the crowd running into the street ahead of him, he saw a car coming through the crowd. Barry watched in shock as the car plowed through the running people, rolling them out of the way. Apparently seeing Barry's vehicle, the car swerved to the far side of the street, hitting more people and roared off toward the Normandie intersection. The screams of the crowd, those injured and scared, filled the night.

Now surrounded by the crowd, Barry could not give chase without also hitting the crowd.

Barry jerked the Explorer to a stop and keyed the radio, "This is Sheriff Four-four, unable to pursue red Chevrolet, early '80's, custom low-rider heading west on Carson, vicinity of Normandie, vehicle suspected of felony hit and run and possible weapons charges. Armed and dangerous. Request assistance. Over."

"Roger, Four-four. Torrance Patrol One-two, investigate suspect vehicle, heading west on Carson, your vicinity. Code three. Over."

Barry did not wait for any more of the radio conversation. He rolled the Explorer to a stop and got out to check on the people down in the street. In the darkened street, his emergency lights cast a strobe effect on the running people. People ran everywhere, screaming, and shouting. It was pandemonium.

Barry reached the spot where a woman writhed on the ground, her legs crushed. Another body next to her did not move.

One of the reserve cops from Carson, a middle-aged black man, ran up to him as Barry knelt next to the injured woman. Barry deferred helping the woman to a nurse who ran up also, and he stood to face the reserve cop.

"What the fuck happened?"

"Jesus, it all happened so quick. They got Harris, I think he's dead. He didn't have a chance."

"Who got Harris? Slow down and tell me." Barry assumed Harris was another of the reserve cops, he had not caught all their names.

The reserve cop, his nametag said Jefferson, was having trouble catching his breath and reporting in the chaos that filled the street at the hospital entrance. "There was some kind of fight broke out in the crowd. Shouting, sounded like all hell was about to break loose. Harris went out to see what was up. It was out by the road, where the others, the cadets were getting the cars to move. All I know is that someone fired from the car at Harris, when he was in the middle of the crowd. He did get off some rounds at them, but I think they got him when they fired the second time."

"Any idea why they fired?"

"Nope. None."

"Well, let's get things back in order, then we'll have to figure out what happened. You help them here," Barry indicated the people down in the street. I'll go check where the shots were fired."

"Got it."

Barry left Jamil and Alisha to direct the cadets and reservists on the hospital's front lawn and went to where the Explorer was parked at the entrance. The injured and dead had been cleared into the hospital and the shooting had dispersed the crowd a bit, but not far. A crowd that is half-full of injured waiting for treatment does not move far, even after what had happened. Barry tried to collect his thoughts before reporting back to dispatch.

"Dispatch, Sheriff Four-four, Over."

"Roger, Four-four, Over."

"The situation at Harbor UCLA is under control, so to speak. We have twelve additional injured from gunshot or hit and run. Five dead from gunshots and one from the car, including Officer Levon Harris, a Carson reserve officer, multiple gunshot wounds. No word on why they opened fire yet, sounds like some kind of fight in the crowd that Harris popped in on. Crowd says they think Harris got one or two shooters before they got him. Any word on the car? Over."

"Patrol One-Two pursued and found the car, abandoned in the traffic jam at Normandie and 215th. One dead Hispanic male, age approximately sixteen, in the passenger seat, no sign of anyone else. Over."

"Do we ... I mean ... normal procedure would be for us to secure the crime scene on something like this until the sheriff's detectives clear it. We're under your control and we can't contact any detectives. And, this is the front entrance to the hospital, you know, we've got a crowd of several thousand here. What are the instructions for the shooting scene? Over."

"Secure any real evidence. It doesn't sound like there'll be much. Take some names of witnesses and then clean up the area. This isn't a good night to get too hung up on forensics. Over."

"Roger. Four-four, out."

Barry hung the microphone on the dash and stifled a yawn. The problem with an adrenaline rush was that it did not last. Barry Warden needed more coffee. It would be a long night.

■

There is a school of thought amongst seismologists that the study of earthquake faults is not the most fruitful place to look to predict future quakes. Although faults do have repeated earthquakes on them, they are merely the scars of old quakes that resulted from the build-up of extreme stress in the earth's crust. If sufficient stress builds up it can cause a quake, either on an existing fault or in virgin territory.

In the aftermath of the 1994 Northridge quake, the sophisticated computer models of the stress build-up between the 1971 and the 1994 quakes on opposite ends of the San Fernando Valley, clearly show that there should have been cause for concern in the Northridge region even though the particular fault that gave way was unknown beforehand.

A similar stress model after the 1994 quake would seem to indicate that the city of Simi Valley just to the west in Ventura County is a place to be concerned about in the future. Computer stress models in the aftermath of the 1987 Whittier Narrows quake raise concerns about the stress build-up in the region to the west of Whittier, the Elysian Park Fault under downtown Los Angeles.

May 7th, 5:45 A.M.

It was supposed to be his shift for trying to catch a bit of sleep, but Barry had not been able to take advantage of the opportunity. Sights, sound and sensations from the day's events had prevented him from sleeping. The seat of the Explorer reclined into a rather decent sleeping spot, the cots in the staff room in the utility building where the two L.A.P.D. officers had sacked out earlier had since been converted to patient space, shortly after Jamil came to spell Barry.

Not being able to sleep, Barry had decided to lay back and listen in to the AM radio and the tactical net to try and catch up on what was going on. He had not had time to pay attention to anything except his own local problems all night. He pulled out his cell phone to see if he could call Kathy. No bars.

So, he was listening to the incessant damage and injury reports, interspersed with calls for assistance, when the call for his call sign came through.

"Sheriff Four-four, Torrance Dispatch, Over."

It took Barry a moment to rouse himself and find the mike, "This is Four-four, Over."

"Four-four. We have been informed via the Emergency Ops Network, that there is a Navy helicopter flight inbound to your location. L.A.E.O.C. says that they have been contacted by someone on the state net and they request someone at your location come up on the Navy frequency. Over."

"Roger. What's the freq? Over."

"One two niner point four. Repeat one two niner point four. Over."

"Roger. What's up? Any idea? Over."

"No. They just asked that you come up and said a navy flight was inbound. That's all we know."

"Roger. Four-four, out."

Barry moved over in the driver's seat and started the car. The Explorer's battery needed recharging anyway, he had been listening with the engine off for a quite a while. He dialed the 129.4 up on the radio and made the call.

"Navy flight, Navy flight, this is Los Angeles Sheriff Four-four, Over."

"Four-four, this is November Juliet Two. And this is a Marine flight, not Navy. Just some of the passengers are Navy. Over."

"Roger. How can we be of service? Over."

"You are the unit at Harbor UCLA Medical Center, correct. Over."

"Roger, over."

"We wanted to check on the whether you were ready for us. Are preparations complete? Over."

Barry waited before answering, trying to figure out what was going on.

"This is Four-four. You have me at a disadvantage. What preparations are you referring to. Over?"

"This is November Juliet Two. We were told by State Emergency Services in San Diego that a work crew would be ready to help unload. Over."

Barry again paused, trying to contemplate what was going on.

"This is Sheriff Four-four. I seem to have been left out of this loop. Could you explain your mission? Over."

"Roger, Four-four, it's understandable, all considered." The voice paused and then continued, "November Juliet Two is assigned as LZC, that's landing zone commander, for Force Recon/First Marine Division. We are inbound on your one seven five at forty clicks. We are a flight of three rotary aircraft with the advance teams from Force Recon Battalion/First Marines and Navy Hospital Camp Pendleton. Our mission is to establish a Navy Field Hospital to augment Harbor UCLA Medical Center. Approximately forty additional aircraft will be inbound within the hour. We do have the right place? Over."

"Roger that. What do you need from us? Over"

"Hospital Commander estimates that we will need a work crew of one hundred fifty to unload and set-up. Do you have sufficient people for that. Over."

"Roger. One thing I do have is plenty of people. Over."

"Our facility charts show two established helipads and a designated alternate landing zone, a parking lot, in the south-central area of your complex. Is that correct? Is the alternate zone going to be clear? That will be our staging area. Over."

"Correct. The two heli-pads are clear. We will get to work and the parking lot will be cleared ASAP. Over."

"Roger. Our ETA is 20 minutes. November Juliet Two, out."

Barry raced through thoughts of everything that needed to be done. Parking lot? Work crew? Notify the medical staff? Keep the crowd out of the way.

Barry decided to try and find the hospital administrator. What was his name? Perry? Then, everyone could pitch in a make ready for the Marines landing.

After the last twenty-four hours, Barry liked the sound of that last thought, "the Marines landing.".

■

*One theory of earthquake prediction is known
as the Mogi Doughnut. Named after Professor Kyo Mogi
of Tokyo University, the Mogi Doughnut is a circular
pattern of increased seismic activity surrounding an area
that is conspicuously devoid of seismic activity. There are
several excellent examples of such doughnuts of minor
earthquake activity forming around areas which were
later hit with sizable earthquakes. To those seismologists
who follow the stress build-up hypotheses, this makes
perfect sense. The doughnut is formed as the stress in a
region builds up until the point when the critical failure
of the fault in the center of the stress causes the release
of the pent up energy in a major quake.*

May 7th, 6:00 A.M.

The thought that the phone was ringing came slowly to Matt
Contreras. He had talked with Gloria for a long time after he got home
past midnight and he was in the deepest phase of his sleep when the
phone rang in the pre-dawn hours.

The fact that the phones were finally working sparked recognition in Gloria. Seeing that Matt was not waking up, after several rings,
Gloria reached over Matt to get to the phone from the nightstand.

"Hello?" Gloria said. She listened. "Yes. Just a minute."

Gloria reached over Matt again and clicked the nightstand light.
The light worked, electricity had come back, too. She cupped her hand
over the phone and said, "Somebody wants Officer Contreras."

Her words, the phone cord in his face and the light in his eyes
finally roused Matt. He took the phone. "Yes. Hello."

"Matt? Crawford, here. Glad I got you. Thought the phones might still be out. Matt, we've got problems. They've ordered an evacuation of everything south of Indio. You've got to get your bird out of Thermal." Captain Hal Crawford was the CHP commander for the Indio region.

"Evacuated. What for?"

"Salton Sea is flooding. Highway 111 is already closed."

"I saw the mud at Thermal last night, but that doesn't seem cause to evacuate."

"Naw. This is different. I heard about that flood yesterday. that was from the quake, shaking the water. But this is a real flood. Got word from state headquarters that everything below sea level is to be evacuated."

Matt's mind raced. He gave voice to the question, "How in the hell ...?"

Crawford tried to answer, "The flood's coming from down in Mexico. Don't know if it is the Colorado or the Gulf. All we know is that everything below the sea-level line is in danger. That sounds like the ocean is flooding in. Don't know, really, just know its sea-level they're worried about."

"How far does that go? The rest of the Valley isn't in danger, is it?"

"We dug up an old topo map here that shows sea level running right south of Indio. Thermal, Mecca, the whole Torres-Martinez reservation, all that is below. We're waiting for a Fax now from Sacramento that should tell us exactly. Anyway, the point is that Thermal is below sea-level. We gotta get your chopper out. State Emergency Services keeps shortening the warning time."

Matt knew that only too well the elevation of Thermal airport. For years he had been one of the few pilots in the country that set his altimeter at a negative altitude every time he took off.

"But, how can I get to Thermal. I'm not gonna leave my car in Thermal, if it's flooding."

"One step ahead of you. Dooley's on Code Three to your house to pick you up. The roads are packed coming north out of the lower Imperial Valley, Salton City and Torres-Martinez, you'd need lights and siren to get down to Thermal now, anyway. He should be up to you in ten minutes."

"Roger, I'll be ready."

Matt turned to Gloria and handed her the phone.

"You need to call your parents. They're evacuating everything south of Indio. Make sure they know to get out. Now!"

"Why? What?" Gloria fumbled for words. What new calamity had occurred that would force her parents from their house on the reservation amongst the lush date palms groves of her childhood home?

Shaving in cold water was strange. The gas water heater was not working. But, Gloria had boiled some water in the microwave and the hot coffee was making amends for chill of the cold shave and of Matt having to clean himself with only a washcloth and a few ounces of cold water. They sat together in front of the television, waiting.

Matt looked at his watch and said, "Dooley's ten minutes is sure stretching out. It must be a real mess on the roads."

"Look at that." Gloria pointed to the screen.

Matt looked over to see a live shot from one of the two Los Angeles stations that were back on the air. The helicopter's vantage point showed the sun rising in the east over a darkened city, the only lights below it were a few streets with cars on them and many glowing squares, indicating the fires.

"That's just how Rancho Mirage looked last night when I flew over." Matt had already gone out into the yard to look around and see if any of the fires from the night before were anywhere near their house. He had seen none, but the smell of smoke was still in the air.

"Holy ..." Gloria said, still entranced by the TV.

Whatever she was going to say was cut off by the sound of the CHP siren coming up the street. Dooley was there.

"Insurance carriers are scared to death they're going to be destroyed by the next major earthquake."
Chuck Quackenbush,
California Insurance Commissioner
(1995)

In January 1994, following the Northridge earthquake, most insurance companies stopped issuing new policies with quake coverage in California. A new federal and state sponsored insurance underwriting program is now in place, but with a high deductible and high premium cost, only a small percentage of homeowners participate. Commercial properties are usually required by their mortgage lenders to participate, but in a major disaster the underwriting capacity of the earthquake program is highly suspect.

May 7th, 6:40 A.M.

Kathy woke up with the thought curiously intruding on her drowsiness that she had actually been able to get to sleep after the hours waiting on the cold, hard floor. And, that her bladder was ready to burst.

She had not gone to the bathroom since leaving home yesterday morning. She had not needed to, with nothing to eat or drink until late last night.

Now, though, the big cups of oriental soup and coffee were making their presence known in her system. Kathy had no idea what to do about it.

Kathy opened her eyes and rolled over. Her muscles rebelled at this, both from the night on the concrete and from the numerous bruises that she had received between the freeway wreck, the street explosion and the alley. Kathy closed her eyes and tried to shut the thoughts out. The pressure in her bladder helped her forget the other body pains.

The muted light of dawn was coming in through the far windows of the workshop. Sally Kim was still beside her, curled up with the baby. Kathy heard some movement in the room. Someone already had the radio going quietly in the corner room.

Kathy wiggled her way up into a sitting position, which exacerbated the need to find a bathroom. Fortunately, Kathy's movement roused Sally, too.

"G'morning," Sally mumbled softly, careful not to wake the baby.

"Good morning. Say, where can I, ah, go to the bathroom?" Kathy asked.

"Oh, you're right. Me, too. Just a sec, I'll show you." Sally carefully slid the blanket from her shoulders and sat up, leaving her baby on the floor. Then she wrapped the blanket back around the baby and got to her knees. The baby stirred, but did not wake.

"Come on, outside." Sally indicated Kathy should follow.

The door at the back of the workshop swung open and Kathy found herself in the alley. The same alley where, a block west, she had been attacked. Sally turned right up the alley the other direction. The air was chilly in the partial light of dawn.

Passing the corner of the workshop, Kathy saw that some of the people from the room, mostly women, were already at work with fires in a couple of steel drums that were cut to make wood stoves. Kathy could smell the start of sausage cooking. Sally kept going across the yard.

Behind a row of poplar trees facing the alley, Sally showed Kathy the toilet facilities. The two turquoise port-a-potties had signs on the doors, clearly advertising "Kim Construction, L.A., CA 90012." An older Korean woman was just coming out of one of the portable toilets.

"Hi, Mom." Sally Kim smiled and turned to Kathy, "Mom, this is Kathy Warden. Kathy, my mother, Yoo Soon Kim."

The older woman smiled and said, "Good Morning. How are you doing?" She intentionally did not offer her hand to Kathy; exiting a port-a-potty, this was understood.

"Fine, thank you." Kathy said.

"Where's the baby?" Sally's mother asked.

"Still sleeping," Sally answered.

"I'll check on him," the grandmother said, heading toward workshop building with a parting smile. Sally rolled her eyes at the over-protectiveness of her mother to the grandson, but only for Kathy's view, after the older woman had left.

Sally headed into the toilet vacated by her mother and Kathy opened the other turquoise door. The chemical smell was strong, but the little booth was clean and apparently new. The Koreans had things pretty well organized for it just being the morning after the disaster.

■

Barry Warden stood watching the line of volunteers complete their "FOD walk down" of the south parking lot. Barry had listened in as a Marine sergeant had quickly explained to the assembled work crew that "FOD" or "Foreign Object Damage", that is, the blowing around of loose trash in a helicopter landing area, could ruin a chopper's engine if sucked into the turbine air intakes. So, the sergeant had organized about half of the volunteer work party, that had come from ranks of those waiting around the hospital, into a long line that walked the length of the parking lot, picking up paper trash and anything else that could cause such damage.

Barry stood at the corner of the parking lot, next to the control station the Marines had set up to direct the landing area. Upon landing at the hospital's regular helipad, shortly after six o'clock, the Marine commander, Colonel Munro, had met with Barry, the hospital administrator, Mr. Perry, and a handful of other people from the hospital to explain what to expect. But, after the courtesy of the initial briefing from Munro, the Marines and the few Navy officers who accompanied them had taken charge and were functioning without any input or help from anyone, except for the work party that Munro had asked Barry and Jamil to gather together. Two squads of Marines had even taken over the security of the hospital complex. The unruly crowd that Jamil had been unable to move with his bullhorn six hours before, moved like obedient sheep to the barked instructions of the flak-jacketed, rifle-toting Marines.

Soon, the whole southern half of the hospital complex and the area around the hospital building itself were cleared. The crowd was moved north to the front lawn and the other parking lots, well away from the one in the south that would become the landing zone. With Holmdahl's help, the Marines had even dismantled two streetlight poles that the Marine colonel thought too close to the landing zone.

As the end of the "FOD" hunting line passed by him, Barry recognized a face. It took him a minute to realize who it was. When he finally did, Barry shouted to him, "How's your daughter?"

The husky man in the tank top shouted back, "She'll be OK, broken pelvis, doctor says she'll mend." But there was no joy in the man's face at saying this. Barry remembered the man saying he had also lost his wife in the quake.

Barry had thought about the incident with this guy as he sat trying to catch a wink during the night. This, plus the shooting out front and the incident with the kids in the temporary morgue had kept going over in Barry's mind. Seeing the man on the volunteer crew, Barry's decision to let the armed assault charges slide, seemed more appropriate. These were strange times. Barry would never have thought a week before about letting a perp who drew down on him with a loaded gun go free, let alone be glad that he had done so.

The thought of this man and his dead wife, the injured girl's mother, again brought to Barry the other thoughts that had flooded him all night. He had no idea how his own wife was. Did Kathy lay injured somewhere, or worse? When this operation of getting the helicopters landed was over, Barry would have to figure out some way of getting word to Kathy and the rest of the family.

The twittering of Marine police whistles brought Barry's thoughts back to the landing area. The Marine landing crew members in their "Mickey Mouse" ear protectors and colored vests had the work crews divided into eight groups, most kneeling at the edges of the parking lot. They were signaling everyone else down with the whistles and hand signals.

Someone nudged Barry's arm. It was Colonel Munro. The lanky, gray haired Marine officer held a pair of the black ear protectors out to him.

"First wave is inbound," he pointed to the sky to the south over Long Beach. "You'll need these in a few minutes."

"Thanks." Barry said. He hung the ear protectors around his neck, like the colonel did.

Until the colonel pointed to where the helicopters were, Barry had paid little attention to the sky, so busy had he been with the affairs around the hospital. Now, he could see in the light of the rising sun that smoke still rose into the sky in many places. Not the walls of flame and smoke he had seen yesterday, but still huge columns ascended from a dozen spots on the horizon and a pall of smoke hung in every direction. In the east the rising sun cut through a red aura on the horizon. The low-hanging morning clouds were tinged with deep orange and red. The sight of the sky so full of smoke explained the burning of nose and eyes that had continued throughout the night.

"Everyone ready?" the colonel asked another officer who stood next to a table with a radio.

The officer gave a thumbs-up sign.

"Proceed," The colonel spoke and then crossed his arms and continued to stand next to Barry, apparently confident that no further action from him was needed to carry out the landing.

The assembled work crews, their Marine handlers and everyone else at the hospital now looked and pointed to the south. The first cluster of olive drab CH-53 helicopters could be seen making their way between the columns of smoke rising in the south. The red glare from the dawn's light glinted on the canopies. Soon several clusters of aircraft could be seen. They seemed to be flying in groups of four.

That number matched the number of huge white "H's" the Marines had painted on the south parking lot. As soon as the last of the parked cars had been cleared from the lot, it had been transformed into a heliport. A windsock was erected. And clusters of indicator lights grouped around the "H's" and other markings that Barry did not understand the meaning of were hastily sprayed on the asphalt.

By the time the first four aircraft descended toward the landing area, the strips of indicator lights were lit up to show the pilots the wind direction and speed. The officer at the radio announced into the radio, "November Juliet Five, you are cleared for landing, landing area Hotel One."

The colonel leaned over and said to Barry, "I've done this a thousand times in my career, but every time I see a force landing like this I get goose bumps. I know it sounds silly, but it always impresses me."

"This morning I can understand completely, Goosebumps, too. It is a damn good sight to see. You don't know ... I kinda feel like we ought to be playing the theme from `Apocalypse Now,'" Barry said this last to Colonel Munro before thinking that Marlon Brando's demented character in that movie had also been a colonel, but this colonel did not seem to mind the analogy, he just nodded.

No further conversation was possible. The thunder of the first helicopter filled the air. The colonel pulled up the ear protectors and Barry followed him in this.

A white-vested landing signalman waived the first chopper, one of the huge CH-53's, into position over the northwest landing spot. With a crescendo of awesome noise, the huge helicopter whipped up a cloud of dust and settled gently to the ground. The doors slid open. A Marine in charge of one of the work crews already had these men running stooped over under the spinning rotors. The crew wasted no time in starting to pull some of the hundreds of canvas bags that filled the cargo space from the chopper and running to the edge of the landing zone with the cargo. Another Marine with a clipboard seemed to be counting bags as they came off the landing zone.

While the first cargo chopper was unloading a second CH-53 was signaled in to the landing area closest to Barry. None of the work crews moved this time. Just a pair of Marines in green vests who ran forth motioning to those in the helicopter, as though directing traffic. The second chopper did not carry cargo, rather, it was a passenger flight.

Even above the pounding thunder of the huge copters' turbines and rotors the shouting of the watching volunteers could be heard. These volunteers were among those who had waited with injured loved ones throughout the night as the staff of Harbor UCLA Medical Center had been forced to refuse to see more patients.

The welcoming cheers for the passengers of the second heli-copter continued as the twenty-odd figures ran awkwardly through the turbulence under the rotors with duffel bags and luggage clutched in their arms. One of the green-shirted Marines trotted ahead, showing them where to go.

It was clear to Barry and Colonel Munro why the first wave of air-mobile military forces off the choppers in this landing had drawn such a cheer from the men of the work crews. Instead of Marines in battle gear, the first wave of this landing were, quite obviously, Navy nurses.

■

The gate to the flight line at Thermal airport stood wide open, the guard shack was empty. Inside the gate, Dooley cut the siren and lights for the few hundred feet to the CHP hangar. As Dooley pulled up next to the hangar, the Sheriff's Huey was just starting to crank up its rotors. The Huey's cockpit was angled away from Matt, so he could not see if Moody was at the stick.

The little red push truck from the airport service company was still parked near the Huey, for which Matt was thankful. He and Dooley would not have to push the Jet Ranger out of the hangar themselves, a hernia producing task. This was but one of the problems Matt had worried about on the run down from Palm Springs to Thermal.

Matt got out of the CHP cruiser and waved to the driver of the push truck, indicating the CHP hangar. The driver nodded.

"Why don't you wait to see if everything checks out, before you take off," Matt said.

Chuck Dooley nodded, "Anything else I can help with?"

"Maybe check with Indio and see if they have any update on how much time we have."

"Roger that."

The CHP helicopter had started up without a hitch and Matt was airborne in less than ten minutes. As he lifted off Matt heard Dooley finishing a check-in with the CHP office on the radio.

"Roger, Patrol Six, proceed to intersection 111 and the interstate. They have quite a jam-up trying to get on the Interstate east bound."

"10-4. Patrol Six, out."

Matt Contreras keyed his mike, "Indio, this is H-Ten, over,"

"H-Ten, this is Indio. Over."

"I am airborne over Thermal, proceeding to Palm Springs. Over."

"Roger, H-10. The Captain wants to know if you can make a loop down along the north shore of the Salton Sea, to give us some idea of what's happening before you head for Palm Springs. Over."

"I had thought about doing just that. I'll let you know what I see. H-10, out."

The morning sun was just coming over the Chocolate Mountains on the far side of the Salton Sea. Thermal was only five miles from northern coast of the Sea. It was in sight before Matt was more than a few hundred feet up.

Matt Contreras had taken off several hundred times from Thermal and many of those times he headed south or east after takeoff. The terrain below him to the south was definitely changed from what he knew.

The little farm town of Mecca was now half-again as close as usual to the shore of the Sea. Matt could see the reflection of water from between the rows of date palms between Mecca and the shoreline. Matt added power and took the jet Ranger up higher to see farther south. He squinted in the morning sun to see the far southern shore of the huge salt lake.

Matt keyed his mike, "Indio, this is H-10, over."

"Roger H-10, Over." Matt recognized Captain Crawford's voice on the radio.

"The water line is definitely rising and it looks like it is going pretty quick. H-10 requests permission to make a patrol of the whole Salton area prior to heading north over."

"Roger, we were thinking the same thing. Proceed, out."

As he gained altitude Matt could start to make out the south shore of the Sea. The usual murky blue-green of the Sea's surface was interrupted in the south half. A mushroom-shaped plume of terra cota red water was pushing north from the southern end of the Salton Sea near where the New River emptied into the sea. In the far south Matt could see that a river of the dark red water, he guessed maybe a mile wide, flowed toward him from the far southern horizon, cutting through the lush green fields of the lower Imperial Valley. The new river flowed through what had previously been the tomato and cotton fields of the Imperial Valley.

■

"A moderate earthquake will probably occur in central California within two or three years, another great earthquake in southern California can be anticipated in the next twenty years, recently increased earthquake activity in the San Francisco Bay Area could be the return to a normal cycle of severe activity, and a damaging earthquake in San Diego is not unlikely."

California Statutes, Government Code § <u>8876.1</u>

May 7th, 7:16 A.M.

Genevieve lay in the fluffy folds of down-filled cotton for several minutes, in the sumptuous semi-consciousness that a good night's rest brings to the morning, before the questions of where she was and why burst upon her. She sat up, looking hurriedly around the Weld's garden room, struggling for orientation and memory. When these came back to her, they came along with depression, and Genevieve flopped back into the bedclothes to consider the thoughts that reality brought back.

■

"Roger, H-10, over." It was Captain Crawford and not the CHP dispatcher who answered.

"Indio, I passed over Westmorland five minutes ago, or what was Westmorland, it's under water on the west side of the flood area, and the water's rising. It's pretty much all water between Westmorland and Brawley. Lots of debris in the water, seems to be flowing pretty fast to the north. I am just coming up on Calipatria now, will report back, out."

Matt had toyed with the idea of going farther south, but the fuel situation stopped him. If he went further he would not have enough fuel to get to Palm Springs and there did not seem to be anyplace left in Imperial County to refuel.

The red-brown water of the Sea had already surrounded the big geothermal plant north of Brawley and was nearly to Calipatria city limits. At the lowest part of the valley, near the south end of the Salton Sea, Calipatria was home of Calipatria State Prison. Matt had kept his altitude high to keep in touch with Indio, but now he went down a bit. He wanted to see what was happening at the high-security prison.

One of the newest of California's many prisons, the pattern of Calipatria modern prison blocks and guard fences stood out on the green springtime landscape of the Imperial Valley. Matt made his turn from east to north and came up on the prison from the south. The sun was now high enough over the mountains to see ground clearly and what Matt saw was worth reporting to Indio.

"Indio, H-10, over."

"Roger, H-10, you are breaking up, over." As low as Matt was now flying, the transmission from Indio was none too clear either. Matt increased altitude as he called back.

"Indio, it appears that the Calipatria Prison is being evacuated on foot. There are several groups of uniformed prisoners walking on the road east from the prison. It looks like they are trying to reach the Coachella Canal. The water line of the Salton Sea is only three quarters of a mile west-north-west of the prison and it looks like they decided not to wait. There are a couple of dark blue and white prison buses on the road, but they've got several thousand prisoners ... Over."

"Roger, H-10, we had not heard about that. We'll report it to

Sacramento."

"Roger, that, those guards have their hands full. If they keep going like they are now, they'll be bivouacking a couple thousand hardened cons in the sand dunes below the Chocolate Mountains by nightfall. The state better send help. Not only for that, but from what I saw, the whole valley, Brawley, El Centro, all the towns are going to be evacuating to the east. It is not going to be just convicts camping in the sand dunes, I'd guess they've got upwards of a hundred thousand people scrambling for dry land down here. Over."

"Roger, I'm not sure anyone might be in a position to help, all considered, but we'll pass the word on."

"We just better hope those prisoners don't decide to blow off the guards and head home to L.A., Indio is the first place they'll hit. And, now that I think of it, there's another medium security prison on the southwest corner of the Imperial Valley, I didn't get a chance to get down that far. I reckon it is on the west side of the flood though. If they follow Calipatria's lead they'll be marching their prisoners toward Ocotillo and the San Diego County line. And I.N.S. has a big immigration holding facility north of El Centro. That would be in the flooded zone. Over."

"Roger, copy, over."

"This is H-10, I am RTB ... Correction, H-10 is enroute Palm Springs, ETA 0815, Out."

As he turned northwest toward Palm Springs, gaining altitude, Matt Contreras saw another curious sight. At the edge of the advancing waters, a few miles north of Calipatria, he could see several plumes of what looked like steam coming up from the ground. Stopping his ascent to look closer, he turned toward the steam.

The steam was clearly coming right out of the ground west of the little town of Niland. He could now see the source of the steam clearly. Several geysers spouted fifty feet or more into the air. At the base of the geysers Matt could see the start of mounds of red mud growing around each geyser, like little volcanoes. The waters of the Salton Sea lapped around the geysers, and but for the growing mounds of mud the geysers would already be underwater.

The curious geyser field, like the flood itself, left more questions than Matt could consider while flying solo. He added power and climbed into the sky headed northwest. Below him the red-brown waters coming from the south seemed to be even farther north in the Salton Sea than they had been on the trip south.

As he flew north, the scope of what was going on below him filtered in to Matt's thoughts. He was seeing something that had not been seen before, at least recently. A whole section of the state, the country, was disappearing below him. His first thoughts about Pompeii did not seem to be really the same thing, but maybe Atlantis legend or the great Ice Age floods that had cut the Grand Canyon and the Grand Coulee area had been like this. Maybe his Indian ancestors had seen this before.

Matt's mind rebelled at the thought of a hundred thousand people fleeing the waters that spread below him. It was too immense to consider.

■

The ornate plate she was handed was something Kathy Warden would keep in a china cabinet, not something you would serve food on to strangers in a back alley. But, Kathy remembered, most of these people were not strangers. It was she who was the stranger here. Kathy took the beautiful plate and a more mundane coffee mug. She followed Sally Kim to the row of inverted milk crates that served as seating in the yard off the alley where the food was served. Sally's mother was already there near where Sally had left the baby in a child's portable car seat.

Breakfast was not a repeat of the "mystery soup" she had been served the night before. Sausage, scrambled eggs, biscuits and coffee dissolved ethnic boundaries. Actually, Kathy was surprised at the food, perfectly prepared and delicious.

"This is great. How do they do it over an open fire in a barrel?" she commented to Sally.

Sally's mother heard the comment and answered before Sally could, "The Park family runs the Seoul Palace restaurant chain. You might say they are pros. I don't think the type of stove matters much to them."

"Definitely not."

Kathy ate the food quickly and without any conversation. Sally seemed to keep quiet around the older Koreans, who now spoke in their native tongue. Kathy was nearly finished when Sally dumped her plate on the ground near the baby, jumped up and ran into the alley.

In the alley, Sally jumped into the open arms of a young Korean man in coveralls. The man spun Sally around and they hugged and kissed. Several other Koreans ran back and gathered around the couple. One of the missing husbands had been found.

Kathy looked back down at her plate and wondered when she would get such an embrace from her husband. She finished her biscuit and made plans for getting home and finding Barry.

■

Barry Warden had lost count on the number of helicopters that had come in, something like fifteen so far, both the huge CH-53's and the other oblong, twin-rotor CH-47's. The initial fascination at the system the Marines had for keeping supplies and people moving from the landing area had dimmed. He was already planning on going to the hospital to check on how everything else was going when he felt someone tug on his arm. He turned to see John Holmdahl in a pair of dungarees and a hard hat.

The hospital facilities manager was holding his ears and motioning for Barry to follow, apparently he wanted to talk away from the noise of the helicopters. Barry followed him toward the main hospital building.

When they were away from the landing area, Barry pulled the ear protectors off.

Holmdahl shouted, "Pete Valdez, you know, the guy from County Public Works, said we ought to let you know. Maybe you can get someone to send help. We think there are some people alive down in the west basement."

"I though you guys said there was no chance. That everything was flattened down there when the floor collapsed."

"Well, we thought … It sure seemed … I don't know. All we know is that two orderlies were searching the central stores room in the middle of the basement for supplies, just before the helicopters came in. They thought they heard someone knocking on the cement joists in the west end of the basement, you know the big pre-stressed beams that run the length of the floor. Valdez went down with one of his men, borrowed a nurse's stethoscope to listen to the joist. They say there is a definite pounding on the beam. Whoever it is responds to their knocks."

"Can they get in there?"

"Not with anything we've got. Valdez wants to know if you can get through to L.A. County Fire, maybe get one of the Heavy Rescue teams in here, maybe cut down from the floor above."

"I'll try, but I haven't even been in touch with my own department since yesterday afternoon, let alone County Fire. You might have better luck on the Emergency Services network the hospital administrator is on."

"That's my next stop." Holmdahl left running toward the main building.

Barry headed for the Explorer again. He did not run though, he did not have the energy. Since the quake he had only had the numerous coffees and a doughnut Jamil had scrounged for him.

He unlocked the Explorer and swung up into the seat. He turned the ignition to switch on the radio and picked up the frequency chart.

"Dispatch, this is Sheriff Four-four, Over."

"Roger Four-four. Over."

"Four-four will be 10-10, switching to County Fire Primary. We have personnel trapped in the collapsed hospital wing at Harbor UCLA and need an Urban Search and Rescue team. Over."

"Is that a new collapse? Over."

"No. From the big quake, we just found out people are alive down there. If you folks know of some way to get a heavy lift team out here, we could sure use it. Over."

"Roger, we'll check. Out."

Barry picked up the freq chart. It took his tired eyes a minute to focus on the tiny lettering for the frequency channel of the County Fire department.

Barging in on another agency's radio net was really not the right way for a deputy to get hold of a fireman, but Barry Warden did not have too much concern for protocol at this point. He knew the duty station of the deputies assigned to the hospital criminal holding facility was in the west basement and if anybody was alive down there, it was a good chance it was one of Barry's fellow deputy sheriffs.

■

"Look, they are going on through," Esteban woke Sybil Perkins with his words.

She opened her eyes on a different scene than she had imagined in the dark the night before. She was fairly familiar with the Baja California geology, but she had no idea when they stopped how rough the terrain ahead was. The jagged red and yellow volcanic cliffs were surrealistic in the warm light of morning.

She saw what Esteban was talking about. Of the several dozen trucks and cars stopped with Sybil and Esteban along the two-lane highway, a few were now pulling onto the road and heading up the incline toward those jagged cliffs.

"Do you think its open?" she asked.

"Who knows? I suppose it could be. They've had all night."

"How far is it to the next town?"

"Oh, La Rumorosa is only ten kilometers straight, but the road, it is very much curved, ah, has many curves. Maybe twenty kilometers to La Rumorosa and another thirty or forty to Tecate. Tecate is bigger and there is a crossing to the U.S. there."

"Enough said, you talked me into trying."

Sybil pulled the lever to raise the seat back to sitting position and ground the starter motor getting the little car started. She soon joined the line of cars and trucks snaking slowly up through the basalt pillars on Mexican Highway 2.

Halfway up the La Rumorosa incline they found the reason for the night's wait down below.

A piece of plywood leaned against the rocks on the side of the road. The words "No fumar" were scrawled in dripping red paint on the plywood. Sybil looked at Esteban. "Why `No Smoking?'"

Next they saw a patch of road cluttered with gravel and rocks. A Caterpillar was pulled into a turnout pushing away the last rocks of the landslide. Around the next hairpin turn the carcass of a green Pemex tanker truck was rolled off the road to the downhill side. The tank was caved in. A boulder slightly larger than the Nissan rent-a-car Sybil drove was wedged against the uphill slope. The smell of the spilled gasoline hung in the air like a threat.

Sybil wondered at the wisdom of continuing up the narrow mountain road.

"Back home they would have washed the gasoline down with a fire truck first, before opening the road," she said.

Esteban looked over at her and raised his eyebrows, "You know, *Senorita* Perkins, it is just possible after an earthquake big enough to collapse the Colorado River delta, that perhaps the fire trucks in La Rumorosa and Tecate have more important things to do than come out and wash down highways. Do you not think so?"

Sybil Perkins pretended to ignore the remark and concentrate on the difficult road.

■

"Yes, and even if we do get the rioters in the Crenshaw district under control during daylight, the word I've heard from everyone is that the whole stretch from Westwood down to beyond Culver City is even worse than around here, in downtown." The cop that James Kim had brought over to talk to Kathy after breakfast had not stopped shaking his head since hearing of her hopes to get to West L.A. Now, he pointed to James, "Your cousin was real lucky to get in all the way from Commerce. There isn't nothing moving in this city. No buses. The freeways are, well, totaled. And she wants to walk to the west side. No way. They say there is a cliff across what used to be Santa Monica Boulevard in Century City."

Hearing something about Century City, Kathy thought of her sister. "How about Century City? Could I get there? My sister works in Century City," she asked.

"You haven't heard about Century City?" the young policeman looked from Kathy to James and back again. "Jeez, I thought you'd know. They lost four high-rises, maybe five, in Century City and the shopping center collapsed part way. If your sister worked in Century City you better hope she got out after the first quake, cause the second one supposedly hit right under there, knocked the buildings around like bowling pins."

James tried to signal with his eyes for the cop to shut up, but it was too late. Kathy's face had gone ashen and she stumbled back, trying to sit on one of the milk crates. James helped her sit down.

The cop tried to finish up, "Sorry, I didn't think. It's been real tough on lots of people. Look, Miss, I'd say if your husband is a deputy sheriff, the best place for you to try is downtown, at the county build-ings. Maybe they can get in touch with someone who knows whether ... you know, who can help. But, trying to get around town, especially across the whole city is going to be hell; really impossible for a while. If you have to, try downtown with the Sheriff's office, but if you can, stay here where it's safe."

The cop looked to James, "I gotta go. Thanks for breakfast, Jim."

James nodded and the cop left. James Kim put his hand on Kathy's shoulder. "You're welcome to stay here as long as you need. There's plenty for everyone. You ought to follow his advice. If your husband is OK, you'll find him. No need to risk your life in this city the way it is now." He paused. "You gonna be OK?"

Kathy shrugged and continued to stare at the ground.

■

The 1960 earthquake in Chile was caused by the movement of a chunk of earth 200 miles wide, 600 miles long and up to 40 miles deep. Over 150 square miles of land subsided beneath the ocean. Although the main quake was on a recognized fault line, the foreshocks and aftershocks involved several other faults, some previously unknown. The seismic sea wave, or tsunami, from this quake hit Hilo, Hawaii fourteen hours later with a wall of water 35 feet high. With a Richter scale estimate ranging between 9.0 to 9.5 the Chilean quake was the greatest ever recorded.

May 7th, 8:30 A.M.

"Don't take this wrong, but I was kind of wondering how it is that we got you here so quick. Glad to have you, but we been screaming for help for twenty-four hours and you're the first local help we've gotten, except for the deputy here and a few cops." John Holmdahl asked the fire captain, Bill Riggs, as he stood with Barry watching the urban search and rescue team outfit themselves. They stood around a large yellow truck that mimicked a normal fire truck except that in place of the ladder it had a crane.

"Well, don't really know, we just follow what they send our way. My guess is that it's a combination of two things." Riggs paused to pull on his headgear, a combination radiophone and hard hat. "First, we weren't doing anybody any good over at the Armada Hotel, you can't rescue anybody from a seven story hotel that falls over sideways. All we were doing was dismantling concrete and filling body bags. Second, and

I'd guess this was really controlling, the boys downtown are probably barely treading water keeping things running. They're so far over their head, with nothing to work with and too many problems, they're just following the check sheets and emergency guidelines. It just happens that you," he pointed at the hospital building, "a major 500+ bed trauma care hospital, fall smack dab at the top of the priority list for assistance from us," Riggs patted his chest, "critical structure rescue and assistance services on the emergency services guideline chart some bureaucrat is using. In other words, you lucked out."

Riggs grabbed a fiberglass equipment case, signaled to the other firemen suiting up and said, "OK, where's the scene? Where'd you hear 'em? Where do you guess they are? Whose got structural plans?"

Barry pointed toward the stairway down from the loading dock to the basement storerooms. Holmdahl pulled a set of blueprints from his briefcase.

Before heading into the building, Riggs turned to Holmdahl, "My men have been working at the Armada all night. Haven't eaten anything. Your kitchen working?"

Holmdahl shook his head, pointing to the sagging west wing, "Nope. Second floor, West. But, we're working on setting something up over at the paramedics training center. We'll try to get something together for you."

"When you do, I have nine cops who haven't eaten either," Barry added.

"I know, and eight hundred staff, and a couple thousand critical patients, and now the Marines and Navy, too. I'm working on it." Holmdahl raised his arms in frustration. Barry led Riggs toward the basement. He was familiar with the route, it was the same every deputy took to get a DUI suspect down to the drunk tank.

■

The primary assets of American financial institutions are the debts owed to the institutions by borrowers, both commercial enterprises and consumers. These debts consist of real estate mortgages, commercial loans and consumer credit card debt, among other things. A few types of debt are protected by some sort of governmental guarantee, like FHA or VA home loans and Small Business Administration loans. However, the vast bulk of the monetary assets of many financial institutions is secured only on the borrowers' and clients' assets and future income, both of which will likely be stricken by the quake. Lack of earthquake insurance by most of these borrowers and possible failure of such insurance will further exacerbate the banks' problems. Even if banks, savings and loans and credit unions are able to survive the immediate cash crunch from a massive quake, their ability to recover from the near total failure of their loan portfolios is questionable.

May 7th, 9:10 A.M.

Gloria Contreras pulled into the parking lot from the back of the lot behind the supermarket. She could see the small crowd gathering at the front of the BankCal building. She parked behind the bank building.

Brian Kowicky was leaning on the hood of his little red pickup truck, talking to Angie Spencer, one of the tellers who sat in her car. There was no sign of Murphy, the assistant manager, or any of the other employees. Brian straightened up as Gloria pulled up. Angie opened her car door to come over with Brian to their manager's car.

"G'morning," Brian said.

"That remains to be seen, but thanks for the wish, anyway." Gloria said as she sat her briefcase on top of her car.

"Let me get that." Brian offered, reaching for the briefcase.

Angie smiled and said, "I didn't know whether to come in or not. I tried to call you at home, but the line was busy."

"Yes. I know, sorry. I was trying to get hold of anyone in BankCal that knows what is going on. No luck. Every phone number for the south region is out of order. I'm going to try some other numbers when I get inside." Gloria locked the car and headed for the rear door to the bank.

"Any idea what's up out front? I thought they put up an out of order sign on the ATM," Gloria said.

"I walked by when I first drove up. They're not lining up at the ATM. They are stretched out at the door, maybe thirty people, waiting for us to open.

"They probably saw that thing on CNN." Angie said.

"What was that? I haven't been watching for a couple hours, getting my parents settled in with my kids at home." Gloria said.

"Oh, they had somebody from the Federal Emergency Management Agency on. They asked him what were the critical things people ought to be worrying about in the aftermath of the quake. He said one of the real important things was to have plenty of cash, since credit card networks and ATMs wouldn't be working for awhile. Then he questioned whether the banks could open at all, for days."

"Great! On CNN? That's all we need, some fool starting a run on cash on national TV."

Brian spoke up, "At least the power is on so you can get the main vault open. You were worried yesterday that we'd have to make do with only the emergency funds in the little safe."

Gloria Contreras shook her head, "That's not much help. It wouldn't take more than twenty or thirty decent sized savings accounts or CD's to use up all the reserves in this branch, even in the main vault. If there is any run at all we're dead. or rather our customers are. The manual says that if it appears that cash reserves are insufficient to carry out a day's operations, the branch manager can close or not even open. Our cash comes by armored car from San Bernardino. My husband flew over the Interstate last night, he said nothing is going to be coming in from the west. Nothing at all. But that's not the biggest problem."

"What's that?" Angie and Brian asked simultaneously.

"I've already called every phone number I can for BankCal in southern California. No answers. If I can't get through by phone, the computers probably can't get through either. If we don't get tied into the BankCal computer net, then we don't need to worry about a run on our cash reserves." Gloria stopped talking as she put her keys in the back door's lock. "We can't have a run on cash if we don't know how much cash someone has in their account."

"Besides," she continued, "We all saw the BankCal building downtown L.A. on television. Didn't you? I don't think there is anything left for our computer to connect to."

"So, what are we going to do?" Brian asked, pulling the back door closed behind them.

"We are are going to start calling the list of numbers in the manual again, someone in BankCal, maybe in northern California, has to have some idea of what we should be doing?"

■

"You won't reconsider?" Sally Kim asked.

"No. I really have to find Barry. And there's no way he can find me here, he wouldn't know where to look." Kathy Warden stood in the yard off the alley with Sally, her husband, Stanley, and his cousin, James Kim.

"The phones have to be working soon. It is not safe. I think I've said that before," James said, avoiding Kathy's eyes.

"Yes, you did, and I deserve the `I told you so' especially after you rescued me and have been so nice to me, a stranger. I can't ever thank you enough. But, I've got to go. Besides, I passed the Pacific Bell building down on Olympic last night, I saw the ruins there, it'll be weeks before they finish carting off the bricks in the street, let alone get the phone exchanges inside working. I have a feeling that things aren't going to be getting better very fast. And they might be getting worse after people find out how really bad everything is. If I am going to get home or find my husband I'd better do it while I can."

"Fine," Sally motioned to her husband. "Stan?"

Stanley Kim reached down and picked up a blue backpack he had set near his feet when he walked up. He handed it to Kathy. "Mom and her friends put this together after I told them you had decided to keep going." Sally smiled.

"What ... ?"

"It's just some food and cans of juice, with some other stuff. In case you need it. I put my address here at Mom's and the phone number in the pocket in case you wanted to get back in touch ... you know, after all this."

Kathy took the back pack and reached to hug Sally. Kathy also reached out and grasped James Kim's arm, but he did not step forward and join in the young women's embrace.

At length Kathy stepped back with tears in her eyes. "Thanks for everything. It's a little amazing to find friends like you folks here in the middle of all this."

"And if you need anything again, you don't be afraid to come back. You know, if things don't work out downtown," James said.

Kathy just nodded and turned toward the alley.

"And remember, stay on Alvarado to Beverly. Beverly turns into 1st and it'll take you right to the County Building.

Kathy Warden again nodded her head and turned for one last look at the Kim family of Koreatown. She turned her head back to the alley before her face showed too much of the fear she had at returning to the ruined streets of L.A.

She hefted the backpack to her shoulders, realizing how she felt like a frightened schoolgirl leaving home. It must be the backpack, Kathy had not worn blue jeans and carried a backpack on the street since high school. This thought, of course, turned her mind to others. How had Granada Hills High withstood the quake? And, her parents home? Her parents?

The cycle of worry and conjecture started anew. But, this time she was able to put it aside easier than before. By the time Kathy reached Alvarado Street she had restored her belief that today would be a good day. She would be able to find someone with the Sheriff's Department who could help find Barry. And that would be the first step to getting life turned around right again.

It was with this thought that Kathy stepped out across the intersection of Ninth Street and Alvarado. The asphalt of the intersection jumped up to meet her step. The 6.7 aftershock that would become known as the "Morning After Quake" rose out of the Elysian Park Fault below downtown L.A. The uniquely powerful ground motion that this particular quake would be noted for knocked Kathy backwards to the ground. The backpack on her shoulders made the angle of her fall align to smash the crown of Kathy Warden's skull against the curb of Ninth Street. Across Los Angeles the Morning After Quake buried rescuers and those residents bold enough to have returned to their quake-damaged buildings and homes to start the recovery.

Kathy Warden's body lay spread eagled in the intersection of Ninth and Alvarado Streets. The thin patina of dust raised by the collapse of the entire row of apartments between Alvarado and Westlake eventually settled down on the area where she had fallen and on her motionless body.

■

An earthquake in 1940 near El Centro, California had a surface displacement in spots of over forty feet. That is, the ground on one side of the surface crack caused by the quake slid forty feet north along the crack compared to the land on the other side of the crack. The U.S. Highway east of El Centro was sliced through cleanly by the quake's fault line and the road segments east and west of the fault no longer lined up with each other. Similarly, the U.S./Mexican borderline slid almost fifteen feet sideways.

The floor of the Imperial Valley near El Centro is marked by escarpments above subterranean faults that show that the floor of the valley has, at various times, settled and/or lifted twenty to thirty feet after quakes.

May 7th, 9:10

Gil Echeverria was starting to worry about his idea to have his family come to Calexico rather than head east on the Interstate with everyone else from Brawley, El Centro and Imperial. Many of the Calexico residents had headed east themselves as soon as word spread of the torrent of water that was flooding the New River.

The reason for his concern was apparent from the main street in Calexico, just ten blocks west of the Echeverria residence in the housing tracts on Calexico east side. The downtown section of Calexico and the corresponding sector of Mexicali had now been washed downstream as the floodwaters cut the chasm of the New River ever wider. The border crossing was gone and buildings in the commercial district were falling into the waters as the undercut edge crept north and east.

Gil now stood with his son, Gilberto, Jr. or "Bert", in the pickup truck bed, watching the awesome spectacle of the flood. Several cars watched with them along with a crowd on foot.

"What you figure? "Bout a mile wide?" Gil asked.

"God, I don't know. Its hard to judge distance like that. But I wouldn't argue with a mile." Bert peered of to the south into Mexico. "When you figure it'll stop?"

"From what I heard from IID before they went off the air. They figure it is the ocean for sure now. So it should stop when the water gets up to sea level."

"You sure about the elevation here? Wouldn't want to have to swim to Arizona if you're wrong."

"I saw the map. All of Calexico is above sea level."

"Yes, but what if it just keeps eating away. you think it might cut all the way out to the house?"

Gil did not answer. He was standing still, feeling the truck rock gently on its springs. Another aftershock, nothing like the big ones yesterday, but fairly strong.

■

The fireman's rotary blade threw sparks out behind it in a rooster tail of yellow and white streaks. Steam rose from where the second fireman sprayed the saw blade with water to cool it as it cut through the reinforced concrete of the hospital floor. Barry Warden stood with Captain Riggs just inside the shattered window frames of the abandoned west wing of the hospital. The sawing was taking place another fifteen feet inside, at a spot where Riggs and Holmdahl had estimated the hallway in front of the sheriff's holding cells would be in the collapsed basement. This was in a direct line up from where the knocks had been heard in the basement joists at the other side of the building.

"Slow work." Barry said to Riggs.

"Yes, nerve-wracking. But there's no other way. Can't tell if the upper floors could take a jackhammer. Don't think it would. Those pillars." he pointed to the round columns along the wall, "are almost all cracked. Couldn't help but be with the way the whole floor dipped in. Probably same kind of pillars down below that gave way in the first place."

From where the two men stood the floor of the hospital slanted up into the dark recesses of the building. They were actually standing on what had been the second floor. This cut into the floor would be the first of two; this one to get into the ground floor cavity and another to get to the basement.

"Too bad you couldn't go in from the side through the basement, like you first thought."

"Yes, but it would have been a gamble. Going in from the side like that you don't really know what is holding up the stuff above you. You poke through the wrong wall and the whole kit and caboodle comes down on you. This is lots safer. Just slow." He was shouting to be heard over the whine of the saw, so Riggs motioned to his ears to show that it was not worth it to talk.

The floor below Barry's feet moved and at the same time the saw blade squealed, showered extra sparks and stopped. He thought the floor had given in to the cutting until he heard the fire captain shout.

"Quake. Everyone out!" Riggs shouted. The firefighter pushed Barry out through the window frame and into the sunlight. Barry kept moving, out away from the building into the hospital driveway. Ahead of him, Barry saw the crowd across the drive running *en masse* away from the hospital. He saw people fall under the feet of those behind. His own run was the same clumsy wobbling gate he had felt during the first quake. This quake had two powerful lurches to it that bent Barry's knees as he ran.

At the far side of the driveway, Barry turned to check on the firefighters behind him. He saw that Riggs had waited at the windows for the last of his four men. When the last man had cleared the ruined building wing, the building could be seen to move. A puff of dust came from the far right side. This was answered by another retort of dust from the left.

Riggs was running with his head looking back over his shoulder. Now he turned and motioned those in front of him back further. His shout of "Back!" boomed over the rumble of the quake. Barry followed Riggs orders, stumbling back a few more paces up onto the embankment next to the drive. Riggs and the firemen stopped nearby.

The quake still churned the ground as Barry, Riggs and the others turned together to watch the building as it attempted to mimic the quivering of the ground. In slow, but increasing motion, the six floors rocked, shuddered and then started to fold inward. The lower floors fell first, jetting a boiling cloud of white-gray dust outward. The dust cloud filled the street.

The dust would have kept the deputy and the firemen from seeing the collapse of the upper floors, had they been looking. Instead, they were diving higher up the embankment away from the collapsing building.

Barry was face down in the grass across the driveway as the vibration and rumble of the collapsing building joined that of the quake, each having a different quality, but both of gut-wrenching ferocity. The ferocious Morning After Quake had ended by the time the last cement had fallen.

Utter silence followed. Even the screams from the crowd seemed to have been stifled for a moment. The billowing cloud of dust enveloped everything, even shadowing out the sun to the east.

Barry could not see the building, or whatever was left of it. The debris had obviously not fallen beyond the driveway, but he knew little else. He rolled to a sitting position on the grassy slope. He could see Riggs and the firemen around him, barely. He restrained the urge to cough in the heavy dust. He saw the firemen pull masks up on their faces.

The dust hung in the air for an interminable moment. Barry's thoughts, as everyone else's was on the huge hospital. Had it really collapsed?

The dust slowly settled, coating everything, swirling. It was the shadow and the streaks of sunlight cutting through the upper levels of the dust cloud that gave Barry the first inkling of the extent of the collapse.

The morning sun cast a square, dark silhouette through the dust. The heavy cement dust accelerated its fall to the ground, revealing the truth that the silhouette had foretold. Most of the hospital remained. Only the already disabled west wing had fallen.

The west side of the hospital was neatly sliced away from the east. The six floors of the east wing could clearly be seen, divided at the central elevator shafts. Barry could see inside down the corridors of the east wing, where people were now rising from the floors, staring incredulously out the open wall toward the western hospital grounds.

A breeze from the north cleared the last of the dust cloud away.

The clear air showed everything in sight, including Barry and the firemen to be a uniform chalky gray color.

Barry sat up straight, feet braced on the grass embankment, trying to look at what had become of the west wing. The debris pile stretched over halfway across the street, but the bulk of it was right where it had fallen. The entire six stories were now no more than ten or fifteen feet tall, a mass of broken concrete slabs and steel rods.

People in the still-standing hospital structure looked out over the ruins. Several figures in white were hurriedly moving patients away from the open wall.

Riggs was slowly shaking his head staring at the ruins also. It was then that Barry realized that any hope of reaching anyone trapped in the basement was gone. The profound regret of this thought mixed rather peculiarly with the realization in Barry that he had been inside the flattened wing a few seconds before the collapse.

Barry sat and watched as Riggs and the other men got up and walked slowly toward their rescue vehicle. Jamil Allen was walking past them toward Barry when he stopped to ask Riggs something. The crowd behind him, murmured and pointed at the wreckage. Barry could not hear Jamil, but whatever he had asked was answered by a somber shaking of the fireman's yellow hardhat. With the response the LAPD officer's shoulders slumped and his gait toward Barry slowed.

To the south, two of the big Marine helicopters were flying in tandem toward the hospital. After the sound of the collapse the rumble from the flying behemoths seemed tame, almost mellow sounding.

Jamil walked up and faced Barry. He said nothing. Jamil put out a hand to help Barry rise from his seat on the embankment. Barry took the hand, pulled himself erect. He dusted himself off, raising a cloud of dust that forced Jamil back a few steps.

"When you're through shaking yourself down, the head honcho Marine, Colonel Munro, says he'd like to see you. Something about reconnaissance or some shit like that." Jamil's voice was tired and drawn.

"Reconnaissance. Of what?"

"I don't know. He asked me and I told him you knew this area better. It's a bit off my turf, San Pedro and Wilmington are my 'hood."

Barry pursed his brow, wondering what the Marine wanted. Together, the policeman and the deputy walked toward the south parking lot, now heliport. Their shuffling feet raised twin rows of dust clouds as they walked.

■

"I am sorry, Senora. It is the law. You can't take a rental car out of the country without a special permit from the rental company. You Americans have the same policy going the other way. You will have to turn around over there." The portly Mexican border guard pointed to a turnout to the right.

Sybil Perkins could see the American customs agents just beyond the border gates. She wanted to argue, but could not think of anything that would work. She pulled into the turnout and started to turn back into Tecate.

"Great. What now?" she asked Esteban.

"Well, you could cross on foot. But, that won't do much good. There isn't anything on the other side, just a little town, you'd still be a hundred kilometers from San Diego, in the middle of the mountains. On foot. Or ..."

"Or what?"

"You could fill up the tank and keep going to Tijuana. Tijuana is right next to San Diego and they have an international airport right in Tijuana or you can take a trolley from the border to the San Diego airport."

"Fine, sounds good for me. What about you?"

"I can't get to Mexicali anyway. I might as well visit my brother in Tijuana."

"Then it's settled. Which way to Tijuana?"

"Back to Highway 2 and then west. But first, perhaps we could stop and get some breakfast."

"Good idea."

■

"Where's Colonel Munro?" Barry shouted to a Marine officer at the landing zone control table.

The lieutenant pointed toward an olive drab trailer unit sitting a few yards away from landing zone. Barry had not been present for the arrival of this new addition, it had obviously been dropped in place by one of the big heavy-lift helicopters the Marines were using. It looked much like an office trailer used by a construction company except for the camouflage coloring. But it was obviously heavily reinforced and big steel cables used to lift it were still in place on the roof amongst the antenna masts.

Barry went over to the trailer. A Marine guard at the door nodded to him. "Everyone's inside, said to send you right in."

From the drab green exterior, Barry had not expected the interior to be as complex as it was. As he went in, he saw a bank of computer terminals and electronics racks on the far wall. The carpeted interior was dominated by a central map table surrounded by Plexiglas status boards. A decorative display of crossed swords and flags on the side wall announced "First Marine Division." Colonel Munro and several other Marines stood around the map table. Pete Valdez, the County Public Works supervisor, was with them. Seeing Barry, Munro motioned him to his side at the table.

"Deputy Warden, thanks for coming. I don't think you've met, General Burroughs, our Commander, and Colonel Margolis, the division Ops Officer," Munro gestured to the two officers next to him. The general across the table nodded and the colonel next to Munro shook hands with Barry. Munro did not bother introducing the lesser ranked Marines.

"I just started explaining our plan to Pete, I'll backtrack to catch you up." Munro shifted a chart on the table so Barry and Valdez could see it. It was a big Thomas Bros. wall map of south-central Los Angeles with an acetate cover over it. The acetate was marked up with lines and areas marked in grease pencil.

Munro looked at Barry, then fingered the map, "Our problem is this. Word we get from our connection to State Emergency Services and the Federal Emergency Management Agency is that this whole operation is going to be bigger and longer than anyone planned. We left Pendleton this morning planning on running a Navy field hospital for a few weeks until the local authorities got back on their feet. The picture is getting pretty clear that it isn't going to be a short-term thing and the military, everybody, Marines, Army, the works, is going to be throwing everything they have into this. Los Angeles doesn't have any water, utilities, phones, nothing ... And they estimate that it could be weeks or more to get everything back. They've got untold tens of thousands of injured and dead. Hundreds of thousands of homeless. Freeways are useless, either broken or blocked. The three airports that we could use in this area are out of service for some time, the runways are rippled and utilities out. Long Beach Airport has reportedly got a cliff running catty-cornered across the runway, our pilots saw it on the way up this morning. We're still trying to get firm word on LAX."

Munro took a deep breath and collected his thoughts before continuing, "It's clear that there is going to have to be some major effort to house and care for the tens or hundreds of thousands of people hurt or homeless. And, the military is going to have to get things going. Probably start setting up tent cities, maybe evacuating people out to other parts of the state or country. Seems the Marines are once again `first in' so we have to set the groundwork for the bigger effort to follow.

"Our foothold here at Harbor UCLA is not going to cut it. Too small an area, just four landing pads. And now that the west wing has cast doubt on the main building, we might as well start out fresh, rather than pounding our square peg into ... you get it." Munro tapped the map at an "x" that indicated the hospital. "That's where you two gentlemen come in. We need to find a proper place to set up, but we don't know the area. You do. Here's what we need. First, we need something with lots of open area for a tents and for helicopter ops. Second, it needs to be fairly central to the whole South Central region, that's our area of responsibility, at least for now. Last, it needs to be secure, shouldn't be too close to heavily populated areas. We hear that there is virtual open warfare in some of the areas to the north." He pointed in a circular motion between the Crenshaw district and Watts. "They've got riots, looting, gang turf battles. LAPD has abandoned everything in here, there's word coming from the state the LAPD got hit real hard personnel wise. Things are pretty chaotic and we're going to have to rely on our own resources a lot. We need your input as to where would be a good place for us to set up our main staging area."

Barry looked at the map before him. A large area was blocked off with black grease pencil lines hashed across it. "What's this mean?"

A major spoke, "That's the estimated `dead zone' from the big gas explosion. Nothing much alive in there and probably all facilities gone, no utilities without rebuilding everything. We figured it would be best to pick somewhere where power and water could at least be foreseeable."

Barry blinked at the map. This `dead zone' encompassed much of southern L.A. County, including virtually all of Carson and much of northern Long Beach.

Before he could say anything else the officer also volunteered, "The red areas are the hot spots from the satellite photos, either burnt out or fires still burning. The yellow are the fault lines from the quakes, as best we know them."

Barry was again taken aback at the extent of the areas so marked. He continued to look over the map. He looked up at Valdez.

"What about Dominguez Hills? Pete?" Barry asked.

"Sure, I was just thinking that."

"What's that?" the Marine general spoke for the first time.

Barry answered, pointing just to the northeast of the red `X' that marked their own location. "California State University, Dominguez Hills. Lots of open ground. Maybe even dorm and classroom space, if it survived the Big One yesterday. And it has got a big golf course and sports fields nearby for tent cities. Even some open, undeveloped land, park land nearby. It's all state owned land and not a lot of buildup around, compared to other areas."

The general spoke again, "Sounds perfect, have we done anything to check it out?"

The major stammered briefly and answered, "No sir. Not yet. Its right on the Newport-Inglewood fault, it was covered by yellow so we hadn't thought of it. If it isn't damaged too badly, it would work out fine."

The general continued, "OK. Colonel, let's get a bird over there to check it out. Take these gentlemen with you, if they don't mind. If it checks out for our purposes, get on the horn with the FEMA guys and tell them what we plan on doing and have them tell the state and local people. Don't ask them, tell them. I don't need to wait for some bureaucrat's approval. Nobody's going to second guess anybody taking positive action at a time like this. If I had waited for Washington yesterday afternoon for an OK, we'd still be at Pendleton picking our noses watching fucking CNN about this. As it is, I sent an `Unless otherwise directed' message to them, somebody saw it and agreed, this morning the President issues an Executive Order telling the whole military to do what I told you gentlemen last night. We've got a couple hundred thousand people in harm's way today, I don't want any Marine officer to be waiting for anyone's approval, except mine. And, if you can't get to me, just do it, and tell me later. Everyone clear on that."

No one spoke. The general turned around and walked out of the trailer.

■

In the 1923 Tokyo Earthquake, the Tokyo-Yoko-hama metropolitan area shifted 15 feet to the southwest in the period of a few seconds. 143,000 people died from the quake and resulting fires. 50,000 buildings were destroyed. The greatest loss of life came from a firestorm after the quake. Damage to roads and fire equipment and the loss of water pressure due to broken underground water mains made it impossible to fight the many fires which eventually destroyed forty percent of the city.

The 1994 Northridge, California quake showed that losses due to explosion of natural gas supply lines was one of the deadliest components of the disaster and certainly one of the most spectacular. In many cases, with water supply cut off, many fire crews turned to the swimming pools for water to fight the conflagrations. In 1995, the fire department of Kobe, Japan stood helpless, without any municipal water, as vast sections of the city burned following their quake.

May 7th, 11:30 A.M.

"Look, Ma'am. I didn't make the rule." The young Santa Barbara motorcycle cop was being respectful, but losing patience, he had said the same thing too many times this morning. The traffic circle was cordoned off so that no one could head downtown Santa Barbara from the east without permission. "No vehicles downtown, unless you've got a pass from the Emergency Services Office. You'll have to turn around. Just follow the traffic circle around and go back the way you came."

Natalie glanced over the where Genevieve sat next to her, raising her eyebrows. She turned back to policeman.

"How do I get a pass?" Natalie Weld asked.

"You have to walk down to the police station on Figueroa. But, I'll tell you now, you won't qualify. Only residents in the downtown area and those with a critical need get passes."

"But this young woman lost everything." Natalie pointed her thumb at Genevieve. "She doesn't have any ID, or money or, anything. She's destitute."

The cop took the opportunity to bend over further and glance over his sunglasses at the beautiful brunette in the passenger seat, but then he shook his head. "That won't qualify as critical. The banks are closed, the DMV on Bath Street is flooded and has waist-high mud, the stores are closed, the Courthouse is flattened. There isn't anybody downtown Santa Barbara that can help her." The cop's patience was gone now. "All I can suggest is to go back home and wait until things get pulled together a little bit. Did you folks try in Montecito? Maybe they did better than downtown in the quake."

"Thank you, Officer." Natalie started to go, but thought of something else. "Oh, by the way, you know anything about elsewhere. Goleta or even Santa Ynez?"

The cop shook his head, "Downtown Goleta is just as bad as downtown Santa Barbara, they say maybe worse, you know it's right on the Goleta Slough, the whole airport area is still under water. And they have a landslide closing 101 at Gaviota Pass and Highway 154 at Painted Cave is out. The CHP says the whole mountainside is gone. Nothing left."

"How about Ventura? Anything the other way down the coast?"

The cop started shaking his head the instant he heard the city mentioned, "Same with 101 at Rincon. The whole freeway settled into the ocean, it's right on the beach in the first place. Santa Barbara's pretty much cut off. Without the airport and the freeways, that's about the only way in or out." The cop pointed to the sky over Alameda Padre Serra, where a large blue helicopter flew to the west.

"OK, thanks." Natalie put the Rover in gear and moved out around the Alameda Padre Serra traffic circle, retracing her way back uphill.

"I guess that explains where you father's been. Probably can't get down from Santa Maria" Natalie said, looking in the rear-view mirror at her son and daughter in the back seat.

Genevieve had been wondering about a `Mister' Weld, but had not asked Natalie. Natalie was a great hostess, but rather closed mouthed about personal matters. Genevieve appreciated this, too many Americans blabbered on about life history and personal matters.

Genevieve had not understood all of the place names the policeman had mentioned, but she understood that downtown was out of the question and Santa Barbara was landlocked, if that was the right word.

"Where to now?" Kiki asked from the back.

"Well, Genevieve said she banks at BankCal, like us. And I wouldn't mind having some extra cash at a time like this so let's try the BankCal out on East Valley Road. Maybe BankCal will let me vouch for Genevieve and get her some cash and bank I.D." Natalie smiled over to Genevieve and when she heard no objections she gunned the throttle up the hill. The Rover's transmission downshifted for the climb up the face of Santa Barbara's Riviera toward the Weld home and the hills of Montecito beyond.

There were several homes with visible damage on the way over to Montecito's "village" area, tilting roof lines, crumbled bricks, but nothing as severe as what happened to Genevieve's cliffside home. In one spot, the retaining wall for Alston Road was collapsed, closing the road down to one lane.

The road curved down into Montecito, lush landscaping lined the sides of the East Valley Road. Natalie and Genevieve saw a front loader scoop shovel working on debris in the Town Centre parking lot before they got a glimpse of the buildings.

Natalie Weld parked in the first parking space off East Valley Road. A handful of men in hardhats worked alongside the scoop shovel. Several sheriff deputies in khaki uniforms and a small crowd of people watched the equipment operator scoop from a pile of blond-colored bricks and load it into a waiting dump truck. Occasionally one of the waiting men would run into the debris pile and retrieve something.

Natalie and her children sat quietly for a moment, watching the men work on the brick pile. Genevieve fidgeted in her seat and then asked Natalie, "What is it we are waiting for?"

Natalie turned to Genevieve and looked with surprise, "Oh, I thought you knew. That," she pointed at the pile of blond brick, "is the Montecito BankCal branch. Looks like we need to think of something else."

Genevieve had never been to this little branch bank closest to her home, Michael had always handled the banking matters. But, seeing the destruction of the bank that Natalie had thought would give her money, Genevieve Dumont felt the return of the depression that had come with the collapse of her house and the sight of her husband's building on television. She sat back in the seat and watched the scoop shovel work.

"What now?" Kiki Weld asked from the back.

Genevieve looked over the Natalie who simply shrugged her shoulders.

■

Everything was apricot colored. But Kathy could not think of the name for the color or understand why everything had such a hue. The small corner of consciousness that noted the color failed to note that "everything" consisted only of the color and the thoughts, the visual memories, that pulsed into that consciousness along with the throbbing pain from somewhere beyond. Sometimes the pulsing bursts of pain would darken the apricot colors to blood red, or with the worst pulses, to blackness, when the pain departed with the color.

Now, from the apricot mush of her thoughts came the realization that something was touching her face. At the same time a searing white light burnt into her from one eye. After a few seconds the stab of light stopped, only to strike again from the other eye.

A deep, calm voice spoke. She knew she recognized the words, but could not put the words' meanings together.

"Marked non-responsiveness left pupil. Consistent with blunt head trauma. Concussion. Scalp contusions, need suturing. Displaced fracture of occipital region requires reduction, prep her for surgery, full head prep. If radiology can get at least a partial skull series, it will help. They up and running yet?"

A woman's voice spoke, "I'll check. Anything else?"

"Yes, tag her for medevac. If she makes it through surgery, she's a candidate to get out of here. The Old Man may be an arrogant SOB, but he is right, Good Samaritan's got to clear some of the beds, we got more coming in than we can handle. Neurosurgery recovery is a good candidate for sending elsewhere. We just don't have the resources."

Hands had been holding her head as the voice spoke what were to her unintelligible words. The hands touched the back of her head and the pain rushed in, pushing her thoughts into the enveloping redness. Just before the blackness shrouded her totally, Kathy felt the curious feeling of someone pulling on her big toe and tying something to it.

■

"F.D.I.C. San Francisco Region, Mr. Pfeiffer's office. May I help you?" a woman's voice said.

Gloria hurriedly took the phone off speaker and said, "Yes, this is Gloria Contreras, branch manager of the BankCal office in North Palm Springs. I have some questions and several people have indicated Mr. Pfeiffer may be the one with the answers."

"Just a moment, I'll see if he is available."

Elevator music replaced the woman's voice.

The man's voice came on in a moment, "This is Marcus Pfeiffer."

"Thank you for taking my call. My name is Gloria Contreras and I'm the branch manager of the BankCal branch in North Palm Springs. I've been trying all morning to get in touch with corporate officials of BankCal and I've been unsuccessful. The only people I can get in touch with are other branch managers who are as in the dark as I am. I made some calls around the banking regulatory circles and I've been told you might be able to shed some light on what's going on or what we should do, you know, with the quake and all."

"Well, Ms. Contreras, that was some pretty good detective work.

The FAX from Washington appointing the receivership is still warm."

"Receivership?"

"Yes. Twenty-seven banks and S&L's headquartered in Southern California, including BankCal, have been put into emergency receivership. Probably more coming, when we get word on how bad the outlying areas were hit."

"What does that mean? What should I be doing?"

"Well, first off, we have some time to put things together. There's a national bank holiday through Monday morning, at least for our area. And, I just heard that SEC closed the securities exchanges a few minutes ago to protect from a sell-off of stocks effected by the quake. I don't know why they let them open this morning, in the first place. Anyway, I've got until Monday morning to get the handle on several hundred bank branches and twenty-seven main offices. Most of which would appear, from television, to be in ruins. You're the first field operations person I've talked to this morning and since you apparently have a working telephone, you would seem to be among the lucky few in southern California. How's everything else for you, any damage?"

"Just some crumbled bricks around the ATM and boarded-up windows. Nothing big, which is lucky considering how close we are to the San Andreas."

"How about operations? Personnel?"

"We haven't heard from our assistant manager or head teller since the quake hit on their lunch-hour, everybody else is OK? Operationally, I guess you'd say we are in a jam, at least for now. Our computers are just a node on the BankCal network. In good times we're connected to a server in San Bernardino and they are connected to L.A. and they ..."

"Yeh, I get the picture. But you've got to have hard-copy daily print-outs. That's required by federal regs."

"Sure, but they're printed in San Bernardino as of close of the bank day and shipped with the armored car bag the next day. The armored car didn't make it yesterday, so we only have the Monday morning printout and its Wednesday morning. That's two and a half days of transactions not on the printouts."

"But you've still got the daily receipts the armored car didn't pick up, so you're really only missing the one business day's transactions. That's a good start at reconstructing your accounts. I suggest you get started. I'll be giving the same instructions to the other couple hundred branches between now and Monday. Your opportune call gave you a head start. I'd suggest you get your people going on a standalone computer and a good data-base program that uses SQL query language. That's what the FDIC staffers flying in from Washington will need to see when they audit each branch prior to starting the deposit insurance payouts, and restructuring."

"It's that bad. You're planning to use deposit insurance ... I mean . . BankCal ... ?"

"From what Washington told me, they consider almost all of the big southern California banks out of action, permanently. The receivership isn't going to be temporary. You and your staff should consider themselves employees of FDIC."

"What about cash for operations? The bank holiday helps for today, but when the line we have outside comes back Monday, we'll be in a jam. These people are going to need money for repairs, food, you know. We only keep one day's cash on hand, and that's one normal day. After a long weekend with no ATM machine, my customers are going to be cash hungry on Monday morning. If I don't get an armored car of cash from BankCal, or FDIC, somewhere, I'll be closing as soon as I open on Monday."

The FDIC executive paused for a moment, "I'm sure we'll have more information for you as soon as we get a handle on the scope of this. If you'll stay on the line I'll have my secretary get your contact information. I'm sure you'll understand we have a lot to digest ourselves, all of your own problems multiplied times several hundred."

"I understand, thanks for your help."

While she waited for the secretary, Gloria reached into her bookcase for the software manual and motioned for Brian to come over to her desk.

When he got there, Gloria had just finished giving the FDIC secretary her office and home phone numbers, as well as her non-Bank-Cal Internet E-mail address. Gloria handed Brian the software manual, "Check the index to see if this uses SQL query language, I think it does. If it does, learn to use it."

Brian smiled, "BD2, no problem, used it in Financial Statistics class my senior year. It has both an SQL module and I think it interfaces with most of the other main database languages."

"Good," Gloria stood up and patted the monitor of the HP computer on her credenza. "It's all yours, you're officially our database expert."

"What's up?"

"Our new boss, the FDIC, wants us to set up a new database, reconstructing our chart of accounts, locally, without the BankCal network."

"Manually? That's got to be thousands of accounts! And, a pretty complex structure, interest compounding, credit lines, we ..."

"No problem, we've got the whole weekend," Gloria said as she headed to get the computer printout binders from the Head Teller's desk.

As she walked off, Brian mumbled, "FDIC? New boss?"

She did not answer.

■

After the 1971 San Fernando Quake, some eighty thousand people were evacuated from part of Los Angeles below the damaged Van Norman Dam. Luckily, the large reservoir behind the dam was safely emptied and a disaster was prevented. There are more than twenty reservoirs in the hills above Los Angeles which could hazard downstream homes and businesses if damaged by a quake.

May 7th, 12:00 Noon

Flying in the big Marine helicopter was like flying in an airliner compared to Barry Warden`s only other experience in a helicopter, the orientation flight in the little Sheriff's Department traffic chopper given to most new deputies. Also, the ride inside the Blackhawk was quiet in relation to the noise it made to the outside observer.

Barry still was not quite certain why the Marines needed to fly around to check on the sites for setting up their expanded operations, but they seemed determined and it did not seem to be his place to question their operations, even if they were asking his advice, as a "local."

Pete Valdez, now wearing his Los Angeles County Public Works windbreaker, was seated beside Barry. Colonel Munro was seated just ahead of Barry, with the other colonel. He turned and spoke after they cleared the ground, "This sure is a nice way to fly. The Marines only have a few of these Blackhawks, equipped to carry passengers, one squadron back in Virginia for flying VIP's and most flag officers in command manage to snag one."

Barry nodded. "How long will the flight be?"

"Well, we`re going to do a circuit down past the Long Beach

Airport and back up to the east before getting to Dominguez Hills. We wanted to see the worst of the damage now that it is sun up. Most of us, the staff officers, flew in real early."

"We going to see the big blast area?"

"Sure are. It should be coming up on the right in just a minute."

Barry turned to look out the Plexiglas window. Just as he was focusing on the scene below, one of the Marines seated behind him let out a long whistle. Below them columns of smoke rose from the charred landscape of the town of Carson and the neighboring Wilmington section of Los Angeles. The few buildings that still stood were the exception. Barry could see hulks of vehicles standing in the streets and along the length of the Harbor Freeway, which they followed south. The high tension line towers that paralleled the freeway were crumpled abstract skeletons. Power lines drooped like cobwebs.

The helicopter banked slowly to the left, leaving the freeway corridor. Barry looked quickly to the west, trying to keep his orientation with the hills of the Palos Verdes Peninsula to the west that he was most familiar with.

Something was wrong.

He knew the area below him. Or at least, he thought he did. Barry's memory of the landscape did not match up with that he now saw below him. He figured he should be seeing the rows of post-War tract homes of Wilmington. The entire view below was a grid of charcoal and black, barely recognizable as city streets. The trees, power poles and structures were either flattened or burned away.

As they crossed over the tank farm that had been ground zero nothing was recognizable. Barry remembered the dozens of tanks that had covered the green hills north of Long Beach. Neither the tanks nor the green hills remained. There were only blackened, unrecognizable shapes.

"You looking for something special? You seem pretty intent on something," Colonel Munro asked Barry over his shoulder.

"Oh, I guess so. We had an officer needs assistance call from a couple of deputies pretty near the center of that yesterday right after the main quake. I thought I might be able to make out the location, but I can't. Don't even recognize the main landmarks, all burnt up like it is."

"I can't even tell what kind of buildings there were. Do you know?" Munro asked Barry.

"Sure this whole area from below us to the south and west was housing tracts. That directly below us and off toward the harbor would be the tank farms."

"I guess that's what went up." Valdez said.

"Don't know. Haven't heard. Is that what they say?" Barry asked Munro.

"Yes. It first came in as a possible nuclear blast, but it turned out to be petrochemical. Probably this tank farm, if that's what you say it was." Munro said.

Someone behind them spoke, "Jesus, you ever see anything like this?"

An officer seated directly behind Barry answered, "Only in a bad nightmare. Or a science fiction movie."

The high-rises to the south in Long Beach were hidden in the pall of smoke, but to the east Barry could just make out the landmark of Signal Hill.

"Should be coming up on Long Beach airport soon." Munro surmised.

"Yes, that's Signal Hill. We should be just southeast of the airport." Barry said, pointing to the landmark hill.

In answer to their predictions the timbre of the aircraft's engines changed and the Blackhawk headed lower to the ground.

"We need to make sure what condition the airport is in. It would make things a lot easier to resupply if we can use the nearest airport here for supply flights," Munro explained.

Barry continued to watch as they descended. The landscape changed somewhat. The stark burned out area with its myriad of smoke wisps stopped and the more normal cityscape reappeared. Even then, when Barry looked closely below him he could see telltale signs of trouble and destruction. Some smoke pyres still rose from the streets of north Long Beach and Carson. Buildings along the arterial streets occasionally stretched out into the streets in piles of bricks and wood.

"There's Long Beach Airport," came on announcement from someone in the cockpit.

Peering forward Barry could make out the Marriott Hotel near the passenger terminal, both of which were standing. Everything beyond the terminal was obscurred by a wall of smoke blown from the north.

"The big fire to the north is the McDonnell-Douglas plant," Valdez explained. "Still burning."

Colonel Munro hmmed a response. He was craning his neck to see the runway area west of the terminal.

Several airliners could be seen on the ground near the terminal. Everyone on board the helicopter looked closely at the main runway, searching for damage.

"Look there. On the east-west auxiliary runway." the young officer behind Barry said.

Barry moved his eyes down to the smaller runway. Now that his attention was brought to it, he could clearly see the jagged scar that cut across the runway and its adjacent taxiways. The morning sun cast a shadow, showing the eastern edge of the crack in the earth was raised above the ground level to the west.

"Looks like about a five-foot lip." Munro said to no one in particular.

One of the other officers answered, "Yes, but it looks like the main runway is clear."

"Let's make sure Air Ops gets down there to talk to them about setting up a liaison office. We'll need them up and operating. Word is that the runways at LAX are folded up like a row of toppled dominoes." the colonel seated next to Munro ordered someone else farther back in the cabin.

"There! At the end of the main runway. Looks like a 737 down." the voice from the cockpit said.

Everyone turned their attention from the airport to look farther north. They could all see it, the white tail and nose cones connected together by a charred skeleton of the airliner, but whatever fire there had been was long since extinguished. Several vehicles were parked around the blackened quadrant of burned grass around what was left of the aircraft.

"You think the quakes caused that?" Barry asked.

"Who knows? Maybe the explosion." Munro answered.

The helicopter churned on to the northwest. Barry was able to follow the crack in the earth from the airport property until it disappeared in the rows of tract houses in Bixby Knolls in neighboring north Long Beach. Even there the rows of identical houses showed the continuing path of the quake's greatest destruction with a wide swath of flattened houses and an abnormally high incidence of smoke plumes and burned out spaces in the pattern of the tract.

Barry watched as they passed over the country clubs and parks, Valdez stood peering over Barry's shoulder out the near window. As the crossed over the Los Angeles River, Valdez exclaimed, "Look at the river!"

"Isn't that the one we see in movies with the concrete walls and bottom." Munro asked.

"That's it. It's never this full. I didn't notice it on the first leg. It's almost over the edges. They must have lost a dam up above."

"That must run all across Los Angeles like that."

"Yes, all the way from the mountains up north. They're losing a lot of water."

"And what else is going, with the water?" Munro asked.

"Here's another tank farm and what looks like the railroad." the officer behind Barry said. The young man seemed to be keeping track of facilities.

"We should be right over Dominguez Hills after this," Barry said.

"Counter race-track orbit. On the stadium." Munro ordered the cockpit crew.

The helicopter swung into a broad right hand turn. From their side of the aircraft Munro and Barry could now see the whole of the California State University campus.

"Looks like they have some damage. One of that cluster of buildings is missing glass, lots of it." the voice behind Barry announced.

"Yeh, but everything seems to be standing," the colonel added.

"Lots of people around," the `spotter' said. "They`d still be in session, first week in May."

"But they won't be anymore, after the Big One. They're not going to have utilities or anything more than the rest of the city. Those standing around are probably just that, hanging around for want of anything better to do." Colonel Munro spoke as though he had made up his mind, he leaned forward and shouted to the pilot. "Take it down, that big plaza by the tan building looks good. Check it out and if its OK, put her down."

Colonel Munro turned his attention back to the window and said, "Now we get to find the Dean and tell him about his new tenants."

"Sir?" the officer behind Barry spoke up. "It's Chancellor, not Dean, and it's `her' new tenants, not `his.' The printout we got from the Internet on the campus shows a Lucille Waters, PhD. is the head honcho. Chancellor Lucille Waters."

"That figures. Let's see the printout."

Munro sat back in his seat, his tone leaving no doubt about the disdain he had for dealing with women, especially ones in authority.

The helicopter gave a gut wrenching lurch as it slowed to hover over the university campus. Barry watched out the window as tiny figures on the ground pointed up at them.

■

Genevieve tapped the receiver on the phone, listening. Nothing. She shook her head at Natalie, "Not yet."

Natalie handed her a mug of coffee and the two women joined Kiki at the kitchen table.

"They said on the TV it might be days before they restored phone service, maybe weeks," Kiki said.

"It just seems so strange to be totally out of touch with the world. Not knowing ..." Genevieve stopped there.

"I guess we should count our blessings that the electricity went back on so fast. They say those poor people in Riverside and San Bernardino may be without any utilities for weeks," Natalie said. "I guess our only critical shortage in Santa Barbara is water. And phones."

Kiki snickered at something.

"You want to share the humor with us?" her mother asked.

"It just sounded so funny, Santa Barbara, right on the beach and with the whole downtown flooded is short of water."

"I think the right word is ironic, not funny. You could be drinking swimming pool water before long, so don't call it funny too soon." Both Kiki and Genevieve rolled their eyes at this.

Kiki changed the subject, "When do you think we'll hear from Daddy?"

"It shouldn't be too long. He'll find some way to get back down from Santa Maria. He's a pretty resourceful man."

"How far is Santa Maria?" Genevieve asked. "I don`t know the area very well, yet."

"Oh, I guess about an hour's drive north, over the Santa Ynez Mountains. You heard the policeman say the Pass is cut off. With Los Angeles such a mess, they'll have to open the roads north up soon, it's the only way out for Santa Barbara."

Natalie Weld knew, as soon as she spoke, that the talk of Los Angeles was not the right thing to say to Genevieve. The woman looked down into her coffee and fell silent. Natalie tried to think of something to say.

"Genevieve, you really have to have faith. You can't assume the worst, until you know more. He could be just fine, you know."

"Yes, he could ...," Genevieve let the thought drift away. Natalie sat up straight, "Is that the front door?"

Her question was answered by a loud exclamation from a baritone voice in the foyer, "Jesus Christ! What happened? Natalie?"

Both Natalie and Kiki jumped up, with Kiki shouting, "Daddy!" Both ran out of the kitchen, Genevieve followed them.

By the time Genevieve got to the foyer, both the woman and the girl were in the arms of a tall silver-haired man. The Weld's son ran in from his bedroom and joined the family hug.

The man, whom Genevieve could only assume was Mr. Weld, Natalie and the children all started to talk at once. "Where were you when . . ?" "How'd you get down?" "Is the rest of the house OK?"

"Whoa? One person at a time." Mr. Weld took charge. "I see you all are Ok? Any damage, other than this?" He indicated the chandelier that still sat on the marble floor. "I opened the door and saw that, I thought ..." As he spoke another tall, handsome man, somewhat younger than Weld, appeared through the front door.

"How'd you get through? The police said everything is closed off," Natalie asked him.

"Well, it's been an adventure. We were coming down 101 after court in Santa Maria when the quakes hit. The CHP turned us back south of Buellton. We tried 154, but it was closed at Lake Cachuma by a rock slide. We waited there for Caltrans to clear it and then learned that the whole Pass was closed. Tried to call, no phones. Well, to make a long story short, we finally wound up back in Buellton in the last motel room in town. Huge traffic back-up in Buellton, everyone headed south on the 101. We heard about how bad Santa Barbara got hit with the quake and tsunami and this morning we hired a helicopter from Santa Ynez Airport. They flew us to the Polo Grounds where we walked over to Ted's house on Padaro Lane. Which, ... Come' n in Ted," he motioned the other man inside, "Which, Ted's house that is, was quite a shock ..."

The other man, Ted, now nodded and smiled at the Weld family and took off his aviator-style sunglasses to look over at Genevieve. Weld continued, "Ted's place was in ruins, just splinters."

Natalie cooed, "Oh my."

Ted cut in, "Yes, wet splinters. Couldn't really find anything, 'cept my SL, sitting right there where the carport used to be. A little soggy, covered in seaweed, a few dings, but started right up."

"That's too bad, about your house, but you're better off than Genevieve ... I forgot, Genevieve," Natalie motioned back to Genevieve, who waited by the kitchen door, "let me introduce you to my husband, Donald Weld, and one of his law partners, Ted Galloway. Don, Ted, this is Genevieve Dumont, our neighbor and house guest, unfortunately the later, since she lost her house in the quake."

Both men nodded to Genevieve, who, rather than crossing the foyer to shake hands, gave a little wave and smile, which Ted returned, saying, "If I have to be a homeless refugee, it is great to be in such charming company."

"I thought Ted might stay with us because of his house ... You have Genevieve in the garden room?" Don Weld asked.

Natalie nodded, "Yes, but we've still got two spare rooms. No problem. You guys probably could use some lunch and coffee. Let's go into the kitchen and swap stories."

Genevieve held the kitchen door open as the others came over.

Ted hurried around the Welds and took the door from her, managing to brush her shoulders and back with his arm. The Weld children and their father went into the kitchen after Genevieve. Natalie took the opportunity of going through last to give her husband's junior partner a quick palm down signal to slow up and tapped her wedding ring.

Ted responded with a churlish grin and a flourishing "after you" motion toward the kitchen. Natalie made sure Ted saw as she rolled her eyes toward the ceiling in mock derision.

■

All of the drapes in the Chancellor's conference room were pulled wide open to make up for the lack of electric lighting. Dr. Lucille Waters, a stout black woman of fifty-plus years, sat at the end of the long mahogany table flanked by two of her assistants, a black man and a young white woman. Colonel Munro sat farther down at the table with two of his officers. For reasons as yet unknown to Barry, the colonel had demanded that Barry and the county public works supervisor accompany him to the meeting. They sat across the table from Munro.

Dr. Waters ebony features furrowed in deep concern.

"Let me get this straight," she said. "The Marine Corps wants to take over my campus?"

Colonel Munro shook his head, "That's not what we envision. Our current needs are just enough room to set up a field hospital and some support facilities. You have about the only uncluttered open space in this section of the city. Your buildings survived the quake better than anything we've seen."

"That's because we knew we were building on top of the fault line. We built them to stay put. And," she paused for emphasis, "we built them to house the thousands of students who have paid for a university education, not for a military base, hospital or homeless camp."

One of her assistants, the stern-faced black man about Barry's age who wore an African tunic rather than a business suit, decided to take up his boss's tone, "At this point, since we are fortunate enough to have escaped serious structural damage, we hope to be able to restore enough services in the near future to allow us to complete the academic year, so the students don't lose out on everything they've worked for since January."

Munro stared into the black man's eyes. Barry could see the muscles in the colonel's jaw tighten and then relax before he said, "Sir, I am not sure upon what you base that hope, but the reality of what I have seen in this city is that neither you nor the rest of Los Angeles are going to be able to restore enough services to do anything other than stop famine and a cholera epidemic, if you're lucky, in the near future," he intentionally mimicked the black official's phrase.

Munro continued, "And I know that millions of citizens have lost everything they have worked a lifetime for, not just a semester of college. The families of half those students you speak of don't have houses anymore and that the jobs that paid the tuition here for those students are probably gone, too. The siblings of some of your students were probably among the gangs that fought pitched battles with the L.A.P.D. in the Rosecrans district last night. My guess is that those students you speak of are eating leftover potato chips and Snickers bars right now, and that in a few days, if not already, your biggest problem is going to be what to feed those students and where to send those thousands of students to relieve themselves on a campus that may not have water to flush the toilets for weeks or months. I assume that by restoring services, you did not think of digging latrines in the lawn outside the girls' dorms."

As the university officials blinked at his words, the colonel continued without giving a chance to respond, "We, on the other hand, have a different, but, I think you will see, integrally related problem. These gentlemen," he waved an arm at Barry and Valdez, "have a collapsed county hospital, Harbor UCLA, and several thousand critically injured people literally laying in the boulevard outside the hospital. I have a fully equipped military field hospital and all the support equipment and staff I need, but there is not room in the Harbor UCLA grounds for us. Our military hospital comes along with a complete field utility and sanitation system. The combat engineers for the First Marine Division have airlift-able generators big enough to power a small city and they are sitting on an airstrip less than an hour's flying time from here. Our field kitchens are set up to feed more troops than you have student body many times over.

"In short, the site where we put our field hospital will have electrical power by mid-afternoon and will be serving hot meals to whomever shows up by suppertime. It will be the first place that receives the supplies and medical care the federal government will be flying in, we'll make sure of that with a couple hundred rotary aircraft dedicated to our needs. And, in the midst of a city in total chaos, our chosen site will have the tightest physical security on planet Earth, the U.S. Marines will see to that. We need your open space and a couple buildings, but we don't come with our hands empty. Now, it sounds like that is a symbiotic relationship to me. Tell me where I'm wrong."

Dr. Waters waited, thinking, then asked, "How do you keep my campus from becoming a mecca for everyone without shelter or who is injured in south L.A.? If things are getting as bad as you say and your offer is such a good deal for us?"

Now it was Colonel Munro's turn to think before answering, "You know, I am not sure I have a good answer to that. It could be a valid concern. I, ah, well ..."

With Munro stumbling for words, Barry Warden, contrary to his natural quiet nature in such situations spoke out, "I guess the only answer for any of us, as public servants, is to ask what brings the highest and best public good. Especially in times like this."

Dr. Waters nodded her acknowledgement. Barry caught a look of approval in the colonel's eyes.

The Chancellor took off her glasses and folded them on the table. She looked from Barry, then to the Colonel.

"If we are going to proceed with this, what exactly do you have in mind?" Dr. Waters asked.

The black assistant protested, "Are you sure we should proceed? We don't have any contact or concurrence from anyone at the state level,"

Colonel Munro was back in form, he did not wait a second to answer, cutting off any reply from the Chancellor, "I have a satellite communications console in my helicopter, I can have you in contact with the Governor's Office in Sacramento in a few minutes, if you doubt your Chancellor's authority to assist us."

Dr. Waters did not give her assistant a chance to answer, "That won't be necessary. But, I'll take a rain check on the free phone call."

With a mutual smile at this last comment, the deal was done.

■

The Aero Mexico ticket agent drummed her nails on the keyboard frame as she waited again for the credit card confirmation. As Sybil Perkins viewed the young Mexican woman she noted the stark difference between the severely precise make-up and overly moussed look of the Latina and Sybil's own rumpled, slept-in-the-car appearance.

At last, this ticket agent shook her head and handed the credit card back to Sybil, shaking her head, "I am sorry Senorita Perkins, it did not go through. Perhaps you could pay cash?"

"It can't have been declined. It's a corporate card for a big American engineering firm." Sybil protested.

"Senorita, I did not say it was declined. It just will not go through, no approval code. Many of the American credit cards have been like that today. It's the computers, or the telephones in America or something. You can understand, with the tremors, you see." The ticket agent smiled at a man standing behind Sybil, acknowledging the delay Sybil was causing for everyone.

"How much is it, in U.S. dollars?"

"The only thing we have left today on the flight to San Francisco is business class. That would be $413.00."

Sybil frowned, she knew without looking she had nothing like that in cash. "And there is nothing else, less expensive, into America, today."

"No, Senorita. The only cheaper regular flights up north are to Los Angeles and they are, of course, all cancelled until further notice. Perhaps you should try crossing the border and trying up at Lindbergh Field in San Diego. Maybe they are having better luck accepting the American credit cards." The agent smiled a final, condescending smile at

Sybil as she reached past her for the ticket of the man behind her. "Next?"

■

Geologists estimate that the typical five thousand foot mountain, such as those ringing the Los Angeles Basin, are raised up to their height by a series of several thousand earthquakes in the range from 6.0 to 9.0. Of course, these thousands of earthquakes are spread out over vast stretches of geologic time, hundreds of thousands of years. Nevertheless, there is every indication that the San Andreas Fault and its sister mountain builders are still in the midst of this age-old process. Given enough time and monster quakes, the Newport-Inglewood Fault will eventually turn Beverly Hills into a mountain top.

May 8th, 4:30 A.M.

The pillow was barely big enough to have served as a decorative sofa pillow, but its plastic liner belied that function. And the coarse woolen blanket was just the right length to pull away from her feet when she pulled it around her shoulders, unless she curled into a fetal ball. When she had tried the fetal ball position, the woman sleeping at her feet had taken advantage of the opening to expand into Sybil Perkin's vacated territory.

Aside from the physical discomfort, the crying babies, babble of conversation and the now-routine rumble of the jets taking off outside the old warehouse building in which Sybil and her fellow refugees slept, had kept her awake virtually the whole night. Only the bone-weariness of her second night sleeping in an odd situation had allowed Sybil to catch the briefest moments of fitful sleep. The rest of the night had been filled with the monotonous re-hashing in her mind of the events of the last two days. Why was it that when you did something out of the ordinary, that your brain insisted on going back over and over it again all night?

The day had not been that great the first time through and going back over it a dozen times lying in the dark, uncomfortable barn of a building was pure misery.

After leaving the car and her Mexican traveling companion in Tijuana and getting turned down for a flight due to the credit card problem, Sybil had spent hours in line at the border, while the American Customs and Immigration agents struggled with a computer system suffering from inadequate power supplies and faulty connections to the outside world. Finally, someone in the bureaucracy had gotten the smart idea to close the border to anyone who could not prove U.S. citizenship or residency without reference to the moribund computer network. This had let those like Sybil Perkins, with her passport, through, but had stranded thousands in Tijuana.

Once across the border into San Diego, things had gone from bad to worse. Sybil had found her way to the trolley that ran from the border to downtown San Diego, but the fluctuating power supplies had shut the trolley system down twice during her trip.

Conversations with other passengers during the ensuing waits on the trolley had given Sybil a picture of the situation in San Diego, as well as second hand information about the extent of the earthquake damage farther north. It was then that she got the sad word that although much of San Diego had escaped serious damage, the reclaimed tidal basin area that served as San Diego's international airport was one of the few badly damaged areas. Lindbergh Field was out of commission.

She also got word of the thousands of refugees streaming into San Diego from the east and north. Interstate highways 8 and 15, respectively, were choked with people either escaping the flooding in the

Imperial Valley or the epicenter of the main quake on the San Andreas in the San Bernardino/Riverside area. She also heard rumors about the dire situation in the whole of Orange County and northern San Diego County. Such rumors were fueled by the fact that every northbound on-ramp on Interstate 5 in San Diego was blocked off.

The trolley stopped short of downtown San Diego, ending at the trolley roundabout in the lower port area. With downtown San Diego also built on low-lying harbor-side land, the word spread amongst those around Sybil that the structural engineers had declared the high-rise area of downtown San Diego off-limits until more studies could be done and the aftershock situation was better understood. There was also word that the Navy port facilities had been hit rather hard by a tsunami right after the quake.

Sybil spent the better part of the afternoon walking in search of someone who could answer her questions of how to get out of San Diego. The city was apparently cut off from phone service and she had experienced the erratic electric power situation. The entire city was clogged with both traffic and people on foot. It seemed that nobody knew what to do.

At length her searching led her to a building labeled Naval Supply Center where her inquiry got her included in a group of non-San Diegans and navy dependents who were sent on a cramped, blue Navy school bus to the Air Station at Miramar. The bus trip had turned into a three hour marathon journey that had included a drive past the toppled intersection structures of the Interstate 5 and 8 junction. Emergency vehicles still labored on fires near the huge freeways. The twisted and missing spans of the overpasses stood as mute testimony to the fact that San Diego had not been spared completely from the fury of the great quakes.

Sybil and the others had finally come to the old Navy warehouse at Miramar Air Station shortly before dusk. They were herded into the building and informed that they would be evacuated to outlying military bases when flights became available. After an interminable time in a waiting line and a perfunctory questioning by a nervous sailor, Sybil Perkins had been given a piece of gray cardboard with a number (178) and the word "Travis" written on it. Each person had been given a can of lukewarm Doctor Pepper, a baloney sandwich and a bag of potato chips. Parents of infants were given a can of evaporated milk. After an embarrassing wait the sailors had also come up with can openers for the milk cans.

Darkness fell quickly and the growing crowd waited in the poorly lit building. Twice during the evening the waiting had been interrupted by the whine of turbines and glare of landing lights on the tarmac outside the warehouse. Those in the warehouse lucky enough to be holding gray tickets with the magic words "Nellis" or "Offutt" and numbers less than two hundred- fifty were directed outside and apparently flown away. More than a few of the gray tickets had been exchanged for cash, with Nellis, in Nevada, being the most valuable.

Just before ten o'clock a group of women who were obviously Navy wives started going through the building handing out the pillows and blankets. When this distribution was finished most of the lights were turned off and the miserable night began in earnest for Sybil and her fellow "guests," as one of the public address announcements had earlier called them.

The night had been filled with false hopes that the roars and whines or aircraft they heard on the flight line at Miramar were for them, but apparently none were passenger flights, or at least not for the likes of the residents of the warehouse.

Sybil Perkins' dreadful night ended with a screeching shriek from the public address system in the pre-dawn darkness. The feedback squeal was quickly adjusted down and an apologetic voice said, "Sorry about that." to the abruptly awakened crowd.

The voice announced, "Would all those with boarding passes for Travis numbered one to one hundred ninety please assemble at the yellow exit light please. Your flight has just arrived and you will be boarding soon."

It took Sybil a moment to realize that the announcement meant her.

■

"No-o-o!" the shrill voice cried out in the dark.

Gloria struggled against her drowsiness, listening for the voice again. At first, she did not recognize the voice, it sounded like a little girl, but it was not Miranda. Then Gloria remembered ... there were two little girls sleeping in the house now. It must have been Jessica.

Matt roused and turned over when Gloria got up, but he did not wake up. Gloria put on her robe and went to the girls' room. As Gloria reached the hallway, Gloria saw a short dark figure enter the girls' bedroom.

Turning into the bedroom, Gloria saw her mother setting on Jessica's side of the girls' bed, stroking the little girls hair. Miranda was still asleep.

Seeing Gloria, her mother whispered, "You go back to sleep, you need to go to work. I can take care of this, she just had a bad dream."

"Thanks. Mom."

Gloria waited a moment in the doorway. She could hear her father snoring in a baritone on the hide-a-bed in the living room. With both her parents and the neighbor girl, Jessica, now living with them, the Contreras household was full.

It was both a good and bad feeling. Good, because of the feeling of love that pulling together in hard times gives you. Bad, because she had no idea what would become of her parents or their house, and no idea what had happened to Jessica's parents. Matt had promised to look into the situation up north of the Interstate near the San Andreas where Jessica's parents had their laundry. They had not shown up yet and Gloria feared the worst.

Gloria decided her mother was right, she would let the older woman handle Jessica. It was going to be another horrible day tomorrow, reconstructing records and trying to prepare for resuming the bank's operation on Monday.

■

The City of Los Angeles has determined that over 80,000 of its buildings, half of which are residences, are of such construction that there is a reasonable likelihood of these being destroyed in a moderately powerful earthquake, on the scale of the 1994 Northridge quake, depending on the location of the quake. If the predicted great earthquake is considered as the basis for this kind of determination, the number can be multiplied many times over, because it would be a rare building which could withstand the maximum forces that the Los Angeles area's seismic faults are capable of. It was decided that the county ordinance controlling the upgrade of these known potential earthquake hazards would be on a voluntary basis. A mandatory program was considered to be "unfriendly to the business climate" and an economic burden to property owners.

May 9th, 7:00 A.M.

The fog was unusual, more akin to what you would expect in San Diego or San Francisco, than Calexico. The morning sun had not cut through the partially overcast sky. It was strange weather for a region where mid-May usually brought the first scorching days of desert summer heat.

Gil Echeverria pulled the pickup to a stop on the canal embankment. He figured the spot was roughly a couple hundred yards from where he had parked to observe the raging floodwaters on the afternoon the biq quakes had hit. He could not be sure though, all of the points of reference except for the canal itself had disappeared. The resulting change of scenery was confusing to Gil's internal sense of location and direction, a sense he had developed over a lifetime of working the ditches and canals serving the farms of the Imperial Valley.

That internal sense told Gil that he should be looking out over fields of sprouting spring crops, but his eyes showed him an expanse of open water that stretched out to the misty fog-shrouded horizon. Just above were the foggy horizon seemed to be, he could see the tops of the western mountains toward San Diego, just barely tinted where the pink-orange light from the rising sun was able to cut through the overcast.

Gil Echeverria had been right, but he found little solace in this. His knowledge of the topography of the valley told him that Calexico would remain above the water as the ocean flooded into the rest of the Imperial Valley. This knowledge had led him to have his children and grand-children come to his house in Calexico rather than joining the mass exodus from the towns of Imperial County into the eastern desert area and on into Arizona.

Now, the Echeverrias and the few others who had remained in Calexico found themselves on the tip of a peninsula jutting out into the middle of the newly huge Salton Sea. Their only direct contact with the rest of America was along this road along the All-American Canal that had been Gil's duty to repair. Now instead of holding the fresh irrigation water in, the levees of the All-American Canal held the waters of the Pacific Ocean away from Calexico. The only other way out of Calexico was south into Mexico, through the earthquake and flood ravaged ruins of the city of Mexicali.

"What's that smell?"

Gil started at the sound of his son's voice. In his contemplation of the scene before him he had forgot about the presence of Gilbert. Jr.

with him. He sniffed the air.

The salt-air scent was mixed with something else, something noxious.

Gil answered his son, "I`d say that is the smell is the smell of a hundred gas stations and farm pesticide tanks in El Centro and Brawley that are submerged and leaking into the water. You remember the big oil tank on the highway south of El Centro that has the sea-level line marked a hundred feet up on its side. Think of how many tanks must have been inundated completely."

"Yes. Look at all the debris from the sunken farms and towns." Bert pointed out into the water.

The shoreline of the levee, like the surface of the water, was littered with floating junk. Wood, plastic and tin cans, Styrofoam chunks, furniture, anything that could float away from a submerged city was now adrift in the Salton Sea. Even a couple of boats, lifted off their parked trailers by the rising waters could be seen floating in the distance.

Bert again pointed, this time off to the south. "Seems to be a strong current to the south. Toward Mexico." He left a question dangling.

In the channel between them and the far shore on the Mexico side Gil could see the water and floating junk moving along, almost like in a river current. Gil thought for a moment and then nodded to himself before speaking. "I'll bet that's the tidal surge. This new Salton Sea is shaped like a lollipop, big area of water, all the way from Ocotillo to the Chocolate Mountains, connected by a real narrow channel to the ocean. When it broke in and flooded, the force of the water cut the old New River channel from a couple hundred feet to a couple of miles in a few hours. Now, I bet every time the tides change its got one hell of a tidal surge, sucking in and out of this valley."

Bert nodded agreement and added, "Not much of a valley anymore though. More like, what do they call it, a fjord."

The two men stood on the levee and watched as the morning sun finally broke through and illuminated their view of the body of water that would come to be known as the Mexicali Channel.

At length Bert turned and looked at his father. He asked the older man, "Dad, what are we going to do now?"

Gil turned to his son, thinking about suggesting they head home for some breakfast. But he saw from the look in his son's eyes that the question was meant to be broader in scope than a simple decision on the morning's schedule. He looked his son in the eyes as he thought.

"Bert ..." Gil Echeverria paused, then moved to put his hand on his son's shoulder. "I really don't know. I've spent my whole life just trying to raise you kids and working for Imperial Irrigation District. Now both you and your sister have lost your homes and jobs. But, thank God, you're all safe and we've at least got the old house. I don't think anyone has any answers to what everyone does just now. We just survive for a while as best we can and see what life brings."

■

California building laws consider an earthquake fault that is less than 11,000 years old (the last Ice Age) to be active faults. Those up to 750,000 years old are called potentially active. Building of critical facilities, like hospitals, is prohibited in the vicinity of a fault considered potentially active. There are also limited restrictions on new buildings directly over active faults. However, the prohibition against buildings in these areas has simply led to the restricted areas becoming natural paths for highway building. Interstate Highway 280 between San Jose and San Francisco precisely follows the path of the great San Andreas Fault for most of the highway's length.

May 9th, 9:05 A.M.

Matt Contreras watched as the video operator cycled and rotated the camera pod from inside the Jet Ranger helicopter. It seemed to be working flawlessly, but strapping anything extra on the familiar aircraft made him ill at ease. The globe shaped camera pod attached perfectly on the forward floodlight rack, but made the otherwise sleek chopper look dumpy. Inside the Plexiglas bubble of the pod the high-tech gyro-stabilized camera looked like a Star Wars weapon system. On the rear end of the landing skid a similar globe was clamped which contained a satellite link antennae that would send the video signal real time to whomever it was in Sacramento that was picking up the bill for this trip.

The crew chief from the CalTrans survey team gave Matt a thumbs up signal. "All set."

"OK. Make sure all your gear is secured with the straps in back.

I'll file the flight plan and be back in a minute."

The flight plan Matt carried into the Palm Springs airport building called for a three leg flight. Palm Springs to Ontario, Ontario to Victorville and Victorville back to Palm Springs. Someone in Sacramento wanted a detailed survey of just how bad the damage to the critical road system, both highway and railroad, into the Los Angeles Basin from the East was. And, they had sent the California Transportation Department contractor crew with their high-tech equipment down and asked the CHP to fly them around. It was a common job for the CHP, Matt had been doing just this on the morning before the Big One, but they had never asked to hang anything on his chopper before. Usually it was just Matt and one of the CalTrans supervisors flying around and looking for any sign of problems.

Matt actually looked forward to the flight and the chance to see more firsthand of the destruction to the West. He filed the flight plan and made a last phone call back to Indio, letting them know he was off.

The first leg of the flight through the San Gorgonio Pass was much the same as his first flight the day of the quake, except for the lack of fires. The scar of the quake through the Pass was just as prominent and the destruction of the three small towns just as obvious. This time, however, when he flew over Banning he knew that his parents were safe at his brother's home in Morongo Valley. The old family home having been abandoned to its damage.

The survey crew leader sat next to Matt, he was a qualified pilot, a civilian contractor that usually did this job in his own aircraft up north, but on this flight paid attention only to his equipment, which consisted of a little television monitor and a joystick controller with which he moved the video camera in the nose pod.

They followed the track of Interstate 10 most of the way, only diverting twice to zero in on critical failures of the railroad bridges and to capture the worst of the surface disruption in the southern half of the Pass.

They left the path Matt had flown earlier at Redlands where they continued up the Interstate 10 corridor toward San Bernardino. Matt kept the copter directly over the highway, hovering occasionally when the structural engineer who was riding in back asked for the high definition camera to be zoomed in on a particular ruptured beam or broken overpass section.

This path along the freeway brought them a few blocks northeast of downtown Redlands. Looking over, Matt could see older brick downtown section of Redlands was largely symmetrical rows of brick piles. But the destruction of Redlands was nothing to prepare Matt or his passengers for the sight of central San Bernardino.

The main commercial district of San Bernardino was just a few blocks north and east of the multi-level interchange between Interstate 10 and 15E. The graceful arching spans of the transition ramps soared a hundred feet off the ground. At least, they usually did.

Matt momentarily thought it was poor visibility that prevented him seeing the prominent four-level interchange by the time he reached the eastern edge of the city. But, he had flown this leg in to Los Angeles many times and he knew from the orientation of the mountains to the north that both the highway ramps and the city's buildings should be showing right where they were not.

The survey crew and the structural engineer were paying attention to the damage on the road directly below them and they did not see the interchange until they were nearly upon it. When they did the engineer let out with a single expletive "Jesus!" forgetting momentarily to tell Matt to circle which Matt did anyway, giving the video crew and himself a full view of not only the interchange where not a single span remained erect, but also the whole downtown area.

It was clear at a glimpse that San Bernardino had taken the full brunt of the worst seismic force possible. Every building, whether one story or higher was flattened. The courthouse, the several bank buildings, the stores, everything was in ruins. The one building in downtown San Bernardino Matt was most familiar with, the BankCal office complex where Gloria's boss worked, was not even recognizable. The rubble piles had merged into one another, especially now as the rescue crews Matt could see scouring the ruins struggled to uncover any lucky survivors.

On the second pass around the downtown area Matt saw that he was wrong. there was one building still standing. The Federal Courthouse stood alone amongst the ruins. For what reason, why it had been spared, Matt did not know.

He was not alone in the skies above San Bernardino. A single news helicopter and one military chopper, a Chinook, also circled at nearly the level Matt was flying and a fixed wing plane was just above them, all apparently checking out the scene on the ground. The airborne equivalent of a gaper's block developed and Matt had to turn away to the west for safety.

"What now?" he asked in the intercom.

"Keep going west. On with the show." The flippant words of the engineer annoyed Matt, but he headed west.

∎

Sybil Perkins had thought about calling in to work from Travis or the car rental place in Fairfield, but with the "refugee" processing at the air force base and the bickering over whether her credit cards were still good in Fairfield, the call had slipped her mind. By the time she got home to her apartment in Sunnyvale, she could think of nothing more than collapsing into her own bed. She had slept through the night.

She regretted not making the call as soon as she crossed the lobby at work. There, on an easel in the center of the engineering firm's lobby were four photographs, of Sybil and three of the other engineers that had been in Mexicali with her. Each photo had a strip of black ribbon across the upper right corner. The ribbons had "In Honored Memory" embossed in gold. Her boss, Cliff Hodges, who had headed the team's trip to Mexicali geothermal field was not among the photos.

As Sybil stood open-mouthed staring at the memorial display, the receptionist jumped up and announced to her, "Sybil, you're alive."

"Yes, relatively speaking. The other three are ... ?"

"Uh-huh. Mr. Hodges called us all together this morning and said you were all missing and presumed dead."

Sybil Perkins stepped forward and detached her photo from the easel.

"I don't know about the others, but it is a bit premature for my eulogy. Is Cliff in?"

"Yes. I think, in his office."

"I'll be there then. And, Deb, you probably ought to call around and tell everyone I'm back in one piece. Knowing this place they're probably taking dibs on my office already."

Deb and Sybil tried to smile at the attempted joke, but the strangeness of the situation and the three other colleagues on the easel made it awkward.

■

Some financial planners advise that investment portfolios be "geographically diverse." That is, investments which are based in any one region are susceptible to natural and economic disasters of that region. It would not be wise to hold California bank stock, California municipal bonds, and California real estate or investment trusts alone, without matching investments in other regions. Each of these would be prone to collapse with the Big One. Likewise, it might be preferable for liquid funds to be held in banking institutions in other regions.

Another investment consideration relating to California's earthquake danger is that of the market conditions in the aftermath. Large insurance companies, pension funds, municipal treasuries and personal and corporate investments may need to be liquidated on short notice in the aftermath of a major quake. Securities might be flooded with selling in the short term.

May 12th, 09:00 A.M.

Her staff was augmented with a police officer, a security guard and an observer F.D.I.C. had sent in from Washington. D.C. She had gone over this moment dozens of times over the last five days. She had trained her tellers over the weekend on how to handle the ticklish situations she could envision. But, nothing could have prepared Gloria Contreras for the sight out the front door of the bank as she prepared to unlock it for the first day of business after the bank holiday.

She could only see fifteen or so people, but it was clear that the line snaked around the corner of the bank and into the parking lot. The security guard was at her elbow. Brian Kowicky was right behind him, relishing his first day as acting assistant manager.

Before she unlocked she turned to the guard and told him, "Remember, just three at a time in the bank. And if we have any trouble in the bank, shut and lock the door."

The guard nodded, "Right. Ma'am. I got that the first two times you told me."

Gloria sighed and nodded herself, "Sorry to repeat myself, I just can't be too careful, today."

She handed the key ring to the guard. As he inserted the key, Gloria saw the crowd in line push forward to the door. By the time he fumbled with the keys and unlocked it, the press against the door was so strong the door would not swing out to let people in. The fingers of those in front clutched at the door frame trying to pull it towards them so they could squeeze in.

"Shit!" was all the guard could say as he tried to get the situation in control.

The Palm Spring police officer, who had been standing back in the lobby, now strode forward and elbowed the guard aside. With his nightstick the policeman rapped hard, three times, on the aluminum door frame, hard enough to worry those close to the door.

"Back off! Away from the door!" the cop shouted. "Get back in line."

Amazingly, this is just what the crowd outside did. Slowly, then all together they backed off. The officer then opened the door and told them, "That'll be enough of that! Stay in line. Only three at a time in the bank. If you try to break the rules, I lock the door. Got it?"

The crowd outside nodded and tried to find their place in line again. The policeman turned and resumed his previous post in the lobby.

Gloria nodded her appreciation as he passed. The guard motioned for the first three people to come in.

As Gloria headed for the tellers' counter she straightened the placard holder that stood in the entrance. The sign in it said:

THIS BANKCAL FACILITY IS BEING OPERATED UNDER THE DIRECTION OF THE FEDERAL DEPOSIT INSURANCE CORPORATION. IT IS OPERATING UNDER EMERGENCY RULES WHICH SPECIFY:

- THE MAXIMUM DAILY CASH WITHDRAWAL IS $500.00 FOR ALL ACCOUNT HOLDERS ON DEMAND ACCOUNTS.

- IRA AND CERTIFICATE OF DEPOSIT ACCOUNTS CAN ONLY BE DRAWN UPON WITH 72 HOURS NOTICE AND ONLY PAID, WITH F.D.I.C APPROVAL, BY BANK DRAFT.

- ONLY LOCAL ACCOUNTS (THIS BANK) WILL BE HONORED.

- NO CASH ADVANCES FROM CREDIT CARDS. NO ATM SERVICES ARE AVAILABLE.

- ALL NON-CASH DEPOSITS ARE SUBJECT TO VERIFICATION OR PAYMENT.

- NO AMOUNTS IN EXCESS OF THE F.D.I.C. ACCOUNT INSURANCE LIMIT OF $100,000.00 PER INSURED ACCOUNT CAN BE WITHDRAWN, TRANSFERRED OR CREDITED TO DEBTS.

- ALL TRANSACTIONS ARE SUBJECT TO F.D.I.C. APPROVAL.

THANK YOU FOR YOUR COOPERATION.

At the tellers' counter the three tellers, the head teller and the F.D.I.C. observer waited as the first customers approached.

As Gloria watched, she heard Jenny explain to her customer that she had no records of deposits in the Riverside Main Street Branch of BankCal. Jenny finished off with saying, "I am sorry sir, we cannot handle that transaction at this branch.

Myrtle, at the second window was shooing away a man who wanted to get a cash advance on a credit card.

Brian was already over at the counter, backing up Terry who was arguing with a farm worker who wanted to cash a check drawn on the Bank of El Centro.

"All you can do is deposit the check and hope it is honored by the issuing bank," Brian explained.

"But you know, we all know, El Centro is flooded. The bank is under water." the worker said.

"How can you expect us to pay you cash for a check that you, yourself, think is going to be dishonored? And you don't have enough in your own account to cover it." Brian asked.

"But, this is my paycheck. Maybe the last I am going to get. Who knows when we will work again? How will I feed my family? Pay the rent?"

Gloria took a deep breath, she could see that this day was going to be everything she had worried it would be.

■

Government studies estimate that a 7.5 magnitude quake on the Newport-Inglewood Fault would critically damage the 88 hospitals within the area of strong motion from such a quake by reducing their capacity as much as 25 percent or 7,000 beds fewer out of a total available of 28,000. At the same time, such a quake alone is estimated will cause up to 21,000 deaths and 80,000 hospitalized casualties.

That is, after a major quake in central Los Angeles there will be four times more critically injured patients than hospital beds.

May 13th, 10:17 A.M.

Captain Joseph Goetz met Barry on the steps of the double-wide trailer that stood in the parking lot next to the rubble of the old sheriff's substation. The middle-aged officer had his left arm in a cast and sling. Barry was standing, looking around the parking lot and staring at the cement footing and bull-dozed pile of rubble that was all that was left of the old building.

"Any idea what happened to my car?" Barry asked.

"You have it parked by the building?" Goetz asked.

"Yeh, where we all parked."

"When the building went it took them all. Mine, too. Everyone had its roof caved in, a few were really flattened. To make room for our new quarters they towed them all out to the impound lot in Torrance, if you want it. Word is that the insurance isn't going to pay, what with earthquake disclaimers and all the insurance companies going bust."

"It feels weird, I haven't been back here since ..." Barry paused.

"I know. I heard good things down the grapevine from County about your work up at Harbor UCLA and helping out the Marines with Dominguez. That's what I called you down here about. Some colonel wrote you up in a report that came down from the state and federal emergency services channels, caught the Sheriff's eye."

"The Sheriff, I heard he was killed in the Big One."

"That's one rumor. No. The Sheriff's alive. And just as hard-assed as ever. Actually it was the L.A. Police Chief and quite a few other top police and city officials that were lost. That's also part of the news I wanted to talk about."

"God! And here I thought all you really wanted for me to come down was to get your hands back on my Explorer or put me back out on patrol." Barry tried to joke, uneasy with the situation of the commander of the sub-station, calling him in to talk about "news" such as this.

"Nah, lots to talk about, but first let's get inside and get some coffee," Goetz said as he turned to enter the trailer, awkwardly opening the door with his good arm.

Inside the trailer was actually much like the Marine general's trailer had been with the maps and cramped quarters, but this was more crowded and ramshackle. Eight to ten people sat at rows of tables made of bare two-by-fours and plywood. The dispatch area had a familiar feel about it, except for the fact that only radio handsets were being used, no phones. The long wall was covered with quadrant maps of the south county. Barry recognized the familiar squarish peninsula of Palos Verdes, the Redondo-Manhattan coastline and the familiar freeway corridors of Interstate 405, but he also saw other maps being looked at by dispatchers with areas of Compton and Lakewood that were far outside the perimeters of the sub-station's normal responsibilities.

A couple of familiar faces smiled at him from the dispatcher and staff desks, but many were new faces, including two dispatchers in Torrance Police uniforms. Everyone was busy, except for three very young-looking deputies who stood drinking sodas near one of the maps. Captain Goetz pointed toward a coffee urn sitting outside a glassed-in office at the far corner, "Grab a cup and have a seat in my office, I'll be right in."

Barry took his coffee and sat down in one of two folding chairs in Goetz's office. He noted that the captain's desk was also a sheet of plywood on two saw horses. There was no telephone, but Barry could see a cellular smart phone sitting on a stack of personnel files.

Goetz came in with his coffee and took the other chair. "How about these posh new offices, huh?"

"Where'd this trailer come from?"

"The feds, FEMA, had them stockpiled out in Paramount. Just waiting for something like this. Same ones they're using out in Dominguez. You've seen 'em. It's amazing that they were so prepared for some things and so unprepared for others, but I guess that goes for us, too."

Barry nodded, sipping his coffee. Goetz put his coffee down and pulled a file from the stack. He opened the file and read a bit.

"You're married. You hear from your wife or family?"

Barry looked at Goetz, shaking his head, "No chance, no phones. We live out in West L.A. My wife's family is in the Valley. My folks are out of state."

"You know their number?" Goetz stated more than asked as he handed Barry the cell phone, "Fringe benefit from the department. It can only call other AT&T cell phones and long distance, none of the local phones are working. Make sure your folks know your OK, maybe they can get word to your wife and her folks. Dial Star-one first."

Barry took the smart phone and dialed the number in Denver, the same number his parents had since Barry was a small boy. After three rings, Barry's look of anticipation turned to frustration. He shook his head and said to Goetz, "Answering machine."

After a few seconds wait Barry spoke into the phone, "Hi, Mom, Dad, it's Barry calling from L.A. I'm OK, at work. But, I haven't been able to get home or reach Kathy or anyone else. If you can, try to get in touch with them and let them know I'm all right. I'll get back in touch with you when I can. Love ya, Barry."

Barry handed the phone back to Goetz, "Thanks. I really appreciate it."

"Least I could do. Too bad about getting the machine." Goetz switched of the phone's power switch and set it aside. "Now, down to real business. Let's get you up to speed on the state of things. I just got back from downtown yesterday afternoon, met with the Sheriff, some state people and some city police officials, what few they have left. I'll try to give you the quick and dirty version."

Goetz shifted his seat in the uncomfortable folding chair and continued, "Seems the top L.A. city police brass and lots of other city people, all the top management staff, were in a community race relations class, you know the ones the Bradley Commission recommended, when the Big One hit. After the first quake. they all evacuated out into the street downtown, just in time to get hit by the second quakes, falling glass from the highrises and Parker Center itself partially collapsed, bad luck. They lost about all of them. Not only that, but the other, smaller city governments got hit real hard, you know about Carson, the whole city government is gone, along with most of the city itself. Well, with thirty or forty small municipalities all in various stages of destruction, physically and organizationally, the state and the federal government, not to mention us in the county and neighboring cities, are having a hell of a time putting things back together. No organization, just chaos, can't get anything done."

"So, the Legislature passed an emergency bill, and the Governor will sign it as soon as he gets back to Sacramento after his trip down south here, to create a single City and County of Los Angeles, like in San Francisco. What that means is that we're going to have one local government to work at the relief and rebuilding. The city governments are going to be folded into the county, hopefully with a minimum of confusion. But, with things so totally screwed up anyway I guess they figured it couldn't get any worse. Not really our choice, apparently the feds shoved the idea down the state's throat and shit rolls downhill.

"Where the city governments are still in place and working, like in Torrance, they'll just continue, but under the county umbrella. The Torrance police chief will be a Sheriff's Captain probably. But, where the city government is dysfunctional, like in Carson, it will be the County's job, our job, to get things back in operation. Which leads us to how you fit in."

Barry raised his eyebrows at this. Captain Goetz reached down into a cardboard box beside his desk and pulled out a plastic bag, which he tossed to Barry. It tinkled as Barry caught it. It was a pair of silver insignia bars.

"The city of Carson doesn't have much of a police force left and they estimate to have lost over half their buildings and population, but the tent city there on the Cal State campus is growing every day. FEMA and your buddies in the military want the civil authorities, which means us, as soon as the Governor signs the bill, to take over the security and eventually the whole camp operation. Like I said, that little love note your Marine Colonel friend sent down the chain got the Sheriff's attention and, with my concurrence, you're being appointed Officer in Charge of the new Dominguez Hills branch, Lieutenant Warden."

Barry fingered the silver bars and said, "I appreciate this, but I'm not sure how much of this is promotion and how much is headache. That tent city is chaos."

"Chaos? You mean like this?" Goetz pushed an 8x10 photograph across the bare plywood to Barry.

It was an wide angle shot. It did not take Barry very long to recognize it. It showed the Harbor UCLA Hospital main entrance area. It was taken before the west section collapsed completely so Barry figured it must have been early on the morning of the second day. One policeman with a bullhorn and a single sheriff's deputy could be seen standing in the street, gesturing broadly with outstretched arms and directing a huge crowd surrounding the stricken hospital. A crowd that apparently numbered in the thousands as seen from the air, totally surrounded the sheriff deputy who seemed intent on controlling the mob. The crowd now seemed much larger than it had from Barry's point of view on the ground.

"The Sheriff gave me that, it sent out by a wire service. Ran on the national wire services, front page on the New York Times. You've sort of become the symbol, the nation's poster child, of the Los Angeles peace officers maintaining control of chaos. Yes, Dominguez Hills is probably chaos and a headache, but as of right now it's your chaos."

"But, all the way to Lieutenant in one bump, isn't there some civil service rule?"

"Not any more. County Board of Supervisors, at least the three they could pull out of the rubble of the Hall of Administration last Tuesday, passed an emergency ordinance letting all County officials fill any slots they need to deal with the emergency. No red tape."

Barry shrugged and said, "Fine, I'll do what I can. What do I have to work with?"

Goetz smiled and nodded, "Those three over by the maps are your patrol staff." He indicated the young officers, two men and one woman, who were standing by the maps. "I guess you can keep the Explorer, we don't have anything else, patrol-wise, to give you. They tell me the camp operations people will have three trailers like this for you, only single-wide ones, for ops and for living arrangements. We have a two-channel base radio and generator set outside in a pickup for you to take up, keep the pickup with you, courtesy of FEMA. The truck also has tactical radios for your patrol officers and other supplies, stuff from the emergency stockpile downtown. Keep someone up on the base radio, Sheriff's Admin Net, all the time you can. And I'll get more information and help for you when I can. Having all the military there at Dominguez Hills should keep things down to earth a bit for you. And, the Sheriff has given all officers in command, that's why the lieutenant bars, the authority to deputize whoever is needed from the public, a citizens' posse to maintain order. Any questions?"

"Yeh, a million, but I'm not sure what they are yet." Barry paused before continuing, "There is one thing. I haven't seen Kathy and she may be all alone. I don't know. Can't get to her cell and... You suppose it would be a problem if I took some time off to get up to our house and check on her?"

"I understand. I went over to my house in Lakewood on my way back from downtown yesterday, hadn't seen my wife and kids since the night of the quakes. You get things set up in the camp and then you take the Explorer up and check on your wife. But be careful, none of the freeways are up and running yet, and the surface streets are real bad, especially since you have to go out west past Inglewood and Culver City. Lucky you got the Explorer."

"Speaking of which, where are we refueling, I'm getting real low on gas."

"The Torrance city yard is pumping gas for all the public vehicles. Over on Madrona, stop by on your way over to the camp." Goetz stood up. "Now, let's go introduce you to your crew."

"They look a bit, aah, fresh."

"Yeh, brought them back from downtown yesterday. New cadets just done with their POST classes at Chase College up in the Valley, their badges are as new as your silver bars."

"I don't suppose there's any chance of giving me anyone with experience?"

"Well, Janet Mortimer stopped in today, she just got out of hospital. Doctors over at the Kaiser Hospital Burn Unit said she could come back on light duty, tomorrow. She's single and found out her apartment was flattened, so she needs a place to stay anyway. She'll be on limited duty for a while, but she's experienced and can help man your base radio. She'd fit in with this other young gal you're getting, so I'll send her up."

"Glad to hear she made it. I heard her call-in right after the explosion, sounded bad. What about McNeely?"

Goetz shook his head slowly. "Too badly burned. Same with Espinoza and Ruppert. All in the one big blast."

"Anybody else?"

"Nine officers in all. Besides McNeely, Ruppert, and Espinoza, we lost Barbara Fuentes and Don Smith when the sub-station went down. Drake and Aguillar were in the office in the hospital basement lock-up, you probably knew about that."

"I didn't know who it was on duty. You know, I was only thirty feet away when it finally came down."

"Yes, Drake and Aguillar. And we never have heard from Morris and Purdy after the quake, we're counting them as missing. But, even so, we did a lot better than some places. I guess the Sheriff still hasn't heard from a couple stations out in the San Gabriel sector."

"What about Sergeant Rivera? I haven't heard from him since he took over the net after the quake."

"Sheriff gave me some silver bars for Rivera, too. I sent him off to Long Beach this morning. Long Beach is missing over half their uniformed officers and most of their command people, between the explosion, the quakes and the tsunami."

"What tsunami?"

"You haven't heard about the tsunami? Hit the whole coast bad after both sets of quakes, but hit Long Beach especially hard after the Newport-Inglewood quake, that was the second big one. Pushed the Queen Mary right up onshore, on top of the Convention Center. Real mess. And on top of that the whole downtown of Long Beach, all those high rises were hit bad, I heard from a briefing I attended with the Sheriff that is was something about the soil and water level particularly under downtown Long Beach, liquefaction, quake turned the ground into so much Jello, or quicksand. Same thing that brought down the four level East L.A. interchange."

Barry shook his head in response to the news. Then, he thought to ask Goetz something else.

"You hear anything about West L.A., Santa Monica?"

Goetz waited a second before answering, "Yes. I guess the second set of quakes hit pretty much ground zero under the north end of Culver City. Lots of fires in the apartment districts, La Brea, Westwood, ... What can I say? I hope you find out everything's OK at home."

"Thanks." Barry put his coffee cup down and tried a perfunctory smile, which neither man believed.

Barry followed Goetz out of the office. The new officers waiting by the maps nervously adjusted their uniforms in preparation for meeting their new boss.

Barry suppressed a smile. Little did they know their new boss had not showered or changed his underwear in almost a week. He involuntarily patted down his own clothes. In so doing noticed he still had the little gift box for Kathy in his pocket, purchased the first day of the quake. It was definitely time to change clothes. He wondered if the camp at Dominguez Hills had showers or laundry facilities, yet.

■

When one looks at some of the names for communities in the Los Angeles area it does not take much insight to see a certain pattern in the list of Mission Hills, Granada Hills, Baldwin Hills, Signal Hill, Dominguez Hills, or the most famous, Beverly Hills. The first two communities on this list are adjacent to Northridge and shared in their neighbor's damage during the 1994 Northridge quake. The latter four all sit astride the Newport-Inglewood Fault Zone with their namesake hillocks clearly marking the path of that massive fault system. Several dozen other place names in southern California reflect this penchant for placing residential communities directly on top of earthquake faults and then naming them after the hilly topography caused by the faults' past devastation. These range from posh Laguna Hills in the south, to Flintridge in the north and in the middle, Hacienda Heights, which marks the center of the other major seismic time bomb under central Los Angeles, the Whittier Fault Zone.

May 14th, 11:45 A.M.

"And to think that we used to cuss the crowded freeways." Barry said.

Jamil nodded, "What I would give for a simple traffic jam or even a Sig Alert, instead of this mess."

Jamil had decided to ride along on Barry's trek to check on his house. A company of National Guard MP's from Fresno had taken over perimeter security duties at the hospital, so the two men took the opportunity to make the trip Goetz had authorized in the Sheriff Department's Explorer.

Barry would never have imagined that a trip from Carson to Santa Monica could take three hours. It was a trip that a Los Angeleno could expect to take minutes on either of two freeway routes in better times. But neither could he have imagined the level of destruction they had witnessed on this journey.

Barry had not been able to use the freeways for more than a few miles at a stretch today. Each time he had tried a toppled overpass had blocked the route. And, the surface streets were crowded and gridlocked in places and abandoned and rubble strewn in others.

They had been warned by an Inglewood cop they met at a road block on La Brea of the near total blockage of the roads and freeways through Culver City and Baldwin Hills and the persistent rumors of impassable streets and sporadic street warfare in the Crenshaw district. The only choice that remained for them was the route that had brought them to the intersection of Centinela and Culver Boulevard, south of Santa Monica. The jam up of traffic here was as bad as they had seen anywhere on the trip north through Gardena, Hawthorne and Inglewood.

The collapsed overpass on the Marina Freeway a few blocks south had stopped all traffic in that direction, gridlocking the intersection already narrowed by rubble from the neighboring buildings. The crowds of pedestrians, most carrying bundles of belongings now swarmed over the stopped cars and trucks, squeezing between vehicles and further snarling movement.

"Where in the hell are all of these people going?" asked Jamil.

Barry shook his head, "I don't think they know, they just know there is nothing back where they came from."

"Think I ought to hop out and try to direct 'em out of the grid lock?"

"It's probably better than sitting here all day, but to break a grid-lock you have to have someplace to shunt the cars to. The only place open is Culver east bound." Barry pointed to the east.

"Well then that's where they'll go. When I clear this lane you pull on up into the intersection." Jamil pointed to the south bound lane of Centinela.

The Explorer was still five vehicles back when Jamil got out to push his way through to the intersection. Barry watched as Jamil started to motion cars and pedestrians one way and the other. Occasionally, he saw Jamil gesture forcefully to prod a driver to move in a direction he obviously did not want to go.

Finally, Jamil got some of the cars on Centinela south of the intersection to back up and turn around enough for Barry to pull the Explorer up into the intersection. He parked in the middle of the southbound traffic lanes and turned on the flashing red lights on the Explorer's light bar.

Jamil shouted over to him, "Good idea, I think it is southbound Centinela that's jamming this up. If we can keep 'em moving east and west, I think it'll clear."

Barry nodded and joined Jamil directing the traffic. They continued to route cars and alternate letting the people on foot cross.

Barry was waving cars from the north side of the intersection both west and east on Culver, when a small black Toyota truck ignored his signal and continued straight across the intersection, heading around the Explorer.

"Hey!" Barry shouted as he moved to block the truck's path.

The truck jerked to a stop, rather than hitting him, which Barry thought for a moment would happen. The truck driver was a young man with two others his age in the seat next to him. The back of the truck was full of luggage.

"I motioned you to head east."

"Yeh. but I need to go south, to LAX."

"The overpass is out over the Marina freeway. You're going to have to head east."

"And what are you going to do if I don't. Arrest me? Take me downtown to a jail that doesn't exist anymore? Give me a ticket? I can pay the ticket with money from a job that doesn't exist anymore. What the fuck are you gonna do to me if I don't? Huh?"

Barry clinched his fist, thinking of another option the punk had not mentioned. But, he held himself back, taking a deep breath.

"Look, being an ass isn't going to help you. And neither is heading south on Centinela. We just came north and had to cross over on Inglewood Boulevard. You want to head south, you're better off heading east on Culver then south on Inglewood."

The young man thought a second then nodded. "OK, thanks. And ... I'm sorry about the mouthing off, I'm just getting really fed up."

"Yes, we all are. By the way, I hope you aren't disappointed at LAX, word is that they're closed down, just military helos and small craft landing, no fixed wing traffic yet. The runways are buckled."

"Gotta try somethin," the driver shrugged.

Barry motioned to traffic behind to stop and let the truck back into the intersection and turn east.

Barry saw that Jamil had drafted a young Chicano man who had been watching from the sidewalk and was showing him the ropes directing traffic. Jamil had given the traffic "recruit" an orange safety vest from the Explorer as a symbol of authority. After a few moments things were going well enough for Jamil and Barry to get back in the Explorer, ready to head north themselves.

"Your recruit seems to be doing a good job," Barry said as he buckled his seatbelt.

"Yeh, I think the good people of L.A. had better learn to handle unmarked intersections better and pitch in directing traffic 'cause I don't think the traffic signals are going to be back in order soon." Jamil said.

"My guess is we're gonna run out of gasoline, before they figure out how to drive through this rubble and without freeways. Looks like half the people are on foot already."

As they traveled north on Bundy and into the apartment district of Sawtelle/West Los Angeles the gnawing angst that Barry Warden had felt for the last week became outright fear. He had seen the random destruction of the housing and buildings across all of southern Los Angeles. He had flown over the worst parts of fire-gutted Carson and North Long Beach. But now, seeing the block after block of charred ruins that had been closely packed apartment buildings and condos of his own neighborhood, we started preparing himself for the worst.

"We getting close?" Jamil asked.

"Yes, just down Olympic to Purdue and then left."

"Damn, ain't lookin' good. Is it?"

Barry did not answer. He was approaching a road block on Olympic and Bundy. It looked like the National Guard had set up a checkpoint. A dozen cars and trucks were stopped. They could see one pickup turn around and head west on Olympic. They apparently were not letting anyone through to the east.

"Why you suppose they're doing that?" Jamil asked.

"No idea. Maybe looting control. It doesn't look like anybody's left in a lot of the blocks. Maybe it's just too screwed up to travel, like down in Inglewood."

One of the camouflage-clad Guardsmen at the checkpoint waved toward the Explorer, motioning them forward. Barry pulled around the stopped line of traffic. The Guardsmen at the checkpoint stood aside and the one nearest them waved them on past the row of sawhorses across the intersection.

Jamil gave a short salute in response to the wave and Barry nodded.

"That was no problem." Barry said.

"Yeh, we can put it on the list of the top ten good things about being a cop. `They let you into disaster zones.'"

A few of the buildings on Olympic still stood, but on either side there were usually either piles of rubble or ashes where Barry expected to see familiar buildings, houses and businesses. A few trees still stood on the side streets, some in the blossoms of spring, but most were charred skeletons or simply black stumps.

A few blocks before Purdue there was a stretch of Olympic Boulevard where everything was blackened. The cars that lined the street were totally destroyed, tires were melted off the wheels, paint completely burned off the vehicles and glass either shattered or melted. Not a single building or tree remained. The asphalt of the street was glossy where it had melted and run. Streetlight poles were even warped by the heat.

"Damn, it got freaking hot here. Some kind of firestorm." Jamil exclaimed. He got quiet when he remembered this was the neighborhood Barry had lived in.

Barry said nothing. He turned left onto Purdue Street. The view was not much different. For many blocks, not a single building stood.

Several blocks up he pulled to a stop, midblock.

Barry's jaw was set as he surveyed the scene. Where the row of townhomes had stood there was nothing but burned timbers and rubble. The townhomes had burned to the ground. Several had the hulks of cars in the garages, also burnt. Other than the cars only the carcasses of washers, dryers and refrigerators still stood higher than a few feet off the ground.

"I can't even tell which one is mine." Barry said. He mouthed numbers as he counted from the end of the row. He stopped at the ruins directly on the right of the Explorer. He unbuckled and got out.

Jamil waited a moment, then followed Barry. Walking up behind where Barry stood at the edge of the charred remains.

"Damn, this is really bad. This yours? Sorry, man. It's really too bad." Jamil fumbled for the right words.

Barry shrugged his shoulders, "Actually, I guess its good news."

Jamil looked askance at Barry, "What you mean, good news?"

Barry pointed to the pile of timbers and rubble on the left and the right, "Our neighbors on both sides had minivans." The blackened remains of the minivans showed as dark lumps in the ashes on both sides of them.

Barry Warden pointed to the space in front of him. "No car in our garage. Kathy wasn't home."

■

Genevieve stood watching the operation with curiously detached interest. Every new load of the crane's bucket brought bits and pieces of her shattered life up from the ruins of her home in the canyon below.

The joy she would have expected from the recovery of her possessions that had laid buried in the toppled house was tempered by the word that her husband's Mercedes had been found, crumpled and covered in debris from the tsunami, by a crew working to clear the Pacific Coast Highway through Malibu.

Ted Galloway, who had joined with Natalie Weld in her shepherding of Genevieve since the quake, had been the one who had given her this bad news about Michael's car. He, together with Donald Weld, had also carefully explained to Genevieve that under the emergency laws the California legislature had passed, and common sense, that her husband should be presumed dead. Ted was also the one who had arranged for the crane and work crew, and now stood directing them for her. Genevieve realized that Ted's attention was something more than the neighborly kindness of Natalie Weld, but in the void of Michael Dumont's absence Genevieve did not mind Ted stepping into her life. Such a thing as this salvage operation would have been impossible for Genevieve, but apparently simple for this attorney who had befriended her. The fact that Ted was handsome, urbane and spoke passable French were just icing on the cake for Genevieve Dumont.

The work crew consisted of three workers down below and two more laborers stood with Ted and Genevieve. The foreman of the work crew communicated with walkie-talkies and directed the crane which deposited the loads it brought up from below on the circle drive that had once led to her house. The crane stood with its support legs extended on Camino Espinazo and its long boom reached out over them. As each load came up, Ted and Genevieve checked it out to see what it contained. Her clothes and personal items went into a growing pile beside the driveway, everything else, salvageable furniture, housewares, and Michael Dumont's personal things, were carried by the two Mexican workers to the waiting rental truck.

Every action by the crane did not bring up a load of possessions, occasionally the workers below would signal the crane operator to lift debris and move it to clear the way for further searching in the rubble. This was apparently what was going on now, as it had been several minutes since the last load.

Genevieve took the opportunity to go through her pile of possessions. The last load had brought up her purse, which had been on the table in the entranceway when the quake hit. Genevieve sorted through the purse with its driver's license, credit cards and, most importantly, the green card and passport, like they were treasures. Which, in fact, they were. The weeks without proof of identity or personal wealth had proven this to Genevieve. The rest of the purse`s contents -- makeup, cell phone, keys -- were just as she had left them the week before.

Genevieve had just pushed the test button on the cell phone when Ted came over and spoke, "The crane operator says we should get back a bit."

"*Pour quoi?*"

"Don't know. Guess they're bringing something big up." Ted said, helping her grab her pile of things and carry them toward the street a bit.

The rumble of the crane's machinery deepened. The two workmen scurried to finish rolling up an Oriental rug that had come up in the load with Genevieve's purse. One of them dragged the rug to the side, off the driveway, and the other, shouting something in Spanish, uncoiled a long length of heavy rope across the driveway.

The straining, deep grind of the crane continued as the identity of the heavy load was revealed to Genevieve. She saw the rear bumper of her forest green Jaguar appear above the lip of the cliff.

As they saw the water draining out of the car as it lifted higher, Ted commented, "I wonder if that water is from the radiator."

Genevieve said, "I am not sure, of course, but I think it was setting in the swimming pool."

Ted nodded and gave an "Ah hah" of understanding.

The crane swung the car in over the drive and lowered it to within a few feet of the ground. It still dripped water. One of the workers ran up and looped the rope around one side of the front bumper and then over around the other side. Each of the workers grabbed an end of the rope attached to each side of the Jaguar's front end and took a strain on the rope as the crane lowered it further.

As the car settled down on the drive, it became clear what the workers were doing with the rope. They were taking the direct weight of the car off the front bumper, letting the car settle back down on its wheels. Finally, the car lurched down onto its springs and the workers moved in to disconnect the steel cables to the crane bucket from the rear end. Ted and Genevieve walked up to assess the damage to the car.

The front bumper was curled into the grill and one headlamp was broken. The entire car was covered with heavy, chalky dust, except for the front half of the hood forward, which had been under water. The roof was scratched and the rear window was cracked, but it appeared that the only major body damage was a long crease in the hood and front quarter panel.

"Pretty decent shape, considering. Huh?" Ted said.

Genevieve just raised her eyebrows. He was right, she had expected worse, but still ... her beautiful Jaguar was a mess.

"You got the keys?" Ted said, motioning to Genevieve's new-found purse.

She reached in and handed him the keys. "Are you sure we should? I mean, what if ..." She could not finish the question.

"What harm is there? We'll only know if we try." Ted said, taking the keys.

Ted unlocked the door and rolled down the window. With a smile, Ted showed Genevieve a "cross your fingers" signal, which she did not understand.

As he keyed the ignition, the starter growled and the car back-fired and belched a cloud of white smoke. Genevieve took a step back.

The starter continued to labor for several tries. Twice it coughed the same white cloud as before.

Ted stopped and smiled at Genevieve. "Actually, I'm surprised it has any juice, let alone start. One more time."

Genevieve smiled back, use of the term "juice" not meaning anything to her.

With the next grind of the starter the Jaguar's engine coughed and caught for an instant. Ted pumped the throttle and tried again.

The car roared to life, albeit coughing and belching the white smoke, eventually settling into a fitful idle. Ted revved the engine twice and then pulled the door closed. He put it in gear and pulled the car forward up the circle drive to the end.

Watching Ted Galloway park her bedraggled, but operative Jaguar, Genevieve had a sense of her life being closer to normal than it had since the quake had dumped her, bruised and near naked, on the very spot she now stood. She still was without a home and knew nothing for sure about her husband's fate, but the uncertainty of the previous weeks was beaten back a bit with the presence of her purse, her bedraggled car and the little pile of personal possessions. A few months before she could never have thought that she could find happiness, or at least security, in such meager things.

■

"Mobile homes are mobile twice during their lifespan. Once when they are being delivered, and then again during earthquakes. You don't want to be inside one during a big quake."

Frank Breckenridge,
former Santa Barbara County
Building Official

May 15th, 2:35 P.M.

Barry had just finished turning the knob and pulling the Sheriff's trailer door open when the aluminum door and the wooden steps started to rock. He could see the new female deputy, Jennifer Winslow, inside the trailer at the computer console rise halfway from her seat, ready, as he was, to react if the tremor was bigger than the norm they had grown accustomed to in the weeks since the big quakes.

The tremor lasted another ten seconds, during which time Barry and Winslow looked at each other, sizing up the aftershock. They had become so commonplace since the big quakes that the city's residents had long since exhausted the need for any casual conversation commenting on each new tremor. As it died away, Barry continued on inside the Sheriff's duty trailer, which now served as the Dominguez Hills police station. Winslow took her seat again. Janet Mortimer was also in the trailer, reading paperwork in the corner. She waved at Barry, who nodded back. The other officers were all out patrolling the Camp or off duty.

"They get that thing up and running yet?" Barry asked Jennifer, indicating the computer.

"Yes! It`s great. The contractor the feds hired sent someone over just before lunch. They've got all the camp residents in a database and they've even got all the disaster recovery centers hooked together on the Internet, like ours is. They've got a database started for all the survivors and victims, a kind of lost and found for people. And its hooked up to the national 800 line they set up for questions about quake survivors from the rest of the country. I found my boyfriend in Azusa and Janet's grandparents."

Upon hearing this, Barry stopped short, looking intently at Winslow. "You like mine up yet?"

"No, I'm still just getting the hang of it, but anyway," she looked over at Janet Mortimer "We thought we'd wait for you." It had been no secret among the deputies that Lieutenant Warden had not heard from his wife after the quakes.

Barry came around the table so he could see the terminal screen. "Go for it."

Janet joined them as Jennifer typed commands into the keyboard.

Barry watched the screen as the welcoming message telling people that this was a service of the California State Emergency Services Department and the Federal Emergency Management Agency made possible by a grant and equipment supplied by Southwest Telesys Corporation. Then there was a warning that the information was exempt from the Privacy Act by order of the President, quoting an Executive Order number. Then, Winslow selected a command from a menu that called for a search by name.

"Same last?" Winslow asked.

"Yes, first initial K." Barry said, answering the other empty blank on the screen.

Winslow entered the information and a moment later a list of names appeared on the screen. The listing was a last-name-first roster of people named Warden from initial K. to Kyra. There was one "K.," one "Katherine A.," a "Kathleen," and two "Katherines."

"There," Barry pointed, "Katherine A., her middle name's Anne."

Winslow highlighted the line and hit the Enter key.

The screen flickered and reconstituted itself as a form showing personal information - name date of birth, address, and various other data. It took Barry only a moment to recognize the "DOB" blank to be Kathy's birthday.

"That's her. What does it say?" Barry stammered pressing toward the screen to read.

Winslow put her finger on the screen, pointing as she read. "It doesn't have a temporary address, is that your home address?'

"Yeh, but I've been there, nothing left."

"Well, it really doesn't say much, except this ..." Winslow stopped talking as she pointed to the "Notes" line.

`Personal effects available at Good Samaritan Hospital.' Barry read, then re-read the line. He blinked in silence staring at the screen.

"What's that mean?" Winslow asked Barry's unspoken question. "The blank about `Deceased' or "Evacuated" isn't checked. Does that mean she`s a patient at the hospital, or what?"

"Anything more?" Janet asked.

Winslow hit the page down key and was answered by a loud beep.

"Nope. That's all." Winslow said.

Barry again blinked at the computer and mumbled, "... personal effects?"

"Let's check the other two Katherines, maybe there's something more." Winslow added as she hit the Escape key on the computer. She moved the computer to another personal information screen. This one showed a date of birth for a sixty year old woman from Pasadena who had been processed through the evacuation center at Burbank airport. Winslow cycled the screen to the next name.

This screen of information also showed the date of birth for Barry's wife. But, this time the screen looked different. It was an inquiry screen. It showed much the same information, but at the bottom it asked anything having information about this person to contact the person listed. Barry recognized his father-in-law's name, George McMurphy, but not the address. Why were Kathy's parents in Bakersfield?

"Her dad is looking for her, too. Guess that answers the possibility that she went home to her parents." Barry's voice was on edge. "Can you print that? I'll try to reach her folks."

"Sure thing." Winslow said, hitting another button on the keyboard.

"Well, thanks. I guess I`d better figure out how to get in touch with Good Samaritan Hospital to see what the hell they mean about her personal effects. If she is still a patient there I don't think they would be advertising that her stuff is available for the next of kin." Barry said as he straightened up from leaning over Winslow's shoulder.

"But if something, uh, you know, really bad happened, they would have noted it. All they said was her personal effects were available," Janet Mortimer said.

Barry reached for the paper being ejected from the printer, "Maybe they just forgot to check the block for deceased." The tone of his voice did not leave room for comment from either woman.

■

The Los Angeles Unified School District received $90 Million in federal earthquake recovery funds shortly after the 1994 Northridge Earthquake. On the second anniversary of the receipt of the funds only $34 Million had been used, showing the even if funds are available, earthquake recovery is a long process. Much of the delay was caused by bureaucratic bickering over whether the funds could be used for projects which had certain earthquake safety aspects, but which did not have safety or renovation of damage as the projects' main function.

May 16th, 8:00 A.M.

Matt Contreras had already gotten in the habit of showering and shaving at work. For some reason the Indio city water system was working, but Palm Springs was still without. From the looks of the Highway Patrol locker room before shift change, he was not the only one in this situation. Matt finished dressing and joined the other officers in the squad room.

The squad room was packed. There were several people in California Highway Patrol uniforms that Barry did not recognize. He did a double take at the Texas Ranger shoulder patches on several other uniforms.

Hal Crawford stood at the lectern, waiting for everyone to settle. With all the seats taken Matt leaned against the bookcase at the back of the room. Crawford motioned for someone to hang a map on the pegs above the blackboard. When this has done he rapped his pointer on the lectern.

"Ok, ladies and gentlemen, let's get settled. Lot to cover."

The group settled down and waited for Crawford to begin.

"You all probably notice lots of new faces and some different uniforms this morning. Our district has been augmented with folks from the Tahoe CHP office as well as about ten officers from the great state of Texas. They are here in answer to California's request for assistance in law enforcement. Word is that other state's officers are coming, but the Texas Rangers' convoy is the first to arrive." The last was cause for a round of mock cheering from the Texans.

"The out-of-state officers are deemed under the Governor's emergency proclamation to be sworn California peace officers with full law enforcement authority. We're glad to have them."

When the chorus of murmurs died down Crawford continued.

"I'll be giving you an update on the situation with the Calipatria prisoners and the local picture in a moment, but I got a FAX from Sacramento this morning that fills in a lot of the questions we've all had about the actual situation across Southern California and I thought you'd want to know."

Crawford picked up the pointer and went to the map on the blackboard that showed most of the southern end of the state.

"The FAX I got covers the transportation situation and the law enforcement implications." He cleared his throat. "Most of you know that the main quake was almost on top of us here, right over here, just east of San Bernardino. There were two other main quakes centered under L.A. proper. Here and here. And lots of other shocks throughout the region. We're all aware of the huge flood of the Imperial Valley. Can't really miss it, considering our little desert town of Indio is now a seaport."

More murmurs interrupted him.

"Transportation-wise, that makes things a real mess. Like you didn't know that, huh? Of course, I-8 through Imperial is closed for good. Here in our district, I-10 is cut off, almost totally destroyed, more on that later. I-15 and all of the San Bernardino Mountain highways are also cut. I-15 is not as bad as I-10, but still out of commission for weeks, or more.

"Farther west, the big interchange at San Fernando on Interstate 5 has collapsed. That's now the third straight quake that has collapsed the same exact interchange. 1971, 1994 and now. Remember the home movies of the truck driving off the span in '71? I'd think the engineers would get a clue soon."

Nervous chuckling filled the squadroom.

"The 5 is also broken farther north where it crosses the San Andreas on the Grapevine. They've graded a new lane there, just finished two days ago. One lane each way. That's about the only clear route into Los Angeles right now. And that's bottle-necked to one lane both at the Grapevine and again at the San Fernando collapse. Farther north, the 101 is cut in three places, Thousand Oaks, Ventura River and Gaviota. No hope there. To the south I-15 is open from Riverside to San Diego, but San Diego is cut off from everything to the east by Interstate 8 being flooded through Imperial. I-5 was closed from L.A. to San Diego due coastal slippage south of San Onofre, but it looks like that is about cleared up. I won't go into details as to what the situation inside L.A. is, you've all seen the TV. Most of their freeways are trashed. You know the rest ... chaos."

Crawford put down the pointer and squared his shoulders at the lectern. "The bottom line is the Los Angeles is virtually landlocked. What that means to us here, and why I started with this rundown, is that the road engineers see the I-10 break just west of here to be the easiest route to open up. The cuts in I-15, I-5 and the 101 are all on hillsides, mountain passes or need big interchange construction to work. I-10 is broken up on flat ground, in the valley. All they think they need to do is grade out the earthquake damage and through down some paving.

"They've already started this. You've probably seen the heavy equipment coming in from everywhere, parking along the Interstate from Indio to Whitewater. It looks like we can count on the biggest, fastest construction job you've ever seen take place right here. We've got several million people getting ready to starve in L.A. and wanting to get out. Until that highway gets opened there's no way to service them, except by air, and that isn't too efficient.

"Now the specifics of our part of this ... Gathering up the refugees that trickle through from L.A. and Imperial will continue. You all know about the camp they've set up at Twenty-Nine Palms. We're going to patrol the construction area as well as we can, considering the terrain, and take any refugees to the shuttle bus service in Morongo. You're OK'd to arrest them if they resist your help. We can't have millions of refugees clogging the routes up. Besides, they're getting to be a law enforcement problem, stealing food in Palm Springs and Morongo Valley, sleeping everywhere. It is better for them and us, if we get them to the camps."

"Now, about the escapees from Calipatria Prison, it looks like we've seen the worst. But, we sti ..." Commander Crawford was cut off by a jarring thump that rocked his lectern and caused those standing to try and catch their balance.

After the past ten days of near constant aftershocks, the C.H.P. officers from Indio and those from Tahoe who were used to the same treatment from the Mammoth Mountain Fault near Tahoe simply stood and braced themselves. They waited out the abrupt, rocking aftershock and watched with the knowing looks of old hands as the Texans scurried into the hallway or looked about wide-eyed.

■

"There you go. Suck on that. You're probably pretty dry. Huh?" The woman's voice coincided with the insertion of a something round and wet into Kathy's mouth.

Whatever was put into her mouth tasted vaguely like lemon, but it had the feeling of cloth to it. The wet lemon-ness of it trickled down into her mouth, which was, indeed, dry.

Kathy smacked her tongue and lips together, spreading the wetness around in her mouth. The relief of the moisture was short-lived. It ended when Kathy realized that she had no idea who had put whatever it was in her mouth. Or why. Or where she was. Or anything else.

Questions flooded into her consciousness. Some had answers, most did not. The first, `What was in her mouth?' could not be answered. Although the lemon flavor was clear, with a corresponding smell, the shape was not. It seemed to be a cloth lollipop. This thought caused her to gag on it, and somebody (who?) pulled it out. To answer the second question `Who?' she tried to open her eyes.

Dried mucus slowed the eye opening, but the same person who had removed the lemon-flavored object now gently stroked Kathy's fluttering eyelids with a warm wet cloth. Kathy demurred to the washing and waited until it stopped to look.

The `who' question was partially answered by a smile from a young woman seated next to where Kathy lay. Kathy blinked at the woman, trying to remember if she knew who this was. At length, Kathy was certain that she did not.

"Who . . ? Wh... " Kathy tried to sit up, but the woman quickly put her hand on Kathy's collarbone, pushing her down.

"Keep calm, lie still. No theatrics. You're in a hospital. Everything is going to be fine."

Kathy looked around. It did not look like a hospital. Above her all she saw was flapping canvas, rippling in an unfelt breeze. She seemed to be in a huge tent. Other people were walking around. Everyone, including the woman talking to Kathy, seemed to be wearing uniforms, camouflaged uniforms.

"How did I ...?"

"How'd you get here? I don't have a clue, other than your chart shows you were med-evacked here from Good Samaritan Hospital last week. You are recovering from a rather nasty knock on the head, skull fracture."

At this, Kathy tried to reach for her head. Both the woman and something taped to Kathy's arm stopped this.

"Whoa. You'll pull your I.V. Just lay still."

The abrupt movement brought a sharp pain to Kathy's head. She moaned and shut her eyes tight.

"There. See. Just relax. I'll see if we can get you something for that. The doctor pulled you off meds until you regained consciousness. Real bad concussion. Maybe he'll give you some painkiller now." The nurse got up to move away, before she did, she added. "You just lay still. I'll be right back."

Kathy Warden obeyed. She lay in the bed, staring at the green canvas above her, wondering how she had come to be wherever it was she was.

As the moments drug on without the return of the nurse, as it seemed the woman was, Kathy thought again of what the nurse had said. `Skull fracture.' Kathy reached up again, but with her left hand this time, which did not seem to be encumbered by anything.

The movement of her arm and shoulder was awkward and strangely slow, her shoulder stiff and painful. Finally, she touched her head. Her fingers recoiled at the touch. Kathy felt bandages and skin. She tried again and confirmed the first touch. The back of her head and the top from halfway back was covered with bandages and tape. The part in front of the tape, above her ears and over to her forehead was smooth, only the barest hint of stubble could be felt there. Kathy's shoulder length hair had been shaved off.

Completely.

Kathy continued to finger her odd feeling scalp. Questions flooded back in again. The questions and her movement incited another round of pain from the rear of her head. She clinched her fist in pain and shock pressing it against her barren pate.

Feeling someone at her arm, Kathy opened her eyes in time to see the nurse inject something into the tube in her right arm. "So, Sally, you didn't mind very well. Had to check out the new hairstyle, huh?"

Kathy wondered why the nurse was calling her `Sally.' Kathy tried to correct her, but all she could say was the first "I" as the warm half-burn of the intravenous drug filled her arm, shoulder, and then her body. Blackness followed.

Lt.(j.g.) Marge Gardner put "Sally Kim's" patient chart at the end of the portable cot, along with the green canvas bag that held the patient's personal property, including the backpack with the address in the pocket from which someone had identified the once again unconscious patient.

■

It is estimated that there are slightly under two million children in public and private schools and day care on any given day in Los Angeles County. With the existing school busing programs, many of these children are in classrooms many miles from home and with Los Angelenos' employment commuting patterns, many parents are scores of miles from home and their children's schools. Even though most schools are considered safe from a structural standpoint during moderate quakes, many educators worry about what the children will do after a major quake. The greater the disruption to transportation and housing, the longer it will take to reunite parents with children. A catastrophic quake in an urban area will result in tens of thousands of displaced, homeless children, many of whom will be reunited with their families only after a considerable time, if ever.

May 26th, 9:10 A.M.

Nurse Gardner was just finishing Kathy's blood pressure check when a Navy doctor walked up with a flat stainless steel pan. It was Dr. Murchison, one of the two doctors Kathy regularly saw in the tent, which she had learned housed women recovering from surgery or critical injuries. The pan gave a metallic rattle as he sat it down next to where Kathy sat on the canvas cot that served as her hospital bed. Kathy could see the forceps and scissors in the pan.

"Time to get those stitches out, its been almost three weeks since your surgery. You've healed up well, don't want to miss any sutures now that your hair is coming back in." The doctor smiled at Kathy, who tried to return the smile, but nervously eyed the surgical implements in the pan.

Seeing her furtive look at his tools the doctor assured her, "Don`t worry, you'll hardly feel anything."

The nurse moved on to the next bed. The doctor positioned himself behind Kathy gently tilting her head forward.

"Is there going to be any scar?" Kathy asked.

"Oh, they did a pretty good job keeping the incision to a minimum, just enough to check on the reduction of the fracture, but if you have someone fingering through your hair they'll probably be able to find something. But, I assume you are not going to keep this stylish butch haircut too long." The doctor spoke as he fingered the back of her head, he ended the last sentence with a snip, followed by a quick twist of the forceps. "See that didn't hurt, did it?"

Kathy thought better of shaking her head while the doctor was prodding her skull, she just mumbled a response. The doctor continued snipping and pulling stitches from the back of her head.

"When will I be able to go?"

"Well, your concussion is better and the last x-rays show the skull fracture starting to knit, and as long as you are careful about not bumping your head, there is not much else we can do for you that you can't do for yourself, if you take care. You have someplace to go?" He ended the question with another quick twist and tug.

Kathy gave a half shrug, "I have no idea. I don`t know how my apartment is. I don't know how or where my husband or family are. I really don't even know how I got here. Last thing I knew, I was downtown L.A."

"The tent city is getting pretty well established here. I hear they have sections for men, women, children and families. You should be able to get someplace to stay there until you can contact your family. When I get done here, you can go check it out. You get yourself a place to stay, I'd say we can release you, not much more we can do for you anyway. It'd do you good to get on your feet and out of the hospital area for a while. You have any clothes besides the hospital gown?"

"I don't think so. Just my backpack. That's how you wound up giving me the wrong name at first."

"Yeh, I remember the look on your face, asking us why we were calling you `Sally' and us thinking you were amnesiac. Sorry, about that. That's one you can tell your grandkids about," the doctor stopped talking as he pulled another suture out, "I'll have the nurse check into getting you something to wear."

The doctor tore the end off a plastic pouch of salve and rubbed some into the area he had finished with on the back of Kathy's head. He dropped the forceps and scissors into the pan with a clatter and stood.

"And the piece de resistance, we don`t want you to sunburn when you go out in the sun," the doctor said as he pulled something from his belt behind his back. It was a blue Navy baseball cap embroidered with a gold "USS Tarawa."

"Your cap. Nah, I couldn`t," Kathy protested.

"Nonsense. I insist. Doctor`s orders. Your scalp has never been in the sun with no hair to protect it. It`s either the cap or I bandage you up again."

Kathy relented, "Thanks."

She tested the cap for fit as the doctor picked up his things to leave. The cap was loose and strange feeling on the newly grown stubble on her head. She snapped the nylon-pegged adjustment strap tighter and slipped the cap on.

The woman in the cot next to her smiled feebly and gave her the thumbs-up sign. Kathy knew this would be all she would get from the woman, who had her smashed jaw wired shut. Kathy smiled back.

"So, you`re getting out, huh?" a voice behind her said.

Kathy turned to see Nurse Gardner. She was carrying one of the blue cotton jumpsuits the hospital staff sometimes wore, socks and a pair of black military boots.

"This is the best I can do for clothes. A military hospital supply room isn't very good for fashion. They say the FEMA supply tent over by the football field has more clothes, underclothes and essentials for the. ... , err, refugees."

"Is that what I am? A refugee."

"Sorry, it sounds bad. I know. I just didn't know what to call everybody. There's thousands coming in, every day."

"Yeh. The world changed real quickly for lots of people."

"I guessed on the shoe size. If they don`t fit let me know. And you'll need this to get through the gate." The nurse handed her a blue paper card printed with "USN Hospital Camp Pendleton, Dominguez Hills Detachment, Grounds Pass -- Kathy Warden."

"We finally got your name right," the nurse said, smiling.

"Ok. And, thanks."

Kathy ducked under the door flap of the tent and got her first view of the tent city that surrounded the hospital. The hot sun after days inside made Kathy thankful for the cap.

Kathy felt odd, sort of tomboyish, in the boots, cap and strange clothes. With no hair, no makeup and the utilitarian clothes she felt somehow depersonalized, like she wasn`t herself. The strange surroundings she saw did not help the odd mood either. And, after three weeks in bed, her legs were weak.

The hospital tent she had been in was in the second row of the identical green tents that stretched back as far as she could see behind her. A chain link fence separated the hospital from the rest of the encampment.

A few hospital personnel moved inside the chain link fence, but beyond was a maze of activity. Lines and crowds of people moved amongst trailers, tents, and trucks. The hospital seemed to be on a knoll above what appeared to be a golf course turned trailer park. To the right Kathy could see what she assumed to be the university field house the nurse had told her about. A small stadium could be seen beyond.

Two armed Marines in fatigues and body armor guarded the gate in the fence around the hospital. The guards waved Kathy through when she showed the hospital pass the nurse had given her.

There seemed to be a main thoroughfare through the camp that ran over the hill past the hospital and down past the field house on the next knoll over. The unpaved track was crowded with groups of people and individuals moving both up and down and across it, interspersed with an occasional vehicle, mostly the big green military trucks. Far down the hill she could see a tank truck spraying a mist of water on the dirt road, trying to keep down the dust that hovered everywhere.

Some of the people who walked with Kathy carried possessions with them. Many of those groups she met coming up the hill carried what were apparently photocopied maps showing them were to go in the maze of tents and trailers. Some of the people wore jackets and jumpsuits emblazoned with "FEMA," a Red Cross symbol or "Social Services." Many wore military uniforms. But, most seemed to be what the nurse had referred to as "refugees." Their forlorn, lost look gave them away. Kathy assumed that her own visage was similar.

Kathy could see a line of people forming on the left side of the road. It rain a couple hundred feet down the hill to a particularly large tent. By the time Kathy reached it she could smell the food. A banner by the tent's entrance announced, "US Army Reserve Field Kitchen, HHC, 144th Field Artillery Battalion." There seemed to be a packed house in the tent.

Kathy could see the huge field house definitely that seemed to be the center of the tent city's activity. The sign above the doors read, "Cal State Dominguez Hills Athletic Facility." Kathy had only a vague idea of where Dominguez Hills was. Somewhere down south in Los Angeles. To someone from the San Fernando Valley, names like Dominguez Hills, Watts, and Compton all merged into an amorphous mass, someplace you only heard about in a traffic report and definitely did not go, except maybe to hit the big shopping mall off the 405 freeway in Carson.

After weeks in bed, the brisk walk down from the hospital and up the next hill to the field house was tiring. A dull ache was pounding in the back of Kathy's head as she got to the field house.

Many of the people coming out of the main doors had the maps clutched in their hands. Kathy now noticed that many of these people also carried stacks of blankets, pillows and a plastic bucket full of things. One group of people was a cluster of four wheel chairs, with the wheelchair occupants holding stacks of blankets and supplies while the others struggled to push the wheelchairs across the well-worn sod.

The crowded lobby led to the basketball arena. The far end of the field house was lined with tables where the blankets, buckets and apparently supplies were being issued. A large crowd of people waited to left side in what appeared to be a snaking line that terminated at a row of tables that seemed to be where the people in line were registering. Several other tables lined the opposite wall. The logos of the American Red Cross and several government agencies labeled these tables.

Two men in orange vests were answering questions and directing people in the lobby. Kathy Warden walked up to the older of these two men, a frail looking man, who nevertheless had quick animated gestures. The man greeted Kathy with a broad smile.

"How can I help you, Miss?"

"I came down from the hospital. Is that the line where we check in?" Kathy asked, indicating the long queue to the left.

The old man blinked in thought and then answered, "Oh, no. You don't want to have to wait with them, that's just for the new homeless people checking into the camp. If you're from the hospital I think they can handle you at the Camp Manager's table. That's the two tables together over there on the right with the FEMA sign. Just tell them you're from the hospital."

Kathy left the man with the feeling that she had missed something, not knowing why it was she wouldn't have to go through the registration process with the other new people, just because she was checking in from the hospital rather than off the streets. But, she did not know enough about what was going on to do anything but follow directions. She went to the FEMA table.

There was no smile from the women sitting behind the FEMA table, just the blank stares of people who had been on duty too long.

Kathy looked from one woman to the other as she said, "They sent me down from the hospital. I was told to check in with you."

One of the women pulled a piece of paper from a stack and handed it too Kathy. As the woman spoke Kathy noticed the woman looking at the military medical jumpsuit, Kathy's Navy cap and what she could see of Kathy's obviously shaved head, "Fill this out and take it to the man on the end of that table." The woman pointed with her pencil toward to other table marked FEMA.

The second woman pushed a ballpoint pen towards Kathy. Kathy took the pen and read the paper. It was printed on photocopied Federal Emergency Management Agency letterhead and turned out to be a form entitled "Staff Information." Kathy was going to question whether this was the right form for her, but several more people came up behind her and one of the women asked her, "Could you move over there to fill out the form."

Rather than interrupt the other people, Kathy moved aside and started on the form. After a lengthy notice about the Freedom of Information Act and the Paperwork Reduction Act, the form asked for her to give her name, permanent address, date and place of birth, social security number, next of kin and numerous other items of personal information. Kathy had no trouble with anything on the form until she got to "Specialty" and "Referring Agency and Point of Contact."

After thinking about it a moment, Kathy decided to fill out her college major in the blank asking for specialty. She wrote "Child Psychology / Early Childhood Education" She had no idea what to do about the other question, so she finally wrote "US Navy, Doctor Murchison" as her "Referring Agency and Point of Contact," since he had told her to come down to the field house.

After signing the form, Kathy gave the pen back to the first woman and went to the man at the end of the other table sitting in front of a computer terminal and printer. He took her form and studied it. He stamped it in a time clock and started to type into the computer. After a moment's pause the printer ejected a form, this one blue with a duplicate just like it. He separated the forms and gave one copy to Kathy. Then he took a photocopied map from a pile and turned it so Kathy could see it. He pointed with his pencil to the map and said, " Good to have you, they have been screaming for help. Children's Services is headquartered right over here," he marked an X on the map, "only a couple hundred feet out the front door and to the left. You can't miss it, big orange colored tent, only one that's orange. Don't ask why, no idea. Give them the blue form. The Children's Services staff are housed with the kids, so you won't need a bed assignment. But you can take this supply chit to the tables in back and they'll outfit you with the basic supplies." He pushed a pink paper toward her.

The man half-smiled at Kathy, "Good luck with the children. Next." He reached for the paperwork from the man standing behind Kathy.

Kathy walked away from the table with a paper in either hand. She saw that the blue one was a rehash of the form she had filled out, but this time entitled "Staff Assignment." The pink form had only the words "Initial Supply/Provision Request - Staff" and her name, "Kathy Warden." If she had thought this would get so formal she would have used her full name, but it was too late now.

Kathy headed for the supply tables, now sure that she had some-how gotten into the `staff' designation by accident, but realizing that it was probably not in her best interests to point out the error. She would go with the flow for a while. Being dealt with as staff was undoubtedly better than being a refugee. Kathy decided to check out the orange tent and then decide what to do.

■

The official state report on the 1906 San Francisco earthquake reports an incident in which a startled cow fell into a chasm that opened up during the quake and was entombed when the rift closed seconds later. This widely repeated story led to the popular conception that an earth will open up and swallow people during a quake. Such an occurrence, although remotely possible, is far overshadowed by more likely seismic hazards.

May 29th, 08:30 A.M.

"And that's about it. Watch out for any sign of gang activity or graffiti artists. And, keep an eye out for the cholera symptoms. We don't want the same mess here as they have in Burbank. If anyone looks sick and they don't want to come with you to the clinic. Just I.D. them and report it to the camp HQ." Barry looked into the faces of his four sworn deputies and the ten civilian "posse" members who now helped out in camp patrols. "Any questions?"

Nobody spoke, so Barry ended with the expected, "Be careful out there."

The sheriff's crew dispersed, mostly out the door for patrol duties. Barry went to his desk, after getting a cup of coffee, and Janet Mortimer went to the radio and computer console.

Barry started sorting through the stack of messages the laser printer spit out constantly; alerts, information bulletins and administrative messages. The computer net was great in that it kept everyone in contact in spite of the continuing telephone outage, but it also generated stacks of useless and esoteric paperwork. To save paper they printed everything in small print, which made the culling task even worse.

Barry was barely through the top pile of paper when he heard a muted exclamation from Janet.

"What's up?" he asked.

"Is your wife a psychologist?" Mortimer asked.

"No, teacher."

Janet Mortimer`s voice was excited, "You'd better look at this. I ran your wife through FEMA's ID program again. What I came up with, I think, is the same birthday as that first one. Under first name `Kathy.'"

Barry rushed over to join Mortimer. He saw the screen, this one different from the two screen types he had seen on this computer the week before. At the top of the screen it said, `Office of Emergency Services - Interagency Government Personnel Registration.' The form had blanks for the last name and first name, and it had a "DOB" and SSAN" that Barry recognized as Kathy's.

The form had a blank for "Position" which listed "Psychology Technician" and several blanks with coded information. The date showed it had just been processed the day before. This screen had a "Notes" section like the earlier screens which showed, "USN HOSP RFRL, ASSGND CPS/DH."

"Damn, that's her, but what's it mean?" Barry asked.

"Well, Lieutenant, my guess is this means your wife started working this week as a children's' counselor for CPS, Child Protective Services, right here in our camp. DH is probably Dominguez Hills."

"But, you gotta be kid- ... CPS is right over in the big orange tent by the field house." Barry looked at the female deputy for a moment, wordless, trying to believe what he had been told.

He left the door to the Sheriff's trailer wide open as he left.

■

Kathy sat, Indian-style, on the canvas tarp that served as the tent floor. Around her in concentric rings, sat her multi-ethnic flock of lost or orphaned children. Two graduate students, volunteers from psychology departments at universities back East, sat on the edges of the cluster of children taking notes.

A little girl with coffee and cream skin and tightly coiled red-brown hair was speaking. "…and Corinne, she's our baby-sitter, had us all stay out in the yard all afternoon after the Big One. It was really scary. There was a big explosion, too. And the fire."

One of the psychologists cut into the girl's story, "Did you see the explosion?"

"Uh-huh. And we felt it in our ears. It hurt."

"Whoosh!" a little boy sitting next to the girl added for emphasis, throwing his arms high in the air, fingers outstretched to portray to explosion.

The psychologist, a young woman about Kathy's age, wrote something on her clipboard. "OK, go on."

The little girl continued with her story of the aftermath of the quake.

Like the rest of Dominguez Hills Camp, the Child Protective Services operation had grown exponentially in the three weeks since the big quakes. It was run by the Los Angeles County government with the help from the Cal State University staff and students. Also, after a CNN story, the rest of the country, as witnessed by the volunteers, had gotten interested in the plight of the children in this and a dozen similar camps.

As time went on after the quake it became clear that their primary purpose was as an orphanage, both temporary and permanent. The joyous reunions the others on the CPS staff told about in the early days had become rarities. The records of most of the twenty children in Kathy Warden's tent showed the parents to be deceased. Many of the children had witnessed the deaths, while others refused to believe the horrible news the CPS workers tried to gently break to them.

Since Kathy had all pre-schoolers, there were a few cases in which children did not know full names of their parents or their home address, so the task of finding parents, even with the computerized search system, was difficult. The CPS workers talked with these children, trying to draw out any item of information that might lead to identifying their parents.

That was what Kathy and the psychologist helpers were doing on this, Kathy's second day at work. Through the guise of a shared story time, they were trying to get a few of the children to open up about their families and homes. A child who might clam up when asked a specific question by an adult, might open up when chatting with his or her peers in a group. The story telling also helped the children come to terms with reality, or if not, it gave the staff and psychologists some insight into where the children's internal defense mechanisms had led them, trying to cope with the disaster.

"Corinne stayed until it got dark. But, then she said she had to go see her family. Corinne said Mommy would come home soon," the little girl stopped and blinked her wet eyes, "but she didn't. She never came back. Neither did Corinne."

"What about your Daddy?" Kathy asked the girl, but she did not hear the answer. Kathy's attention was drawn to the man clad in khaki and green who was sauntering toward her tent, down the path from the big orange CPS Admin tent. As she looked up at the man, she saw him break into a run. Kathy leaped from the ground and had matched the man's stride by the time she ducked under the tent flap. They met in a wild, spinning embrace in the path between the children's tents.

"Oh, God, Kath I though you…," Barry said, hugging Kathy.

Kathy could say nothing, she just nuzzled her face into Barry's chest, her arms around his neck.

The long embrace might have lasted even longer, but Barry realized they were not alone. The two were surrounded by a herd of twenty children, all squealing and jumping around their teacher/surrogate mother. The orphaned children were sharing in Kathy's joy in a way that only they could.

As Kathy looked about her, Barry said, "I take it this is your brood."

Kathy just nodded and then pulled Barry close again.

Barry looked down into Kathy's face, "God, it's good to …"

Kathy caught Barry's quick glance at her close cropped hair, and she nervously fingered her head.

"I, uhh …. ," Kathy mumbled.

"New hair style. Huh?" Barry smiled.

"Yeah, long story."

"Yeh, I'll bet."

Their gazes locked. The gazes turned into grins and they clutched each other again. As they hugged, the two graduate students started gathering the children back into the tent.

As Barry and Kathy finally pushed each other out to arm's length, Barry whispered, "Happy Anniversary."

"What?"

"Happy Anniversary. May 29th. It's our anniversary."

"Wow, you really know how to pick a great anniversary surprise."

A look of realization came to Barry's eyes. "Gosh, I forgot." He took his left hand and felt inside his jacket pocket. He took a small gift box out and handed it to Kathy.

"What's this?"

"Anniversary gift. I was buying it when the first quake hit. It has been in my pocket ever since."

Kathy opened the box and fingered the earrings. "Great choice, especially now."

Barry looked questioningly at her, "Why especially now?"

Kathy gave Barry a sarcastic smile, "With hair like this, earrings have extra importance."

As she spoke, Kathy finally had a chance to look closely at Barry. She fingered his collar and asked, "What's this?"

"Oh, yeah, Lieutenant's bars. I've got a pretty good story, too."

The two enjoyed each other's arms for another moment. Kathy saw the female graduate student smiling and motioning her away from the tent, freeing her from duty.

"Let's get out of the middle of things here. We've got a lot to catch up on. Can I buy you a cup of coffee? We can swap stories."

"Coffee. I didn't think there was any coffee left in L.A. Especially in this camp."

"Sure, you just got know who to ask."

■

A survey of San Francisco residents after the Loma Prieto earthquake indicated that a very small percentage considered the earthquake threat a reason to leave. Most residents indicated that the opportunity and lifestyle that California offered outweighed the risk of seismic problems.

July 14th, 6:15 A.M.

It was not easy to hide anything from one another, living in a single bedroom in the one of the sheriff's staff trailers. The sound of Kathy retching in the bathroom woke Barry.

Barry was quickly at the bathroom door, "You OK? Can I get you anything?"

"No!" was the curt response from Kathy.

In a few minutes, Barry heard the sound of gargling. Shortly, Kathy came out.

"You're sick. We've got to get you to the clinic," Barry said, pulling on his uniform pants.

"I'll be fine."

"No, there's cholera going around up at the Burbank camp. And, lots of other stuff going around. You probably got something from your kids. We can't take any chances."

"Barry, I'll be fine," Kathy said, "If you must know, I've already been to the clinic. I'll be fine."

Barry put his hand on her shoulder, "So, what is it? What's wrong."

"Nothing's wrong. Just a little stomach upset. And, it is not anything I could catch from my kids. Nothing to worry about."

"Nothing to worry about? But...." Barry looked askance at Kathy.

"A little bit slow on the uptake this morning, huh, Lieutenant?" Kathy looked at Barry with raised eyebrows, waiting, as a look of surprise and then joy crossed her husband's face, when he finally understood the cause of Kathy's stomach disorder.

July 14th, 3:30 P.M.

With a perfectly manicured maroon fingernail Genevieve pushed her hair away from her face. Genevieve could feel Ted watching her as he walked up. She looked his way and smiled. She slid her hips to one side and canted her knees to the right so that the sides of her long, slender legs would get the benefit of the afternoon sun. The location of her new home in Hope Ranch, west of Santa Barbara, made afternoon the best time for sunbathing.

Ted was carrying an iced tea glass. He sat it down on the table next to Genevieve' chaise lounge and took the towel off his own shoulders. He was going for a swim.

"Thank you, you're a dear." Genevieve said. He was.

"You feel that little tremor a few minutes ago?" Ted asked.

"Tremor? No? I don't think so. They come so often, that I hardly notice them anymore."

Ted nodded as he prepared to dive into the pool. The chaos of the quakes was past. Life was good. The estate that Michael Dumont left behind made Genevieve as wealthy as she was beautiful. While reasonably well-to-do himself, Ted Galloway's law practice income was miniscule compared to the funds he found when researching the late Michael Dumont's affairs for Genevieve.

Their lives seemed to naturally intertwine. She had no wish to handle the financial affairs of the estate or Michael's companies, Ted liked nothing better. Genevieve nestled herself into Ted Galloway's care (and adoration) and he accepted everything she offered, physically and financially.

Genevieve's natural inclination to return to live in France after the quakes was countered when Ted bought her the new home in Hope Ranch, with her money. The home was elegant, situated atop a lovely green hillock, high above the ocean, and appointed for a queen.

Genevieve was assured that the new mansion was as safe as any home in California, not a stilt or cantilevered deck in sight. The afternoon of hobbling barefoot and nearly naked up the road after the Big One was almost forgotten the first time Genevieve walked across the plush carpet to the veranda and the gorgeous view of Hope Ranch and the Channel Islands out in the Pacific.

The geology underlying this lovely hill in Hope Ranch was of no concern to Genevieve, it was too wonderful a life to worry about such things. The Mesa Fault that had created her lovely, green hillock was of no importance. Life was good.

■ The End ■

ABOUT THE AUTHOR

KEVIN E. READY

Kevin E. Ready is currently a government attorney in California, where his duties include being legal advisor to a law enforcement agency. He has served as a commissioned officer in both the U.S. Army and Navy. He holds a bachelor's degree from of the University of Maryland and a Juris Doctor degree from University of Denver. He was an intelligence analyst and Arabic and Russian linguist for military intelligence and was decorated for activities during the Yom Kippur/Middle East War. He served as an ordnance systems officer onboard a guided missile cruiser off the coast of Iran during the Iranian Hostage crisis and later served as a combat systems officer for a destroyer squadron and as a tactical action officer for a carrier battle group. He also was the command judge advocate for a major military weapons command. Kevin was a major party candidate for U.S. Congress in 1984 and 1994.

Kevin is the author of several books and editor of a translation of the Koran. He lives in the Santa Barbara, California area with his wife Olga and their children.

Please visit Kevin's Web site at: http:// www.KevinReady.net

Kevin Ready's other books are available at:

http://www.SaintGaudensPress.com